JAMES MIRANDA BARRY

❖ ❖ ❖ ❖ ❖

Patricia Duncker

A catalogue record for this book is available from
the British Library on request

The right of Patricia Duncker to be identified as
the author of this work has been asserted by her in accordance
with the Copyright, Designs and Patents Act 1988

First published 1999 by
Serpent's Tail, 4 Blackstock Mews, London N4

Website: www.serpentstail.com

Set in 11pt Bembo by Intype London Ltd
Printed in Great Britain by Mackays of Chatham, plc

10 9 8 7 6 5 4 3 2 1

— CONTENTS —

For S.J.D.

❖ ❖ ❖ ❖ ❖

This is as strange a maze as e'er men trod,
And there is in this business more than nature
Was ever conduct of.

Shakespeare, *The Tempest*

A surgeon should have an eagle's eye,
a lady's hand and a lion's heart.

Sir Astley Cooper,
Professor of Surgery at Guy's Hospital

— PART ONE —

The House in the Country

THE MAN WITH A MOUSTACHE sweeps me up in his arms and bangs me down upon the balustrade. A huge puff of smoke floats out of his mouth. As if he were a dragon. There is a chain hanging from a pin only a few inches away from my nose.

"Dragon. Gold."

"Stand to attention when you're addressing me, my girl." He peers into my eyeballs. I see that his eyes are grey, but flecked with gold. "You don't look like your mother yet, you know. But there's hope that you will."

Is he wearing a uniform? Gold shiny buttons and a silk cravat? I put out my fingers and touch the gold. I unleash a strange smell: herbs, musk, forests. And the weariness of immense distances.

"Travelling dragon." I look up at him, already in love with his adventures. "Give me gold."

"Gold? You little mercenary! Well, well. Don't think I didn't offer all that to your mother. Estates, servants, riches, a world of luxury. She wouldn't have me. Wouldn't. Even her damned father advised her to reconsider. Another mercenary bastard. She'd promised herself to the other one. Would you believe it? Promised? Who in God's name makes or keeps promises at the age of sixteen?"

The General has lost his audience. I am now peering over the side of the balustrade. What can I see? A torrent of yellow flowers, falling, falling into a large basin. A stone dolphin with two putti astride, laughing forever, their faces turned in different directions. A little spurt of water. And circle upon circle of reflections. My face, far below me, shimmers, vanishes, shimmers, gone. The General hauls me upright.

"Easy there. Don't you fall off. Your mother will say that I had a jealous fit and pushed you."

The dragon is giving out small, equal gusts of smoke. I stare hard at his moustachios to find the fire. The little brown poker is too small and thin to produce all that smoke. But come to think of it, the more brilliant the fire, the less smoke. I remember a perpetually blazing corner of the nursery and sit thinking of the dolls on the window sill and the inevitability of tea-time. The dragon unties the chain of gold and carefully fastens it around my neck. He has huge hairy fingers and wears an elaborate heavy ring. But his fingers are gentle, hesitant, insecure. He lays the chain flat, free of my lace collar and red curls.

"There you are. You asked for gold."

I understand at once. The dragon is asking me to be his friend. We will be friends forever. We will have adventures together.

"Dragon." I reach up to put my fingers into silk, my head into smoke, my nose into gold. The General kisses the top of my head.

"Francisco! I thought you'd kidnapped her."

She is there. My Beloved. All her smooth pink scents, the prickle and stab of her jewellery, the rustle of her silks, the curl of her lip, a pearl in each ear. Now I am perched on her hip, my plump legs astride her waist. I look down at the stone putti in the fountain beneath us. They are riding dolphins. I kiss the shelving pink curve of her jaw and cry out in her ear.

"Look! Gold."

"Now who gave you that?"

Her face is inches away from mine. My Beloved fingers the chain.

"Mine," I say defensively. Hoping we can share it later.

"Of course it's yours. Francisco, you mustn't give her such expensive things." But I know from her tone that she is only pretending to disapprove. She looks up at the dragon. He is twice her size. She is so beautiful to touch. I finger her skin, her pearls. She is mine. She smells of lilacs and powder. The dragon is enveloped in a dense cloud of smoke.

"Come down into the garden. They won't miss you for twenty minutes. Don't look so suspicious. Bring that child. How can I be guilty of any gross improprieties if you've got the child in your arms?"

I am swept away into the shrubbery.

Here the earth smells of leaf mould and damp. Drops of water in sunshine become a cluster of brilliants on the rhododendrons. I stare at thick green rushing towards me at eye level. The woman says very little to the man. My Beloved holds me as if she were drowning. But I am looking up, up, up at a vast gulf of blue. Beyond the green cathedral, spangled with pink and purple flowers, into an eternity of luminous blue.

"Blue. Mine," I shriek in her ear.

"Shhh, darling."

The dragon is talking to her. Above his low muttering I hear the creak of leather, the cracking of twigs. Now my Beloved is my faithful mare. We are charging towards a gap in the enemy ranks. I dig my heels into her pure white flanks as we sweep past the poised Frenchies, with their green faces and their pink flowering guns. One of the rhododendrons has been transformed into a general. The colossus with the explosion of purple in his cockade must be Bonaparte himself. I flash my sword at him. He wants to steal my chain. My mare shifts beneath me.

"Don't kick, sweetheart."

We sweep towards the gap. My standard-bearer is in front. Smoking. Galloping. We come out of the shrubbery and my mare falls beneath me. But we have escaped the French. Here, all before us, are English fields. Cows standing, chewing, staring, in the spring sunshine. The white fence is a network of shadows on green. Above, the eternity of blue, and all before me, the vastness of this world.

"Why don't you run about a little, my love?"

I have lost my army, my horse, my weapons. But I have escaped the French. As I always do in my dreams. I see my Beloved, growing a little smaller, laughing, laughing. Suddenly I have fallen over a grave.

It is a large mound of earth moving slightly at the edges. It is a small grave, not yet decorated with a slab and a name. But it is opening. I sit quite still to watch the resurrection of the dead and my buttocks are growing damp. The earth sarcophagus is cracked across. There is a huge fissure in the lid of this grave, as if the last day had already been announced and the spirit had escaped. I peer superstitiously into the crack, but see only lichen, earth and broken stone. I sit staring at shining wet oceans of green and a trembling grave. This is a child's grave. A child even younger than I am. A child who never knew her Beloved. But she is coming back, struggling under the weight of earth. I lean forward to help. This is a mistake. I catch sight of her claws and pink nose. Quickly. Quickly. She descends back into the grave with a flurry of wet, crumbling earth. I am nearly in tears with disappointment. My dragon must dig her up. My Beloved must find me a baby. I look round for reinforcements. I demand help.

The dragon has quenched his fire. They have both fallen over, like toppled, coloured columns. He is trying to gobble up my Beloved. His moustachios encircle her soft face; one giant claw is fixed in the back of her head, disturbing her gorgeous torrent of ribbons and curls, his other claw is clamped about her waist. No, it is rising, rising carefully towards her left breast. His back arches above her as she falls prone on the grass. Crushed. Her white silk is being eaten by his grey and red stripes. I love her. And he is killing her.

I let out a great wail.

The dragon lets her go. A little. But she is in no hurry to come to me. She enjoys being eaten. She wants him to consume her. She has lost the use of her legs. I increase the volume and frequency of the wail.

At last my Beloved is sweeping across the green meadows towards me. My Beloved, her hooves pounding the earth, her mane flying, her blue and pink banners trailing in the wind, her eyes flashing as she catches sight of the tiny grave.

"Oh, my darling love. It's only a mole. Did it frighten you?"

Yes, it did. The dragon is not to be trusted. He will eat you if you let him too close. I look up mistrustfully, my eyes filling with tears. But my Beloved is not bleeding. Nor is she covered with bites. She has escaped the dragon's claws. I can see him puffing gently on the horizon. If he comes any closer I will steal all his gold. Yes, all his gold.

But as we scamper back towards him I lose all my fears. They fall away. I have what I want. My Beloved's hand in mine. Warriors we are. Comrades. Lovers. I will give her all the dragon's gold. And we will live forever, alone in a cave, somewhere behind the gulf of blue.

"Chooses her moments, doesn't she?" remarks the General.

Suddenly I want to confide in him. Now that my Beloved is completely mine once more.

"Dead babies." I point towards the grave.

"I haven't tried to kill you yet." The moustache twitches. "In fact, for the sake of your mother I will give you anything you want, child. Ask."

I stare. I have understood. The dragon has become an ancient, leathery, well-travelled magician. He is going to offer me three wishes and this is a test: of my honesty, my breeding, my honour.

My Beloved intervenes. She is not talking to me.

"I never forgot you. I gave her your name."

"She could have been mine in more than name, woman. In fact, can you swear to me that she is not my child?"

Of one thing I am quite certain. I do not belong to the dragon. But he sinks his enormous hairy fingers into my Beloved's arm. I am too fascinated by his rings, glinting in sunlight, to begin screaming. But as his fingers release her flesh I see small indentations, blue becoming red.

My Beloved bites her lip. I snuggle into her skirts, triumphant, fingering my gold chain. All around us is a world turbulent with spring light. I am delighted; for I have the distinct impression that they are quarrelling about me.

❖ ❖ ❖ ❖ ❖

I watch the firelight making patterns on the tiles. The tiles are black and white marble in the shape of huge diamonds. I try to make my two hands fit completely into one diamond. And they do, easily. I hop like a rabbit from diamond to diamond, each time making sure that my hands never touch the black. If they do touch the black, even the slightest part, something terrible will happen to me. My thumb inadvertently crosses over the forbidden line. And at once my game is finished. I have arrived in a soft, warm stream of red, orange, gold. It is a turkish carpet.

An obstacle presents itself. Four decorated legs in curving black and gold. I hide behind the sofa and peer into two close masses of silk, which are geometric, like the tiles, one is black and one is white. The ladies' knees are touching. One of them has dropped her glove. I settle down beneath them, their personal voyeur, their spy.

" . . . a scandal. Well, these days just something of a scandal. I hear she didn't wear her widow's weeds a year. I don't care what she does. Her husband didn't leave her a penny anyway. It was all entailed to the cousins. And knowing her she'd want the best black silk. Or not wear black at all. But for the look of the thing . . ."

" . . . mind you, he'd always been her lover. She met him years before. He used to visit our family. And the Barrys were well-connected. She was torn between the two of them when she was sixteen and really very marriageable. The General went off to fight with the French against England and there were tempests of tears. All kinds of carryings-on. He may be twice her age, but he's a very handsome man. Well, dear, don't look so startled. I'm old enough to say so. Lady Melbourne thinks so too. He's wealthy, talented . . . Of course, he has quite shocking political opinions. He always did have. But even radicalism is perfectly fashionable, if you have enough money to carry it off."

"Isn't he from the Americas?"

"Venezuela. Or somewhere like that, savage and exotic. But wealthy, my dear, with estates, servants, horses, gold. And of course he's very well-travelled. I heard him say that if the French invasion had suceeded in '97 it would have been the best thing that could have happened to us. He thinks the world of Bona-parte. And because he fought on the side of the French he's a marked man in this country. But he has too much money for them to touch him. Mind you, he's watched. All the time. I have that on the very best authority. Oh yes, he's a Papist. And it's rumoured that he's had that child baptised. The Barrys were Catholics. But what with all his revolutionary sentiments and French principles he's probably out of favour with the Papists too. Well, you can see why she's in love."

" . . . Jeremiah Bulkeley was a better catch when she was

sixteen. Or at least she thought so. She wasn't quite so adventurous then. And had all the usual illusions. She was just a little country girl. The General had run off to the wars and the Barrys weren't rich. But, as I say, they were always well-connected. No, she couldn't have expected to do better than Bulkeley then . . ."

"She's free to marry the General now if she wants to. Then she could be received everywhere. Well, perhaps not everywhere . . ."

"My dear, I'm not sure he's the marrying kind. And she has some very odd notions."

" . . . and there's that red-headed child of hers . . ."

" . . . that's Bulkeley's child all right . . ."

" . . . if not my brother's . . ."

" . . . my dear Louisa, you don't suggest . . ."

" . . . I'm in a position to know and I'm afraid I do . . ."

" . . . General Francisco de Miranda and Mrs Bulkeley. No, no, we are disgracefully early. Please don't apologise . . . May I introduce . . ."

I watch the flicker of my Beloved's dancing slippers as she crosses the tiles. I flatten myself out onto the rich, warm surface. Her satin slippers look like the tropical butterflies Francisco described, with brilliant golden wings, and spots of black, disappearing suddenly by magical cryptic colouration on the surface of a tiger lily. She arrives on the carpet and her feet vanish. This is my choice too – vanish, or be sent to bed.

Overhead I hear the muffled slither of politeness. I have blocked up my ears. If I cannot hear I cannot be seen. I survey the battlefield: to my right, leather boots and dancing shoes, frills, flounces and furbelows, straight ahead, chaise longue legs, two, not very solid-looking, to my left, an armada of fire irons, logs and flames. The door is too far away. There can be no escape. I am a spy. I will be shot. Francisco says that spies are always shot. At once. Without trials. I will therefore fight to the death.

No need. The boots creak backwards, giving me a better view of elegant light trousers, and my Beloved's graceful ankles, revealed briefly as she turns, the hem of her shawl trailing across the surface of black and white diamonds. A great gust of cold as the other hall door shuts and the winter pours in from the outer world. I slither away towards the umbrellas and coats and discarded bonnets. Pause in the doorway, then a rapid escape to the bottom of the staircase. Hide behind the sideboard.

The double doors are open into the downstairs dining room. This is one of my favourite rooms. So long as I don't crash into anything I am allowed to wear Francisco's slippers. These are at least ten sizes too big for me, but I can wedge my feet into the toe and use the open flat backs for ballast. Then, gathering speed on the diamonds in the hall, I can slide from one end of the dining room to the other. Rupert bows ironically low. Polishing the oak boards again, Mademoiselle? I'm glad to see that Mademoiselle takes such an interest in the housework. Rupert thinks that I am monstrously spoilt. He says so. Then panders to my desire for sweet cakes, dipped in sweet wine. Only men work for Francisco. We used to have a maid. But my Beloved had no more money to pay for her. So she left. Then there was no more money to pay for the house. So we left that too. Now we live with Francisco.

The dining table is being laid for supper. There is a huge centrepiece of flowers and fruit, surrounding a small statue of the goddess Flora. Her robe is made of flowers and she carries golden apples in her basket. She is a warm fountain of gold among the white china and dead silver soldiers. I stare at the glasses I am forbidden to touch. Each one has a different face etched in fine swirls. I know all the faces. I have stared at their scratched features, at their grimaces, at their earrings of grapes, their goat-like beards, their ivy-covered rods, their sneers. I want to touch the faces. I am forbidden to touch.

So much I desire is forbidden.

Disgruntled, I check both hall doors, drawing-room door, kitchen door, give myself the all-clear, and then begin the long ascent of the staircase, keeping close to the shadows, counting. The stone stairs are uneven, but I know every step. The candles are lit on the half-landing. The fine glass shades are clear, polished. Salvatore cleans them every day. Francisco bought them from a theatre in Venice that burned down. It was there, just one week before, that he had heard one of the most famous castrati of his age, singing. He explained to me in great detail what a castrato was. It sounded wonderful. You were specially chosen, then you remained a boy forever with a voice borrowed from God and became famous, fat and rich. You never turned into a woman, nor did you die in childbirth.

There is a horsehair cushion on one of the little sofas on the landing. Now it is my saddlepack. I tighten the girth, running two fingers underneath to make certain that my horse is comfortable. I put my feet through the fat stone bannisters and line up my cannon on the front hall door. I have to be both the gunner and the mounted guard. Every so often I change roles. So that my muscles do not freeze up. Up here the hall fire has very little effect. But I cannot be seen. I can pick off anyone who tries to get in. All the guests who have been invited by Francisco and my Beloved are here now. I count out a convoy of elegance and snobbery. Anyone else is an enemy invader. They will be picked off, ascending the staircase.

But no one comes. Rupert and Salvatore are working downstairs. Far away, in the drawing room, the music begins. But I must not abandon my post or fall asleep. At all costs I must guard the door. The intruders may poison the dogs, murder Rupert and Salvatore with machetes, cutting their throats at once so that their screams are inaudible, swarm up the staircase. I am the last outpost of defence. The city depends on me. I stand guard. But no one comes. I begin to doze off, clutching the stone bannisters. My arse is getting cold. The candles gutter above me.

Suddenly I am awake again, staring at the huge picture that is always there, halfway up the staircase. A man and a woman lean close together. They are vast, giants on Olympus. She holds him close to her. Her fingers are entwined in his long black curls. She shows him her naked breast, her nipple appearing pink between the tresses of her torrent of golden hair. The figures are two solid masses of pink and gold, a gigantic expanse of rich merging flesh, looming far above me. Their nakedness shimmers and gleams in the candlelight. His mouth almost touches hers. For a moment I am terrified. Francisco and my Beloved. They have become monsters. Then the world turns black.

"Why aren't you in bed yet, child?"

Francisco has stepped out of the painting, dressed in seconds, and is relieving me of my duties.

"Will you take the second watch?" I murmur as he disentangles my legs from the cold stone diagonals of the staircase. If he takes over my post he will not be able to climb back into the picture. Yet again I have rescued my Beloved.

"I'm on duty all night, soldier."

Now his moustachios are against my face, his arms around me. I hold on tightly, just in case he tries to get away.

"You are my prisoner. Don't try anything," I give the orders here. He strides up the stairs, two at a time. There is the library, also lit by candles, brown, red and black leather volumes with a gold globe on the top of one of the bookshelves. The wooden ladder is there for a second, then vanishes as we turn the corner. The terrible painting sinks beneath us. I lean over to see whether it is torn at the edges where Francisco stepped out. But now it is too far below us, it is becoming too dark to see. The nursery is engulfed in shadows. We have reached the top of the house.

"You can't get away from me," I mumble accusingly.

"You've taken me prisoner, have you? Right, I yield." Francisco lays me out flat upon my bed. He removes my boots.

"Jesus, Mary and Joseph, child, your feet are freezing."

I used to sleep with my Beloved. She used to warm my feet. Since we came to live with Francisco I have been banished to the nursery. There are compensations, but sleeping alone is not one of them. Francisco gives my toes a bracing rub.

"All right, soldier. Get in. Wriggle down."

"Will you tell me a story?"

Anything to keep him here. And out of the painting.

"Which one do you want? The escape across the marshlands? The battle with the alligator? The Mohammedan brigand who saved my life?"

"Tell me the story of the picture on the staircase."

"No game, soldier. You're not old enough for *The Rape of Lucretia*."

"No, no. Not the one with the black horse. The big, big one with the woman and the man."

"That's *Juno and Jupiter on Mount Ida*. They were the King

and Queen of the gods. But Juno was playing a very clever game. You see, there was a war on between the Greeks and the Trojans. All because Paris had run off with Helen, the most beautiful woman in the world . . ."

"Is she more beautiful than my Beloved?"

"No, of course not. Juno wasn't pleased about this, so she was on the side of the Greeks . . ."

"Why wasn't she pleased?"

"She thought that married people shouldn't run off with people they aren't married to, so . . .

"But you said . . ."

"Listen, soldier, do you want this story or don't you?"

"But . . . all right . . . go on."

"Juno was on the side of the Greeks and Jupiter was backing the Trojans. So she was hoping to seduce him off to sleep so that she could arrange the war without any interference. She asked Venus, the goddess of love, for help and Venus gave her a secret potion made with the dew of plants from the forest. And Jupiter was overcome with drowsiness and love . . ."

I don't hear all the story. But I have the impression that Juno and the Greeks are going to win. And so I am reassured. This is my Beloved's doing. My Beloved is always on the winning side.

❧ ❧ ❧ ❧ ❧

I hear her step, somewhere in the room. I smell warm roses in sunshine. She has been dancing. Her hands are damp.

"Is that you?"

"Shhhh, darling. Sleep now. It's nearly morning."

But I am wide awake.

"Did you dance all night?"

She laughs softly.

"Most of it, yes. When we weren't eating supper."

"Do you love me?"

"More than anyone else in the world."

This sounds sufficiently extravagant. But I want more.

"But do you love me the best? More than Francisco?"

"Well, it's different. You can't really compare."

This will not do.

"But if you had to choose?"

There is no hesitation.

"I would choose you."

"Mmmmm." I snuggle back down into the dark, satisfied. But there is one more question.

"Who painted you and Francisco on the staircase?"

"On the staircase?"

"Yes, enormous."

She laughs again. She has gathered up her shawl. She is leaving.

"That's Juno and Jupiter. Not us. And that was painted by your uncle, James Barry. Now go to sleep, my love."

But she is lying. I know she is. It is them.

❖ ❖ ❖ ❖ ❖

I knew who James Barry was. And I was afraid of him. He hated children. He had the reputation of being cantankerous and unreasonable. He was not often in the house. When he was there he ignored me. He usually ignored my Beloved too. He only talked to Francisco. But I spied on his passage through the hallway, up the staircase, into the library, out of the French windows, down the garden walks and into the bushes. I watched over his steps. I hid behind the great ornamental chest which contains the logs to watch him stump into the drawing room. I tried to remember all his swear words. I practised them in secret, on my own, hiding in the gardens. I counted the holes in his stockings. His wig smelt of linseed oil and ashes. I was afraid of him, but I was also fascinated. There was one particular thing about him which held me in thrall.

He looked like me.

And so I began to stalk him. After the night when I saw his painting move I began to lie in wait for him. I stared out of carriage windows. I hunted the walkways in the park, keeping low to the ground. I followed my Beloved's steps. I checked her daily collection of visiting cards. I listened out for gossip. James Barry was my target, the focus of my imagination.

When I knew James Barry he was an old man, stocky, robust, heavy on his feet, violent with the servants, rude to rich men, and ruder still to ladies who believed in religions. His lined face was impeccably shaven, his eyebrows thin, arched, aristocratic, his glance an inferno of desires.

Barry came to find Francisco. I had seen him from the school-room window, where I was sitting in a draught, learning Latin verbs by heart. I looked down through the early leaves which had just begun to thicken and shine. I saw his shabby hat bouncing up the gravel four floors below me. I knew Francisco was out. James Barry was hammering at the door. I crouched and slithered, calculating every distance crossed in relation to the sight-lines up the staircase. I must not be seen. Out of the schoolroom and along the landing, I uncoil steadily, oozing like liquid jelly, one step at a time, flat on my belly, all down the staircase. My Beloved is coming out of the upstairs drawing room; a breath of warm air accompanies her steps. I freeze into a wooden pilaster and become one with the tall clock in the corner as she patters down before me.

Salvatore opens the door. Spectacular, majestic in his bad manners, Barry drops his hat on the bench, refusing to wipe his muddy shoes on the scraper, and marches into the house, leaving a handsome trail of prints all across the immaculate sequence of black and white. He sees my Beloved and grunts the most minimal of greetings. She increases the speed of her descent, but he does not wait for her and stomps away into the downstairs breakfast room. Wherever Barry goes he leaves a trail of dirt. I wait for her to close the door, and for Salvatore to sweep up the mud on the hall flags. Then I continue upon my spiral down-wards. By the time I have flattened myself against the breakfast-room door they are having an argument. Unfortunately, James Barry is winning.

"Ask your husband's family, girl. I've told you. Not a farthing. Not one damned farthing . . ." Barry's voice is sharp with irri-tation. "She's not my responsibility. Can't you save something out of the housekeeping? Doesn't Francisco give you enough?"

"James, this is a family matter. It ought to be. Can't I even discuss it with you?"

"Oh, don't bother me, Mary Ann. If the child's clever she'll make her own way in the world. And a better marriage than you did. Let her amuse herself. You're like a harp with a single string. One long irritating whinge . . ."

I could hear one of them fiddling with the fire irons. That meant that their backs were turned. I risked the door. One of the great advantages of being small and thin is that you can ooze through doors like a flat shadow. I sat holding my breath, crouched between the piano leg and the curtain, when the door, which I had failed to re-shut properly, blew open. They both turned quickly away from the fire. My Beloved was pale, with two red spots, high on each cheek. She stepped across to the door and shut it firmly. Barry pulled one of the chairs closer to the fire. He spat a sizzling gobbet into the flames, then farted as he settled into his seat.

"Shall I ring for tea?" he asked rudely, as if nothing was the matter between them. My Beloved sat down upon the sofa, ignoring the bell rope, her back straight.

Barry chuckled, grunted, bit his lip, stared into the flames.

"I have enemies, Mary Ann. They are jealous of my success. Yes, my success. You may not see me as a success. But even if every door in London was locked against me they would still envy my work."

Then he began to stare at her. She remained seated in silence while the fire snapped and shuddered. For a few minutes neither of them said anything. Holding my breath involved an enormous effort. I began to dribble into the curtains. Suddenly she rose and tugged at the bell rope. All the drapes shuddered. I feared discovery. Barry watched her every movement, as if he saw her bones beneath the skin.

"Sit for me again, Mary Ann," he cried out with terrible intensity. She sprang to her feet. She was facing me. The two red spots in her cheeks flooded out to her ears and down her neck.

"No," she shouted. And she rushed out of the room, creating a huge gust of air which lifted the curtain and exposed my toes. I felt the tug of her skirt and pelisse, billowing out like a sail as she passed. The double doors slammed behind her.

I peered at the vibrating doors, astonished and impressed. Francisco and my Beloved never shouted at each other. When they discussed their affairs, especially the account books, there was a good deal of laughter and kissing. But she occasionally shouted at me. Barry had made her shout. He not only looked like me, he had the same effect upon my Beloved. As the vibrations from her departure gradually ceased Barry settled back into his chair, then he drew out a pipe and a leather pouch of tobacco. He chuckled to himself. I tried not to breathe. He puffed away quietly for about twenty minutes, accumulating a blue haze by the writing desk and the huge Oriental vase with blue shiny dragons, their faces like Pekinese dogs, which Beloved had told me never to touch. Pins and needles developed in my knees. I was on tiptoe, my single eye pressed to the crack in the curtains.

I grew bored with watching the lines on his face, the creases on his hands, the frayed edge of his coat, his stringy greying hair poking out from the offensive smelly wig, and the mud slowly drying on his tattered shoes and stockings. He was less frightening when he was closely observed. His hair had once been red like mine. I could tell from the thin streaks tied back behind his ears. But it was straight, as Beloved's would have been had she not spent hours with papers and curling tongs, persuading it to froth and whirl into beautiful curls. Barry clearly spent no time whatsoever on his toilette. He was neither handsome nor glamorous, he wore no jewellery and no frills. He was uncompromisingly plain.

Suddenly he was on his feet, four strides across the carpet and his fist clamped to the back of my neck, flesh and collar and all.

"Come out, you jealous little bastard or I'll pull you out by those damned red curls!"

I began yelling at the top of my voice as he dragged me onto the hearth rug. I knew at once that he intended to put out my eyes with a red-hot poker.

"Silence," he thundered, and boxed both my ears.

I shrieked and struggled. Barry picked me up by the belt and suspended me over the fender. The flames were barely two feet away and Barry's face was bloated and purple. I bit his wrist as hard as I could. He dropped me at once with a tremendous roar and reached for the poker. I somersaulted backwards on the rug, ready to run. Barry was upon me. The double doors flew open with a crash. Handsome, laughing, magnificent in his military uniform of unknown origins, every inch a revolutionary general, Francisco was standing in the doorway, peeling off his gloves.

"Well, well, James," he said, "am I interrupting a family discussion?"

❖ ❖ ❖ ❖ ❖

"You mustn't bite your uncle," my Beloved reproaches me gently, "whatever he says to you."

"He made you shout too," I counter.

"And you mustn't spy on your elders." She flushes slightly, reopening the abandoned Latin verbs. "Let's try *confiteor*."

"Was he really my father?"

"Whatever gave you that idea?" she says sharply, but I am watching closely and she has turned slightly pale. "He's your uncle. He's my brother."

"But I never met my father."

"Yes you did. You just don't remember him. You were very small when he died."

A pause. I am still looking at her intently and my Beloved picks up her embroidery. She bites her lip. Then she continues.

"Won't Francisco do? He's like a father to you."

"He's not my father. He's my commander-in-chief."

"But that's what fathers are." At last relaxed, she laughs. I persist gently.

"He's my General. Not my father."

But she was right too. Francisco had become a father to me and I loved him for it. I wanted to give in to her. I wanted her to win. And so I recited the verb *confiteor*, through all its conjugations, without hesitation or mistake.

❖ ❖ ❖ ❖ ❖

It was Francisco who taught me to read and to write. He taught me geography, history, philosophy, Latin, Greek, German and Spanish. We read the classics together. I read Homer in Greek long before I read Pope's translations. We also studied botany, but his books were about the plants in South America. All this information was exotic and marvellous and proved useless when

I was confronted with English hedgerows. Every morning, even on the mornings when they had had guests or had been to the theatre the night before, Francisco would be waiting for me in the library, and I would stand before him and recite whatever I had learned, before we proceeded to the next lesson. Learning was like building a cathedral. There was a proper order in which to construct the building. Francisco had a masterplan. I never doubted that. I learned many things by heart. Francisco said that it was important to learn with all your heart. And to know things, so that whatever else was taken from you, if you were a prisoner, or a hostage in the mountains, you would still guard many things that were secret, that only you would know. Knowledge would always protect you from destruction. He told me that it was more important to be clever than to be beautiful.

Beloved also heard me recite everything I had learned. Often in the late afternoons, when she was getting dressed. I loved to deserve her lavish praise. She never praised without kissing. And she taught me French, because he said she had a charming accent, which I would do well to acquire. But I never learned dancing, drawing, embroidery or theology. James Barry said that I had never learned any morals either. I heard him say so. And Beloved turned pink again with rage. But she didn't say anything. That was years later, when I didn't need her to speak up for me.

Francisco would wait for me in his library and when I appeared and saluted formally, legs together, back straight, keep your elbow parallel with your ear, that's right, he would always ask the same thing: "What's the news from the front today, soldier?" turning his face to the fire so that all his colours matched the bindings of his books, red, grey, brown, black, gold. His lamps had special safety devices, which snuffed them out, in case they were overturned. But he ordered a fire in the library, even in July, because he loved and treasured his books so well. That was one way I knew he loved me. He let me read his books.

On the lower shelves were ranks of huge encyclopaedias with blue and black leather bindings, dictionaries and books on natural history with hand-coloured engravings. Each image was separated from the facing page by a soft detachable sheet of absorbent paper. I was allowed to look at them if I could prove that my hands were clean. Francisco had travelled the world, amassing trunks of foreign languages and images. He had great hard-backed portfolios of maps and diagrams, architectural plans, political cartoons and anatomical explanations. He had an enormous collection of scrolls, some of them in Arabic and Hebrew. I was shown these on special occasions, but never allowed to touch them, no matter how clean my hands were. They were covered in a strange white powder, which slaughtered approaching insects.

"In the tropics there are tiny beetles which burrow right inside the books. You find every page covered with tiny holes," Francisco explained as I sniffed his deadly powders speculatively, "but this keeps them off. Go easy on the poison, soldier. It's not snuff."

Francisco read mostly poetry and philosophy. He loved both Rousseau and Voltaire. When we were together alone in the evenings he read Shakespeare aloud, trembling with passion or shaking with laughter, changing voices for every part. Even if I didn't get the jokes, I laughed with him. When he was quite carried away, he lovingly stroked all the buttons on the front of his uniform and made them shimmer and vibrate in the lamplight. I watched the dark hair shining on the back of his hands. He told me that he had learned to hate tyrants by reading Milton and he made me recite long passages from *Paradise Lost*. The passage that I loved best was the creation of the world. The tiny print swam before my eyes as I clutched the blue and gold text and spoke the words by heart as the lion struggled into being out of the cloying earth. When I looked up, Francisco was gently turning his huge globe of the pendant world, his hands full of tenderness and his eyes full of tears.

We spent hours perched on his moving wooden steps, a smooth spiral in shining elder with two platforms, one halfway down and one at the top, where we could sit on different levels and read to each other. Some of his books were locked up, and others were chained to the shelf. I gazed at these sinister, silent volumes, and the iron convent grilles which separated me from the rows of white vellum. Here was my forbidden tree, my fruit.

"You'll read them, soldier," said Francisco, "when you're old enough."

Once he took down a vast volume on South America and spread it out before me on the lectern. We had reached the chapter on the conquest of the Incas. Francisco never taught me one thing at a time: this was to be a mixture of history, geography and revolutionary politics. Slavery, torture and war had precise and graphic meanings for me long before I was ten years old. As he told the story of his continent and his peoples, Francisco became impassioned, distressed and enraged.

"With my own eyes, child, I have seen the Cross of Christ dishonoured and abused. Simple holy people forced down upon their knees to kiss the jewels hanging from the hands of the priests. We have grown rich and fat off foreign wars and the slavery of our fellow men . . .

"Our own dignity depends upon the love and care we have for others. If I do not care for my brother, I become less human . . .

"Love is not a feeling, child, nor even the passion of lovers, which always seeks only its own gratification. It is the act of caring, of giving, the act of protecting the weak, the helpless, the imprisoned and the desperate. Love is the hand raised in defence. You cannot love and keep your hands clean . . .

"The Church is founded upon a monstrous lie. No priest is closer to God than a simple peasant who cannot read or write, but drives his goats across the common pasture in the mornings . . .

"Do you think that God speaks in Latin? Of course you must learn Latin. To read Virgil, Ovid, Lucretius, Propertius, Tacitus. And you must learn how to interpret passion from Catullus. But you must never confuse sexual passion and the deeds of disinterested love. And you must read your Bible in plain English . . .

"When you fall in love, soldier, remember this. Passion is a form of madness. You will lose your way in the forest. Love is true dedication and service to your fellow human beings. That will bring you joy, ecstasy and suffering enough. Love will bring you closer to the people you serve and closer to God . . ."

My Beloved stood before us, like Judgement in the doorway, with a draught tugging at her skirts.

"You'd be less sentimental about the people if you had to deal with them every day," she snapped. "Twelve bottles of the

Portuguese dessert wine are missing from the cellar. Salvatore denies all knowledge of the matter."

"Love is sharing all your worldly goods with God's people," I suggested.

Francisco rose up in a burst of irritation and snatched the cellar keys that were swinging from Beloved's fingers.

"Who has duplicates?"

"You. And Salvatore."

"Hmm." Francisco stalked out of the door and down the staircase to negotiate a confrontation between idealism and villainy. My Beloved sat down beside me in the firelight, and smiled in a warm, late-afternoon conspiracy.

"Well, my dearest, I'll give them twenty minutes to accuse, shout, simmer and bicker. And then I'll ring for tea. Where had you got to?"

"Here. The speech by the Spanish governor."

She peered at the drawings of ecclesiastical torture apparatus in use upon several unfortunate Incas, sketched from life.

"Darling, is this quite suitable?"

"Francisco was telling me that it was all lies, because the Spanish intended to defraud the Incas of all their rights and land and force them to turn Christian. He said that real love showed itself when you treated your defeated enemy with generosity. He says treachery and deceit are the worst vices."

"Francisco is a soldier, darling. And a man of honour."

"Then you don't think he's right?"

I climbed onto the arm of her chair, coming closer to her scent. I could see the fine hair on her cheek and her skin warming in the reflection of the flames. The library rearranged itself around her; all the books turned to face her, the maps fluttered in their soft tissue, the bust of Shakespeare winked, the music, neatly arranged in folders, began to hum softly to itself. She was the Queen of Wands, the Witch of Beauty, my Beloved. I gazed at her. She smiled. And my adoration became ecstasy.

"Listen," she said, "you love your General. You want him always to be right and to know everything. He is a man who believes in liberty, the freedom of the people from Church and State. He has travelled the world and is very well-read. You want to believe every word he says and to be exactly like him. You will be. I promise you that. But remember that he is also a rich man. And the rich can afford to forget what things cost. Francisco will give you all he has. But you will also have something else, which is what I will give to you. You will know the cost of the real world, the price paid for Francisco's ideas. And who usually pays."

I didn't understand her. So I asked another question.

"Who stole the wine?"

"Salvatore, of course."

"How do you know?"

"He sold it to the innkeeper at the Dog and Duck to pay his gambling debts. He hoped I wouldn't notice."

"How are you so sure?"

"Do you think I don't know what goes on at the Dog and Duck?"

"Will you dismiss Salvatore?"

The penultimate housemaid had been dismissed for stealing. And she had denied it all, even the conclusive incriminating evidence, with a good deal of screaming in the kitchen. Francisco preferred men in his house anyway, so that it was more like a barracks.

"Heavens, no. I'll deduct it from his wages over a year."

"Is that what Francisco means when he says that real love is being generous to your defeated enemy?"

My Beloved laughed.

"Begin reading, my precious. Here."

❖ ❖ ❖ ❖ ❖

There were two washes: the small wash, half a day, supervised by my Beloved, her keys rattling as she rationed out the soap, and the great wash, which was carried out like a military operation, by Mrs Blake and Mrs Booth.

A great wash in the household happened every two weeks. The event lasted all day and took place in the washhouse, which stood between the kitchen and the side door leading into the vegetable garden. Its windows looked out onto a small sunny yard where a bevy of scrawny cats gathered on the gravel, awaiting the regular leftovers. One had a sinister milky eye and was called Nelson. But the others had no names and would not be touched. I often sat in the doorway while the wash was going on, flicking pebbles at strategic objects in the yard: a derelict mangle, a rusting bucket. The cats either chased the pebbles or menaced me. Inside the washhouse were two vast stone sinks with wellworn, pale, wooden washboards, streaked with grey. In the corner chimney was a small wood stove with a brick surround on which we placed a huge cauldron for boiling whites.

If I escaped unnoticed from the nursery or lessons in the library I was allowed to fill the cauldron and help Salvatore light the fire. Then I could watch the back door and listen for the bell which announced the joint arrival of Mrs Blake and Mrs Booth. They were enormous: red-boned Amazons of tremendous proportions, who arrived in bonnets and mufflers, shawls, aprons and clogs. They had political opinions. They accused Salvatore, to his face, of being a French spy. He ignored them.

"He can't possibly be a French spy," I said. "He comes from Venezuela."

"That's what you think, my lad. But he could still be working for the Frenchies. You don't think Bonaparte would be so stupid as to employ a Frenchman, do you? That's too obvious. No, he's too clever. Much better to use someone from the Americas. Someone nobody'd suspect."

"But you do suspect him, Mrs Booth. So it hasn't worked."

Like all children, I was relentlessly logical.

"Well, I have my suspicions. But that's because I'm nobody's fool." She unwound her shawl, which smelled of sweat and woodsmoke, and laid it down beside the mangle in the washhouse. If I helped with the wash I was allowed to feed sheets through the mangle. Sheets, pillowcases and underwear were boiled hot to kill the bugs. The rest was washed in icy water which we purchased from the neighbour's well. Mrs Blake never said anything except "Down with the King" from time to time, to get on Mrs Booth's nerves. My Beloved often said that Francisco employed political eccentrics who would never be employed anywhere else.

"But that can't be true," I argued. Mrs Blake and Mrs Booth did the great wash for all the other houses all down the street.

Next time they came I made trouble deliberately, and asked Mrs Booth outright whether she thought that Francisco was a French spy too. His past was certainly against him.

"Never," she thundered. "Your stepfather is a gentleman."

This was the first time that I had heard him referred to as my stepfather. My Beloved was there with us, bent double, her hands filthy, organising the wood to stoke the bread ovens and the washhouse fires.

"Did you become an honest woman and marry Francisco? Without telling me?"

Her ears turned red. Then she boxed mine smartly. Mrs Booth chuckled into her soap suds.

❖ ❖ ❖ ❖ ❖

She may not have been married to him, but my Beloved managed every aspect of Francisco's household. She never lay about in bed drinking chocolate like some of the ladies whom we visited. She nosed around in cupboards and kept an immaculate ledger of household accounts. She had two books. One was her rough copy, which had lots of crossings-out and figures scrawled in different colours. The other was in ravishing italics, with no mistakes. This was the one she presented to Francisco for inspection every Friday morning. I don't think he ever added up the figures; he just admired her handwriting and kissed her fingers. She could have been accumulating a small fortune, for Francisco was very generous with his money. But she always insisted that it was very important for women to be above and beyond all suspicion in matters of honour and matters of money.

"You must always be able to account for every hour and every penny." She placed her blotter carefully on her final addition. Mrs Booth said that there were only two authorities to whom women were accountable: God and their husbands. I repeated this. My Beloved exploded.

"You must never marry! Never! I forbid it."

Then she burst into tears.

I promised her never to marry. I was so anxious to reassure her, that I never asked her why.

I was nine years old at that time.

❖ ❖ ❖ ❖ ❖

I did not see James Barry again, after the biting incident in the breakfast room, for at least half a year. He may have come to the house late at night. My Beloved may have visited his studio. Or he may have been travelling abroad. She never mentioned him. I never heard him announced. He didn't leave visiting cards. I went through the collection on the hall platter. But that didn't mean that they hadn't seen him or that he hadn't come.

That spring I studied hard: Italian, French, botany, history, Latin and mathematics, at which I excelled. Francisco was delighted with me. But I still never learned how to draw, press flowers into delicate arrangements or execute passable water-colours, and I didn't have a dancing master. I realised that other children learned these things and that I was being given a selective education. That was the year we set up a telescope on the back lawn and spent hours gazing at the stars. Francisco named one constellation after another. I too learned how to read the strange invisible lines in the sky: Orion, Ursa Major, Pleiades, the seven sisters clustered together, see, see how clear they are.

"The secrets of heaven and earth, soldier, are engraved in the tiniest things, in the ants you never notice until you lie flat on your stomach in the grass, in the great formations of the clouds and in these distant specks of light, which are the source of so many myths and dreams. The greatest mysteries of all are written in the hearts of women and men. Look, there's Mars, the bloody planet and the God of War. The brighter one on the left. Hold on, I'll lift you up."

Francisco lifted me onto a stool, to stare out into the blurred void. He wanted me to grasp this distance, this immensity, without fear. He wanted me to feel that my small spot of earth was the point from which I had the right to watch the whole world and all the worlds beyond. I remember the gleam of his pearl cufflinks, which shone in the pale dark of a London garden.

Francisco brought me up to ask questions and to insist upon my right to know the answer.

We packed up the house at the beginning of June, just as our city garden unfolded into a torrent of colours.

"Where are we going? Where are we going?"

"To Shropshire," said Francisco, "to spend the summer at a big house in the country with a very eccentric friend of mine – and your mother's. He's wealthy, learned and amusing. He's the eleventh Earl of Buchan. There will be other children there and you will enjoy yourself. And you'll be seeing your uncle, James Barry."

He paused. He looked at me hard. Then he laughed.

"And whatever you do, don't bite him again. Understood?"

Yes, sir.

❖ ❖ ❖ ❖ ❖

My Beloved complained all the way to Shropshire. She complained of the heat, the inns, the beds, the coach, the roads, the mosquitoes, the food, her fatigue, my fidgeting, Francisco's equanimity. I gathered from all this that she did not want to visit the country at all. But I was transfixed by white blossom and fresh, glimmering green. Down all the muddy roads, throughout all the counties, beside every turnpike through which we passed, a lavish, floating mass of white pushed against the carriage doors. I sat pinned to the grimy windows, mesmerised by the unending flood of hawthorn and cow parsley, fresh in the damp sunlight, breathless beside this glamorous, sinuous, seductive green. The whole colour of my world, illuminated by June shafts of heat, was green. Thatched roofs, brick walls and roses always gave way to green; even the beggars seemed less menacing as they emerged, tattered and haggard, from the wall of green. My city eyes were drunk with green. I fell in love with a spring that I had never seen before, my first green spring.

"Don't you remember Shropshire, soldier? Or the house?" Francisco tucked my curls into my cap so that no one would see how short my hair had been cut.

"How could he?" snapped my Beloved. "He can't have been more than three years old."

"It was where I first met you," he said, "and I was very jealous when I realised that Mary Ann loved somebody else. Even a red-headed little body with ginger freckles, like yourself."

I saw nothing, trying to remember; just a stone balustrade, two fat cherubs astride a stone dolphin, and a golden chain.

The house in Shropshire was enormous, but we arrived after dark. I was asleep in Francisco's arms when we trotted into the park. I only half remember the uneven outline of its massive bulk. I don't remember the people standing on the great steps under the perpendicular Tudor chimneys, but apparently they were all there to meet us. I didn't like to think that someone had looked at me when I was asleep. Francisco carried me up all the long staircases to bed. I fell asleep again, convinced that I was in one of Piranesi's *carceri*.

My room was at the top of the house and I awoke in the early dawn to a cascade of birdsong and chilly, damp sheets. I was still wearing my vest and short trousers. My other clothes lay in a heap on the floor and I was dangerously hungry. I pissed in the chipped blue chamberpot which was kept under the bed. It had a sinister yellow stain all round the rim. I tried not to notice, pulled on yesterday's clothes and set off to explore the house.

It was a monument of dull mirrors and chipped gilt. I crept through the shadowed spaces, but all my initial precautions were worthless, as it was a house where children were ignored. I caught sight of Rupert descending the cellar staircase as if he had lived there all his life. He nodded, winked at me, and disappeared into the vaults. The kitchens were in action, with a good deal of shouting going on above the slit throats of dead poultry, as yet unplucked, and the large vats of milk, which a woman with huge red hands was skimming off, dipping her fingers into the cream from time to time. I stole two bread rolls still warm from the ovens and ran for my life. No one took any notice of me. So I slithered on, past pantries, up back stairs, into a room hung with foul-smelling linen and a row of full chamberpots awaiting attention. I inspected their washhouse, twice the size of ours. I tried the door of the dresser. Locked. I hid in the broom and bucket cupboard while the butler cleaned the fish knives and candlesticks. He muttered to himself while he did it and never saw me. I willed him to see me, but he never once looked round. I finally reached the drawing room, which had four sets of French windows, opening out onto endless damp lawns and a distant ha-ha.

I was discreetly trying out the sofa springs when the great clock, whose face was painted with sentimental pansies, suddenly gulped, whirred, breathed and struck eight o'clock. Beside the clock, on a shining table, under a thin glass dome, stood an authentic, once living fox, stuffed, dynamic, with its teeth bared. Beneath one triumphant paw, a dead rabbit lay stretched out, bloody and bizarre, its glass eye fixed on heaven. I gazed at this for a long time. It was very odd to see the natural world, murderous but frozen, presented as a decoration in a family drawing room. I pinned my nose to the thin dome of glass and watched it mist over slightly, as if the animals were breathing. Francisco did not have any curiosity cabinets or geological collections, only books. I peered into the dome, anxious to verify my suspicions that the moss and grass under the fox's handsome lifted brush were in fact made of slit waxed ribbons.

I never heard him come in. I simply felt his hand clamped to the back of my neck. I was twirled round like a marionette, my feet clear of the ground, and found myself eyeball to eyeball with James Barry.

He hissed into my face, with a little spray of spit, "If you try to bite me again, I'll knock all your teeth out."

There was a terrible pause. He put me down and whistled quietly for a moment, but he did not relinquish his grip on my collar, and he began to stare into my face with grim fixity. Close to, I could see that his teeth were yellow and rotten. His breath smelt of alcohol and tobacco. He crouched above me triumphantly, staring so hard that I became convinced he was counting my freckles. Gradually, I became less afraid and stared back. The old painter was masticating like a feeding beast. I watched the black hairs in his nostrils quivering as he chewed.

"I'm sorry I bit you, sir," I said finally, and my voice came out firm, but one octave too high.

"Never say that you're sorry for the things you meant to do, child."

He paused and went on chewing and staring.

"Come and visit my studio, before your eyeballs crack."

He put out his hand. It was perfectly clean, soft and white; the skin around the fingernails was cracked and scarred. I understood that this was a genuine gesture of friendship and so, without hesitating, I put my hand in his.

James Barry's studio was on the north side of the house, facing the hill and a huge mass of rhododendrons, which had finished flowering and now formed a darkening phalanx of thick and sultry green. The floor was of polished wood and around the two huge wooden scaffolds which supported his painting there was a mass of crumpled, stained canvas sheeting. His paints lay in disarray on a long table, with a variety of dishes and bowls. I saw a pestle and mortar made of marble, both stained with red. The room was vast and cold, and stank of varnish and turpentine.

I didn't look at the painting, but out of the great windows. In the rushing shadows and bright bars of sunlight crossing the gardens, I saw rabbits bouncing in the grass and above them, a roaring, seething mass of green.

"Come and have a look from here." Barry gestured towards the painting. "You're too close to see it by the window."

I stepped back. Parts of the stretched canvas were naked and raw. Across the grimy, unpainted spaces he had drawn careful lines in faint blue crayon: designs for faces, a horse's arched neck and splayed mane, a staircase on which stood two large classical pots, decorated with grimacing satyrs, just like those on our wine glasses at home. They were partly blocked in with thin paint. I stared, but could not make sense of the fragments. The whole refused to appear. Barry pulled me a little further backwards and set me on a high stool. He was surprisingly strong. I was now on a level with the images before me. And then the action of the painting began to take place. It was Rome, built on the hills in the pale, diminishing background. In the foreground, a battle of sorts. Here were huge Roman figures with straight noses and reddened muscular thighs, flat swords, arms raised in slaughter, or embracing pale, gleaming mounds of naked female flesh. The blood, blond hair and undulating breasts surged and rippled into patterns. It was the scale of the painting that sickened me. Too large, too brutal and too close to my face. I stared. Then shut my eyes.

"Well?" Barry was unperturbed. He now stood very close to the painting with his back to me, peering into the layers of paint. "Well, child?"

"What is it?" I kept my eyes firmly shut. Tell me, I don't want to look for myself.

"It's an historical subject. Naturally. As are all the greatest paintings. You know your history, don't you? Can't believe that Francisco hasn't taught you about the rape of the Sabine women and the founding of Rome."

I opened my eyes. Once explained, the flesh looked less menacing. Barry ignored me and began working on one huge enfolding Roman arm. Reflected sunlight flickered for an instant on the studio walls. I could hear the faint chime of bells from the domestic quarters in the household. I gazed at the stony Roman profiles, the dimpled jaws, full cheeks and fixed grey eyes. It was oddly frozen, each figure embalmed in gleaming colour; even the tortured female forms seemed suspended, like scientific specimens floating in spirits. I gazed at the static canvas for a long time. And there the figures remained, monumental, immobile, and as lifeless as the volcanic bodies at Pompeii.

"What's rape?" I asked finally. It was clearly slightly different from butchery.

"It has two meanings, both of which are current here," said Barry, without looking round. "What does *rapere* mean in Latin? Answer quickly."

"To seize or to snatch."

"There you have it," Barry commented, beginning to scratch gently at one point of the painting with a tiny razor. "*The Rape of the Sabines*. But it also means to have carnal knowledge of a woman without her consent. I don't think that the Romans were given to asking anything politely. Anyway, all societies are based on the seizure, slaughter and slavery of women, child. You ask your mother."

I reflected on this information for a while, but I had the fixed

idea that carnal was something to do with meat and thus formed
the opinion that the Sabines were obliged by the Romans to eat
meat, after having been strictly vegetarian. Francisco had read
Horace with me and so I was under the illusion that the Sabines
all lived on farms.

"Here she is. Your mother."

He stepped aside so that I could see the dark, luminous face
of a woman in white, escaping from the painting. It was my
Beloved, younger, but just as slender, quick and graceful, her
hand half raised to protect her face, her dress torn, one breast
exposed; she turned, mouth open, crying out, her curls falling
loose down her back. But she was getting away from the Romans;
a long, empty alley of cypresses stretched stiffly before her. The
painting would soon no longer contain her. I smiled, and Barry
understood my smile.

"Ha. Yes. That's Mary Ann. Always finds a way out, your
mother does. Surprised she got caught pregnant with you, really.
Or that she didn't put paid to you with pointed twigs or by
swallowing cockroaches. No morals, that woman. Just brains,
plenty of brains . . ."

Barry went on talking, but more to the painting than to me.

"She's beautiful now. When she's not in a temper. But ten
years ago she was very, very beautiful. You don't look like her at
all. More's the pity for you . . .

"She used to sit for me. When I couldn't afford models. I put
her in every painting. As Juno, Pandora, Cordelia, Eurydice . . .
I painted her as Chastity, as Fertility, as Liberty, as Artemis, as
Aphrodite, as the Angel or the Maenad. In *The Education of
Achilles* you can just see her beyond the Centaur, a pale wraith,
gazing back from the darkness, excluded and envious. She isn't
going to be taught by Centaurs. There's an odd mixture of
cunning and envy in Mary Ann. You can't see her face, it's her
body I've painted . . .

"I wrote to her, almost daily, during all the years I was in
Rome. Why didn't she wait for me? I'd have sent for her as soon
as I was in a position to do so. I'll never forgive her for that
cretinous wretch Bulkeley. A waste, a waste . . . I sent her presents
when I had the money. Patterns, stuff, silk, the best lace I could

buy from Cambrai. She wanted to travel too, of course. And Father wouldn't let her. All the education she ever had was what I taught her. And what she taught herself. You're a lucky little bugger to have Francisco to teach you. He'd take great pains with you. And he's good to her. But it was through me that she met both Erskine and Miranda. Damm her. She'd never have been anything if it hadn't been for me . . .

"I made her what she is, child. But I never made her a whore. She did that all by herself. The woman survives by trickery. Disguises. Who is Mary Ann Barry? Mary Ann Bulkeley? Even her own child will never know. There she sits, nice as pie at the dinner table. Smiling at the men. Pretending to be up on society conversations. The woman wears every face I've ever painted . . .

"I've made love to that woman in oils, child, year after year, and she's always hated me for it . . ."

Suddenly he swung round and glared at me, jabbing the air between us with his brush. The Romans looked out of the painting, swords raised.

"What does she say about me? Mind you speak the truth."

There was another terrible pause. I spoke perfect truth.

"She never mentions your name to me, sir. And when I ask anything about you, she changes the subject."

"Ha!"

Barry growled at the Romans, thrusting his nose into a pile of turpentine rags. He said no more. After some minutes had passed in silence and gentle scratching, I climbed carefully and silently down from the stool and crept away into the bowels of the house, closing his studio door behind me.

❖ ❖ ❖ ❖ ❖

The house belonged to the servants in the early mornings. Some of the scullery maids and kitchen boys were my age or only slightly older. I looked at them all with haughty curiosity, spied upon them from cracks and knots in the pantry doors, the tops of garden walls, from behind the dresser. I was desperate with loneliness. Sometimes they giggled and pointed. But mostly, they carried on working or laughing amongst themselves and ignored me. By mid-morning neither my Beloved nor Francisco had appeared and my misery was complete. I had prowled through the stables, cackled at the chickens, eaten a cucumber from the greenhouse and broken one flowerpot. No one wanted to play with me or to be my friend. In fact, I had no idea how to approach the kitchen boys. In London I was used to living with four self-preoccupied adults, but they always had time for me. Francisco gave up part of every day to teach me. I invented my own worlds when I was alone. I knew no other children. Now I was marooned in a mansion of possible acquaintances, none of whom I had managed to meet. I sat down on top of the ha-ha in a pool of gloom, gazing at the distant purple hills of Wales.

Then I saw something white rustling in the long grass beneath me. Hastily, I assumed battle stations, took aim with my stick and prepared to defend my position.

"Halt! Who goes there?"

A small, dark-headed girl with a dimple in her smile and a gold gypsy ring in her left ear came out of the grass with her hands up.

"Drop your weapons," I commanded.

"Haven't got any," she said, but she was carrying a ball of white in her left hand.

"Give me that." I still had her covered.

"Catch." She flung up the bundle and swarmed up the sheer face of the ha-ha with rapid agility. Her knees and her apron were covered in grass stains. She worked in the kitchens. I had seen her very early that morning, scouring carrots. She sat down beside me as I laid aside my rifle and undid the bundle. It contained two pairs of white silk stockings.

"Just trying them on," she explained, "but they're too big yet. I'll keep them till I'm grown."

"Whose were they?" I already knew they were stolen. The dimpled smile was unabashed.

"Who'd you think? They belonged to the Missus. I'd never lay my hands on your mother's stockings. Hers don't have darns. But Lady Elizabeth won't miss them. She's got dozens. They're ever so rich."

She pulled at my short curls in several different places and gazed at me anxiously.

"Is it really true you're Mr Barry's natural son?"

I flushed bright red with embarrassment and shouted, "It's not true. My father's dead. He died before you or I were born. And now we live with the General and I'm not a son."

I hesitated. I had never been dressed as daughters usually were and was therefore swaying in limbo between the safe worlds of either sweet ribbons or breeches.

"No offence meant," said the kitchen girl amiably. "My mum's no more married than yours is. Are you really a girl? Prove it."

I couldn't think how to prove it.

"Don't be silly," she giggled, "show us your prick. If you're a boy you've got a prick and if you're a girl you've got a hole. Like skittles. Look." And she pulled up her apron and skirts to reveal two plump dirty thighs and a blossoming triangle of soft dark hair. She looked proudly down upon the display. It was more difficult for me to remove my breeches, but I began undoing all the buttons. I fumbled with nervousness and fright. She twitched impatiently at this lengthy operation and before they were half undone she pushed my muddling fingers aside and thrust her hand down my pants. It was a most perturbing sensation. For a second she looked at me, puzzled and amazed, her fingers moving on an exploratory voyage between my legs. Then she burst out laughing, withdrew her hand and kissed me.

"Well, you're a sort of a girl, I suppose. But definitely not like me. Perhaps you're a girl dressed up as a boy? Or a boy that's got enough girl for it not to matter too much either way. Well, I'll tell everybody that you're not Mr Barry's son after all."

"Yes, tell them," I said tearfully, floundering in a pool of ambiguity.

"Don't cry. Boys don't cry. And anyway, it's not sad. He's an awkward old bugger and I wouldn't want him for a father. But it is funny that you look just like him."

"That's because he's my uncle. You can look like your uncle, can't you?"

"Then that'll do as an explanation." She gave me another hug and wiped my eyes with the hem of her apron.

"What's your name?" I asked.

"Alice Jones."

She never asked me mine.

"Come on," said Alice. "I'll show you the new kitchens."

The rain had begun. We ran all the way.

Through the dining room, down the back passage, left by the pantry, down one flight of stone steps, behold a cream door with a large hatch and a little shelf to lean on, too high for either of us, stop, listen, turn the knob, slide in.

David Erskine had invested in a new range with a boiler at the back to supply both the kitchens and the scullery with hot water and steam for the warm closet and steam table. There was a tap at the front and a kettle beneath. The kitchen itself was a furnace of good smells. A very large, handsome woman was extracting a currant cake from its hoop. The solid, rich black mass descended with a thud onto the scrubbed wooden table and the cook prodded it expectantly. Alice clung to the end of the table and peered at the cake. There was a boy I'd never seen before snoring in the corner.

I stared at the mass of new pots and the dripping pan, all larger and more lavish than anything we had at home. There was an old iron skillet with which the cook had clearly refused to part, but it was redundant beside the handsome copper stew pans hanging on the wall in descending sizes, all with their own polished lids. My hunger had reached starvation levels. Apart from the two bread rolls, I had eaten nothing since seven o'clock on the previous evening.

"Any chance of a small pie each?" asked Alice.

Cook didn't look at her. "Get the grater and prepare the nutmeg. Then we'll see."

No promises.

Alice knew where everything was kept. She pushed me onto a stool by the table, then climbed up to reach a tin on the dresser. The tin was not marked. The one next to it said CURRY POWDER and next to that was a large bottle of anchovy essence. David Erskine liked foreign foods. So did Francisco. I was quite sure I wouldn't.

Alice washed her hands before energetically settling down to grate fingernails and nutmeg into a fine dust.

I looked around. Two plucked ducks and a goose were

hanging naked over the sink, their limp necks a spectacle of tragedy. Cook saw me looking.

"You'll be happy enough when you eat a bit of those tonight," she snapped. "And they're a lot cheaper than what your master pays in London. We only eat our own. That foreigner you've brought with you, who's so brown you'd think he was born in a desert or in Africa, says that a good goose in town costs five shillings. He says his name means Saviour. Blasphemous, if you ask me. I shouldn't be surprised if he was a French spy."

"Everybody thinks that," I admitted.

"Then it must be true," cried the cook triumphantly. She began her elaborate decorations on the cake.

I was beginning to understand the force of general opinion.

"Pies, please," said Alice, handing over a little dish of grated nutmeg.

Cook extracted two small meat pies from the pantry and we sat on the back porch, just out of the chilly rain, munching our spoils.

"Are you older than me?" I asked doubtfully. I rather thought that she was.

"Yes. Lots. I'm four years older than you. You're ten. We asked the man from Africa. But I'm small for my age. I know my birthday. It's written down in the parish register and the rector put on his spectacles and read it out to me. Mum says he's a good man. He writes down all the children in the parish whether their mum is married or not. So everyone is officially born and no sermons or questions. There's some people who don't like it that we're in the same book as them. People round here think that they're as good as Londoners . . ." Now she looked at me, impressed, suddenly remembering that I lived in London.

"Can you get your mum to take me on? I'm desperate to get to London, but if I didn't have a situation my mother wouldn't let me go. What's it like? Speak truth."

"Noisy and dirty," I said, mired in truth.

This was not the correct answer.

"But aren't there grand buildings? And great wide streets? And bands? And the King? And parades?" Alice didn't have any images against which to test my words. She gazed at me in disappointment. I was not delivering the goods.

"There's the Lord Mayor's Day parade," I suggested helpfully. "That's very grand. But in winter there's fog all the time and mud in the streets. We live in a street near the park, where there are trees. It's only when you go east into the city that it smells. And it's full of beggars and thieves."

Alice was alarmed.

"But theatres? And musical evenings? And fine ladies in dresses from Paris?"

"Oh yes. We have all that in our house." I brightened up.

"Do you dress up?"

"Not for the visitors. I just watch from the staircase."

"Like us," said Alice. So I wasn't special after all. "Sometimes I serve the cakes at tea, but not often. Cook says I'm never clean enough. And Harold hates me."

Harold was David Erskine's butler, whom I had seen polishing the fish knives. An unexpected equality was now established between us, so Alice moved on to the personal questions.

"I'd like to wear boy's clothes too, but Mum wouldn't let me. Can you read and write?"

"Yes."

And suddenly a real passion flashed into her face. There was no hesitation, only desire.

"Teach me."

"All right."

"Starting today. I'll find you. Promise. You're staying all the summer. I'll kill myself if I can't read by harvest. Oh, promise you'll teach me. Cross your heart and hope to die. Give me my stockings. They're in your pocket. Don't tell. Kiss. No silly, on the mouth. Cook says boys kiss girls on the mouth, not the nose. Don't forget. Don't you dare forget."

And then she leaped up and ran away across the kitchen yard through the rain, past the gate in the wall to the vegetable garden and on down the brick path to the stables. She didn't look back.

❧ ❧ ❧ ❧ ❧

The bright morning had sunk into a soggy grey torrent of chill rain. It was still raining when we all sat down to dinner at four o'clock. My Beloved had insisted on walking through the shrubbery in her galoshes and had come back with her skirts and stockings dripping and spattered in mud. The geraniums on the terrace bowed down, shedding their petals, and the pansies folded up. All colour vanished, then the countryside did too. Nothing remained, just one grey sheet of rain.

The mistress of the house was not beautiful. She looked old, but kind, and she wore formidable layers of white lace, all of which vibrated as she walked. When I first saw her she was shaking in the hallway, and demanding fires in all the rooms.

"Ridiculous weather for June," she said to me, for I was crouching on the staircase. "We shall all die of boredom. Come on downstairs, child, and let me look at you."

I descended slowly, one step at a time. She waited, staring, clearly surprised by my appearance. When I was within reach she put both hands on my shoulders and looked at me hard.

"Well," she said softly, "Mary Ann's little baby. Her only child . . ." She suddenly kissed me on the forehead. I hate it when adults touch me. They never give any indication that they are going to do so and they always smell peculiar. I sat down on the last stair, overwhelmed by the stench of musk and powder. She smelt like a damp cupboard full of linen. But she laughed out loud and drew me to my feet again.

"Come along, my dear. I haven't set eyes on you for nearly six years. But that's not because I didn't want to see you, nor for lack of invitations. You've grown up into someone quite different from what I had expected. Have you eaten anything at all today? Francisco went out shooting and then it came on to rain . . . they must have quite forgotten all about you. Would you like to bang the gong for dinner? Then you can go into the drawing room and tell them all that dinner is served. I always bang the gong and no one ever moves."

She took my hand and rattled on cheerfully, handing me a giant drumstick and introducing me to a gong the size of a cathedral door. It was engraved with intertwining Chinese dragons and serpents. I hammered its glossy sides with zeal and then pranced ahead of the moving caravan of lace into the drawing room.

But there my tongue was tied. The fox and the rabbit had been joined by people I had never seen before and one of them was even more extraordinary than the lace tower. She was wearing a loose black silk dress with a tight high collar, and her hair was scraped back into a mean little roll at the nape of her neck. She wore neither powder nor paint, but had a pale, faintly yellow skin. Her face was timeless, unlined and utterly still. It was her stillness that unnerved me. Everyone else in the drawing room was talking, or waving their hands. Even my Beloved was smoking; an elegant white clay pipe, dappled with love knots all round the bowl and down the stem. But this woman sat quite still in the midst of them. And looked at me.

"Lost your voice, sweetheart? Don't bother. Here, I'll call them all." And the lace woman clapped her hands, so that a little shower of powder fell down upon my head. I stared at the black silk woman in alarm as the chatter surged on above me. She finally moved, very slowly, like a serpent uncoiling, and rose to her feet. I flung myself into Beloved's arms.

"My darling, have you been amusing yourself? Have you broken anything?" she asked gently, giving me a hug.

"One flowerpot," I confessed.

"Met any other children, soldier?" Francisco was beside her, his long legs stretched out towards the fire.

"Yes."

I did not like to admit that I was already under contract to Alice Jones for reading lessons. They all began to disentangle themselves from their sofas and chairs. I edged away from the rustle of black silk and placed myself carefully between the white lace tower and my Beloved. Their voices rang above me as I sat staring at rows of silver cutlery. It was the first time in my life that I had sat down to dinner with the adults.

"Did you wash your hands and face, soldier?" whispered Francisco, as the master, David Erskine, who looked like a stringy mass of red flesh and white whiskers, rose to say grace.

"Yes," I muttered.

" . . . *per Jesum Christum Dominum nostrum*. Amen."

I was staring at the coil of black silk with her still hands and steady gaze. She was either a spectre or a debt collector. And now she was staring at my uncle, James Barry.

The old painter shuffled in halfway through grace and took his place behind his chair at the end of the table, wiping his brow and thick lips with a paint-spattered handkerchief. He drank his soup without looking up once, making terrible slurping noises. No one rebuked him, as Beloved would have done if I had been the one to slurp. I understood very little of what they said. They talked, laughed, gossiped, argued, disagreed. Every so often one of them would claim everyone's attention and hold forth until another interrupted. Sometimes one of them, usually one of the men, told a joke and the whole table rocked and chuckled. Then they all paired off and talked very earnestly to the person next to them. David Erskine rapped his glass, which tinkled like a tiny bell, and made a short toast and they all rose up, dropping their napkins and snagging their chairs on the carpet. Francisco poured a mouthful of wine into my glass and I watched it shining like fresh blood, afraid to drink.

Outside, the rain attacked the terrace and poured out over the rims of the gutters, creating a thick waterfall in front of the windows and rushing in a little river down the mossy steps. The cupids astride the dolphins soon found their naked toes bathed in water. I slid down from my chair between courses and pressed my nose to the windows. The world was swallowed up in an unnatural early dark. Candles were lit on the table and all around the room. Now they were talking politics, peace and war, and the necessity for both. Barry described his journey across the Alps, chewing his mutton chops at the same time, so that we could all see a mess of meat at the bottom of his mouth. He talked, indifferent as to whether anyone was listening or not. Then David Erskine told us how much he had paid for a huge oil painting of the St Gotthard Pass and Barry told him that there were no landscape painters of any significance left in England and that he had certainly been cheated. I was listening to the rain, the wine glass's dangerous crystal pressed against my lips. And the black silk serpent was staring at the white tower of lace, forcing her occasionally to smile, nod or glance anxiously down the table at my mother. Our hostess was not at ease. But I was used to this. This was the world of women and men, who always seemed to be demanding something of one another, implied rather than honestly spoken out loud.

I lost interest in their long significant glances and eager chatter and thought about Alice Jones. I tried to remember how I had learned to read. And I found that I could recall the exact moment, when I had taken my finger away from the printed line of *The Arabian Nights*, realising that now each word followed the next effortlessly, flawlessly, in a vast ascending curve. But that was after several years of trying. Start with the alphabet. A is for Apple. B is for Bird. C is for Cat, which has eaten the Bird. D is for Darkness, where no one can see her. E is for Emerald, which she wears on her breast. The black silk serpent was wearing a large green brooch just beneath her left collarbone. And now, once more, she was staring at me. But I had grown bolder, and I stared back through the red glow of my crystal wine and it looked as if her face was on fire. As I watched she smiled ever so slightly, and raised her glass just a little, in an almost imperceptible toast. It was a wry, small smile, breaking her stillness. And then she winked at me.

Before I was ten years old, I had learned, as all children do, to watch the shifting winds, to learn the high tides of adult friendships, adult loves. But now I was at last knowingly implicated in the intrigues of the adult world. The serpent woman had presented me with her visiting card. I looked down at the wine in the glass. And, almost imperceptibly, I blushed. Our complicity was complete. But the agreement had not gone unseen. Francisco had watched the serpent wink. And at once he leaned down to cut my meat, which lay cold and congealing in a mixture of fat and gravy. I held on to the edge of his coat, and stared into my plate.

When the ladies rose to take coffee in the drawing room Francisco pulled back my chair too.

"Hop it, soldier. Off to bed. And don't bother your mother. Can you find your way up all those staircases?"

I nodded and fled.

On the second landing my arm was seized by a pink scrubbed

hand hiding under a sideboard, which, by coincidence, also had painted pink legs.

"Hssssst."

It was Alice Jones.

"You haven't forgotton?" She scurried up the staircase just in front of me, increasing speed with every step.

"No, but I don't have many books in my room. I've looked."

"One will do. Any one. Surely once you've read one you can read them all?"

"Some're more difficult. Like the Bible."

"I've already learned most of that by heart," declared Alice breathlessly as we reached the room at the top of the stairs in total darkness. "Or at least, all the bits that really count."

There was only one candle, but someone had lit the fire, so that the small room was alive with leaping shadows. The smell of damp had gone. Outside the rain battered against the windows. Alice climbed straight into bed with all her clothes on and without removing her boots, while I undressed clumsily, desperately nervous, and fumbling with all the buttons. No one came to help me. There was no water in my pitcher and the morning's piss was still floating in the chamberpot. I had been completely forgotten.

"Come on. I've not got that long," said Alice, balancing both pillows behind her head.

I picked up the book with the largest print, which was *Pilgrim's Progress*, and climbed into bed beside her.

"*As I walked through the wilderness of this world, I lighted upon a certain place where was a Den, and I laid me down in the place to sleep; and as I slept I dreamed a Dream. I Dreamed, and behold I saw a man clothed with Rags, standing in a certain place, with his face from his own house, a Book in his hand, and a great Burden upon his back.*"

We read the same passage again and again, learning the alphabet as we went. Alice learned to recognise three words. BOOK. WORLD. DREAM. Then the candle burned down, flickered, vanished into a smoking pool of greasy tallow and went out. Alice was already fast asleep.

❊ ❊ ❊ ❊ ❊

The storm blew itself out in the night. When I awoke there was sunlight behind the curtains and Alice Jones was long gone. Her side of the bed was cold and the only trace of her visitation was a dry sliver of mud on both sheets. The room too was cold and I now faced a chamberpot that was dangerously full and occupied by a large, floating turd. The murky water in the basin was left over from yesterday. I gave my face and ears a perfunctory wash and sped away down all the long staircases, straight to the kitchens.

Alice was watching the bread rise.

"D-R-E-A-M. Dream," she said, smiling. And pinched my cheek. We sat happily on the bench, swinging our legs and chanting the alphabet. A is for Apple. B is for Bird. C is for Cat. D is for Donkey. E is for Elephant. F is for Fox. G is for Garden . . .

I crouched among the sprouting dahlias, eating bacon rinds and bare toast, the first of many loving and edible presents from Alice Jones. She explained that this was all advance payment for the next lesson.

"I'll find you in the gardens as soon as they've eaten their luncheon. Cook says I'm to serve and help clear. But I'm not in the scullery today. Swear that you won't forget."

"I swear." We clapped each other's hands in rhythm. I had made my first friend. Indeed, I was already in love with Alice Jones.

The adults spent hours eating or lounging in armchairs. Sometimes there was a burst of activity and they all dressed up and went out, riding and shooting, or visiting the neighbours, in capes, hats and feathers. I was never taken with them. If it rained they sat in melancholy groups, emphasising their imminent demise from utter boredom. In the evenings, I dozed on the window seat, while they sang, danced, flirted or played cards. Dinner was a nightmare of anxiety. Sitting in between Francisco and Beloved I was painfully visible. I tried eating as little as possible and refusing to look up.

At night Alice kept me awake in a frenzy of sentences, sometimes frustrated, once bright red with tears, she insisted on every single word by John Bunyan. She upbraided me if I did not know their meanings. I was obliged to consult Francisco on the finer points of Protestant theology. But Alice would not be defeated. And she would not give up.

Gradually, towards the end of June, the summer weather pulled itself together, took hold and closed in. The days were transformed into a burning fiery furnace and the nights were breathless and sweating. We reached the Slough of Despond. The adults fanned themselves and sought out agreeable breezes. They organised boating parties and parasols. James Barry had nothing to do with any of their activities. He went on painting.

Alice ran to and fro with iced drinks. We loved the ice house, with the great blocks wrapped in sacking. Cook taught me how to hack little pieces off with a hammer and an ice pick. When I wasn't helping Alice I lay flat on my stomach in the shrubbery, spying on the wild life with Lady Elizabeth's purloined opera glasses. The rabbits basked on dirt mounds in the evenings and the dogs were far too hot to chase them. The dew steamed on the grass in the early light, the air lost its freshness at once and the heat grew steadily. The people working in the fields covered their heads with broad hats and scarves. The hot rotting smell of the cut hay and the buzz of flies accompanied my lethargic adventures. I lay with my feet in the stream that encircled the meadows before ending its course in David Erskine's ornamental pond. I often saw him, strolling in the meadows, pausing to inspect his ducks. He was always cheerful and gentle when he spoke to me. He had lumps of stale bread in his pockets which I could feed to the aggressive flotilla. If the bread was not immediately delivered the creatures climbed out of the water and pursued him across the lawn, bellowing. The old earl had holes in his stockings. He and James Barry were the only men in the company who still wore wigs and his also stank of ancient powder.

"Is he really very rich?" I asked Alice.

"Mmmmm," she said, chewing grass and staring at the open book before her, "very, very rich. Richer than all the kings like Belshazzar and Nebuchadnezzar. He owns all Shropshire and most of Staffordshire besides. All the villages, churches, farms, woods, parks. Occasionally he sells off a bit of land to pay for his gardening improvements. What does this mean? Here."

Alice could spell every word now, but couldn't yet link them into coherence.

"Why doesn't his wife mend his stockings?"

"Lady Elizabeth? She's much too grand for that."

"But he's got holes in his stockings."

"Does it matter?"

Alice looked at my feet. I no longer wore stockings or shoes and my sunburnt freckled legs were as dirty and strong as those of Alice Jones.

"Come on," she insisted, kissing me on the nose, not the mouth, and then biting it a little, "help me with this bit."

❖ ❖ ❖ ❖ ❖

The afternoons in late July beat all previous records for burning airlessness. The lawns turned brown. The wood in the window frames dried, shrank and split, the paint peeled away. The kitchen yard bricks stayed warm under our bare feet till far into the night. The cattle dozed in the stream, their tails constantly flicking at the flies; even the chickens clustered idly in the shade. Alice was confined to the dairy by her mother, in case she got sunstroke, and put to scouring out buckets. Beloved suddenly remembered my existence and ordered a daily siesta. The clocks talked to themselves in the silent still household. Only James Barry went on painting day after day, despite the climatic excesses. My room was high up, under the eaves, and by four o'clock the dark air inside the shutters was intolerable. I went out into the glazed white light.

I scuttled, sweating, through the green mass of rhododendrons on the north side of the house. There was an overgrown avenue which was always in the shade and eventually led back to the great studio where James Barry worked. I got out my opera glasses to spy upon him. He was there, half turned towards the windows, brows drawn together, hardly moving before his colossal canvas. I watched his slight movements, the muscles of his face twitching. The sweat from my forehead blurred my sight. Gradually I realised, from his shifting glance, that there was someone with him in the studio. His eyes always returned to the same place, just out of my sight. He was copying someone onto the canvas. He gave commands. His lips moved. I watched the mystery enacted in dumb show. Whoever it was remained hidden by the rhododendrons and was outside the reach of my glass. I persevered, fascinated. Barry made a large gesture, raising his right hand, wiping the sweat from his face. A shadow moved slowly on the far wall of the studio. Then, into the double blurr of my opera glasses, majestic as any diva, rose the figure of a naked woman. Her loose curls were tied up above her bare shoulders. She yawned, stretched, her breasts rising as she did so. Then, unclothed, but perfectly at ease, as graceful as if she were entering a ballroom, the woman walked across the floor and stood beside James Barry. She leaned against his shoulder. And there they were, grotesquely unmatched, Polyphemus and Galatea, both peering at the canvas.

It was my mother.

I started to crawl closer, keeping the glasses fixed to my sweating slippery nose. I had never seen her naked. She only had a bath once a week. And I had usually been scrubbed in the first bath and put to bed. I had never been able to imagine her like this, naked, but standing there, talking to someone who was fully clothed. Her backside was perfect, two pearl ovals, like gigantic eggs. Barry hardly glanced at her. He was pointing to something in the canvas. She stepped back, folding her arms over her stomach, rubbing one foot against the other. James Barry leaned into the canvas as if the huge structure was a sail, and he was now ready to put about. My mother stood behind him, listening, yawning, stretching from time to time. Barry made a curt gesture with his palette knife, and then, frowning, irritated – I knew that expression so well – she moved back to her original position, outside the two blurred, inflated circles of my glass. I buried my face in dead leaves and warm, moist earth.

From time to time I looked up. Barry went on painting. I knew that she was there from the ferocity of his glance. He looked at the painting, and then he looked at her, unhesitating, unforgiving, without pity. She was becoming one of his forms, awash with pigments. I sniffled into the leaves. I hated her. I hated him. I was bitterly jealous. I wished that I knew how to paint like James Barry.

A line of ants moved across the leaves. Two or three ran counter to the flow, greeting every third or fourth ant in a flurry of nodding segments. Do they have names? I asked Francisco. Ants aren't individuals, he had said, they're a system. Then he had paused thoughtfully and added, Actually, human beings are a system too. We are governed by invisible natural laws and whether you can see this or not depends on your perspective.

But I felt myself to be outside every system.

And then I fell asleep, my nose deep in the dead leaves of the rhododendrons, my sleeve traversed by ants, the opera glasses clutched tight in my damp hand.

❖ ❖ ❖ ❖ ❖

A black padded foot and a bare white ankle turned me over with a shove, as if I were a dead animal. Someone in fine black silk with a yellow face leaned into the overgrown shrubbery, grasped me by the shoulder and gave me a vicious shake. Too close to mine was the still, unlined, unpowdered face of the serpent. The same wry smile with which she had so disconcerted me was fixed across her jaws. She picked up the opera glasses and stared at me for a moment, unblinking.

It was evening, but no longer bright. The air had changed. It was as if we were looking at one another inside a bell jar, like stuffed animals in a vacuum. The light behind her black outline was lurid, orange and purple, like a painted apocalypse on a church wall.

"Were you spying on your uncle and your mother?"

Just in case the end of the world, when all lies would be exposed and added up, was close at hand, I spoke the truth.

"Yes."

She smiled again and slowly extended one long and sinuous hand. She wore no rings. She was not really female. She was not natural. I decided that I would look her up in Francisco's gigantic illustrated volume: *Miraculous Encounters with Creatures of the Occult and the Cabbala in Exotic Lands, or The Further Adventures of Lemuel Gulliver in The Vales of Faerie.*

"Don't judge her. She does it for you. She does it all for you."

I took the woman's hand. The heat around us held its breath. She dragged me through the bushes, pulling the branches away from my face. I only reached her elbow. She was uncannily tall.

"Are you a widow?" I was not being impertinent, only attempting to account for the black, which no one else was wearing.

"Goodness me, no. I never married. I'm in mourning for my father, who died three months ago."

"I never had a father."

"Oh yes you did, you just don't remember him."

"That's what my mother says."

The serpent smiled again, ironically. I looked up at her.

"Do you know who my father was?"

I asked as if I was only half interested and trailed after her, dragging a stick. If she thought I didn't much care she might tell me something. But she said nothing. Twigs snapped beneath her feet, deafening in the stillness. The heat swayed, suspended in the peculiar light. We came out onto the lawns and saw that the sky had gathered itself up into a concentrated purple darkness. I heard the horses stamping in the stables, and caught sight of a man rushing away with an armful of rugs. Then a long jagged arrow of yellow flame, accompanied by a deafening crack and a rush of wind, descended into the kitchen garden, slicing through the ruthless rows of strawberries and lettuce. I clamped my hand more firmly into the serpent's scaly grasp. She never quickened her step.

"We've all been sent out looking for you, child. One of the kitchen girls said you were lost."

The light became fantastical and horrifying. The house loomed before us. I pulled at her hand.

"Let's run."

"No need."

And her timing was perfect. Just as we reached the terrace the first huge drops struck my shoulders. I saw my Beloved, now fully dressed and jewelled, rushing across the drawing room to fling open the French windows and welcome us home, as if we had returned from the wars.

"Don't say anything to her. Ever," hissed the serpent, bending down towards me. "Promise." This was an order, not a request.

"All right."

The rain exploded on the terrace.

❖ ❖ ❖ ❖ ❖

Alice always knew what went on in the house. At first, I was too proud to admit that I had no information. Opera glasses were poor substitutes for valets, chambermaids and kitchen talk. Servants in the house passed through the corridors like ghosts, with breathtaking impunity. They could be dismissed at any time. Yet they were the keepers of incredible secrets. This was all that I had in common with Alice Jones: forbidden knowledge and powerlessness. *"But now, in this Valley of Humiliation, poor Christian was hard put to it; for he had gone but a little way before he espied a foul fiend coming over the field to meet him; his name is Apollyon. Then did Christian begin to be afraid . . ."*

"A-F-R-A-I-D," Alice spelt out the word. Now she easily recognised the words that came again and again. But she was still blocked by combinations of letters that she had never seen. Sometimes she got so frustrated that she attacked the book. Bunyan had developed a dent on his spine from her pummelling. We were sitting on an empty wagon in the farmyard. Once we were facing Apollyon, I asked about the black serpent.

"Tell me about the black silk woman who looks like a snake."

"Louisa Erskine. And she does look like a snake. I'll tell Cook."

"But who is she?"

"She's the master's younger sister and the mistress's special friend. They all grew up together. She's here sometimes six months together. She used to come with her father. He used to be the master. But he went all peculiar and gabbled and raved. When he was old and sick she looked after him. Then he died."

"She said he died . . ."

"She's not bad. Last year she combed all the lice out of my hair. It hurt something terrible. And she can be a bit frightening. She caught me stealing some Turkish Delight from the drawing room last Christmas. And she beat me black and blue. Don't do anything that drives her to hit you. But she never told anyone. Not Harold, nor my mother. I thought she'd tell. I was dead scared. I went on tiptoe for at least a week. She never told. I'd already prepared a long speech for Mum if I got dismissed."

"But everybody steals . . ."

"Yes. But there's a sort of stealing allowance that you can't go over. And you must never get caught doing it."

"Salvatore stole some wine from Francisco once to pay his gambling debts."

"What happened?"

"Francisco threatened to kill him. Not dismiss him. Kill him. For personal betrayal. Then he got given a second chance and Francisco paid all his debts."

Alice laughed.

"My mum says your General's a gentleman. Here. Go on. Next bit."

"You'll like the next bit. There's a battle.

"*So he went on and Apollyon met him. Now the monster was hideous to behold; he was clothed with scales like a Fish (and they are his pride); he had wings like a Dragon, feet like a Bear, and out of his belly came Fire and Smoke; and his mouth was as the mouth of a Lion . . .*"

"Wonderful," cried Alice, "F-I-S-H. I've seen that on the Menus. F-I-S-H. Fish. Teach me the rest. Why's he called Apollyon and what does it mean?"

"Don't know."

"See. You don't know everything."

"I never told you I did. Francisco says Apollyon rules the Kingdom of This World."

"I've never wanted any other, for all that Mum sings about the Blessed Other Land in Chapel." She looked down at the words, as if she could see the monster in the book, and stretched out her toes so that they passed over the hard line of shelter in the shade and emerged into the sun.

❦ ❦ ❦ ❦ ❦

Dinner began at four. There were dreadful delays between courses. I was eating up my pile of vegetables and potatoes, on

Francisco's orders. The sun was still on the lawns, but by then it was almost six o'clock and the heat was beginning to ebb. David Erskine remarked not only my existence at the dinner table, but my activities in the house. I almost choked.

"Francisco, did you know that this child is brewing rebellions in my kitchens?"

"Is he?"

"He's teaching the scullery maids how to read."

Everyone laughed. I turned appallingly, guiltily red.

"Isn't that so, young chap?" inquired David Erskine encouragingly.

"Yes, sir," I gulped, almost inaudible. Caught.

"What are you teaching them, sweetheart?" demanded my Beloved, a little angry and defensive.

"*Pilgrim's Progress.*"

Everyone laughed again. The still black eyes of Louisa Erskine were fixed upon me. I was being devoured.

"*Pilgrim's Progress* won't lead to revolution, David," laughed Francisco, "more's the pity."

"Mark my words. It'll be *The Rights of Man* next and don't tell me that he hasn't already got every word off by heart."

Now they were laughing at Francisco. I was let off the hook. Only Louisa was still looking at me. She smiled slightly. She said nothing. When the ladies rose to leave for coffee in the drawing room I rose with them, clutching the edge of my mother's shawl. But as I passed him David Erskine leaned out and caught my hand. Close to, his face was deep red, full of white hairs, holes and black spots.

"Don't worry, my dear. You teach the girls to read. I'm all for it."

His breath stank of rotting teeth and old food. I slunk away up the staircase, embarrassed and furious.

* * * * *

August stretched out before us: a march-past of blazing days and late-afternoon thunderstorms. David Erskine, in smock and peasant trousers, convincingly dirty, departed into the fields, to direct the harvest himself. Only his mouldy wig differentiated him from his tenants. The adults sometimes went out to watch, but always gave up early in the day, and trailed home complaining of exhaustion, sunstroke, nettle rash, brambles and stomach ache. Alice and I worked side by side in the vegetable garden. We fed the rabbits, ducks and chickens. The other children, whether older or younger than Alice, never disputed her exclusive right to my attention. One afternoon, her mother marched up from the village to look at me. She was nursing yet another squalling baby. I backed away from the bundle. So she handed it over with the announcement, "Alice is the third of nine. Five living. Praise the Lord!"

She must have been several years younger than my mother, but she looked older, fatter and ferociously healthy. She went to chapel, not to church, but insisted that the vicar baptise all her children for their father's sake, and attended all the major festivals, much against her minister's advice. The church services were sometimes attended by Papists, whom David Erskine most unwisely tolerated as visitors in his household. Close proximity might well lead to a lifelong contamination. Alice's mother had strong views on the rights of women. She thought they ought to be allowed to preach in chapel. On these and other issues she was often at variance with the elders, who nevertheless persisted with their dear and erring sister. Why she persisted with them was less clear.

Alice and I stood side by side in the stable yard for the presentation. Cook came outside to watch.

"So this is Mrs Bulkeley's famous tomboy daughter we hear so much about," said Mrs Jones, after a long look. The new baby began to grizzle pathetically. She handed it over to Cook.

"You should wear a hat, child, with your complexion. Look at her, Cook. She's one enormous freckle. Alice, get a hat from the dairy."

Alice always obeyed her mother. She rushed off. Mrs Jones pinched my cheek. I objected, but decided that I liked her.

"I hear you're teaching my eldest to read," she announced at last.

"Yes, ma'am," I admitted cautiously.

"Well, I'm grateful to you. I can't read myself, though my

husband can. But girls should be taught properly. When she can read I want you to go on helping her. Can you lend her books?"

"Yes, ma'am," I agreed. Books were very expensive. Francisco never allowed any of his books to be taken past the library door. My mother had her own small collection on a shelf in her boudoir. Volumes weren't allowed to stray from one collection to another. I wasn't sure how I was going to steal the books for Alice, but I was sure it could be done.

"Thank you, child, and I hope that your stepfather intends to continue your own education."

"I think so. I haven't asked him."

Suddenly she blazed up and spoke very sharply. "Your mother must insist upon it. You're dressed up like his son, not his daughter. You can claim a son's privilege."

She spoke with the same passion, the same gestures, Alice had used when she had asked me to teach her to read. Alice returned with a large straw hat and clamped it onto my head. The baby began wailing. Mrs Jones sighed and took the child from Cook.

"Off you go, children." We were dismissed. She kissed us both goodbye and we rushed away. I noticed that she smelt of fresh grass and warm hay, much cleaner than the adults in the house.

"That's my Mum," said Alice proudly.

❖ ❖ ❖ ❖ ❖

There was a summer ball at the house every year, held on the last Saturday in August, to celebrate Lady Elizabeth's birthday. It was a jolly, unsophisticated affair to which all the local families were invited. The Erskines were not snobbish and invited absolutely everybody, so that the social confusion was considered slightly shocking. Alice described the last one with zest. She could remember who had drunk too much and been sick, whose stockings had descended, whose stays had had to be loosened, who had danced all night, and with whom, who had fallen asleep in the library, only to be discovered next morning with their head in a fruit dish, which of the glasses had been broken, and what they had had to eat in the kitchens. The children were not only allowed to watch, we were allowed to dance. I solemnly asked Alice Jones for the first dance. She said that she would have to consult her little book. We spent the rest of the afternoon stitching one together, so that she could consult it.

My Beloved's exotic plant catalogues had arrived from London and she was busy choosing new specimens for her conservatory. I boasted that I had asked Alice to dance, and been accepted as her principal dancing partner. My mother looked at me thoughtfully.

"You ought to wear a dress for the ball, dear. People do talk."

I had never worn a dress before.

"I can't ask Alice if I don't wear trousers," I protested. "We'd be two girls."

My mother was baffled.

"But you must wear a dress. I've bought the material. You're growing up now. It's not correct otherwise."

"I won't." My temper was rising. Obscurely, I realised that my ambiguous clothes were what had made me special and interesting in the eyes of Alice Jones.

"But, my darling . . ."

"Won't!" My ears went red. I was fighting for the right to remain interesting. I faced her, chin up.

She suddenly smiled, her eyes full of love.

"Sweeheart, don't be angry. You're the image of my brother."

I hammered her knees with my fists and all her catalogues fell to the floor. The black silk form of Louisa Erskine abruptly uncoiled out of the carpet.

"Don't attack your mother. It's very impolite."

I left off, abashed.

The serpent looked me up and down, then came to a decision.

"We can go into town tomorrow, Mary Ann, and buy some more material and buttons. She's so small it really won't take long."

I was to go to the ball in smart blue regimentals, dressed as a soldier. Costume was much more acceptable than disguise. Alice was thrilled. She had always wanted to dance with a soldier. The 13th Light Dragoons had passed through the country some months before and broken every heart in the village.

On the day of the ball two families arrived mid-morning on a fleet of donkeys, causing immense excitement. David Erskine was seen running across the fields without his hat, to greet them.

The kitchens were much too hot. Alice and I were on duty killing flies, a task which we performed with great zeal, breaking off at regular intervals to rush upstairs, stare at all the new adults and children and criticise their clothes.

"Mrs Sperling's lost some more teeth. Did you notice? Last Christmas she made whistling noises when she drank her punch."

I had no idea how many teeth Mrs Sperling used to have. Alice praised and condemned like a court ambassador constructing a society column. She pointed out one of the magistrates, and revealed that he frequently beat his wife.

"Does your stepfather ever hit your mother?" Alice asked curiously.

"No! Not ever!" I was scandalised.

"That's interesting," said Alice. "She had a black eye once. I didn't see it, but it still gets talked about. And it was given out that she'd fallen down in Mr Barry's studio and had an accident. My dad hit my mum once. She hit him back and burst his eardrum. He's deaf in one ear now."

My favourable impression of Mrs Jones was confirmed, but I had no time to brood over the origins of my mother's black eye, for here was the magistrate's wife and her smile, too, was ruined by her missing teeth.

"Maybe the magistrate knocks her teeth out?" I suggested.

"Oh no," said Alice, "they just rot."

The orchestra arrived in two carts, demanding ale at once, on account of the heat. There were fiddlers tuning up in the stables and a new harpsichord unloaded through the French windows on the terrace, upended in the drawing room and carried through into the great hall, where the dancing was to take place. Two gigantic vases of gladioli were standing to attention on either side of the mirror above the fireplace, and all the doors stood open, into every room of the house. A Babel's tower of tiny flies blocked the main doorway and the drugged blooms of Lady Elizabeth's geraniums overflowed the window sills. We rushed ecstatically up and down the kitchen stairs, shrieking. The house was full of laughter, arguments and delicious smells. Francisco was surrounded by ladies, all alive with fans. There was no sign of James Barry.

The men setting up the tables in the orchard had gouged a channel through one of the lawns. The head gardener was hysterical and had to be dissuaded by Elizabeth Erskine herself, resplendent in sweet muslin and looking younger and more joyful than she had ever done before, from settling accounts then and there. I heard her praising the healing power of rain, but as it hadn't rained for weeks and might never rain again, her reassurances sounded far-fetched. At four o'clock the first round of eating began and the household paraded out into the orchard, stumbling and giggling in the rough grass, supporting one another and then falling over deliberately, rushing back inside for fans and parasols. Alice and I scurried back and forth from the orchard to the kitchens, too excited to eat, intent upon our role as spies. We saw two young people who had slipped away, kissing in the shrubbery. I was all for exposure, but Alice said that it wasn't a scandal, as they were engaged to be married.

"It's only a scandal if they're married, but not to each other," she explained, "and sometimes not even then if it's been going on for ages and everybody knows."

The adults ate, laughed, talked and sang, sitting under the trees in the golden light. They looked happy and innocent. Or at least I thought so. Alice didn't. But then, Alice understood more of the world than I did.

At last the orchestra took their places on the creaking stage in the great hall and began tuning up. They sat sweating behind a barricade of fresh flowers. The great hall was not often used. Beyond it was the portrait gallery, burdened with pictures of long-dead members of the Erskine family caressing numerous horses and dogs which had held honoured positions. The curtains smelled of damp, and ivy had almost covered two of the windows. Alice had told me which members of the family were bankrupts or murderers. There they hung, unsmiling, blackened beneath layers of varnish and grease, all looking equally culpable. Now both the great hall and the portrait gallery reeked of beeswax and honeysuckle. And as we danced in on a faint breeze, we heard the glass chandeliers chiming in the draught.

And here are the refreshments, laid out in coloured rows: jellies, fruits, iced cakes, chicken and fish sandwiches, expensive white wine wrapped in linen and iced punch in huge silver bowls with devil's spoons. I guarded the food, stiff in new trousers with the regimental stripe and far too hot in my military jacket with brass buttons. Everyone described me as charming. Mrs Emmersley, the vicar's wife, told my mother that she had been quite convinced that I was in fact a mechanical doll, perhaps even a musical one, as I was so realistic. The fashion then was for flat shoes and loose dresses. Gentlemen's trousers were daringly tight. I suspected Francisco of wearing a corset, but I couldn't prove it. Alice said that we could hide in his rooms, inspect his chests and find out. He was glamorous, foreign and shockingly radical in the eyes of the country people. So everyone wanted to dance with him. There was the odd minuet and even a mazurka, but for the most part we danced country dances, with the top couple calling out the dance as they chose. This meant that no one was left against the wall; everybody danced, until they sank onto chairs fanning themselves, the survivors stamping with gusto. As the night went on and the candles guttered there was a good deal of ogling, flirting, squeezing and pinching, accompanied by shrieks and giggles. It was very indecorous, very uninhibited. The women's ribbons swirled in the reels and I danced with Alice Jones.

Alice was cleaner than I had ever seen her. A layer of sunburn must have been rubbed off. She wore a light blue dress and dark blue ribbons cut out of one of Elizabeth Erskine's cast-offs. She had no shoes on, but nobody noticed. She knew all the dances and bullied me into position with shouts of "No, left hand, silly!" and "Quick, down the other way!" For most of the dances we swopped partners in every set for the different steps and sequences. One moment I was cavorting like a dwarf around Elizabeth Erskine, then gazing adoringly at my mother's beauty, the next clasping once again the cold hand of the black serpent. My uniform was stuck to my back with sweat, fear and excitement.

Supper was announced at midnight.

"Look, look," cried Alice, gorgeous in her ribbons and her audacity, "Mr Barry's wearing a clean shirt."

❖ ❖ ❖ ❖ ❖

We had both fallen asleep behind the sofa in the drawing room when I felt someone gently shaking my shoulder. The curtains gaped apart. Outside, the earth was in the grip of a metamorphosis, the dark was already lightening into a deep grey-blue. The cattle shifted, ghostly in the fields.

"Wake up, child, you must come with me now." It was Louisa, cold, unhurried, dark against the slow dawn.

I disentangled myself from Alice Jones and followed the black outline of the woman, drowsy and confused. I could hear the music, still thudding in the great hall. She led me out into the gardens. The chill hit me in the stomach and the face. I gulped cold air and shivered. The grass was wet with dew and spiders' webs hung from the flowers. The statues loomed, pale and fragile, above the yew hedges in the Italian garden. The yew remained a solid block of darkness, darker now than the night sky. Louisa stepped firmly into the maze.

The maze was on the east side of the house. We often played hide and seek there in the afternoons. It was a perfect square, each avenue parallel, a duplicate of all the others. There was nothing sinister about the maze. But I had never breached the labyrinth at dawn. Now it was uncanny, the hedges giving out a strong scent, the earth glimmering beneath our steps.

I smelt cigars. From the core of the maze, where the fountain bubbled at the feet of the goddess, rose the blue-grey cloud of smoke. We stepped into the heart of the maze, into the last square, and there, sitting round the fountain, was the triumvirate of cigars: David Steuart Erskine, Earl of Buchan, General Francisco de Miranda and James Barry, RA. They all looked very powerful and very drunk.

"Here she is," said Louisa quietly. She let go of my hand. I thought I was dreaming. Francisco opened his arms to me. I clutched onto his uniform, which stank of sweat, alcohol and my mother's musk.

"Well, my dear," said David Erskine, "we've been discussing your future. We can't waste you. You're a very clever child. Something has got to be done."

James Barry stared at me. He said nothing, but puffed convulsively at his cigar. His shirt was no longer clean.

"Listen, soldier," said Francisco, "would you like to study properly? At a university?"

"Yes," I whispered, suddenly feeling sick and shivery.

"Well, that's what you're going to do. There's just one thing that you'll have to remember from now on. You never will be a girl. But you won't find that hard. You'll just go on being a tomboy."

The light was gathering strength. I could see their faces now. These were men who were getting older, fatter, grey-haired; the adventure of their lives was already undertaken and achieved, their roads already chosen. Now they were choosing for me.

"From now on you're going to be a boy. And then a man. Your uncle and I are giving you our names. And David's volunteered to be your patron and your guardian."

David Erskine laughed hoarsely. It was a wonderful idea. A trick, a masquerade. A joke against the world.

"I'll put my money where my mouth is. And gladly. It's about time I did something for you, child. I'm your banker from now on." David Erskine chuckled wickedly to himself. He loomed over me in the lightening blue.

"Welcome aboard, James Miranda Barry. You'd be wasted as a woman. Join the men."

Then they all laughed.

❖ ❖ ❖ ❖ ❖

All around us, the entire village and every single member of the household, whether chapel, church or Papist, bellowed out their thanks to God. David Erskine, Earl of Buchan, had a three-line whip out for the harvest festival, so that we would all be obliged to marvel at the size of his pumpkins. A row of them burgeoned on the altar, enormous, orange and opulent. Bouquets of wheat and barley were fastened to the pillars down the aisles, purple Michaelmas daisies and fountains of goldenrod sheathed the pulpit, baskets of apples, tomatoes bulbous as clenched fists, ginger lilies with huge protruding stamens which the Reverend Emmersley described as unsuitably suggestive, were massed upon the altar steps, tea roses, delicate but unscented, were wound round the crucifix, Christ's crown of thorns blossomed in the autumn sun. Mysteriously, a keg of cider, last year's, was positioned near the font.

We thought about our sins. But not very seriously.

We asked Him to forgive us as we forgive those who trespass against us. Alice was convinced that this was Jesus's warning against persecuting poachers. She had at last understood the sign on the gates by the woods: NO TRESPASSING. She asked to be forgiven for two rabbits and a pheasant.

"What happens to the fruit afterwards?" I whispered.

"The vicar gets to eat it all. Some goes to the curate's family." Alice gazed regretfully at her cucumbers, bottled in vinegar. The choir belted out the Gloria, Mrs Emmersley conducting, her head on one side and her elbows gyrating like windmills.

As the vicar picked his way through the mass of farm produce towards the pulpit to give thanks at length and to exhort us to do thou likewise, I noticed my mother getting out her sewing. She and Louisa were absorbed in a frenzy of tailoring. I was to have a whole new wardrobe. My new life had begun. My red curls were already cropped even closer to my head and I was stuffed into Alice's youngest brother's shirt. The vicar was talking about valour and the progress of the war in an unknown foreign part. He had explained the meaning of sacrifice and was getting on to the importance of tradition when Alice began tugging at my sleeve.

"Come on," she hissed. "I want to read the last bit. I practised last night. You can tell me if I've got it right."

"Where are you two going?" snapped Mrs Jones, as we disrupted the entire row.

"He's got to piss," lied Alice calmly, putting all the blame on me.

We scuttled out of the church and round to the vestry, jumping all the graves. Alice had hidden the book under a cassock. We settled in amongst the clerical robes, once Alice had checked through the pockets of all the coats. Out came the book, battered, dented, grass-stained, some pages loosened, smelling faintly of chicken shit.

"I see myself now at the end of my Journey, my toilsome days are ended. I am going now to see that Head that was crowned with Thorns, and that Face that was spit upon for me."

Alice moved her finger from one word to the next, slowly, intoning the text. One word after another, like a rite chanted. Through a crack in the door we heard the vicar doing the same thing.

"I have loved to hear my Lord spoken of, and wherever I have seen the print of his Shoe in the Earth, there have I coveted to set my Foot too . . ."

I held my breath, willing Alice not to make any mistakes. She was shaking with excitement and pride.

"I may give those that desire it an account of what I am here silent about: meantime I bid my Reader Adieu."

"That's right! You can read, Alice, you can read!"

She hugged me till my bones cracked.

"I want to try a French novel next."

Glory be to the Father and to the Son and to the Holy Ghost, As it was in the beginning is now and ever shall be. World without end. Amen.

— PART TWO —

North and South

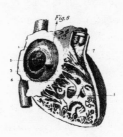

JAMES MIRANDA BARRY was ten years old when he signed the Matriculation Roll of Edinburgh University in December 1809. He paid two shillings and sixpence for his university library ticket out of his own pocket, spoke to no one, turned up the collar of his greatcoat, which almost reached his ankles, and walked out into an icy wall of rain, becoming sleet. He was small, pale, red-haired and very quick to lose his temper. He lived at 6, Lothian Street with his mother, an elegant lady with a fine profile and impractical ideas, and her companion, a sinister woman called Louisa Erskine, who was known as The Black Widow in the butcher's shop. They lived in absolute seclusion. Their landlady reported that the widow and the mother sometimes spent their evenings shouting at each other, that the mother wrote and received several letters every day, and that the boy was a studious little chap, who said nothing and read a lot of books.

This was the general opinion of the household at 6, Lothian Street. The neighbourhood awaited further information.

❖ ❖ ❖ ❖ ❖

2nd January 1810

To General Francisco de Miranda

My Dear Sir,

In a letter I had the honour of receiving from my inestimable friend and patron Lord Buchan he says that in consequence of your kind enquiries about my health and pursuits he did not conceal his pleasure that I had applied myself so assiduously to all the subjects in which I am required to acquit myself to the best of my ability. Under your personal tutelage, for the which I am most grateful and bounden to you, always, Sir, I first made acquaintance with chemistry, botany, anatomy, Greek, natural and moral philosophy, to the which I must now add medical jurisprudence and two optional subjects upon which I have already embarked, that is, midwifery and dissection. Dr Fryer, who is to supervise the payment of my allowance, assures me that you are known to him by reputation and that he had been introduced to you, my dear General, upon your arrival in this country. I could not help telling Dr Fryer what a treasure you possess in London and how often you permit me to partake of it – needless to say, I mean your very extensive and elegant library. Excuse my troubling you with this letter but I could not deny myself the pleasure of wishing you many happy returns of the New Year in which my mother Mrs Bulkeley and Miss Louisa Erskine join with me. I must beg the favour when you see Dr Fryer to tell him that Lord Buchan desires me to say that we drank his health at his house in George Street this day week. Neither Dr Fryer nor anyone else here knows anything about Mrs Bulkeley's daughter and so I trust, my dear General, that neither you nor my esteemed uncle will mention in any of your correspondence anything of my cousin's friendship and care for me.

I remain, Sir, your admiring and obedient servant,
James Miranda Barry

Dissection was carried out on the remains of the unfortunates who had died either in the poor house or on the gallows. James Miranda Barry studied dissection as a private pupil with Dr Fyfe, who still wore a pigtail and was himself a relict of the previous century. He was well known in the town and reputed to encourage his medical students with personal chats and mouthfuls of hard liquor. The aspect of the corpse at the first meeting of the dissection class was so horrible that one of the pupils alongside Barry fainted away. He was a young man called Jobson. Barry caught the boy in his arms to prevent him gashing his forehead open on the edge of a table in the laboratory, then put Jobson's head firmly between his knees and massaged his temples. The grim chill in the room ensured that Jobson's unconsciousness would be a temporary affair.

"Pull him out of the way, Barry," snapped Dr Fyfe. "It's always one of the big ones who goes down. Now the muscles of the arm, pitifully shrunken in the case of this subject . . ."

Barry dragged Jobson into a corner. His face was quite white, indeed a little grey around the nose and mouth. Barry was convinced he was going to be sick.

"Come on, old chap," he whispered, "you'll be all right. Try to swallow."

"Oh God," Jobson gazed blankly up at an equally pale freckled face. "It was that white liquid which came out when he made the incision. White blood . . ."

"It's not blood," said Barry, pedantically.

"When you've finished pretending to be old ladies, gentlemen, you will be good enough to return to the dissecting table. And if you can't be sensible, don't chatter."

"Ohhhh," groaned Jobson, and his head sank down again.

"Hang on." Barry clutched his hair.

They sat silent on the floor, leaning against a rough scarred bench. Barry looked up at the specimens floating in huge glass jars. There was a sequence of foetuses, in different stages of development, high on the top of a locked cupboard. The first was a grotesque monster, an enormous elongated tadpole with tiny clutching limbs; the last looked like a sleeping child, ready to awaken. He could not see the corpse on the table. The other pupils crowded round. Dr Fyfe's pigtail wobbled aggressively. It was freezing in his dissecting room. Barry felt the draught under the door. The doctor had his shirt sleeves rolled up over his jacket cuffs. He was talking about the muscles in and around the stomach. Barry ached to see what he was doing.

"Come on. Try to get up. Are you going to be sick?" Barry's sympathy was now diluted with impatience. Jobson looked into the grey eyes, pale face and ginger freckles inches from his own. Barry's hand was ice cold, but firm. They crept round to the side of the table near the feet of the slippery white cadaver. It no longer looked human, but was shrunken and smooth like a withered eel. The shrivelled genitals resembled aged and inedible giblets. Jobson shuddered again at the evil solidity of the corpse, Barry's frozen hand clasped tightly in his own.

"You watch now, boy," said Dr Fyfe to Jobson, "and remember

everything you see. When you're operating, you'll have to work fast. There'll probably be some miserable soldier groaning beneath you. And you won't have much time. How many methods are there of dismembering this fragile and delicate building? And how many more to be invented? Listen. Watch."

The doctor caressed his knife. In fact, there was a separate course on military surgery, but the internal geography of all men was much the same. Dr Fyfe nodded curtly at Barry, who already promised to be a good student. No nerves at all for a child, well, he looks like a child. But then, most children have no feelings, finer or otherwise. Or don't appear to do so. What a row of pale, blank faces! Amoral savages, the lot of them.

❖ ❖ ❖ ❖ ❖

Barry's coat remained much too big for him. He never appeared to grow. His ears vanished below the collar as he pulled himself into the sleeves, then clamped his hat to his red curls and made for the door. Jobson caught up with him on the steps.

"I say," he cried, "don't run away, Barry. I want to thank you."

"That's all right. Excuse me. I must go. My mother waits tea for me."

"Can you come out on Sunday?"

"I don't think so. I've got to study."

"Just for an hour after dinner? You're never at the club. We could go to the river."

"I'm sorry."

"Oh, go on. Ask your mother."

Doubtful, hesitating, Barry suddenly relented.

"All right. I'll ask."

❖ ❖ ❖ ❖ ❖

The lodgings they inhabited gleamed with a hideous gold and green wallpaper, whose stripes were too close together, so that the family appeared to be imprisoned in a radiant cage. The furniture argued with the wallpaper, retaliating with a vulgar abundance of gold braid. Had it not been for the prospect of moving house yet again, Mary Ann declared, she would have cancelled the tenancy, whatever the penalties. Even if it had meant paying one quarter's rent. But it was not only the ludicrous vulgarity of the wallpaper which depressed her. She hated the climate and built fires fit for Joan of Arc.

Their trunks had preceded them and were evenly distributed throughout the rooms with distressing finality. There was to be no escape. Louisa swept into the oppressive, musty sequence of ugly crowded rooms, each a masterpiece of bad taste, that was to become their home. She looked around cautiously and then pronounced, "Well. Hideous. But it will have to do."

The air in the city was clear, hard, and very cold. Louisa walked out in the early morning. She paced the wide streets, arranged all their regular orders with the butcher and the green-grocers, hired the cook and the housemaid, and came to terms with the domestics after a good deal of hard-headed interrogation. She insisted that they should be able to provide written characters and, whether the prospective domestics could read or not, that they should be possessed of a mimimum of instruction. She attended public lectures, took notes and even asked questions. She went to exhibitions unchaperoned. Mary Ann, who was much more conventional, and cautious of other people's opinions, accused her of causing a public scandal and attracting attention wherever she went.

Louisa paused, her scorn surfacing. "My dear Mary Ann, I will be forty this year. Women of forty cannot cause public scandals, however hard we try. You attract far more attention by living like a recluse than you would ever attract in the public street. If you will forgive me for saying so."

Mary Ann turned pale, then red, then screamed. Louisa swung round to leave the room and found the child standing shaking in the doorway.

"Please don't quarrel with her," said a small firm voice from the bottom of an overlarge collar. Louisa stared for a moment, then laughed.

"Persuade her to go out, James. You have more influence than I do. She'll break her own spirit pacing the cage."

Barry took his mother's hand with great courtesy, but familiarity, as if she were an affronted courtesan who had been offered too little money. Then he made his request like a gentleman.

"Will you do me the honour of accompanying me to the river walks this Sunday afternoon to meet my fellow student and recent acquaintance Mr Robert Jobson?"

"Darling, you mustn't take such risks."

"But it looks odder if we don't see anybody. Louisa's right. We've got to give the impression that we have an exclusive circle of friends. If you just avoid people, they'll think we're peculiar. Or hiding something."

Mary Ann shrugged, all her frustration, boredom and misery expressed in the line of her shoulders and the dull sheen of her curls.

"I'll book a box at the theatre," Louisa said suddenly, stepping up to Mary Ann and kissing her before she could resist, "and you must get dressed and come with us, my dear. I'm sorry I was sharp with you. Look at that wallpaper. If you stay here, cooped up with that pattern for one evening more, the green and gold stripes will kill you."

❖ ❖ ❖ ❖ ❖

James Miranda Barry stood behind his mother's chair, stiff and polished like a toy soldier just lifted from the box. He looked down at the gold chain around her neck, which Francisco had given her, and felt its duplicate hidden far beneath his ruffles and studs, against his own skin. She was still wonderfully beautiful. Other people were looking at them. The theatre was hot. Mary Ann and Louisa fanned themselves complacently, enjoying the undisguised interest and rustle of attention. In the first interval a messenger appeared with a card on a salver and bowed to Mary Ann.

"Dr Robert Anderson presents his respects to you, ma'am, Miss Erskine and Mr Barry, and begs permission to wait upon you in your box."

Louisa raised her eyebrows. Anderson was a well-known literary figure in the city. She had attended his lectures on Scottish literature and philosophy. He was an editor with considerable influence. He was a man other men sought to know. They were less anxious for him to be introduced to their wives and daughters.

The play included a terrifying mad scene and a tempest on cymbals and wind machine. During the deafening horrors of the storm, in which the heroine swayed upon the battlements, Louisa and Mary Ann had a swift, almost inaudible conversation.

"No, I don't know him, but Francisco does . . ."

"Yes . . . I'm sure it's all right . . ."

"I think David must have had a hand in this . . . he'd not want the plan to fail . . ."

"The child will say as little as possible . . ."

"He's the one with the very distinguished whiskers . . . the girl on the left is his eldest daughter . . ."

"Oh heavens, he's coming over . . ."

The rest was drowned by theatrical screaming.

Barry had ordered iced drinks for his mother and Miss Erskine. While the juggling interlude was proceeding on stage, Barry paid for the drinks. All his formulas were perfectly correct, but his voice was stilted and nervous. As he negotiated the process of command, the barrage of distinguished whiskers loomed over him.

"Good evening, young man. I'm a good friend of Lord Buchan, and delighted to meet you."

A giant clasp engulfed him. Barry's manner often appeared to be disconcertingly rude. He rapped out his comments brusquely, to disguise his fear.

"And a good evening to you, sir."

Robert Anderson had been ready with his bluff, affable patronage and found himself confronted with a gleaming stare, as if he had just encountered a magic toad, awaiting the kiss. He peered down at the tiny, immaculate character, who stared back. The silent pause was just slightly too long to be polite. Finally, puzzled, and not a little curious, Dr Robert Anderson introduced his daughter.

"Isabelle, this is Lord Buchan's ward, James Barry, who is studying medicine with Dr Fyfe. Barry, this is my eldest daughter, Miss Isabelle Anderson."

Barry bowed and kissed the girl's hand with a swish as if he were an Austrian archduke. She bowed too, utterly serious, towering above him. Then she giggled.

The meeting in the box passed off extremely well, and a good part of the theatre enjoyed the incident, rarely in mid-season having new faces about which to gossip. Barry was pronounced quite a little gentleman and Dr Robert Anderson inspected Mary Ann's very charming naked shoulders with undisguised admiration. Well, one way and another this was all very interesting. Lord Buchan's ward. If a wealthy aristocrat with no children takes a growing child under his wing, that usually indicates a near relationship that cannot be openly acknowledged. But David Erskine is nearer fifty than forty and this ravishing girl with the creamy shoulders would have been no more than a child herself – unless, no, this is her child all right, the auburn colouring and the grey eyes are a perfect match. And Louisa is an ageless old lizard. I saw her at the back of the hall when I was giving those lectures. The audience always think you don't notice them, but you do. There she was, always in the same place, sitting as still and watchful as a snake by the rabbit's hole. I wonder why she never married. Ah, Mrs Bulkeley, may I have the pleasure . . .

Dr Anderson insisted that his carriage would be at their disposal when the performance was over. Mrs Bulkeley, Miss Erskine and Mr Barry accepted graciously. An invitation to dinner was already prowling in the wings when the orchestra struck up. There was a good deal of bowing and withdrawing. Mary Ann and Louisa had enough material for an hour's whispering.

The last act began.

Our heroine was dying amidst Gothic ruins. She was beyond medical help. Her mind was shattered forever. She saw spectres of the loved and lost flit amongst the ruins. Her bandit lover, in peril of his life, muffled in dozens of cloaks, appeared on every part of the stage, broken by a gigantic grief. He was recognised by the ancient nurse, who must have been clairvoyant, as he was now "horribly altered" by duelling scars and a wild forest of beard and moustachios. He admitted all his crimes, a catalogue of horrors.

"Yes, I have sinned greatly! But I have also loved with the force of tempests and volcanos! My passions have outrivalled

Nature! In a world of little men, I alone have withstood the blast. On rocky crags, in stealth by night, I have performed the justice of the avenger . . ."

Barry was entranced.

"That's all translated from the German," whispered Louisa.

"Justice?" The nurse wrung her hands. "How dare you speak of justice? You who have tormented peaceful sleep and flung your gauntlet in the face of God! Behold, my mistress, her mind adrift in the storm of her love for you! Thou wretch! Unworthy scoundrel! Thy fate awaits thee! Bend your proud heart before your judge – your God!"

"God's justice was not mine," snarled the desperado, and the audience gave a delighted gasp.

Little torches fluttered in the wind machine. There was a bell clanging offstage. Our heroine's family arrived, swords drawn. The brigand took her in his arms. She appeared to awaken from a stupor. She knew him. She flung her arms around his neck. In her first moment of lucidity since the second act, she cried out in thrilling tones, "Rodolpho! At last. I am in heaven. For neither man nor God will part us more."

Terrible pause. She launched into the "Daisy Song", which they had sung together as infants, and which had been her chorus in her madness. The relatives closed in, forming a wonderful tableau, lit by glittering torches.

"Rodolpho, my dearest . . ." The song ended in a gasp, a convulsion and a wonderful dying exhalation, which thrilled every spine in the house. Rodolpho let out a terrific groan and then arranged her corpse in an artistic pose upon the boards. The doomed hero froze for a moment, his weapon lifted, so that during the thunderclap the public got the full benefit of the scene in all its pathos.

"Nevermore!" he shouted. "We shall part no more, beloved! I am thine forever!"

He cast his sword aside, whipped out a dagger, plunged the instrument into the midst of the cloaks and buckled with a mighty cry. The circle of torches closed around him and the curtain whirled across the stage.

The audience roared their approval. Yes, indeed, the last act, with all its horrid stage effects, was a work of power and magnificence.

"I think that the song was rather better done in the London performance by Mrs Siddons," Louisa hissed above the applause.

Barry realised that he had bitten his tongue during Rodolpho's suicide and that his mouth was full of blood.

❖ ❖ ❖ ❖ ❖

The Anderson barouche arrived on Sunday at two, driven by a professional coachman with a postilion seated on the rumble. Mary Ann gasped with pleasure when she saw it waiting at the hall door. Their landlady became a flutter of politeness as they descended in their fine dresses with impeccable hems, pelisses, bonnets, top coats and fur muffs. It was windy, but not yet cold. Mary Ann was taking no risks. She kissed Barry's nose, which was all that was visible, as she throttled him with a gigantic scarf.

"Keep very close with your new friend Jobson, darling," she advised. "Thank Heavens Lord Buchan has sent us a protector."

This was the plan. Barry was to be delivered to the park, where he would promenade for an hour with his peers, then make his own way to the doctor's house in George Street. The child had learned the geography of the city very rapidly and insisted on his independence. But he never ventured into the rougher parts of town. For Barry attracted attention wherever he went: his coat was too huge, and his figure too small. He looked like a very well-dressed dwarf that had escaped, in full costume, either from the stage or from the circus. Sometimes children ran after him in the street, shouting and throwing pebbles. Mary Ann despaired of rendering him inconspicuous. And Barry's surprisingly volatile temperament did not help. He picked fights with impunity whenever he suspected that people were jeering at him. He was ferocious in his solitude.

The barouche paused at the park gates and Barry climbed down.

"Take care, my love," Mary Ann cried after him as he vanished among the barren walks, untouched by spring.

Jobson was waiting on the bridge, whittling sticks with his

knife. They shook hands solemnly, like tiny ancient generals who have agreed on a truce.

"Got a knife?" inquired Jobson as they hunted for suitable pieces of wood on the muddy banks along the river, slipping on the dead leaves. Barry produced an assassin's implement with a double blade.

"That's a splendid murder weapon." Jobson admired the knife. "Who gave you that?"

"A South American revolutionary general," said Barry, who always spoke the truth if he was asked a direct question.

"Go on with you," chuckled Jobson.

"I'll probably be going out to join him in Venezuela when I've finished my studies," Barry insisted. "He's there now. He's not coming back till the end of the year."

"I'd like to travel too," said Jobson, "but we've both decided on the army, haven't we? We should sign up for the same regiment."

Barry hesitated. Then agreed.

"Look at this one," cried Jobson. He held up a bit of wood that boasted a keel. "It's a schooner already."

The winter afternoon gleamed silver. The river was a thick, cold rush of lead. The tree trunks shone brown and damp in the fading light. Barry slithered down to the edge, his boots sinking into the mud. Jobson, watching from the bridge, gave the signal and Barry launched their frail, fresh-created arks into the flood. Then he scrambled up the bank and raced through the trees towards the bridge. Jobson was scanning the waters, his hands turning his eyes into two small telescopes.

"There they are! Look, Barry, look!"

Two small, shaped sticks jabbed and curled in the eddies. Barry's face glowed a little from running. His coat now bore a dark rim of mud. Jobson looked down at the boy's tiny blue knuckles clutching the iron railings and suddenly noticed the size of Barry's hands. Dr Fyfe had stressed the advantages of a small, delicate hand for their bloody profession. The grey wind caught the sticks, pushing them out into midstream. The light flickered over the river as Barry's stick lunged forwards, blocking the other's path.

"You're winning," cried Jobson, generous in his enthusiasm.

Barry peered down into the cold grey waters, feeling the wind on his neck, the damp in his boots.

"But yours hasn't got stuck. It'll get to the bridge in the end."

They paced the empty gravel walks. The greenhouses were locked. The marsh-plant garden which was, in fact, a university botanical experiment, had been subdued to a barren flat patch of mud with small yellow signs bearing Latin names. Nothing broke the surface of the dark, tilled earth. Nothing sprouted alongside the evergreens. The two boys hunted assiduously for signs of life, getting colder and colder as the afternoon closed in. Dusk gathered around them, slate grey at a quarter past three. The city sounds ebbed. A solitary bird shrieked against the approaching dark. They stood, flinging pebbles into the pond, watching for ice at the edges as the temperature dropped, but the circles of cold still formed their eternal rings, pushed outwards, and vanished.

"I've got to go." Barry was sinking into the sadness of winter afternoons.

"Pity."

They walked towards the gates.

"Would you like me to teach you how to box?" asked Jobson, as they stared at each other before parting.

Barry was so small; for his own safety he should learn how to fight. For a second the grey eyes gave nothing away. If Jobson expected enthusiasm from this child he had learned to admire, he never got it. Barry weighed every proposition with sinister cautiousness. Then the boy spoke, peculiar, quaint and courteous.

"Yes, thank you, Jobson. I should like that very much."

He offered Jobson a frozen hand.

"Done." Jobson shook hands heartily. Then Barry was gone, invisible almost at once in the grey sinking light.

❖ ❖ ❖ ❖ ❖

James Miranda Barry made a note of what he had done that day.

Rose at 7 a.m.

Read a treatise on the liver until 9 a.m.

Breakfasted with Mary Ann and Louisa. Quarrelled with Mary Ann about her remaining in Edinburgh.

Attended lectures and transcribed notes.

12–1 p.m. Walked the wards at the lying-in hospital with Dr Fyfe.

1–3 p.m. Dissection in the anatomical department. Did Jobson's share for him too. Jobson contrives to mislay one of the feet. It is discovered in a bucket.

3–5 p.m. Dined with Jobson at his lodgings.

6–7 p.m. Attended Dr Fyfe's midwifery lecture. Attended anatomical demonstrations.

9 p.m. Supper with Louisa and Mary Ann. Made it up with her. It is decided that she should speak to Dr Anderson and see what can be arranged.

Worked till midnight.

❖ ❖ ❖ ❖ ❖

Mary Ann did a sum. She added up how much it was costing to keep Barry in surgeon's fees, lecture courses and medical instruments. The boys had to register as surgical pupils and pay separate lecture fees for every course they attended. Barry had spent eight guineas on books in one month.

"Look at this, Louisa," she cried, waving the figures in the air, as if the bailiffs had already been summoned.

"Hmmmm." Louisa checked all the figures reflectively. "Thank God we're not paying. Write it out neatly and send it all off to David. The child really is doing extraordinarily well. Something of a relief, isn't it? Otherwise David would begin to think that this was becoming an expensive joke. Do it tomorrow. Put out the lamp, Mary Ann. Come to bed."

❖ ❖ ❖ ❖ ❖

There was no effective heating system at the lying-in hospital. A large fire with a cauldron suspended above the flames was perpetually bubbling in one corner of the ward. But it made no difference. The air remained chilly and menacing. Everything was ruthlessly clean. The corridors were vaults of polished cold. Barry's knuckles emerged blue from his cuffs, his hands clenched tight as he pattered along at Dr Fyfe's coattails, avoiding the little shower of powder which descended from the bouncing pigtail. The patient was a lady of quality who lay groaning in a little alcove, surrounded by curtains. They could hear her breathing in great hoarse gulps as they approached. The boiling water and lukewarm towels were ready. The nurses hovered. The waters had broken, but the lady had failed to cast her child into the world. The baby was coming, coming. Her breathing accelerated into a yell. Barry clenched his fists even tighter.

"Well, madam," said Dr Fyfe briskly, "it looks as though we shall have to give Nature a helping hand."

Barry observed the patient closely. The most remarkable aspect of her case was that she changed colour completely every ten minutes, from a deathly white as her breathing ebbed, then, as the pain of her contractions increased, she was translated into a deep shade of burgundy red. Dr Fyfe took her pulse. He listened to her heart. Then he made her cough, so that he could listen to her lungs. He felt her brow. She was sweating profusely with wasted effort. Her sweat-stained lace robe was now speckled with wig powder. She smelt like a cowshed. Jobson, clutching Barry's elbow, murmured that she was a very fine lady, and very rich. Dr Fyfe refused to visit the great houses, no matter how much he was offered. Let them come to me, was his commanding refrain. And come they did. The fine lady began screaming. Dr Fyfe pounced and seized her in a wrestler's arm-lock.

"Come along, madam. Get up."

The students stood aghast. This was unheard of and probably fatal. The nurse in charge of the ward tried to intervene.

"Doctor! I hardly think . . ."

"Out of my way, woman. Barry, take her legs."

Barry seized the fine lady by her ankles and planted them on the floor.

"Now," commanded Dr Fyfe, as if they were confronting the garden broad walk, "we shall take a turn about the ward."

She left off screaming as they began to walk, her nightgown trailing behind her, and began a deep, rhythmic, undulating groan.

"That's it. Better at once, eh?" reassured Dr Fyfe. The procession began to tour the long arched hall.

"Barry, get a shawl for her shoulders. Jobson, refill the gin jar. Nurse, have the water and the scissors ready. We shall be there in less than twenty minutes."

He thundered commands and his troops took up their battle stations. The woman faltered.

"Steady as she goes," cried Dr Fyfe. "One step at a time." She changed colour again as the blood rushed to her face.

"Yell your head off if it helps," Dr Fyfe shouted above her screeching wail of pain.

"Barry, take her other hand. Mind out, madam, he's got hands like an Eskimo."

She gripped Barry's tiny arctic fingers and screamed. They marched three times round the ward, then –

"Oh God, it's coming! It's coming!"

She doubled up.

"Don't hold back, woman. Push, push, push. Blankets, one of you! Quick."

They swept the woman through the curtains and hurled her onto the bed.

"Push! Breathe! Scream! Push! Breathe! Scream!" yelled Dr Fyfe, as if he too were giving birth. "That's it. Breathe. Push. Push. Push. Exhale – push that child out with your breath. That's right. Knees. Hold her knee up, Barry. Bravo. Give me a son, woman, push – "

The baby's head was already in the doctor's hands, and already dusted with powder, like an ancient rite of baptism.

"Push, woman, push!"

Barry grappled in a medley of flesh, sweat, blood and powder. The event was ferocious, ungainly, undignified and profoundly dramatic. Dr Fyfe's hands, which had been scrubbed white, immaculate, were now covered in blood that was pouring over his cuffs.

"Scream! Push! Breathe!" he yelled. "That's it. That's it, madam. We're home. We're there. We're home! – Let me introduce you to your first son."

He was grappling with the fleshy cord. The creature was

bloody, reddish-blue, and wizened. It entered the world, screaming. The sexual organs appeared to be enlarged, unnatural. Yet the woman's face was extraordinary. The afterbirth shot out, like a ghostly slime. She hardly noticed. There she lay, her genitals mangled, bloody and exposed, her huge breasts ugly and unbound, sweat trickling into her hair. Barry gazed at her face, which was pale, relaxed, ecstatic with relief and joy. Dr Fyfe laid her child upon her breast, wrapped in a warm towel. She kissed the doctor's bloody fingers and he looked down at her with satisfaction, as if she were the most beautiful woman he had ever seen.

"There you are, my girl," he cried, triumphant.

Jobson clutched Barry's hand and burst into tears.

❖ ❖ ❖ ❖ ❖

Jobson began teaching Barry how to box in a converted shooting gallery, which was as cold as the dissecting room. Mary Ann protested. Barry insisted. Louisa sat with her eyebrows arched and her lips curled.

"Well, don't take all your clothes off, child," she commented, weary with arguments, as Mary Ann gave in.

Jobson stripped down to a singlet and breeks. Barry wore his shirt under his waistcoat, but undid his collar and studs. Both were small boys, but Jobson was still a good head taller. Barry looked like a well-wrapped mutant. Nobody bothered to watch them. There were other young men who presented a more entertaining spectacle.

The old shooting gallery had a creaking wood floor, solid stone walls in peeling whitewash and lime, and great rooflights, covered in cobwebs. Jobson's cousin ran the establishment. He was a robust, red-faced man of forty with blackened front teeth, which he attributed to drinking down the granite in his home town of Aberdeen. There was a rudimentary gesture towards washrooms at the back of the gallery, nourished by a sequence of pipes and barrels fed from an iron tank on the roof. The tank froze solid for a week or so every winter. Once the downpipes had split inside the building and flooded the gallery. There were still high-tide marks left along the walls.

The gallery echoed with different sounds. Two other men were boxing in a medley of thumps and grunts. On the far side there was a fencing class. Four young men in a line, white ghosts, their faces masked, formal as nuns, moved forwards in a sequence of lunges, twists and arabesques, pushing against phantom opponents. The fencing master was French. He had a tightly corseted figure and a very fine moustache descending elegantly on either side of his white lips. His face was covered in a strange white powder, like a clown, which made his ears look obtrusively red. He rapped out his commands in French. The young men pranced before him, their weapons shimmering, all at exactly the same angle.

Barry kept his arms firmly across his body, raised, defensive.

"You musn't just retreat, man," cried Jobson, pounding his ears. "Attack! Look, like this. Quick jabs. Left. Left. Are you left-handed?"

He danced backwards. Barry was excellent at dodging quickly. He bounced back and forth, a tiny freak on springs. His rapid breaths showed white in the dusty air. But he never came close enough to place a decent blow on Jobson's chin or ribs. They took a puff on the bench, steaming like horses. "What's the matter, Barry," demanded Jobson, puzzled. "You've usually got plenty of aggression."

Barry looked at his strangely magnified, bandaged fists and said nothing. Ever since they had begun their regular tour of the lying-in wards, James Miranda Barry had become increasingly uneasy. The cadavers procured for the medical school by the occasionally glimpsed, much-imagined resurrection men were white, empty and purely horrible. He looked down at their pitiful shrunken nakedness with indifference. Their past lives and lost histories, whether a story of murder or starvation, were not his concern. But when he was faced with a living woman's bodily abandonment in the unselfconscious and bestial act of giving birth to monsters, Barry recoiled into himself. For this child, courage had become a daily necessity. All his life, he had watched, as if from the inside of a closed jar, the adult world of sensations, passions and desires, unjudging, shut out by his innocence. Now he was shut out forever by the very fact that enabled him to move, to act, to meddle with the privilege to which he had not been born. He watched the women, heavy as animals, bred to give birth, again and again, year after year, until they were either exhausted or dead. They heaved and screamed, terrible in their unloveliness, doing something they needed no training to do. Like day labourers, they flung forth their achievement, red and shrieking or pale, blue and cold into the waiting world. In the public hospital many of them died. Barry had closed the eyes of one poor woman whose unclaimed body was doomed to a mass grave.

At first he had hated them, repulsed by their smell and greasy, stringy hair. He had marvelled at Dr Fyfe's tenderness and bitter grief when one of his patients, mother or child, fled from him to God. Barry had seen the doctor bowed upon his knees, his face buried in the bloody sheets, praying and weeping like a child. It was another man, surely, who hacked at the cold stomach of a corpse on the dissecting table, demanding of the pallid Jobson what would be found in his stomach were he to mount the assault there.

Barry feared the living, not the dead.

He was no longer at home in his stunted body. This unease pervaded his gestures, his gait, his habit of taking stock of his surroundings, as if he feared the approach of an assassin. He shrank from Mary Ann's embraces. He hated to be touched. He wrote long stilted letters every week to General Francisco de Miranda, addressing him formally, as if they had never met, and detailing his activities with copybook precision. These were his military reports from the front on which the overall strategy depended. From Louisa he kept his distance, and he referred to her as "Miss Erskine", or "my mother's companion". He mentioned no other relationship. The students jeered at him occasionally, then begged him to help them with their notes or drawings. He was guarded in his façade of perfect impersonal manners. He never drank in public. He confided in no one.

James Miranda Barry had cold hands and cold eyes. Only Jobson dared to take his arm or thump him on the back.

Barry now realised that the physical intimacy of boxing was

beyond him. He looked at Jobson ruefully, breaking the long silence.

"I don't think I'll ever be any good at this. Would you teach me to shoot?"

❖ ❖ ❖ ❖ ❖

They walked back to Jobson's rooms. Barry felt uncomfortable, prickly with sweat turning cold on his back.

"Have a tot." Jobson rummaged with the lamp. His rooms were always warm, filled with reddish glows and a huge fire. He had a landlady who mothered him. Reluctantly, as if he regretted the loss of its protection, Barry dropped his overcoat onto a chair.

"Not much for me. Here, I'll pour in the hot water myself."

They settled on the rug, backs against their chairs, their fingers almost in the flames, muffins balanced on the toasting forks. The two boys were intent as medieval devils in the apocalypse painted on the church mural,

"Copied your notes? Have some more whisky. That won't taste of anything."

Jobson was at ease. He leaned back, his mouth open. Barry noticed a light prickle of hair on his upper lip.

"I say, Barry, when we're at the hospital, do you get – you know what I mean – are you ever afraid or excited?"

Jobson wanted to talk about sex.

"No," said Barry. "I often feel a little sick."

"You're a cold fish, you know," said Jobson, after a minute or two.

"Am I?"

"Mmmm. No nerves. And no feelings either."

Barry suddenly became very alarmed. He straightened his back and said, with devastating formality, "There are some subjects, Jobson, which must never be broached between us."

Oh Lord, thought the other boy. Now I've offended him. Then he looked at the pale face, ginger freckles and red curls, and saw all the mortifying seriousness of a child. He was overwhelmed with pity. And took an even greater risk. Drawing both of Barry's still frosty hands into his own, he spoke with dreadful, embarrassing sincerity.

"I owe you a lot, Barry. We shall in any case always be friends, won't we? Whatever happens?"

Barry retrieved his hands from Jobson's claws as quickly as was decently possible and said, from a now unreachable distance, "I hope so, Jobson. That would give me great pleasure."

That night Barry dreamed that he was lying in bed, with Dr Fyfe bending over him. The good doctor's wig was askew and the powder was descending in showers. Well, Barry, menaced Dr Fyfe, plucking at the sheets, let's see what you've got to give me.

Barry awoke screaming.

❖ ❖ ❖ ❖ ❖

Jobson began teaching Barry how to shoot. Barry's cold eye and steady hand proclaimed him a natural marksman. Within a month he was a crack shot with a rifle and had made quite extraordinary progress with a set of duelling pistols.

❖ ❖ ❖ ❖ ❖

Even this far north, the hawthorn was fully draped in bridal blossom when Mary Ann and Louisa left Edinburgh by the eight o'clock coach. It had been arranged that Barry was to lodge with Dr Anderson until the end of his short summer term, after which he was to spend the long holidays on Lord Buchan's estate. They stood, all three of them, taking a last look around their gaudy rooms. The trunks, books and hatboxes had already been taken down. The rooms were becoming anonymous, girding themselves to threaten the next occupants.

"Well," said Louisa, putting on her gloves, "thank God it's over, and we've escaped from that wallpaper alive."

Mary Ann afflicted Barry with advice and dietary prescriptions. He listened patiently.

" . . . and keep up your guard with Dr Anderson. He's a charming man, but so far as I know David Erskine has told him nothing. So it's best if you keep to yourself. Mind that you do. And be careful in that dreadful shooting gallery. You know, Louisa, if this child doesn't kill himself, he'll kill someone else . . ."

The two women climbed into the coach, their faces changing

in the flickering sunshine. They paused to peer at the other passengers, who were shrieking their goodbyes with vulgar enthusiasm. There was a sheet of liquid mud across the yard, so Barry stood at a little distance, forlorn upon the stable cobbles, among the sacks of grain and broken-down farming implements. Mary Ann turned to wave.

"Louisa," she hissed, "I'm terrified that he's going to start while I'm away and not there to help or to show him how to organise the cloths. He'll have to wash them or burn them himself. He's eleven years old. And he hasn't started yet."

"You've surely said all that's necessary . . ."

They broke off as an old man climbed into the coach, raising his hat to them.

"Don't worry, my dear." Louisa finished hitching her blanket underneath her toes. "I'm sure he'll be all right."

"Did you check our trunk? Is it on board?" Mary Ann twitched the curtains aside and peered out at Barry's ludicrous hat and jacket. His shoes were heavy with mud and his trousers were too baggy. They hung in folds about his thin legs. He always looked extraordinary, no matter what garments she proposed. She felt the tears on her cheeks. Suddenly she began wailing uncontrollably.

"Oh, Louisa, I shouldn't have done it. He's alone now. He'll always be alone. I've done that to him. And now I'm leaving him too. I'm abandoning my only child . . ."

"Nonsense," snapped Louisa, panicking. Mary Ann never cried. "Pull yourself together. Some of us manage perfectly well on our own."

"Take my handkerchief, madam." The old gentleman proffered an enormous square of green silk. Barry, now perched on a grain sack, drumming his heels, had been mesmerised by the raucous drama of departure. He looked up, saw his mother crying and went red to the tips of his ears. As the coach clattered out of the yard he was too ashamed and embarrassed even to wave. Mary Ann lost her child in that moment as she vanished into a sentimental fountain of silk and tears. Louisa's yellowing face, shut like an ageing book, was the last thing he saw. But he had the distinct impression that, for the second time, knowing and complicit, she had held his glance and winked.

And so it was that James Miranda Barry, aged eleven years and two months, found himself alone, for the first time in his life, with no adults directly responsible for him. He looked up at the city, dark upon its assembled hills, and sniffed the chilly spring air in the crowded courtyard. The wind smelled of horse shit and molasses. He was free. He unbuttoned his coat and took a deep breath. Then he marched off in the direction of the hospital. There was nothing in the boy's face or step to indicate that he was not perfectly sure of himself.

❖ ❖ ❖ ❖ ❖

Barry's silences at dinner were terrifying. Mrs Anderson went in for elegant conversation on intellectual subjects and daring floral arrangements. Her husband informed her that their young house guest was really quite a genius and under the very special protection of Lord Buchan himself. Mrs Anderson found it hard to believe in Barry's genius. So far as she could see, he had no conversation. She was not in the least interested in the subject of his thesis, written in Latin, on the hernia of the groin. He had already begun this work, and, if pressed, explained. Mrs Anderson was very interested in Lord Buchan's domestic situation and household management.

"It must be charming – their country home, I mean, for we have often visited them in London. A little grand, perhaps? Do tell me, Mr Barry . . ."

Barry explained that the front hall always stank of the farmyard, and that hens sometimes covered their eggs in the coat cupboard. Geese were allowed on the front drive and so were the guinea fowl. He remembered that Lady Elizabeth liked pots and was often to be found upon her knees among the geraniums. Lord Buchan knew everybody, and didn't care who sat round his table as long as they were energetic and interesting. He often played billiards with the local doctor. Barry couldn't comment on the drawing-room chatter because he spent most of his time among the servants. Dr Anderson chuckled at his wife's disappointments and suspected Barry of being a wicked little devil under his carapace of total seriousness. His daughters, set on by Anderson, urged Barry to describe his thesis, *De Merocele*, until even the doctor began to wonder whether the conversational turn was quite suitable. Anderson regarded Barry as a curiosity, living proof, if any were needed, that the old radical aristocrat, David Steuart Erskine, was capable of bizarre aberrations. When the ladies withdrew Dr Anderson found himself staring at a white-faced child, who neither drank nor smoked.

"Barry," he said, getting a grip upon the situation, "I find myself in something of a parental position with regard to you."

"Yes, sir."

"So you won't take it amiss if I offer you a little advice?"

"No, sir."

"It wouldn't do you any harm to try a little port and a very small cigar."

"If you wish, sir."

"It's not as I wish, my lad. It's the done thing."

"Yes, sir."

Barry drank the undiluted port as if it were poisoned, and choked over his cigar in a professional way.

"Keep it level, lad," advised Dr Anderson, "that's the trick."

They got through the ordeal, painful to both, in silence, apart from the doctor's occasional peremptory suggestions. He assured Barry that they would try again on the following evening. After twenty minutes, they joined the ladies. Miss Isabelle Anderson played a little upon the spinet and Barry turned her music for her, standing bolt upright. But his conversation was a disaster. A polite enquiry concerning his medical studies from an unfortunate visitor drew forth a description of his new course on military surgery, giving more detailed information about gangrene and amputations than the company could possibly have wished to know.

❖ ❖ ❖ ❖ ❖

Barry went back to the house in the country at the end of May, a month or so following his mother's departure. As the coach jolted south the seasons appeared to advance. The chestnuts swayed darker in the hedgerows. A field stretching back from the

gate basked in cowslips. The grass loomed waist-high by the river
bottoms.

Barry's cheek bore a purple mark where he had leaned against
the worn leather seat and been jolted back and forth while he
slept. The landscape rose, sank and swayed as the coach clattered
on, like an unstable ship caught in a big wind, and the child,
battered with exhaustion, half dreamed the thick hedges, the
brambles massed with white flowers and the great trees, their
candles glowing, now white, now rose-pink, in the hesitating
sunlight and the rushing shadows. As the shade hardened and
deepened, they arrived at The Green Man, crouched in caked
mud at the northern end of the village. Barry's trunk was
unloaded and he sat solemnly upon it by the back door of the
inn, waiting for the trap that would take him the last five miles
to the house.

He remembered some of the faces he had seen over a year
ago. But no one recognised him.

"Would you like to sit inside, sir?" suggested the ostler, who
was impressed by Lord Buchan's arms painted on the trunk.
Barry stepped into the half-dark of the pub's small dining room,
laid himself out upon the cushions and fell instantly asleep.

Someone was shaking him.

"Excuse me, sir," said the housemaid in his ear, "but there's a
young lady outside. And she says she's a friend of yours."

Barry sat up, rubbing his eyes. But she hadn't waited for a
reply. She was already beside him, her black curls swinging with
enthusiasm. Her kiss had the force of a slap, her earring was cold
against his cheek. It was Alice Jones.

"I couldn't wait. I've just run all the way from the other side
of the tollhouse. In bare feet too. I cut my left toe. But I just
had to be the first to see you."

Her dirty left foot landed on the seat beside him. It was
indeed bleeding.

"Can you quench the flow?" she demanded.

"You must have got that expression out of one of the books."
Barry smiled shyly, producing his handkerchief.

"One of the ones you sent? I've read them all. The rector lets me have a go at his library now. But I'm only allowed to borrow one book at a time."

Barry called for clean water and washed her grimy foot. Her toe now looked like a decorated parcel. Alice gazed at him, delighted.

"But it's wonderful. Wonderful," she giggled. "You're perfect. No one'd ever guess."

She leaned over and kissed him again.

"We'll go out courting. You're smaller than me, but I can pretend you're Napoleon."

Barry reddened slightly. She noticed at once.

"But I think of you as James. My special friend. I always did. So it doesn't matter what size you are. I'll always love you. Did you miss me? And are you pleased to see me?"

"Yes. Very," said Barry, rigid with embarrassment. She took his hands in hers, insisting on their renewed complicity.

"Is it really true that you've chopped up corpses? What do men's broomsticks look like when they're dead? Do they just shrivel right up? Old Mr Ellis died. I could've looked when my mother took me round because they were busy washing the body and he shat himself when he died, just at the very moment, so that the blankets had to be burned. My mum had to see to that. But I didn't dare. Oh, you must tell me everything."

"I can't believe that you didn't dare." Barry was amused.

"The trap'll be here in a moment. Let's go and wait in the yard." And she dragged him to his feet.

In the late-afternoon sun he screwed up his eyes and, over-coming his shyness, looked at her carefully. Tall as wild nettles, sunburnt, black-haired, her waist and hips slender and supple, her gold earring glimmering against the black. She wore an old faded blue skirt, a baggy white shirt, several sizes too large for her, with fine smocking and a torn sleeve. She was four years older than he was, so she must be fifteen.

Barry was amazed at her strength. She took the other end of the trunk and heaved it into the back of the trap with no difficulty whatsoever.

"We've started the hay," she smiled. "You'll come with us tomorrow, won't you?"

And all the way back to the house, accompanied by the last crescendo of birdsong, she talked and talked, his hands firmly clasped between her own. David Erskine was waiting in front of the house, unkempt in his old waistcoat and shirtsleeves, his white hair bare in the fading sun.

"Well, Barry . . ." he said, staring.

Barry held out his hand.

"Good evening, sir. I trust that I find you and Lady Elizabeth in the best of health."

The old man roared with laughter. As he stood there rocking on his heels, Alice made her escape.

"Well, Barry." He clamped the tiny white hand in his own. "Come here, young man. But it's excellent, excellent. I can't believe that it's reading lessons you'll be giving to that young scullery maid of mine who's too pretty for her own good. Come in, come in. Elizabeth!"

He yelled for his wife, stumbling into the dark, rustling hallway.

"Our young man has come home at last."

❖ ❖ ❖ ❖ ❖

The household took the presence of David Erskine's young ward for granted. But not without comment. One school of thought concluded that he was probably a changeling. He was somewhat uncanny, and certainly not a normal child. Cook started a rumour that Barry was in fact a hermaphrodite, a story which Alice hotly denied.

"Well then," said Cook, offended, "if you're so sure of yourself, what is he?"

"Everything a gentleman should be," said Alice haughtily.

Cook threw a basin of water at her and Alice abandoned the scullery to the enemy. But Alice was right. Barry took his place among the gentlemen. He drank with moderation, but he could hold his liquor. He smoked a pipe. He went out shooting, and his performance in the woods astounded both David Erskine and the gamekeeper. He always handed one of the ladies in to dinner, and then sat in a ferocious, diminutive silence beside her. No matter how charming the lady, Barry's morose monosyllables never varied. He might be a perfect gentleman, but he could not learn how to talk nonsense in an amusing way.

"Medical studies," declared Elizabeth, once Barry was safely buried in the library, well out of earshot, "have turned him into a German. Ask him a question about goitres or dropsy and he comes out with the textbook."

"But he's very quaint and serious." Mrs Emmersley defended the boy, who had sat next to her, transfixed, for several hours. "I think he's adorable. All his buttons always done up tight. His manners are so formal and polite."

This was the judgement of the vicar's wife, who was secretly convinced that, if Barry was not actually made of wax, he must be David Erskine's bastard son, and said as much to anyone who asked.

Barry locked himself in the library and worried away at his thesis. Dedicated and correct, his daily rhythm never altered. His politeness was chilly and invariable. His only friend was Alice Jones.

And this friendship ripened like the pumpkins in the garden. Alice talked, invented, dreamed. And Barry clasped her version of the world to his breast, like a wrecked sailor. He felt that he had been locked up in a box. She made him understand the ways in which he had been set free.

"First of all, you've got to travel. General Miranda's in Venezuela, isn't he? I looked it up on the rector's missionary chart. They don't have any workers in God's vineyard there. It's all gone over to the Catholics. But don't you see, you'll be able to go and visit him. It's ever so easy. Passage on a ship as the ship's doctor, maybe? No questions asked. Now I'll be lucky if I ever get to London . . .

"Your General's got rich friends. Now that's what makes it easier for you . . .

"Well, you can't do much about what you're born into. But after that you've got to get pushing . . ."

Alice was an advocate of the meritocracy. She was all in favour of Barry's proposal to join the army. She was jealous of Jobson. She demanded every detail of their lives in Edinburgh. She had views on Dr Fyfe. She derided their appalling wallpaper. She studied his anatomical drawings with ghoulish zeal. Barry was her advance guard into unknown territory. He was gathering intelligence. And she awaited his return like an experienced spymaster. In the afternoons he worked alongside her, hoeing the weeds among the lettuces, slaughtering slugs, searching for eggs in the hay barn, plucking the ducks under the ramshackle lean-to by the farmyard water trough. When Barry sat with the adults, silent and caged, he was dreaming of the mass of chick-weed, spearwort and marsh marigolds down by the stream, where he sat in the warm grass, listening to Alice Jones.

❖ ❖ ❖ ❖ ❖

It was another extraordinary summer. All the doors stood open and drops of water formed on the cold damp flags in the dairy. The house breathed out winter damp and the wallpaper in the dining room turned yellow in great patches and began to curl up above the skirting board. Immense redecoration operations were mooted over supper, colours were discussed and patterns sent for. The adults lay upon the terrace, indolent, limp and smiling.

The first crop of hay was rapidly whirled into stacks. The grass was long and green to the base of the stalks. On Great Acre it was left to wilt gently for several days, giving out the thick sweet smell of putrefaction. At first it was decided to cut one field at a time and not risk the weather, but as day after day rose upon thick, wet dew steaming in the still heat, the cows standing in the river and the low buzz of flies haunting the stairways, the bailiff and the farm manager consulted some of the older tenants who knew the weather signs, and then decided to cut all the hay. David Erskine forbade Barry to spend the mornings in the library for an entire week and he was ordered out to work on the land. The master and every able-bodied member of the household mowed in massed lines, moving slowly across the great fields, like the Israelites advancing on Jerusalem. Alice inspected and directed the boy's every move, bound up his blisters when they paused to drink, lent him her old hat and swore that his backache would ease off. The scythe and the rake were far taller than he was and he felt his muscles stretched in all directions.

Alice strode down the straight swathes towards the trees, her brown toes gathering long stalks between them. She could tell who had cut every row by the style and height of their cut. Alice was a connoisseur. She had been born on the estate. She had grown up on this land. All around her, for field after field, she was able to name her world. Down at the stream, they dabbled their feet in cold, clear water, raced flowers over the eddies, and Alice gathered wild parsley and milkwort to make blue and white garlands, which always dropped to pieces when she arranged them on Barry's head, crowning him as if he were Caesar celebrating a victory. Sometimes they fell asleep in the grass, waking up chilly and itching, their clothes damp beneath them. It was here that Barry first tried to express his own doubts at what he had become. He no longer confided in his mother, or asked for her opinion. His infrequent letters could have been written by a stranger. He now trusted no one but Alice Jones.

"It's odd. I sometimes hear my own voice. Talking at an immense distance. It's like being two people. One is out there, talking, maybe even arguing with someone else. Like Jobson. We often argue. And the other is crouching underneath, all tensed up, waiting to spring."

Alice wasn't listening.

"So it's very odd. It's like being an actor."

Alice's egoism triumphed at once. "Now that's what I've always wanted to do. Act in a real theatre. Not just charades. Dress up like a lady. Be a lady. Or be a soldier. Or a madwoman. Tell me again about the play in Edinburgh. Was Mrs Chiswick as beautiful as I am? Was her dying sigh really so very thrilling?"

"Well, she looked quite different, with her white robes all torn and her hair down. Her hair wasn't curly like yours is. It was all red. Deep red and flowing."

"Don't be silly, James. On stage you can have hair any colour you like. She was wearing a wig."

Alice chewed a long stalk of fresh grass. Barry saw a thin shaft of green sticking to her front tooth.

"You have to be born into an acting family. The stage and the paint have to be in your blood. How can I acquire the right sort of blood, James?"

She leaned over, peering into his grey eyes. "Tell me how?"

"Alice, I sincerely wish I knew. I don't think that you can become something you're not. And now I feel like two people. One of them is true and one is a charade. I don't know which one is real. And mostly I feel that neither one really exists."

Barry waved his hands in the air, gave up trying to explain and began chewing his fingernails. Alice did not believe in the truth of the body. The truth, so far as she was concerned, was what you could get away with. She sat up straight, eloquent with revelation.

"Oh no. Don't you see? It's all changed. How can I explain? Look, when we first met I wanted to know what you were, because I couldn't be certain. But now I am. Now you're really a man. Soon you'll be a real doctor. You can be a gentleman. Last year was a game. It isn't a game anymore. Now it's the real thing. Games are all finished."

Barry looked at her hopelessly.

"You've got to change your way of thinking. That's all. What'd be waiting for you if the General and Mrs Bulkeley had brought you up as a girl? No real studies. Just a little French and piano playing. Maybe botany and flowers. Never any corpses to chop up or babies to haul out into the world or horrible diseases to cure. You'd have to go out in carriages to keep your feet clean, wait around for gentlemen to notice you and end up marrying someone old and rich and boring . . ."

"Mary Ann made me promise never to marry," protested Barry.

Alice continued undaunted with the dire tale of women's lives.

"Did she? That's odd. But if you'd been a woman you'd have done it anyway. And then when you were married you could never go anywhere unchaperoned, because it wouldn't be respectable. Whereas now . . ."

She gazed up into the huge, flecked green ceiling of sunlight and shadow above them, dreaming of oceans and continents where the people were painted black, or wore nothing but feathers. Or the Arctic waste where ice cliffs, breaking free from the uninhabited mass, plunged into the freezing seas. The world was all before them, beckoning.

"Louisa goes everywhere unchaperoned. You aren't trapped. And you're a girl."

Barry looked at Alice's feet. They were never clean, and servants were not called upon either to have morals or to be respectable. They surveyed one another, assessing their different states.

"That's true. I'll get a better situation now that I can read. And you'll teach me to write more than my own name. But I can't go where I like. Not yet. Nor do all I want to do."

Alice pulled Barry's hat down over his nose, which was peeling, and picked greenfly off his collar.

"Maybe you've got to think a bit like a Freemason. You're part of a secret society. You're gathering information. You're learning all the things that you can use. You're out for yourself alone . . ."

"Like you," Barry grinned.

"All servants are spies," retorted Alice, "That's normal. You have to know things. Otherwise you wouldn't get on."

"We aren't children anymore." Barry felt the flaming sword of Eden at his back.

"So much the better." Alice never had any regrets. She rolled towards him, her eyes glittering.

"I'll teach you women's secrets. It's all easy. There's not much to learn. And you'll teach me what men know."

Her excitement was infectious. She gazed at Barry. She expected everything of him.

"If I was you, nothing'd stop me."

He believed her. And all around them the buzz and whirr of the insects crackled in the silence. Barry saw the dragonflies flit, dart, hover and vanish on the churning green surface of the stream. Alice's nose was an inch from his own.

"Like I said," she repeated, "nothing."

❖ ❖ ❖ ❖ ❖

Some way away from the track back to the house, well out of Cook's yelling distance, lay Alice and Barry, reading in the long grass. They were invisible to passing eyes; even one of the men in the carts returning home would have been unlikely to notice them. They were reading novels. Barry was reading in French, a volume purloined from Louisa's bedroom, guessing words he didn't know. Alice was reading an old Jacobin novel, from which the cover and the title page were missing. By now she knew all the words.

"Listen to this, James. *'Madam, I have waited long enough for your reply. I can wait no more . . .'*"

Alice clutched her forehead dramatically.

" *'Sir, you have had your reply. I am of the same mind that ever I was in the dignity and safety of my father's house. Did you imagine, that, sequestered here, I would willingly yield to your desires?'*"

"What's 'sequestered'?"

"Locked up, idiot. Don't interrupt."

Alice stretched out one bare sunburnt arm, pushing her unwelcome suitor away from her. He promptly turned into a rapist.

" *'Madam! Look not upon me so. I am a man, with all the passions of a man. You will make me desperate.'*"

" *'Ha! And do you think that if you were to make yourself master of my person you would become the master of my mind? Nay, sir, you are deluded. Mind is the source of liberty, the rose of human freedom. Mind has a ductility like water. It can pass through stone walls, locked doors and prison bars . . .'*"

"Get on with it, Alice."

"But that's what she says!" Indignantly. "If a man wants you and is determined to have you, just think otherwise and you'll see it all differently and so will he."

"My arse!"

Alice giggled. "Shut up. Listen."

" *'I speak not of virtue. How should I be ashamed? No violation can ever touch my honour, sir. I can never be conquered by force.'* This bit's really good."

"Does he do it?"

"What?"

"Rape her! As in *The Rape of the Sabine Women.*"

"No. He caves in and rushes back down the stairs. Then he

gets sick and she goes and sits by his bedside and educates him in the powers of the mind."

"How do you know? You haven't got that far."

"I read the last chapter to see if she dies."

Insects buzzed indifferently across the text. The children were harassed now and again by a persistent horsefly. Barry lay biting his nails. Alice chuckled peacefully as the heroine persuaded the villain that all attempts at rape would avail him naught. He duly tottered back down the stairs to his decline. Then Barry found a passage that presented an adequate sexual challenge.

"Alice, listen. Here's a bit where it all happens. I'll translate it.

" '*The Marquis fingered the lock for a moment, then slipped silently into Céline's darkened bedroom. He could hear the girl breathing gently behind the curtains. There was no sound from the adjoining chamber. He found the bolt'* – I think that *verrou* means bolt – '*and pushed it home.*' "

"Who's in the adjoining chamber?"

"Céline's mother. It all happens in a château. Lots of rich aristocrats at a country houseparty. Before the Revolution happened. They flirt like mad at dinner, then go on walks and boating trips, a bit like they do here, only in more expensive clothes, and then at night no one sleeps. They just creep round the corridors, hiding behind tapestries and trying to get into one another's bedrooms."

"Just like here. Only you can hear all the floorboards creaking and we don't have any tapestries. Why doesn't the mother wake up?"

"I don't know. Wait a minute. She also admires the Marquis. She's made that quite clear. So he's been flirting with the mother in order to pass his time with the daughter. Listen.

" '*As he parted the lace curtains, a shaft of moonlight fell upon the lovely sleeping form. Her robes were disordered and he discerned the pale curve of her bosom beneath the silk.*' "

"Oh, yes. That's good," cried Alice.

" '*As she stirred in her sleep her lips parted and she murmured a name. He pressed closer. Was it his name that she whispered, betraying her dearest desires?*' "

"Well? Was it?"

" 'The Marquis, ravished in turn by her innocent abandon, her vulnerable loveliness, paused as he bent towards her soft face. Am not I the first, he thought, to pluck this Lovely Rose. She must be treasured, cherished, savoured . . .' "

"You can't savour roses," said Alice.

" 'His lips softly brushed the maiden's cheek, then, as he gently plucked the lawn aside and bent to kiss her throat, the nymph stretched out her arms to embrace him. Into her dream he melted, caressing her soft loveliness . . .' "

"Sounds wonderful," said Alice, stretching out in the aspect of an expectant Psyche.

" 'The Marquis was in raptures. His lips closed upon the piquant summit of her naked breast, and now his goal, that Heavenly Seat of Pleasure, was even within his grasp. His fingers were entwined within that Soft Foliage that had scarce begun to burgeon, and gently voyaging into the remoter reaches of the Beloved Promised Land, he found that Cave of Sweet Delight. His gentle touch had met with no resistance. He knew himself a welcome traveller, and he did enter there. The maiden yielded up her Rose with passionate abandon. The Marquis was within moments of achieving his desires, when suddenly – ' "

"I knew it! The mother!" Alice, mistress of the plot, diviner of events, the sibyl of all narratives, sat up shrieking.

"You've got it, Alice. He bolted the wrong door."

"Cheat. You read on ahead too."

"I had to. To translate."

"Quick. Tell me what happens."

Barry fluttered the pages, his nose puckered at the pale French print. Alice was sitting astride his thigh, leaning down, peering at yet another language, whose hieroglyphics were still unyielding and opaque.

"He gets away with it! Look. The girl pretends to wake up and yells when the candlewax falls upon her arm. Ouch, Alice, you're too heavy. Look here –

" 'The Marquis, overcome with emotion, drew the outraged lady aside . . . Madame, I dreamed that I held you in my arms. I never doubted that we had an understanding and you, so generous and loving as you are, had consented to put an end to my sufferings and to bring me to those Delights, after which I have so sadly languished. My passion *was welcomed! I was greeted with answering tenderness! What sweet scents and moist warmth were here . . .'* "

Alice rode Barry's thigh like a jockey, urging him on with a makeshift grass whip.

"Quick, quick. How does it end?"

"How'd you think? He goes off to bed with the mother."

"Better an old hen than no white meat at all."

Alice fell off into the grass, displaying a mass of grubby white petticoat and bare, brown legs.

"Kiss me, James. Pretend you're the Marquis and I'm the delicate maiden."

Barry thumped his arm down across the girl's chest.

"There's a beetle creeping up your left leg and aiming straight for your bum," he whispered, in a voice thick with menace.

❖ ❖ ❖ ❖ ❖

DE MEROCELE

*Do not consider my youth,
but consider whether I show a man's wisdom.*
Menander

TO
GENERAL FRANCISCO DE MIRANDA

with the author's eternal gratitude and admiration,
remembering always the father's solicitude, interest and care,
with which he has generously supported
every endeavour on the part of the author,

&

to his benevolent and magnanimous patron

DAVID STEUART ERSKINE
EARL OF BUCHAN

in whose debt the author shall always be,
This Thesis
is respectfully dedicated.

JAMES MIRANDA BARRY

Barry showed Alice his thesis, beginning with the dedicatory flourishes, the rest written in Latin, each page full of wonderful italic curves. Alice put on a clean apron and clogs in honour of the occasion. She read the dedication aloud, several times, but refused to touch it because she had been scrubbing potatoes. They stood together, in front of the lectern in the library, hovering on different levels of the steps. Alice was attentive and silent for about half a minute. Then she wrinkled her nose.

"Hmmmm. Well done, James. I'll stick to English, I think. I've copied out that passage from *Gulliver's Travels* which you set me to do. Though I don't see why I have to learn to spell Houhynhmn. They don't exist. Why'd you have to write in Latin? Nobody speaks it anymore."

"You just do. Everybody does. And you have to defend it in Latin too. But it's very formal. Like delivering prepared speeches."

"I see. It's tradition." Alice was both sceptical and astute. "I don't think much of tradition," she added in tones of decisive rejection.

"You represent the modern spirit," said Barry sadly, "progress at all costs."

"You've got to have progress in medicine. So that we die off less."

Alice wiped her hands on the pockets of her apron. Then she kissed Barry on the cheek. He trembled slightly at her warm touch upon his habitual cold. Outside the shut rooms with their smell of leather, termite powder and ancient dust, the summer sun glittered on thick banks of straw, spiky in the fields. This year's crop was already home. They were gathering apples in the orchard. Despite the lateness of the season, Alice had a batch of new arrivals.

"Come and see the chicks."

Alice's chickens were part of her economy. She took a percentage on all the eggs and live poultry which she sold in the market. David Erskine was trying to develop cooperative projects with his tenants so that the estate would increase its yield. The theory was simple. Each tenant had the right to a small profit from the increase in the estate's revenues, if the new crops, one of which was Dutch Brussels sprouts, a new variety of doubtful provenance, proved successful. If the sprouts flourished, Lord Buchan threatened his agent with acres of tulips, purchased from the same dealer. Tulips were fashionable, especially dark ones with dull stripes. The Master truly believed that if the tenants had a vested interest in a successful harvest they would work harder and better. In practice, popular resistance was total and inflexible. The farm workers suspected a trick that would rebound upon them. David Erskine put on a clean waistcoat and made a radical speech from the mounting block in the stableyard and everyone dutifully gathered round to listen. A reference to "our courageous brothers in the colonies" proved to be a mistake. Cook instantly detected revolutionary sentiments, emanating from France, and muttered about the kitchen that the Master was forgetting his place. Others said that it was a plot to keep them away from their own land and make them work harder on his. Alice said that of course the Master would do better than they would. But then, he always did anyway. That was the order of things. She negotiated a separate deal on her chickens with the bailiff. Although disappointed at the negative scepticism of his tenants and domestic staff, who felt excluded from any arrangement that would clearly only benefit the field workers, David Erskine was nevertheless heartily amused at the acumen of Alice Jones. He suspected Barry's ingenuity behind her. But in that he was wrong. Alice called upon Barry's skills, to which she had no claim, and exploited tham all she could. But she never relinquished her intellectual independence. Barry might know more than she did, but it was Alice who knew how to assess the weight and significance of rumours, events, whispered conversations, looks and smiles. She knew when to insist on having her own way and when to leave well enough alone. She knew how to flirt without consequences, how to cajole, persuade. She knew when to accept and when to refuse gracefully. She guarded her virginity with the vigilance of a poacher overseeing a rabbit trap. And she advised Barry to do the same.

Alice was his Virgil, his guide through the infernal kingdoms. He had given her all the education that she had, but it was he who asked her opinion, her advice, her views. Concentrated and rapacious, Alice applied herself to the acquisition of knowledge.

But she remained critical, unintimidated. She bit hard on true gold and spat out false coin. She mistrusted easy answers and long words. She ate well, slept well, and never remembered her dreams. Alice looked outwards at the world. She accepted the immutable, being an excellent judge of what was in fact immutable, and put her shoulder hard against everything else. Hers was a philosophy of dailiness. She neither anticipated events nor regretted them. But she saved money. Money was the trump card she played against the future, the only card with which she could not cheat, the victor's card in her hand.

❖ ❖ ❖ ❖ ❖

James Miranda Barry was terrified of sex. Particularly if it occurred outside the pages of a book. It was the serpent at his feet. It would be the moment of his unmaking. Men and women of no ambiguity must be kept at arm's length. He never laughed at the kitchen jokes. He never understood the kitchen jokes. David Erskine's groom was a hideous man called Joss. His teeth were rotten and his fingernails were foul with ingrained manure. He drank neat gin for hours, without flinching. He made most of the kitchen jokes.

The groom decided that Barry needed to be taught the more fundamental truths, given that the General's away at the wars, and the poor little midget clearly isn't even given to fiddling with his own broomstick when the candle's out. Joss trapped Barry in the coach house, a cavernous, dusty enclave filled with battered elderly carriages, some of dubious construction and indifferent suspension. The relics were now managed by a team of very successful spiders who left an ornate trail between the tarnished brass lamps and split seats. What's a man's best weapon in the bedroom battle? Well, one fine day, my boy, you'll kiss that Jones girl right here where her throat meets her sloping breasts and right here where her nipple sprouts pink from those dark circles, and don't think that she doesn't let me suck them till they're stone-hard points when she's in the mood and feeling bored, and if she lets you close your mouth round those delicious little orbs, you'll find that your gun is so loaded that white smoke is oozing from the barrel, and what should you do when that's the case?

Why, lift up her skirts, prise the target apart with your fingers, that's what she wants, that's what they all want, and don't you listen to any of them that try to tell you otherwise, stick your gun down the hole as far as you can, and fire, fire, fire. Nothing like it. Sets a man up for the day. Puts a grin on his face and a bounce in his step. And if she's let you do it once then she'll want you back down there pumping away, often as you can take time out to reload.

Joss roared with laughter at Barry's frozen, scarlet face, and prodded the boy's groin suggestively. Barry stalked straight out of the coach house to find Alice, his cold fists clenched with insulted dignity. Alice was busy counting chicks to make sure that she hadn't been robbed. The mother hen pecked at her bare, brown arms as she collected little balls of twitching fluff and packed them into a straw-bedded box. Her fingers closed delicately around the fragile specks of gold, twittering with anxiety. She met Barry's glance, which was now a pale white glare, fixed with rage and fright.

"Ten, twelve, thirteen, fourteen, fifteen . . . all right. They're all there. Now tell me what's happened."

Barry narrated the incident, hesitated, then reported the fact that the groom had also given him a bold tweak between the legs to make his points clear. To his horror, Alice burst out laughing.

"Oh dear, James! You can't join the army and be serious about things like that. Why, it'll happen every day. Anyway, Joss is a rogue. My mum warned me. He gets you alone among the buckets then lifts up your skirt, right up, to keep it out of the molasses, he says, and puts his hands in between to see if you've got anything sticky, there where you shouldn't have. I'm surprised that he didn't insist on undoing all your buttons to see if you've really got a rod or just a mass of feathers . . ."

Two huge tears rolled down James Barry's cheeks.

"Oh, don't cry, James!" She bundled the chickens into the hutch, an armful of pecking and fluttering. "Come on down to the stream."

The September sun warmed the dark, ploughed earth. Alice washed her feet in the river, then dried them on her apron. The air's chill tongue licked her skin. She looked up at the changing willows shivering in the stream, and into the cool, vast quiet of England, the cattle standing by the green shallows, their white flanks streaked with gold, and above the great vault, guttering white high in the blue. James Barry lay beside her, following her gaze into nothingness. She sighed, feeling the burden of his curious innocence: this child, knowing and unknowing the things that Alice had always been able to whistle up towards her, or brush from her skin with her fingertips.

This boy's first love had been the slender woman in muslin and ribbons, who had carried him firmly on her hip. His second love, the huge courageous revolutionary general with his prominent nose, widening girth, heart as boundless as the seas and all the distances he travelled. His third love was Alice Jones. He rolled onto his side to gaze at her black curls, tucked behind the golden ring. Slowly, he reached out and turned the ring gently in her ear. She put her fingers over his and smiled at the chill of his touch. Come into the garden, my sister, my love. Behold, thou art fair, my love – also our bed is green. The beams of our house are of chestnut and the rafters of willows and fir. Let him kiss me with the kisses of his mouth, for thy love is better than wine.

❖ ❖ ❖ ❖ ❖

Scenes from Shakespeare! Now there was mist coating the cedars in the park and the purple-blue clouds of Michaelmas daisies had been imprisoned with festoons of string. The gardeners were planting experimental tulips on the other side of the haha in the early day, and the swifts were already massed on the roof tops. James Barry was due to travel north within the week. And his departure was to be marked by Scenes from Shakespeare. There were still sufficient numbers of languid adults loitering in the household to make up a party of courtiers and mechanicals. We are all going to perform the last act of *A Midsummer Night's Dream*, with the audience seated in front of the first winter fire in the Great Hall, surrounded by trays of soft cake, roast chestnuts, and sweet wine. The boy will play Robin Goodfellow. Won't that be charming? He's quite perfect for the part.

But he wasn't. Caparisoned in a rich costume of lace and velvet with pale silver stockings cut off at the ankle, Barry was to scamper through the Hall at the head of a troupe of fairies, non-speaking roles supplied from the stock of kitchen help, who, once scrubbed and dressed up could pass for wee folk of the magical kind, blessing this house, invoking the powers of darkness, only to banish them forever.

Now the hungry lion roars
And the wolf behowls the moon . . .
Now it is the time of night
That the graves, all gaping wide,
Every one lets forth his sprite,
In the church-way paths to glide . . .

Barry had already learned the part by heart. But alas! As soon as all eyes were fixed upon his tiny pallid face and open mouth and once the assembled household, radiant with expectation, leaned forwards to hear him, he was metamorphosed into a wooden mannikin, whose clockwork innards were on the brink of extinction. He struck an unlikely pose, one arm rigid at the hip, and chanted the words inaudibly, punctuating the poetry with a sequence of querulous gulps. Alice covered her face with her hands. The company shrank in their chairs, or looked into their glasses.

"Oh dear," gasped Elizabeth, as he ceased his undifferentiated mutter, "and you've even taken the trouble to learn the wretched thing. What a dreadful shame. That won't do at all."

Now no one could imagine James Barry engaged in a light-hearted frolic through the corridors with a gaggle of laughing fairies at his heel. The idea had to be regretfully abandoned. No, Puck the mischief-maker was simply not Barry's role.

"Never mind, darling. We'll think of something."

Barry could not endure being patronised and stalked out in a huff. Alice dashed after him, her wooden clogs ringing on the stone floors.

"We could end it all with '*Lovers, to bed; 'tis almost fairy time,*' and just forget about Puck."

"But then the boy has no role at all."

David Erskine lit the candles. Dusk was closing early upon them now, and all the trees were filled with a dark twittering. They could hear the ducks crying through the twilight, far away among the browning reeds. The dogs lifted their heads for a moment, then subsided again with a sigh. Their fur smelt feral in the first hot wash of flame from the green logs.

Elizabeth stared at Alice, who was shyly hanging in the doorway, unsure of her place without James. She had failed to persuade him out of his temper and he was sulking on the cellar steps, his arse getting steadily colder from the moist brick stairs. Scenes from Shakespeare! Use another play. One where my dearest James can just sit there, as he always does, gazing at Alice. That's it! *Why, how now Orlando! where have you been all this while? You a lover! An' you serve me such another trick, never come in my sight more.* And he has damn all to say and that pert little maid will turn all the men's heads. Just the courting scene. Utterly suitable! We need someone to play Celia. Grace Sperling. She'll do. A bit mouse-like, but we can draw her out of herself. Alice will pout and flounce quite charmingly. She's grown tall this summer and holds herself well. James can coach her in the part. But he only comes up to her shoulder. Won't he look ridiculous as Orlando? Oh, what does it matter? It's a breeches part. He can lie among some greenery and no one will notice how small he is. The gardeners can construct the Forest of Arden in half an hour. Then we can have it all in the background for the *Dream* as the play comes indoors. Yes, yes, that's it! And so it was decided to abandon the fairies, who were not normally allowed in the house anyway and whose honesty was doubtful. The butler, who had foreseen that the awful task of supervising the delinquent magicals would have fallen upon him, was mightily relieved. And here comes Alice! *The wiser, the waywarder.* I can hear her saying it. *Make the doors upon a woman's wit, and it will out at the casement; shut that and 'twill out at the key-hole; stop that, 'twill fly with the smoke out at the chimney.* There it is. As you like it.

"Alice. Come here, my girl. Come here at once."

Scenes from Shakespeare proliferated like a camel with an uncommon row of humps. Alice, whose talent for showing off in public proved little short of miraculous, was given the final word. She was to speak the Epilogue from *As You Like It* at the end of this hybrid performance, thus transforming two plays into one.

Everyone was over-excited. The adults rushed up and down stairs, showing one another their latest costumes and wailing for their lost figures. The gardeners constructed a large wooden wall which proved too heavy to move, and a sickle moon, like an ineffective knight's shield with a handle on the back, painted an unreal shade of ochre. Starveling was supposed to carry the Moon, lest the audience should mistake his identity. Then David Erskine read the play carefully and announced that Moonshine should have a lanthorn, dog, and bush of thorn, because it says so, here, Act 5, Scene 1, can't any of you read? It doesn't say anything about a model moon weighing forty pounds.

None of the dogs in the household was sufficiently reliable to be presented on stage. Alice and Barry cut one out of stiff black paper, dug out of the old painter's studio, then reinforced it on one side with batons, and set it up on little wheels. It took them two days to construct this thing and it looked grotesque. They were so delighted with the monster that they led it everywhere around the house. Its straw whiskers began to fall off, leaving a suggestive trail behind them, like bread crumbs in the fairy tale.

Everyone was involved in the performance. Thus the division between spectators and players ceased to exist. Theseus and Hippolyta, the Master and the Mistress, naturally, sat in the front row with the jeering courtiers all around them. During one of the rehearsals Moon really did lose his temper, yanked the paper dog's lead a little too violently and pulled its head off. Desperate repair work was carried out on the spot, amidst an orgy of recriminations. Alice was accused of being insolent to one of the house guests, who, not realising that the beast was a domestic construction, created with love, had vilified the prop designers. Not my fault, Alice defended herself, if the Retort Courteous was received as the Countercheck Quarrelsome. David Erskine was enchanted, for she quarrelled by the book, and he found in her favour.

Barry and Alice learned their scene by heart within a day, but found themselves mortally inhibited by Grace Sperling's censorious Celia. "Pretend she's not there. She doesn't count for anything. I'm the one you should be looking at," snapped Alice. And the insignificant Celia, slightly tearful at Rosalind's brisk dismissiveness, sank into anonymity upon her rustic seat, clutching her bonnet.

The performance took place by candlelight in the Great Hall. Most of the audience were in full costume with whitened faces or bizarre masks, like the *commedia del arte*, escaped for the evening. And many were already roaring drunk, ready to shout and cheer, whatever the event. Barry wore a suit of lincoln green with a hat that collapsed over his nose, weighed down with bright red feathers. He hurled it into the air when he saw Alice, dressed as a brown leather huntsman, her legs revealed to scandalous advantage, nonchalantly carving hearts on a forest log.

"Good day, and happiness, dear Rosalind."

The household howled and clapped their approval at this suggestive scene. For the hero was perfect, if a little small, and his lady was provocatively moody, tantalising in her more coming-on disposition. Barry lay at her feet, delivering tentative interjections as Alice stalked back and forth among the autumnal branches delivering her cynical lessons in love, every gesture making a persuasive case for eroticism and perversity. The household was bewitched. O Alice, thou art translated. A glamorous boy looked her public in the eye, tweaked the nose of her plain little coz, whose startled look was quite unfeigned, as this cheeky pantomime had not been agreed in rehearsal, and declared in a voice lavish with innuendo, that her affection had *"an unknown bottom, like the Bay of Portugal"*. Her audience stamped and roared. Barry, languishing on moss, was merely a foil, an occasion for this boy-girl's barefaced offering of sex to every member of the audience, well warmed by David Erskine's mulled wine.

And wilt thou have me?

Ay, and twenty such.

What sayest thou?

Are you not good?

I hope so.

Why then, can one desire too much of a good thing? (This to the assembled company, with an insolent wink) *Come, sister,* (Celia was dragged off the log) *you shall be the priest and marry us.*

The audience cheered. Barry's ears burned beneath his curls as he knelt down beside her. The play was too much to the point. Alice did not believe in the love that swam Hellesponts, dared Grecian clubs, and dragged beautiful gods down from their horses to seduce them. But Barry did.

The kitchen staff never saw the performance, because from every feast someone is always excluded. And so they demanded an encore after supper. The scene was less suggestive, for Alice wore her skirts again, but Grace Sperling, that one restraining factor, had been abandoned in the drawing room. The two principals had drunk so much spiced wine that they performed with wild, drunken panache to a chorus of cheers, yells and lewd enthusiasm.

Alice climbed onto a stool and addressed the assembled kitchen, along with all the pots, tankards and crockery.

"*If I were a woman, I would kiss as many of you as had beards that pleas'd me, complexions that lik'd me, and breaths that I defied not . . .*" Here, she put out her tongue at Joss, who was leering from the inglenook, "*and, I am sure, as many as have good beards, or good faces, or sweet breaths, will, for my kind offer, when I make curtsey, bid me farewell.*"

She lifted her skirts provocatively, and bowed only to Barry.

"Show us your cunt!" shouted Joss, leaping up. Cook rapped his shins with a poker. Alice jumped off the stool and ran for the door, dragging Barry after her. In the kitchens nobody bothered. It was accepted practice in the household, or at least it always used to be when the old Master's sons lived at home, that the young gentlemen carried on with the scullery maids.

PART THREE

The Painter's Death

I CATCH SIGHT OF MYSELF in a long, ruffled sheet of sea water and I am fearfully humiliated. There stands a small, peculiar figure, dressed in a scarlet jacket and grey trousers, with a full-length overcoat trailing across his narrow shoulders. The coat is too long and the figure looks grotesque, a puppet dressed in a carnival costume, a caricature of the Evil Baron, who will crack a whip five times his length to summon up his unfortunate peasants. I look more closely at the shifting slab of water. No, I am not mistaken. The dwarf is crying, and his tears are slipping away into the freezing wind, blown far off into the salt wastes and grey waves. These are the last days of March in an evil spring. I wait for the wind to restore my composure. When my tears are dry, I turn round to look at Jobson, who is hundreds of yards away. He is smoking on the wharf, his buttocks stowed neatly into a nest of ropes. I cannot see his features clearly. But I know that he is watching me. He has learned to leave well alone, so he does not approach, but in the ebbing light he can still observe me, wandering along the Solent shore.

I no longer know the difference between grief and frustration. And so I walk the damp sand at twilight, biting my lips, skirting the water's edge. The tiny moulds of my worn boots hover and vanish. I walk slowly back, hunched, eyes down, elbows tucked close to my side, marking the retreating tide. Here lies a faint line of white, broken shells in the grey sand, here a sunken piece of smooth, pale wood, with a dark knot like an eye, blackened, gouged out. Battered and abandoned, wooden fishing pots, the ribs cracked and splintered, a mass of shredded canvas sunk into the sand, a bleached skull protruding, the teeth uncannily human.

I try to pluck the skull from the sand and the bones fall to shards and dust in my hands. Everything I touch dissolves. Here is the long shelf of grey rocks, darkening now, the light folded across the pools.

I turn to step carefully over the slippery rocks. I stop, bend down and stare into one of the long fissures which decorate this strange, jagged formation. I recoil at once. I thought that I had seen the flickering of transparent crawfish sliding between the mass of uncoiling, green weed. But when I stare down I see a yellow face, mouth open, the sweat streaming down either side of his nose. The face gapes back. I know that I am seeing two things at once, but neither will disperse in the pool's reflection. As I watch, the muscles tighten into a terrible grimace, then slacken, as the eyeballs turn over and the man dies. I will not flinch. I peer down into the salt crevice. And all I see is the murky slap and smack of the sinking edge. A thin trace of green slime that had trickled from the man's mouth unfurls into the rock pool as the tide sucks back. It is only seaweed, floating in the tides. I shake my head fiercely to displace this image of the face drowned in death, not water. I retreat, slipping on the mass of grey pebbles left wet by the lapping surf. I look back towards the wharf.

The dark sweeps rapidly up the beach. Jobson must still be there. But I can no longer see him. All I can see are the black tarred slats of Portsmouth barracks, a square hulk against the fading sky, beyond that the church tower and immovable weather-vane, rigid with rust, no matter how insistent the wind. Here is the white shed open to the sea, housing the lifeboat, the upturned ovals of the fishermen's skiffs, the painted pale roofs of the out-houses, where the daily catch is sold, all sinking now into darkness. As I watch the cottages along the front, a woman appears, wearing a white apron. I can see the outline of her apron. I hear a voice, calling, calling. I set out, back up the beach, my small boots slithering and sinking in the wet grey sand. I have regained my composure, my habitual calm. They shall not see that I have been crying. My tears would tell the world that I am not invulnerable, unfeeling, vain.

Jobson looms darker in the twilight, but he does not speak

until I am already mounting the steps, pulling myself up by the sticky grey ropes threaded through a sequence of iron rings. The steps are slippery, with a long drop on one side. I try to rise up with dignity, but have some difficulty doing so. Jobson is irritatingly sympathetic.

"I say, James, don't take it so hard."

"We shouldn't have lost him. We were there three days. He passed the crisis last night. We have no excuse."

"There may have been some secondary infection."

"No doubt. But we should have foreseen that too."

"Tropical fevers are very unpredictable."

"But he had been ill at sea for over a week. That didn't kill him. That anyone manages to survive our farmyard of a hospital is beyond me. We will have to create an isolation ward. There will be other cases. And not necessarily from the same ship. I want buckets of disinfectant by the door and shallow footbaths for anyone going in and out. Either you or I, but not both of us, will take charge. I want to see every single man who was aboard that ship. Are you certain that the quarantine rules were followed exactly?"

Jobson nods. I accept his invitation to settle on the ropes beside him, while he loads his pipe with coarse tobacco. I outline my plans.

"Check that all the infected linen has been burnt. And I want that building scrubbed down from top to bottom, so that the planks are as clean as a butcher's block. Make them use salt water."

"Yessir," says Jobson affectionately. It amazes me that he has never resented the fact that I am his superior, his commanding medical officer. I register insincerity and flattery at once. Jobson never flatters or wheedles. He never expects favours. He never presumes on our long acquaintance. His affection is sincere. He pulls me to my feet.

"Good God, James, why are you always so cold? Your fingers are like chilled swabs."

We walk home, arm in arm, to our lodgings with the widow in Bridge Street. We can see the lamp refracted through the leaded diamonds in the window of her front parlour. She has dainty little curtains with a lace flounce, which she washes with fanatical dedication every six weeks. The light flickers onto the muddy street and reveals the outline of a ferocious-looking man, waiting by the horse trough. The widow is peering out. Tonight there is no fog. And she can hear us coming. The squelch of our boots in the early darkness betrays us. The widow rushes out onto her step.

"Dr Barry! There's an urgent message from London."

I can hardly make out the features of the man who stands by the horse trough, but I can appreciate why the widow will not even allow him into her kitchen. He smells. The night is quite still, so I ask her to bring a candle out onto the step. While we are waiting in silence, all three of us stand staring at each other. Jobson puffs pleasantly enough on his pipe. I can see very little of the messenger, but he seems to be a colossus. His smell is constituted of old clothes, sweat drying on an acrid unwashed body and a faint tang of excrement. I set great store by my ability to read smells. I am used to the smell of disease. It is a very useful clue in diagnosis. The candle arrives. I lift the fluttering light high above my head, so that the man's great nose, crowned by a hairy wart, glows red in the night. I notice at once that he is embarrassed and intimidated.

"Well?" I demand curtly. "You may speak now."

This is the one thing that the messenger finds hard to do.

"Y-y-y-y-our m-mother, sir. S-s-s-s-ent me w-with this."

He produces a tormented scrap of paper, still sealed with the emblem of the Miranda family. I break the seal and read the letter by candlelight, standing outside in the cooling dark.

It is not dated. There is no address.

My Dearest Love, James Barry is dying and has asked for you. He is very agitated. We cannot calm him. He has eaten nothing for days. Our physician does not expect him to outlive the week. Louisa has been here. He will not see me, but I am dealing with the house. The filth is indescribable. Francisco is expected back within the hour. The funeral arrangements will be quite dreadful. I am counting on you. Come at once. MA.

I hand the message and the candle over to Jobson. The widow twitters on the step. I peer up at the messenger. He stutters wordlessly, appalled. A gust of foul breath descends upon me in a cloud.

"S-s-s-she didn't a-ask for an a-a-a-answer, sir. S-s-s-he said I was to a-a-a-a-company you back. I've already a-a-a-arranged horses, sir."

Curiosity is already overcoming his awkwardness. He is staring at my uniform. I wave him away in irritation.

"Return in an hour."

The widow leaps forward.

"Oh dear, Dr Barry. I hope it's not bad news."

She hopes that it is. She wants to hear details of catastrophes and disasters. Why rent rooms to military doctors if you don't want dramas? The widow thrives on fantastic tales. Jobson hands them out. She believes him. I nod her sympathy into the distance. She retreats in hushed mutters, back into her tiny glowing parlour, and the messenger recedes into darkness.

"Jobson, don't take your coat off. We must go straight to the hospital."

We squelch our way back down the black street, unable to avoid the horse shit and dank, stinking puddles. Somewhere far off we hear the first cry of the night watch. I tap Jobson's elbow.

"I must give you my detailed instructions for the fever ward before I go. It will be your sole responsibility. And I shall expect to hear from you every day. If there should be more than three fresh cases before the end of the week you are to notify all the army authorities at once and create a complete *cordon sanitaire* around the port. I will come back at once, whatever my uncle's situation. He is an old man. He does not need me to show him how to die. And I want that mad woman released. I will sign the order tonight myself. And one of our men can escort her home to her mother tomorrow morning. To her mother, mind, not to that husband who brought her in. With any luck he'll be so drunk for the next few weeks that he'll have forgotten all about her."

"But she was exceedingly violent . . ." Jobson objects.

"She certainly resisted being chained to the wall in a shed," I snap back. "Wouldn't you?"

"Yes. But we had two witnesses."

"Her husband's friends. If I were a judge I'd have had them thrown out of my consultation cabinet."

There is a pause between us as we negotiate a thick lake of mud.

"I'll take full responsibility."

I relent a little and take his arm under mine. Jobson replies with a protective squeeze. He has grown so much taller than I over the years that he always assumes the role of bodyguard. I proceed through the murky streets accompanied by this disproportionate bear of a man, who has all my confidence and affection.

Jobson is a good doctor, perceptive and sympathetic. But he does not ask himself difficult questions. He is too inclined to give way to accepted opinion. Most of the unfortunates who creep into my weekly clinic for the townspeople, or who are dragged there by their families, think that they have fallen victim to sorcery, magic and spells. Groans are interspersed with maledictions and confessions, all purporting to explain their sores, tumours, fevers and diarrhoea. What is disease? Disease is a form of reprisal. Or is it God's judgement?

I find my atheism especially helpful in my work. I am a doctor, not a priest. I believe in hygiene, not morals. My military patients are not permitted to have an opinion on their maladies. I am the officer in charge of their disease. And I will supervise my uncle's dying. His dying at least shall be achieved with painlessness and grace. I shall escort him politely out of this world.

✤ ✤ ✤ ✤ ✤

We are not the only night travellers on the road to London. By midnight the drizzle has begun again and we overtake carts that are barely visible in the darkness. The messenger insists on riding ahead, so that I remain downwind of his persistent stench. But gradually the cold night air disperses his trace so that I am left to contemplate the bare spikes of hawthorn pushing against our shoulders and thighs. We make slow progress past the farms as our horses flounder in the mud by field gates and turnings, but once we are on open downland the chalk trail before us emerges clear in the wet gloom. The moon is there, somewhere above us, wrapped in a thick veil. We proceed at a brisk trot. The reins are slippery in my hands, the horse snorts and shudders beneath me. We both shrug off the damp, trickling onto our shoulder blades. I feel the creature's withers ripple and shiver.

I endeavour to silence my anxieties. *"If I laid my head upon my pillow without having dissected something in the day, I would think that a wasted day."* I smile into the darkness, remembering my old teacher's comment. Well, he can't reproach me. I may not have dissected anything, but I have not laid my head upon my pillow either. When I am old I will be able to say, with great pride, I was a pupil of Astley Cooper. Sir Astley is a fearless surgeon. I try to follow his example. Yet I am afraid of what lies before me, anxious at what I have left behind, and impatient of this moment of transition. My master's words are always in my mind. *"The quality which is considered of the highest order in surgical operations is self-possession; the head must always direct the hand, otherwise the operator is unfit to discover an effectual remedy for the unforeseen accidents which may occur in his practice."* My entire life has been a perpetual encounter with unforeseen accidents. Remain unruffled, or at least appear to be so.

What lies before me at the end of this damp gallop through the dark world would ruffle any man. My uncle is dying. He is the kind of man who is as likely to die of bad temper as of one particular illness. He alienates everybody with his opinionated belligerence. That Mary Ann should scuttle over his threshold, bearing sheets soaked in lavender, is little short of miraculous. He has not addressed a civil word to her in years. That he should call for me, however, is not odd. We have learned a mistrustful respect for one another. But I have seen very few men face death calmly, at peace with the world and themselves.

I am not afraid of death. We have gazed steadily at one another too many times for that. But it is still not easy to watch his arms encircling the young, who cower like terrified animals. Even the old, grizzled with terror, flinch from his grasp, clutching one more hour of pain to their failing hearts. I am a doctor. I stand beside death, measuring myself against him, evening the odds. Sometimes I can prise his fingers loose from the flesh that he so tightly grips. But even as he turns away I know he will return, again and again. He can be held at bay. He can never be defeated. One day he will return for me. No, I will never be afraid of death. We know one another too well.

But there is someone in that household whom I am afraid to meet.

I have not seen Alice Jones for two years. She writes occasion-ally in response to my letters: odd mixtures of formal copybook sentiments and tirades of unorthodox opinion, all laid out like a formal garden, in an impeccable sloping hand. Her letters demon-strate all her social aspirations, yet betray none of her energy, her obstreperous bright life. None of the things which make me love her. I write to her regularly. Every month. I try not to fill up the pages with diseases, commentaries on dissection and moral admonitions. But often I have little else to offer or report. The only way I can express my affection is by writing these long, repetitive letters. Alice must know this, for she maintains the connection, despite the huge differences which separate us now.

Alice is desperate to escape from her class altogether. She begged my uncle to take her to London. So far as I know he pays her little enough in wages. It is to her credit that she did not want to rise by the traditional method, from the scullery up to the parlour, via the bedroom. My uncle is lecherous enough, but Alice, while she has no time for virtue, has too much good sense to let him do more than peer down her bodice or pat her on the bottom. Alice wants all the trappings of prosperity. She wants fine china and Asiatic carpets. She wants hand-stitched good linen, lace from Cambrai and a shawl, several shawls, from Benares. She wants silver cutlery and a tea caddy that locks. She wants a kitchen with two stoves, one she can walk straight out of once she has ordered dinner. She wants a conservatory with oranges. She wants to travel abroad now that the wars are over.

Alice does not appear to give a damn about being received in good society, which she never could be, no matter how brilliant a marriage she makes. To sit on sofas beside dowagers with sagging chins certainly doesn't form part of her plans. No, Alice wants *things*. She wants objects on tables and shoes in cupboards. She wants wagon-loads of bibelots, hand-painted, engraved and inlaid. She wants to please herself with chests full of new toys. In short, Alice wants to be vulgar and rich.

Education is a means to this end. Not that Alice is not curious. She wants to know more or less everything I do. I send her a large parcel of books every quarter. And she reads the lot, very carefully, from the Dedicatory Preface through to the Index. Her letters, once she has got past the cautious formalities of greeting, puzzle me dreadfully, for she writes as if we were strangers. Or as if I was a benevolent guardian, interesting myself in a poor relation. Then she delivers brisk reports of her findings. These too make for very curious reading, because her opinions are unconventional. I write back, full of pompous and, yes, somewhat conventional advice. She tells me not to be too sure of myself.

Alice makes periodic raids on James Barry's library too. He accused her of stealing Repton's *Fragments on the Theory and Practice of Landscape Gardening*. She produced the book and apologised for borrowing it without permission. My uncle upbraided her roundly, then demanded, "What the devil do you want with a book about gardening, woman? You live in the middle of London."

"I was studying how to construct a maze" was Alice's unrepentant admission. She reported this conversation without irony or comment, in her perfect copybook prose. Nobody knows what my uncle made of this. Does Alice already have extensive plans for her country estate, to be laid out in the elegant style of fifty years back? One thing Alice and I have in common is our deliberate, calculated practicality. We are not utopian dreamers. I make the best of wherever I find myself. But my life, my profession, to which I am dedicated, were chosen for me. But is that not true of every son with the good fortune to be born into the richer classes? No one chooses their origins, and, as Alice has always made abundantly clear, she would not have chosen hers.

I hear her voice, clear in the cold night. *"No one gets dealt the same hand of cards, James. It's how you play your hand that counts."* Her words, not mine. But Alice has not got a drop of honesty in her fingertips when it comes to cards. In fact, Alice does not operate on the principle that games are played according to rules. She plays to win, and will cheat if she has to. But I have always adored her unscrupulousness. It is so bare-faced, so guiltless, and so effective. It is an extraordinarily attractive quality.

The most fantastic aspect of Alice's ambition is her complete lack of fear, her confidence in her own abilities and her certainty of promotion. I am told that she has grown into a beautiful young woman. Francisco has seen her. He tells me that she is now much taller than I am, and that she has huge dark eyes and dimples when she smiles. She always did have an especially underhand method of delivering both the dimples and the smiles together upon her unsuspecting public. In the wet chill of dark, just before the sky shifts from black to deep blue, I imagine Alice Jones, standing on the front step of James Barry's house, in a white apron and cap, and smiling when she greets me.

The messenger has pulled up at the wash house just outside the next village on the road and is waiting.

"T-t-t-there's lights at t-t-the Three Tuns, sir. Would you be w-w-w-w-wanting a hot drink?"

"Yes. The horses could do with a rest."

We stumble into the yard. Someone comes to the back door with a lantern. It is too dark for me to see the mounting block in the yard and the innkeeper's boy witnesses my rapid and ungainly descent into the mud. My uniform does a little work in re-establishing my dignity. And I am shown into a moderately clean parlour with a good fire. It is half-past six in the morning.

I hear that there was a hard frost on the downs and that the Alfreston coach was overturned while making the descent. No serious injuries were reported and they had decided to sit it out until dawn. The woman offers me hot, spiced brandy. I see that my fingers are quite blue when I peel off my gloves. She is larger than I am and keeps curtseying, so that she can look into my face. Her own is not a pleasant sight, pock-marked, with a mottled nose, many teeth gone, and those that remain are covered with an evil stain of brown.

On the window of the staircase the woman keeps a pot containing a little mass of spring flowers. These she had prudently culled to escape the frost, and they are the only things at the inn which do not stink of tobacco and urine. I find the messenger also drinking brandy in the kitchen. He is so closely tucked into the fire that his leggings are smouldering. The colossus leaps to his feet as I come up to him, almost dislodging one of the pots on the range.

I tell him to rest. We too will wait for dawn. James Barry will not die today. If he is able to swear at Mary Ann and savagely refuses to eat, he is not yet in the arms of the angels. Nor will one hour or two make much difference. I am not superstitious, but I am seldom wrong in my premonitions. I never discount my intuitions. No good doctor ever does. They have saved too many lives.

Back in the parlour I draw up a stool, stretch out upon the settle and doze off. It is well after eight when I am awoken by an assiduous cockerel and the first hint of watery light, creeping down the bricks in the yard outside. The woman is nowhere to be seen, the candle has burnt out and the fire is a depressing pile of black embers. I stand up, every bone aching, and stagger down the smoky passage to the kitchen, where all the *dramatis personae* of the previous night are lying, fast asleep.

I wake them all up by riddling the range, then we sit down round the table to eat mutton chops for breakfast. I try not to notice the ingrained filth, inches deep, coating every surface in the kitchen.

❖ ❖ ❖ ❖ ❖

The first sign of London, as we approach across the fields from the south, is the smoke, as if there was a giant conflagration some way ahead. The air is so still that it is not dispersed. There is a white frost in the shelter of the hedgerows. I watch the crisp line retreating under the first touch of the sun. Here the primroses are well past their best and falter sadly on the muddy banks. But I can hear the chiffchaff in the woods. Yes, it must be the end of March if that tiny bird is raising such an echo all around us.

A beggar appears carrying two dilapidated wooden buckets in a contraption round his neck which looks like the upper part of the stocks. One of the buckets is rotten and could hold nothing safely. He leans out and catches hold of my stirrup, begging for alms. The horse pulls back against the hedge, sinking a little into the overgrown ditch. The beggar and I stare at one another. He is foul, ragged and trembling. I realise that he is partially blind: one eye is glassy with mist. His speech is unintelligible, a sort of uhuhuhuhuhuhuh. Yet his outstretched open hand is a gesture with an unmistakable meaning. I steady the horse, which tramples near the beggar's naked, filthy feet, and lean down to place a few coins in the leathery palm. One of his fingers is sliced off at the first joint, but the uneven stump closes with alacrity around the coppers. Suddenly, his speech clears.

"God bless you, sir" rings out in the early air and he bows so that the buckets touch the earth. I see that he is attached to this bizarre harness with a rope, as securely as if he were strung up upon a gibbet. Yet he turns away, the buckets swinging wildly out of the perpendicular, and strides off down the muddy lane, a free man, until I can see only the greasy crown of his hat disappearing beyond the hedgerows. We cross the turnpike just before the village from which the beggar had come, and find ourselves swallowed up in a river of pilgrims on foot and in carts, leading donkeys, pulling barrows, all making their way towards London.

It is after midday when we arrive, dirty and exhausted, in Castle Street East, where my uncle's house can at once be distinguished by the dirt upon the windows and the general air of decrepitude and neglect. I peer about for a point in the road that will not mean landing in a vile morass, churned up by carriage wheels. The rain, which spared us on the first part of our journey, now begins again. I slither down into the murky swamp and gain the pavement as quickly as possible. The messenger waits patiently to lead my horse away to the mews, two streets away. The house is a target for street urchins. The front is strewn with the dried and shrivelled corpses of various animals, waste paper, fragments of boys' hoops and lost toys, some of which have doubtless been hurled at the windows. A black and white cat, recently dead, its fur matted and wet, lies upon the projecting sill of the parlour windows. Its unfortunate predecessors, some now reduced to skeletons, are lying at the bottom of the area steps. A smeared tract in my uncle's writing is stuck there in place of the glass pane. I try to read it, but apart from the opening proclamation, which announces that the occupant is the victim of a general conspiracy, the words are illegible. I am immediately surrounded by a group of ragged boys.

"Soldier! Look, soldier! A soldier's come to arrest the Jew!" They shriek and smirk, jubilant.

"The man who lives here is a distinguished artist. He is not a Jew."

I mount the steps. The gang begins chanting, "Jew, Jew, Jew, Jew," and circles the entrance.

"He's a wizard. And a Jew." The tallest child contradicts me. Then they fly off down the street, shrieking.

The door bursts open and there stands my mother, as slender and arrestingly beautiful as she has always been. She is wearing a filthy apron, headscarf and gloves. My heart turns over. She drags me over the threshold and embraces me with joy and relief.

"My dearest child, come in, come in. Shut the door. The street is not safe. Those children have actually stoned me on the doorstep."

"Mary Ann, there is a dead cat lying on the sill outside the parlour window."

"Oh, don't state the obvious. It's been there a week. What do you expect me to do? Throw it down into the area with the others? Listen, I have had a cot bed delivered from home. He has no furniture, just a bedstead. The kitchen was unspeakable. He won't be moved. He tries to get out of bed and go on working on his canvases, if he's not watched. Louisa has been wonderful. One of her women, Mrs Harris, has tried to make something of the range so that we have hot water and fires in at least two of the rooms. Francisco won't let me stay overnight, as you might imagine. Mrs Harris sits up beside him. That was her husband who came to find you."

"Where is Alice Jones?"

"Alice? Oh, God, Alice! She ran off seven weeks ago. And not empty-handed either."

"Ran away? Where is she?"

"Gone to a street corner in the Haymarket for all I care. She took a box of precious stones your uncle brought back from Italy. The box itself was inlaid with gold and pearl and worth at least ten guineas. Mind you, it was his fault. He had precious little left for her to steal."

"Alice was never a thief. Or at least she never stole valuable things." I remember a pair of white silk stockings.

Mary Ann shrugs, dismissing Alice to the oblivion of the city, and leads the way downstairs. The floorboards are bare; piles of rubbish stir in the corners. We feel our way downwards, into the dark, through the murky air. The kitchen door no longer has a handle, only layers of string threaded back through the keyhole, to prevent the door from closing forever. A smell of damp and rot pervades the kitchen, but it is at least swept and I catch the odour of washed, clean sheets floating on the dryer above us. This is the first fresh thing I have encountered amongst the detritus of abandonment and calculated degeneration. Mrs Harris sits by the back door on a stool. Her hands are worn, but clean. Behind her the back garden presents a jungle of brambles, punctuated by wrecked furniture. I see the remains of a washstand poking up through fresh nettles.

"He flung it all out. Months ago." Mary Ann's energy is suddenly retreating like the Thames tide. "Oh, James, it's all so wretched. Nothing I do makes any difference. He just abuses me. Calls me a whore, then demands to see Francisco, and when Francisco does come he demands to see you. He pisses in the bed on purpose. I can't bear it. I can't bear it."

She bursts into tears. Mrs Harris pumps more water into one of the pots, shaking her head. Her eyes are faded and tired.

I take my mother in my arms. "Don't cry. I'll deal with him."

James Barry is dying as he has always lived, unreasonably, and without the slightest concern for anybody else.

I drink a bowl of bitter black tea. Then I pull off my boots. The messenger appears out of an invisible path through the nettles, carrying my small bags and my medical chest. He stands at the door. Mary Ann stares, puzzled, as if she has never seen him before. I whisk her away.

"Come, let's go and see the patient."

I pad up the stairs behind her. On the first landing the doors are open and I see canvases stacked against the wall, the great wooden frames stretched like scaffolding beneath them. The back windows are blacked out with rough woollen blankets. Even in the gloom the paint stains across the floor are clearly visible. A small assembly of plaster-cast classical statues huddle in the drawing room. A discus thrower, Venus, with neither head nor arms, a reduced version of the Laocoön, with some segments of the serpents lost forever. They stand stark white, vulnerable and naked, frozen in the dusty light. There is a single sofa still there, broken down on one side so that wood and horsehair protrude, like intestines from a ripped belly. Outside, it is raining heavily.

Mary Ann waits for me on the stair.

"It's all like this. Filthy. Empty."

The partitions have been removed in the upper storey. In the front room a huge canvas stands covered with a ragged sheet. I recognise Minerva, noble at the centre of the painting, surrounded by angels. I can see her helmet through a rent in the cloth. But a low growl catches my attention. Behind me, buried in an iron bedstead which supports his shrivelled body, lies what already looks like the remains of my uncle, the painter James Barry. His face is yellow and grizzled. He has not been shaved for many days. His hair is grey and lank, the hacked locks stuck to his temples. The broad fleshy face and mouth are now pinched and tight, the eyes sunken beneath the dark hoods, pulled close like blinds. His face is already in mourning. I imagined that he had heard our steps, but he is asleep, his breaths coming in a series of laboured grunts and mutters.

On a plain stool beside the bed stand a candle, a cup and a saucer, a glass of water and a book with the pages doubled back, as if someone has just ceased reading to him. It is a volume of Walter Scott's *Poems*. I stroke his forehead gently. It is damp, but not hot. The fever is not upon him. The room is bare, but I smell nothing, apart from the faint scent of turpentine which masks the odour of urine. This is odd, for the smell of death is unmistakable. My master is not here. But he is coming. We must make ready for his approach. I examine the sheets and blankets, both of which are scrupulously clean. I peer into his chamber-pot. There are no traces of blood in his thick acrid deposits. Old people's urine has a far stonger smell than that of the young. The old painter's offering is malodorous, but normal. A doctor learns to read the body's effluvia: sweat, excrement, phlegm, slime, these are the hieroglyphics I am learning to decode. James Barry is dying of bad temper and old age.

"Shall I bring up your medicine chest?" Mary Ann whispers.

"Yes. Do."

I know that she wants to get out of the room. Even in his sleep my uncle bullies and intimidates her. She slips away, leaving me alone with the dying man and his last work. It will be Mary Ann who inherits his estate. Such as it is. This sketchbook, this painting. I pick up the open sketchbook, which is leaning against the wall. The fire stutters. My uncle's face, shadowed and melancholy, one hand raised to his temple, stares back. His lined, sad cheeks and fixed frown are roughly drawn. He leans upon the same volume of Scott's *Poems* that lies beside his bed. Where is the mirror? This is drawn from life. For a moment I am much moved by the artist's poignant witness to his own disillusionment. But straight away I suspect him. This is Barry's vision of himself, victim of all the world's conspiracies. He has enemies everywhere, all desiring his downfall and working, insidiously, passionately, to destroy his life, his work, his reputation. Why, the last time I was here he declared that he could not go out because the Academicians were planning to murder him. But at least he still had some furniture. No doubt he had conclusive evidence that all the chairs were impregnated with some kind of malfeasance, a concoction invented by his rivals, and therefore hurled the chairs into the garden. We must call a priest and give him the last rites. The old bugger must have a very multitude of sins to confess.

I step softly over to the great painting, which blocks out all the light from the street, and begin to pull back the ripped sheets. Something that looks suspiciously like blood stains one side. I breathe in the scent of fresh oil, with an odd gust of relief. This smell of art will always be more powerful than the smell of death. This is peculiar, but comforting. I hear screeching from below and then the sound of water being poured over the front steps. Someone is doing battle with the street boys, who were probably trying to add another corpse to the one on the window sill.

I study the mighty torso of the God of Fire. Here, next to Minerva, is Hymen with his torch, to the far left Apollo and Bacchus, fat-stomached, wreathed in vine leaves. And this heroic chest, hairless, shimmering, must belong to the King of the Gods. The pose is suitable. I step back to judge the scale. The painting is enormous, around ten by eighteen feet. I suddenly know what this painting means. My uncle's handwriting, crabbed and mad, swims before me.

I have been shut up at home with a cough. However, thanks be to God, the time has hitherto not been totally lost: the *Pandora* is finished and also I have, just before the cold weather set in, finished very much to my satisfaction a very large print of it, and a written account of the subject, which is also finished, tho' not yet copied out for the press . . .

This was the last letter which he sent to me. The *Pandora*, my last best work. The *Pandora* is finished. A beautiful curved stomach and warm thigh shimmer fleshy in the gloom. This is *The Birth of Pandora*. I now remember that a journalist, who has had a glimpse of this picture, described her as the most perfect female form that pencil ever produced. I stare suspiciously at perfection. She is nearly naked, tended by the Graces, one of whom ties her sandal. Her head is thrown back, revealing the long line of her jaw. I recognise the classical chair, here inlaid with gold, upon which she sits. The original is now lying upside down in the back garden with a bramble growing through the seat. With a quiver of horror I realise that I know the woman too. He has exactly drawn the curve of her breasts, the gentle heaviness of her thighs and the fine length of her leg. Her face is turned away, gazing up at the sombre austerity of Minerva. But I have no doubt. This is a painting of Alice Jones.

For a terrible moment I stand transfixed by the figure and its implications. She was never his housemaid. She was his model. And what else was she to him? Was that why she stole the box of precious stones? She had not been fully paid for whatever she did, and so she helped herself.

Inevitably, my eye is drawn to the crowned Fates, who are preparing the box of evils with which the gods will send her forth into the world, armed to inflict wretchedness and perdition on all mankind. But our own Pandora has already departed from Olympus, clutching the box.

"Cover it. Cover it. I can't stand to see it. I shall never paint again."

The voice comes from the mattress-grave as James Barry levers himself up onto his elbow. His face changes colour, from yellow to white. As he cackles out this frail command, Mary Ann and Mrs Harris appear in the doorway, carrying a dish of warm water and my medicine chest. Barry is transformed into a savage corpse, Lazarus risen in a fury.

"Get out, you old hags! Get out! You want me dead. You stinking Erinyes, crawling up stairs and crouching in corners. Get out, you Irish slut."

He spits venomously at Mary Ann. The gobbet falls on the floor at her feet, and she stops short, furious, terrified.

"Lie down, uncle. You're working yourself up to a stroke."

I lay the dying man carefully back upon his pillows and indicate to the women that they should put down their burdens and go. Barry growls as they scuttle away onto the landing and down the bare staircase; then he closes his eyes. I sit beside him on the bed. Now I can smell his body. His old flesh is rancid. The stench of putrefaction is upon him. I take his hand gently.

"They are trying to kill me," he murmurs, clutching my hand in his terrible claw, "trying to kill me. Ungrateful bitch. When I gave her everything I had . . ."

So far as I know James Barry has never given Mary Ann a penny. I wonder if he is referring to Alice.

I do not believe in bleeding fevers. In any case, Barry is not at present feverish, although his breathing is laboured and rasping. We might try an effusion. It would be no bad thing for him to sit up. He closes his eyes once more and I sit patiently beside him, waiting until his savage grip upon my hand relaxes.

The English do not take kindly to intimate physical examinations. For my part I would never let a doctor touch me. Yet intense observation of the suffering body will yield more material for an accurate diagnosis and an effective remedy than any other method. Most patients are either hopelessly inarticulate or irritatingly garrulous. They cannot describe their symptoms in any detail or indeed sensibly. So often I have been confronted with old women or young soldiers who complain of indeterminate internal pains, are absolutely certain that they have an enlarged spleen or a floating womb, and demand treatment accordingly. I am reduced to the most bizarre subterfuges to determine what is actually wrong with them. In the case of the wealthy whom I sometimes have the misfortune to advise, it is almost always overeating and lack of exercise.

I quietly procure a strange series of wooden tubes from my medical chest. Barry must not see this. If he does he will probably fall victim to an immediate cardiac crisis. When I have screwed all the parts together it is a simple wooden cylinder, around nine inches long. Stealthy as a burglar, I pull back the sheet and lift the fouled edge of Barry's nightshirt. His skin is wrinkled and grey, his genitals pitiful as a shrivelled seahorse. The priest must be sent for. His death cannot be many days off. I apply the larger end of the cylinder gently to his heart and the other end to my ear. The effect is magical. I can hear the rapid clatter of his heart with far greater clarity and distinctness than I could ever have done by applying my ear alone. But it is as I had feared. The pulse is uneven, flickering, unstable. I wait for twenty minutes, then lift him gently onto his side. Even so diminished, his unconscious limbs are heavy and awkward to shift. He groans terribly, but remains insensible. I listen carefully to his lungs, or at least to what remains of them. They are filling up with fluid. It is as I feared. He almost certainly has pneumonia.

I call Mrs Harris and ask her to build up the fire and to change my uncle's shirt. We must keep the room quiet, warm and clean. As the woman gently strips the old painter, I notice that he wears a small phylactery round his neck, no doubt containing a word from the scriptures, after the fashion of the Jews, or a holy relic. My uncle is, after all, a very private man. Whatever he thought of God, he certainly never raised the matter with me, either in intimate company or in public. Yet he was pious in his observance at St Peter and St Paul. I am now relieved that

I was never obliged to make candid agnostic statements, which would clearly have disturbed him. Yet if ever there was a candidate for hell-fire it must have been James Barry. I tell Mrs Harris to send for the priest. She whispers to me that the General has passed by and taken Mrs Bulkeley away. Her husband is fetching provisions. We are alone in the house. I tell her to go straight to the church. Then I sit down again beside my uncle in the bare rooms and failing light, exhausted.

I wait until I hear her negotiating the second landing, before I quietly dismantle my stethoscope and consign it to my chest. Humankind is invariably hostile to improvements, innovation and change. Or at least, that has been my frequent observation. Most people believe that physicians practise a form of black magic, and I was, still worse, trained as an army surgeon. Mrs Harris would probably not be amazed to find me sticking pins into a wax effigy of my uncle after the manner of some West African tribes. My stethoscope is a new invention, brilliant in its simplicity, created by my French colleague, René-Théophile-Hyacinthe Laënnec, a pupil of the famous Dr Bichat. He has been physician to the Salpêtrière hospital for almost a year now. I have visited him there, and found his methods remarkable. I was even a little jealous at the extent to which he is given a free hand in his experiments, when I am everywhere strangled by bureaucratic inconveniences. I have been privileged to read the first part of my distinguished colleague's *Traité de l'auscultation médiate*, which he hopes to publish in a year or two. It is a significant development in our knowledge of diseases of the lungs, a real scientific advance from Bayle's work on phthisis. Yet Bayle was a great favourite with my master, Astley Cooper, because his work was based on dissections, accompanied by immaculate drawings.

I keep my stethoscope hidden for the moment.

James Barry chokes slightly. I put my arms under his and lift him upright on the pillows. He opens his yellowing, watery eyes and peers back at me, seeing me as if for the first time.

"It's you," he whispers, "you've come."

"Yes, uncle. I've been here some time."

We stare at one another for many moments. I listen to the

rain against the windows. His face takes on its habitual tense sneer. He looks better.

"Uncle, I have sent for the priest."

"What the devil have you done that for? I'm not dying yet."

"Not immediately. But you're very ill. I thought the priest might have some comfort to offer you."

"Hypocrite. You don't even have a soul."

I smile down at the old man, who is working himself up into one of his rages. He is quite right. He won't die yet. The human will is an uncanny thing. James Barry is, for some reason best known to himself, refusing to die. I am reminded of Barnadine, called to execution. Arise and be hanged, Mr Barnadine. To which he replied, "I'll not die today for any man's sake." I reflect on the non-material elements of my being.

"Am I encumbered with a soul? No. Perhaps not according to my scheme of things. But if souls exist, then I certainly do have one. And you will do whether they exist or not. It's an article of the Faith. Come on, uncle. The host will do you no harm. As your doctor I can guarantee that."

"Don't speak lightly of holy things, young man," Barry snaps. I take his hand, very gently.

"And don't you be angry. The tension is bad for your heart."

We sit in silence. The fire snaps and light rushes up the wall and across the image of the *Pandora*, now carefully re-covered with the damaged sheeting. I think of the dead cat on the window sill, its limp whiskers awash with rain, and the state of siege in which my uncle appears to live. I want to raise the question of Alice Jones, but I have no wish to distress him. James Barry begins to speak, hesitantly at first, with long pauses between his breaths, then slowly gathering strength.

"I asked for you. I wanted you to come. I don't trust anybody else. Dammit, we made you what you are. David paid for you. Francisco brought you up. I gave you my name. Without us, you wouldn't exist. We have some rights over you."

Suddenly he looks at me, a clear sharp glance, full of undisguised family pride.

"You're a real soldier. A real soldier. Yes, you're the real thing all right." This distended grimace is as close as he will ever come to a smile.

I smile back. He changes tack. His mind is adrift in a high wind.

"Get back the box, boy. Everything's in the box that bitch carried off when she left."

"What was in that box, uncle?"

But he is now too angry to be coherent.

"The box. Damm you. The one she took. And keep that whore out of my studio. Up with her skirts and spreads her legs for any man with a rod to shove up her. She doesn't pick and choose, either. Titled lords and kitchen boys. They all went prancing through her bedroom. Anyone, anyone could have her. I had her myself, thousands of times, there, there and there. And all she gives back is a dose of clap. I hope her cunt rots!"

"Calm down, uncle. Drink this."

I mix two drops of laudanum with the tepid water, which has at least been boiled more than once. I am trusting that opium will calm his obscenities and ease his breathing. But by now, he is raving.

"She's gone. With a man dressed up like a Christmas tree. And that black widow who hides down passages used to open all the doors. Bundling her into men's bedrooms like an unpaid pimp. What was in it for her? Unscrupulous witch. Twenty years ago she used to do it. Did they think I didn't know? Night after night."

Alice is barely twenty-one. So she cannot be the subject of these ramblings.

"What do you mean, uncle?" I ask quietly as he swallows the soporific.

"That foul slut, of course. Who stole my box."

"Then who is the black widow?"

Suddenly, I know that he is talking about Louisa. But his mind has lost its aim. He gives a little jerk, as if attempting to fix his concentration. His gaze wanders the length of the draped painting. He raises one finger and stabs at the darkening figures of the assembled gods.

"That whore! That box! James, you must find that girl and get back my box."

He slumps back. I touch his forehead and cheek and find that he is feverish again.

"Uncle, don't try to talk. Don't. Be quiet now."

I hear Mrs Harris creeping up the house, and the heavier tread of the priest behind her. The room is lit only by firelight. I have had barely two hours sleep in the last days. I stagger to the door. My trousers are smeared with mud and my white stockings grimy and foul with constant wear. I leave my uncle in the sinister hands of the Catholic Church and slither down, aching and depressed, onto the last step of the dusty stairs.

A gust of cold and smoke rushes into the hall as the door flies open. Two giant strides and I am in his arms.

"Soldier! You're under orders. I'm taking you straight home to bed."

It is my commanding officer: General Francisco de Miranda.

✤ ✤ ✤ ✤

I am surprised at how little has changed in the house. Here are the tiles, black and white, immaculate, no leaves or clods of mud scuttering across the patterns, here is the French sofa, with oil lamps shaped like torches, rising up on either side. Here is the hall fire, well tended and blazing. Here are the polished boards of the dining room and the heavy oak table, too heavy to be fashionable, with plain straight legs. Rupert and Salvatore look exactly the same, and they treat me with the exaggerated respect reserved for gentlemen.

"Good morning, sir. I see that the sea air is treating you well." Salvatore's English is almost unintelligible beneath his Spanish accent, but there is no hint of irony nor even a tinkle of knowing recognition. James Barry is right. I am the real thing. Salvatore and I grin at one another. The past unfolds, like a descending curtain, perfectly smooth, with the seams invisible.

"Was there anything else besides this letter from the hospital? I have asked Mrs Harris to send for me at once if there is any change in my uncle's state. Don't forget."

No messages.

But there is an enormous breakfast, real chicken and ham pies, cold tongue, boiled mackerel and sheep's kidney, sausages, bacon and poached eggs, boiled eggs, still very warm, wrapped in a padded muffler, toast, muffins, butter, jam and marmalade, and here is Rupert, carrying tea and coffee in shimmering silver pots. I look gloomily at the laden table. Diet has, unfortunately, become one of my obsessions. My visit to Paris was filled with the undignified contradiction of my learned colleagues discoursing on the need to cultivate a frugal palate, the *sine qua non* for a healthy old age, while gorging on oysters and pâtés swimming in fat. We all agreed that we were killing ourselves, but no one rose from the feast. This is not rational, it is not even sense. Francisco's table has always reflected his tastes, too much meat, too few vegetables and no coarse bread. He loves food. My wealthy patients present me with a remarkably constant spectrum of diseases: heartburn, gout, colic, apoplexy, degeneration of the liver, topped off with a bleeding rectum. The causes? Salt meat, protein excess, animal fat, alcohol in vast daily quantities, overeating, possibly sodomy, smoking and inertia. They want to be sent off to the spas and hydros where they can continue their cheerful round of gossiping, drinking and general debauchery. They do not want to be told to limit their consumption to a quarter of their usual daily intake, to smoke no more and to walk several miles every day. I have a reputation for being ferocious with my patients, for taking no prisoners and showing no mercy. All I do is tell them the truth.

It is extraordinary how much money people will pay to hear blunt advice that they will never follow. At least my patients in the barracks hospital are obliged to take orders from me. But in this house I must obey my commanding officer, and consume a gigantic breakfast. I attack the boiled mackerel, which is delicious.

Mary Ann appears. Her face is bleached with tiredness.

"Did you find your clean linen?"

"Sit down. And eat something. You have no colour in your cheeks."

"James, I can't go back to that house. I have nightmares. You've heard him. He shrieks abuse at me when he's coherent. And sometimes even when he isn't."

She covers her face.

"Eat something, I beg you." I serve her a little cold chicken and toast.

"What does he say about me? What does he want of me? What can he possibly want me to do?"

She is near to tears. I take her hand.

"Listen, Mary Ann, he makes very little sense now. Neither to himself nor to anybody else. And you're quite right. All that comes out is a flood of obscenity. He cursed the priest – and the last rites. But he'll sleep a lot now until he dies. His lungs are slowly filling up with fluid. I'll make sure that his suffering is not excessive. All we have to do is wait."

I pause.

"I suppose he hasn't made a will?"

"Oh, God knows." She flings herself upon the cold poultry, swallowing mouthfuls without paying much attention to what she is eating. "All he'll have to leave are debts. Did you know that David Erskine has galvanised the Society of Arts? They've raised £120 to rehouse him and give him a fresh start. He'll never live to enjoy any of that."

"No, he won't. When I first saw him I didn't believe that he could last three days. But he has a savage will. He may die very slowly."

I say nothing for a moment or two and we crunch toast in the spring sunlight. The first breach in the smoking rain has come. The light pushes back the drapes, thickens the dust on the panes, leaving bubbles glittering in the glass, and sends one broad tendril across the white damask to play with the rings on my mother's hands.

"Mary Ann, he is very distressed about that box Alice took with her when she left. There was something in that box which was of great significance to him."

"It was quite valuable. I don't know how much the stones were worth. Oh, why bother? She'll have sold them all by now."

"We must find Alice."

I have spoken my desire.

Mary Ann bites into her toast, indifferent. I butter another slice and pretend to hand it over.

"Have you any idea where she went? What she intended to do?" I dangle the slice of white toast like a bribe. Mary Ann snatches instead at the tender bread.

"None whatever. Unless she's run off with a company of actors. She was learning Shakespeare in the kitchen."

"Shakespeare!" I drop the toast onto my mother's plate, pour her more tea and press the sugar cubes upon her.

"Oh yes. Something entirely suitable. Katharina the Shrew. Which would only encourage her to grow more unscrupulous and saucy than ever."

"Mary Ann, tell me about this."

An odd urgency in my tone makes her listen and concentrate for the first time.

She had gone to visit James Barry, who had sent an urgent message to Francisco. It was Candlemas, the second of February. The old painter had vomited during the night and was being excessively persecuted by the street pranksters, who had sealed the keyhole on the front door with mud and pebbles. Francisco was away in the country for a few days and the roads were frozen, so Mary Ann and Rupert, finding the front door barricaded, were obliged to approach the house through the wild back garden. Rupert hacked out a path through the frozen brambles. The trees were white with frost. Mary Ann tore her sleeve on one of the branches. The back door flew open and there was Alice Jones, standing on the step leading into a warm, well-swept kitchen, which reeked of fresh bread, smoked meat and spices, clutching James Barry's copy of Shakespeare's comedies.

Alice was pert and gracious. A servant who gave herself airs, according to Mary Ann's tart judgement – "She would have quoted French at me, if she'd dared" – but she led the way up into the house, ushering my mother into the studio and departing with an insolent curtsey. She left Mary Ann arguing with James Barry and strutted back off down to the kitchen.

An hour later, finding that the bell rope was either broken or ignored, Mary Ann came quietly down the kitchen steps, and from the top of the last landing, saw Rupert, far more comfortable than he had any business to be, reposing in a high-backed chair with cushions, his feet on the fender, gazing indulgently at

Alice, who, without the prompt, was in full Shakespearean self-surrender. There she was, the stormy heroine, the tall nut-brown maid, the handsome scowling Katharina, going to the extremes of submission. How far deep in love must she have fallen with her Petruchio, that she will place her hand beneath his heel!

> *Fie! Fie! unknit that threatening unkind brow,*
> *And dart not scornful glances from those eyes*
> *To wound thy lord, thy king, thy governor . . .*

Rupert was thoroughly enjoying his promotion to the position of Eastern potentate.

> *Such duty as the subject owes the prince,*
> *Even such a woman oweth to her husband:*
> *And when she's froward, peevish, sullen, sour,*
> *And not obedient to his honest will,*
> *What is she but a foul contending rebel,*
> *And graceless traitor to her loving lord?*

Alice is an egalitarian revolutionary from every button on her bodice right through to the sinews of her calculating heart, but according to Mary Ann's description, she delivered this speech in tones of unregenerate sincerity, representing the rapture of abjection with alarming conviction. Radiant and beautiful, her black curls escaping, she turned from the two kitchen chairs which had served as Bianca and the Widow, appropriately struck dumb and reduced to vessels of service, and down she went upon her knees before Rupert, whose self-indulgent smile glittered with satisfied masculinity, such as can be witnessed all the world over whenever women abandon some small part of their estate.

> *My mind hath been as big as one of yours,*
> *My heart as great, my reason haply more,*
> *To bandy word for word and frown for frown;*
> *But now I see our lances are but straws,*
> *Our strength as weak, our weakness past compare,*
> *That seeming to be most which we indeed least are.*

Then vail your stomachs, for it is no boot,
And place your hands below your husband's foot;
In token of which duty, if he please,
My hand is ready; may it do him ease.

And here she bowed, in one graceful swoop, dimples discreetly arranged, her cheeks glowing, to place her hand at any man's disposal. Rupert, forgetting himself, rose up from his chair, caught Alice's hand, wrist, waist, hip, and pulled her into his arms. Rupert always was a clever bastard and clearly goes to the theatre more often than we think. And I know of no man nearing forty, and being that way inclined, who does not like to kiss a pretty girl of twenty-one. But Rupert had the line pat.

"Why, there's a wench! Come on, and kiss me, Kate."

Mary Ann has seen quite enough. She stalks over the threshold, like the bad-tempered widow in the pantomime.

"I take it that your rehearsal is now over. Mr Barry and I would like some tea, Alice Jones."

A week later Alice was gone from the house, clutching her infamous Pandora's box. I listen carefully to Mary Ann's narrative, but say nothing. My next move is clear. We must search the theatres.

❖ ❖ ❖ ❖ ❖

The weather improves. A spring wind pushes the smoke of London aside and dries the mud in the streets. There is so much coming and going in the house of James Barry that the street children are held at bay. Francisco orders the dead cat to be removed from the window sill and the house set to rights. The broken panes at the front are repaired and the rooms thoroughly washed and scrubbed. The house confronts the spring, barren but clean. The old painter rallies a little. He is very weak, but his breath is no longer desperate and rasping. For a man of his age he has a remarkable constitution. I spend four or five hours with him daily. On the fifth day, I risk speaking to Francisco about the missing box, and Alice Jones.

We are sitting in his library, where we have always sat, surrounded by his books and maps. He has not changed. His great mane of hair, a little greyer, thinner perhaps, his girth, a rounder, more generous world, bearing witness to his good table, and he tends to suffer from toothache in the mornings; but in all essentials he has not changed, and neither has my love for him. Francisco's outspoken generosity was always my standard, the measuring rod by which I judged all else. Francisco is a man with no mysteries. His unthinking insistence upon candour, honour, openness, gives his outline a solidity I cannot hope to match. He is a man without shadows. I am like my mother, a woman of secrets. I have been forced to hide from others' eyes. I am a ruthlessly private person. I have locks on all my doors, yet I am required to perform, with all the candles lit, day and night, upon the public stage.

"You see, soldier, secrecy is always in someone's interest. And obfuscation is the hallmark of monarchy."

Francisco has always been a republican and never afraid to say so. Quite how he marries that to his role as a good son of the Catholic Church and a faithful devotee of the Virgin Mary is beyond me. He explains that the Virgin is the head of the armed forces in his country and that they implore her to intercede on their behalf with the god of battles before marching off to engage the enemy. I gaze at Francisco adoringly, my stepfather, my General. He is clearly off his head. He is a South American by temperament, all principles, passion and glory. And I, his adopted child, am made of the cold North, a less appetising mixture of brains, calculation and the brisk chill of reason.

There is a faint smell of beeswax and leather, and a stronger, haunting richness: the smell of seasoned wood. Francisco never burns coals in his library fireplace. Coals create black dust. There is a silhouette of Mary Ann, framed in plain silver, perched on the left of the mantelpiece and a small bust of Shakespeare. I look at his unlikely pointed beard and rounded cheeks, much-stroked and well-remembered. This is not the face of a man who indulged in any kind of passion, let alone its extremes. Mary Ann once told me that Shakespeare is like a vast, still lake, in which the passing world is brilliantly reflected, but whose waters remain opaque, untouched. Francisco took another view. This equable opacity was in itself suspicious. A man who takes everybody's part and sees all points of view can have none of his own. Shakespeare was therefore a man without morals or faith. "Look how intelligent his villains are!" snaps Francisco. "Why, they're the most attractive dogs in the pack.

"And yet, my dear child, we know more about him than we do about any of the other dramatists of the period. He was the Stratford grammar-school boy who went off to London, made good, accumulated capital and came home to buy land, settle down and bully his wife. Look at that face. I know a fat, grasping bourgeois when I see one."

"But we don't know what Shakespeare really looked like. What about the other portraits? The romantic one with the pearl earring?"

"Shakespeare would never have worn an earring!" Francisco thunders forth his righteous indignation. An earring? No, indeed not.

Yet I enjoy my General's unusual version of the Natural Child of Genius, partly because it is so unfashionable. I conclude that it is Francisco's Venezuelan origins that give him so strange a perspective on our national poet. He was critical, even when we read the plays together, years ago. He performed all the villains' parts. His Iago was terrifying. But he still preferred Milton to Shakespeare, and said so, often. Yet he insisted on proper respect for the Bard, to be shown at all times. When I made the bust of Shakespeare cross-eyed, by filling in the corners of his blank white eyeballs with pencil, I was heartily spanked.

Now, the bust and I stare at one another. I think of Alice, whose intelligent duplicity must match that of her master-playwright, Shakespeare himself. Is she my Katharina, pretending to subscribe to a passive obedience she has certainly never demonstrated in any other aspect of her life? How else could the drama end? The untamed shrew? I could not answer for its success upon the stage.

My childhood is far behind me. Yet the library is still so familiar. Every polished wooden surface, the lamps with their automatic snuffing devices, the fire-screen with lion's feet, the comfortable chairs with wooden lecterns that swivel in their copper holders. This is Francisco's temple to the written word, the church within which he worships every day. I gaze at this brave man whom I have loved so much, this man whose first gift, a golden chain, is still warm around my neck, beneath my tightly buttoned collars and fine waistcoats, and my heart clenches hard, like a fist. My passion for my mother has ebbed and changed. This woman has made the best of her life by not always telling the truth. She propagates an official version of events, in which some things will not, do not, cannot, happen. I no longer believe her. Yet she has always fought for me, defended me – and made demands upon me. I have never had my mother's confidence and gall. But now I stand outside her sphere. I can move in the world more freely than she could ever do. I watch what she says, what she does.

I send my mother money. I never ask why she needs these sometimes substantial sums for her private use. Francisco is a rich man who would deny her nothing. But this is a woman of secrets. Mary Ann possesses all kinds of information, which she will not share. And now I mistrust that beautiful, languid radiance, that gorgeousness, so luminous beneath Francisco's loving glance. I mistrust that loquacious charm at the dinner table, that capricious, transparent loveliness, the glitter and wit of her fashionable observations, that intelligence and acumen. My mother is a woman who is performing a part. Her acting is so perfect that she only abandons the stage when she is alone. I have rarely seen her without her wigs and paint. But I have watched Mary Ann sitting silent, imagining herself unobserved, sunk in her own meditations, and her face was blank. I judge this chill mask, which registers no emotion, no expression.

The blank face vanishes when I stand before her.

But now I contemplate my General, off duty and at ease, his features tranquil in repose. He is looking into his *Quarterly Review.* This man's face, with his characteristic enthusiasm and serenity, is the same face that would consider the world, were all humanity obliterated, and were there only green fields before us, and a hare, sitting up.

Francisco sighs with contentment. He must therefore be reading poetry. He is. Go on, read it aloud to me.

Again beguiled! Again betrayed!
  In manhood as in youth,
The slave of every smiling maid
  That ever lied like truth.

Well, dearly was each lesson bought
  The present as the past,
What love some twenty times has taught
  We needs must learn at last.

Francisco gazes peacefully at woman's eternal infidelity. I fully expect him to advise me never to trust the fair sex and their confiding smiles. So before he can moralise on the subject of women, as all men often do, I ask for his help.

"Francisco, we must find Alice."

"Alice Jones? Barry's kitchenmaid?"

"And his model, if the *Pandora* is anything to go by. I assume you didn't notice. She stole a box. Did Mary Ann tell you?"

"Yes, I believe she did. I can't recall what was in it."

"Well, I think Alice is trying to become an actress. It was always her ambition."

I tell him everything I know. He listens carefully.

"Then, my dear, if we want to find her we must begin by going to the theatre."

❖ ❖ ❖ ❖ ❖

We take our seats in a private box. I am squirming with irritation. Francisco's idea of research is that we should enjoy the play while Rupert probes the nether reaches of the house. Rupert does at least know what Alice looks like, and if anyone finds her it will be Rupert. But Alice can hardly have transformed herself into an actress overnight. As in every other profession, success in the acting world must surely depend on your family origins and who you know. On this reckoning, Alice is nobody at all.

I brush the dust from my uniform. The city I knew as a child is changing beyond recognition. We negotiated our way carefully from Hyde Park Gate, through an endless building site, hazardous with pits, scaffolding and piles of bricks. The streets are now paved and clean, from Portman Square all the way into the city. The evening is wonderfully lit with oil lamps, and the first warm days are alive with people, out walking or spending money. The city itself is like the setting for a play, freshly painted façades and well-orchestrated crowd scenes, where there is always an event to observe.

I look round the theatre and find that a good many people are staring back at us. Francisco is magnificent in his blue uniform, topped off with a mass of medals and a cockade of feathers. I notice my scarlet coat is flecked with mud, and, seeing that we are being intently studied, from some quarters with the aid of opera glasses, I try to prosecute my cleaning operations discreetly. I shall never get used to those twin trumpets, malicious curiosity and gossip. I can even hear the conversations: that's the son, who trained to be a doctor. And somehow they all know that David Erskine, eleventh Earl of Buchan, foots the bills. How fiendishly important it is, to know who pays. Mary Ann sits between us, in white silk and blue ribbons. She is well past thirty now, but at a glance she has all the fresh beauty of a young girl. There are people in this theatre wondering how she does it: herbal creams or Faustian pacts. Francisco looks old enough to be father to us both. The round of theatre visits commences. A young man opens the door of our box and bows. I cannot hear everything he says to Mary Ann, who leans towards him, smiling, for the music has begun.

The first scene is a forest, the lighting very startling. At the theatre in Edinburgh we had huge chandeliers hung directly over the stage in the old-fashioned style, but here the lights pour forth, sepulchral, from the wings. Our heroine, pursued by her father and brothers, has missed her rendezvous with her banished love, and is convincingly terrified by the looming branches, realistically rustling, suspended from unseen agents, and the terrific Gothic pile protruding through the verdure behind her. Can these be the ruins of the convent where my sainted mother sought refuge so many years before? Yes, yes, they almost certainly are those very horrid walls, which harboured once a noble woman crossed in love. She pours forth her grief to the audience. I begin to think that there is only one play put on in all the theatres, which must contain all the elements of M. G. Lewis's *The Monk* to ensure its success. Our heroine will shortly run mad and we will all be thunderstruck with surprise. But no, Mary Ann is whispering to Francisco that there is a stunning breeches part and we are to see a new actress, who has all London at her feet, but that she, Mary Ann, once saw Mrs Jordan in the part, and even past her best, for her waist is now quite stout, she was so charming and her legs were as lovely as ever, we shall not see the likes of her again, for there is none to equal her. This play is by Mrs Joanna Baillie, now all the rage in Drury Lane, and involves a gaggle of gypsies and a violent horde of brigands in the pay of the wicked count. It is described as a "Romantic Mélo-drame". Judging from the intermittent roars and humming from above, the rabble are here too, enjoying themselves. They cheer on the gypsy dancing. They applaud the songs.

I cease to follow the play and gaze, mesmerised, at the audience. Why, all the world is here, not on the stage but in the house. Here are the rich laden with jewels, lawyers, city men, with their entire families, young beaux on the make, ogling the women, the young women painted up, selling their bodies, and not even waiting for the interval to do it. I gaze carefully at the prostitutes, afraid to see Alice among them. One of the more saucily indecent doxies catches my eye and winks. I stare back, fascinated.

The stage machinery hums and creaks. The scene is set outside a cottage in the forest, where the virtuous count, an unlikely character, if ever there was one, assists in the rescue of the honest peasant's beautiful wife from the lecherous villain, only to discover, O Horror! that it is his cousin in disguise, with whom he once exchanged vows of love, but swore to renounce because of the enmity between their fathers, yet this was but an excuse, as, unbeknown to both the lovers, the old nurse had revealed to the aged count, his father, now deceased, that the child had died at birth and the babe substituted was of noble origins, born, in a convent whose ruins even now haunt the ancient forests where we dwell, to a woman, sir, whom you know alas! all too intimately, and thus, the young count, virtuous and unspotted though his soul might be, adored the woman who was, in fact, HIS SISTER.

She is not, of course, really married to the peasant.

Mary Ann has forgotten Mrs Jordan's performance and is clearly enjoying herself. The loving friend of the disguised maiden fleeing her father, an ogre from a fairy tale, is disguised as a woodcutter and has such shapely legs and such a daringly short green tunic that we all quite forget ourselves as she prances on, wielding an axe, to a universal roar of eulogy. This then is the star of the evening, the real heroine, who can actually solve this impossible plot. Why hasn't she appeared before the fifth scene? Oh, she did? That was the girl who rushed down from the battlements, swore to be avenged (upon whom?), and at all costs to find and protect her beloved friend, who, lost and abandoned, wanders in the forest. I missed all that. I must have been looking at the audience. Ah! Thank God – another song.

Mary Ann knows how to attend the theatre. She pays just enough attention to the events on stage and the events either in the boxes opposite or in the stalls beneath, to follow any intriguing plot developments in either sphere. Another young man has acknowledged her. I catch her very gentle, gracious bow. Several necks swivel to see what lucky gentleman is known to the beautiful Mrs Bulkeley. She opens her fan with a snap. I sigh with relief that I will never have to learn how to play with such fragile objects, whose purposes are largely decorative concealment. Yet I watch my mother managing the theatre, with undisguised admiration.

The entr'acte arrives. Mary Ann agrees to sip a little chilled lemonade. I am suddenly confronted by a gentleman with an alarming waistcoat and huge staring eyes behind tiny round glasses.

"Mrs Bulkeley . . .(bow) . . .General Miranda . . .(a still deeper bow) . . .Dr Barry . . .(an odious stare) may I take the liberty of enquiring after your uncle's health? We have heard the most alarming rumours at the Society of Arts."

I have no idea who this is and he has not introduced himself, but the enquiry is clearly addressed to me, which is not a little rude, for the old painter's sister and close friend are also present and I am clearly the youngest of the party.

I draw myself up and arrive at the level of the buttons on his midriff.

"I am afraid that I have not had the pleasure . . ."

Mary Ann, ever the seamstress when it comes to a breach in good manners, does the honours at once.

"James, may I introduce the painter Mr Benjamin Robert Haydon."

No doubt someone else who hates James Barry, and with justice.

"Thank you, sir, for your concern. My uncle is very weak and not expected to live long."

A flurry of condolences and anxieties rings around the box. Mary Ann explains that we left him not two hours ago, and that he is comfortable, as comfortable as we could expect, but yes indeed, weak, very weak, too weak to be fractious and objection-able. Would he be able to receive a visit? As his doctor, I think not. Any excitement or agitation could be fatal. Mr Haydon deeply regrets. He had always regarded Barry as a master, whose greatness has never been fully acknowledged. I incline my head gracefully on my uncle's behalf, but wonder how anyone can acknowledge the greatness of someone given to vilifying his patrons, at some length, in his public lectures. Mr Haydon stays longer than is either usual or polite, and, while paying the con-ventional compliments to Mary Ann and Francisco, continues to stare enquiringly at me. I begin to loathe his little round spectacles and become disconcertingly abrupt.

When the orchestra strikes up and the play begins again, Mary Ann squeezes my hand and whispers, "My darling, you appear to have inherited your uncle's temper. I thought that you intended to hussle Mr Haydon out of our box."

"He struck me as an ingratiating charlatan."

"But he's very highly thought of. Sir George Beaumont paid at least £100 for his *Macbeth*. And *The Assassination of Dentatus* was ecstatically praised in *The Times*."

"Shhhh, you two," says Francisco, as the heroine flings herself to the ground, weeping, upon finding the honest peasant's cot burnt out by the brigands – here are the smouldering walls – and the little plot of land abandoned. The dog, a real one, licks her face, thus demonstrating the fidelity and affection of our dumb companions, to offset the treachery of our relatives. He gives a most touching performance, and earns a roar of applause. Enter the woodcutter with the exciting legs. We all breathe sighs of relief. Whenever the woodcutter enters the fairy tale, whatever sex she is, all will shortly be well, and the wolf is as good as dead. Woodcutters belong to an honourable profession, with a reputation for heroism.

I concentrate on the plot, which is about to be unravelled. The last act takes place in a church, which is wonderfully painted in perspective, with side chapels, one on each flap, life-size looming saints, an image of the Mater Dolorosa surrounded with candles, and ghostly chords upon the organ to complete the illusion. Our heroine is discovered, ever the victim, upon her knees, begging for someone else to intervene and resolve her desperate situation. This really is the tradition of Monk Lewis. We are bound to have a ghost or two. And sure enough, one of the statues becomes luminous in the fluttering half-light and begins to stir. Can it be? Yes, the spectre of the late departed mother, for this is her tomb, with the arms of a noble family thereupon, who watches o'er her beloved child and speaks in hollow tones from beyond the grave. Beware! Beware! The ghost has a very original way of moving, and appears to glide on little rollers. For once the entire audience is transfixed by the action upon the stage.

Our heroine in breeches, armed with two pistols, a rapier, a cutlass, a slingshot and a large stick, storms into the nave. We are discovered! We must flee at once! Too late! The brigands rise up from behind the plaster-cast tombs. One, in an arresting theatrical effect, pushes back the slab and surges forth from the tomb itself, masked and armed, all ready for the resurrection. We all gasp, thrilled.

The breeches part draws her sword and prepares to die for her friend. But no! Behold! Forth from the confessional, flinging off the white cowl of the Order of the Little Brothers of the Penitent Thomas, thus providing definite proof that *cucullus non facit monachum,* the cowl doth not make the monk, steps the virtuous count in lace and jewels, rapier at the ready, prepared to take on forty brigands. Standing astride the mother's tomb and drawing a dagger from his boot, he reveals his identity.

"I am the Chevalier of Valdevenant and I charge you on your lives to yield, or my sword shall find the heart of each of you. This maid is mine and by her sacred mother's head I will poignard the first who dares . . ." etc., etc.

I am very struck by the fact that his announcement arrests the action completely. Say who you are, and every situation is instantly reversed. The balance of power is irrevocably upset. Murderers are frozen in their tracks, ghosts vanish and everybody listens.

"You haven't followed the plot, darling," whispers Mary Ann. "It was the utterance of his name."

"I can see that, dammit – but why?"

"The brigands are being paid by the Marquis of Valdevenant to do away with the maiden, who is really the sole legal inheritor of all his lands and castle. They aren't being paid to murder his son and heir."

"Oh, do keep quiet, Mary Ann," hisses Francisco, who, like a child, has tears in his eyes as the lovers are reconciled. Half the house applauds and the other half weeps at the affecting scene.

But what of the heroine in breeches, who has risked all to save her beloved friend? What will become of her when the loose ends are tied up? After all, she has delighted us with her songs, her beautiful legs, and dazzlingly short tunic. Surely she must have some reward? She is swearing eternal friendship: they never will be parted. Yes, yes, we know all that. Ah! Here comes the noble cottager who was burned out by the brigands. Aha! He wasn't a cottager at all, but the banished younger cousin of the Marquis, who was in on the secret of the disguise all along and had lent the woodcutter the rapier which she has just so proudly sheathed. The brigands have melted away, while we get down to the nitty-gritty of identity revelations. The erstwhile cottager drops to one knee and declares his love for the wood-cutter. A sentimental sigh shudders through the house. She cannot refuse, nay, she must not, for we all want the closing song and the pantomime.

There is a good deal of shouting from above us and flowers are thrown energetically at the principals. We leave the box before the pantomime begins, for I want a report from Rupert on his theatrical researches and one from Mrs Harris on Barry's condition. But as we descend the marble staircase, Francisco is collared by several of his acquaintances, one of whom wishes to introduce him to the dramatist herself, and I find myself looking up at the soft, effeminate jaw of the persistent Mr Haydon.

"Dr Barry, may I be so bold as to call upon you at your London residence?"

He will call, whatever I say. He has the intent and predatory look of a man who will not be refused. I nod and sweep past.

Rupert is holding the carriage door for Mary Ann.

"No luck, sir," he shakes his head at once. "No one's ever seen or heard tell of her. But a woman among the costume makers said that she could be at Bath or York. One of the provincial companies might have taken her on for their summer tours."

I will not be deflected or discouraged.

"We must find her, Rupert. If it takes us the rest of the year."

I cannot believe that so flamboyant and energetic a character as Alice Jones will ever sink without trace. Alice is one of life's entrepreneurs. We will find her at the gaming tables. She plays to win. She cheats. She wins.

❖ ❖ ❖ ❖ ❖

James Barry creeps towards death an hour at a time. When he is awake he is obnoxious and impatient. His incontinence is now chronic, to such an extent that it can no longer be intentional. I employ another woman to help Mrs Harris. The sheets are boiled daily in the kitchen and the stairs creak with the continued rise and descent of both women, bearing cauldrons of hot water. James Barry refuses to be moved. He also refuses to see Mary Ann. Inexplicably, her banishment causes her to overflow in great pools of grief. He demands continually to see Alice, but has ceased to insist upon the recovery of the box.

"Bring her home, my boy. Bring her back to me," he whispers, with shuttered eyes. I send Rupert out, night after night. But every morning he has no news. He hears nothing.

The spring blossoms all over London, and in Hyde Park Gate the dawn comes with shrieking birds. On still days the stench of London smoke and burning rubbish from the labyrinths and hovels which exist, disconcertingly, alongside the mansion houses and beautifully gardened squares, drifts towards even the most gracious and beautiful drawing rooms. Beggars with more exotic, running, fly-blown sores than I have ever seen, present themselves on doorsteps and at street corners. David Erskine employs two footmen, full-time, to chase them off. The clubs and drawing rooms of London society scarcely acknowledge their existence. Yet these freezing, ragged, barefoot children, who so torment James Barry, emerge from the lower depths behind Castle Street East, like invading demons, for a brief sojourn above ground, and then return to the abyss from whence they came. I watch, fascinated, as they fling themselves, like defeated goblins, down alleys and over walls, jeering and shrieking. I cannot imagine their lives.

Mr Haydon proves, unfortunately, to be a man of his word. When he is announced in Francisco's household, Mary Ann and I are out, trotting past the dusty bushes in Hyde Park. He leaves his card and undertakes to call again. Which he does, even earlier on the following morning. I am standing before the mirror in the drawing room, preoccupied by Jobson's report from the hospital. I have no time for the importunate Mr Haydon.

"Dr Barry, I would be honoured to accompany you to your uncle's house."

This man is like a fly in summer. He cannot be dislodged. I am silent while the cab lurches and jolts towards the city. But nothing deters Mr Haydon. His conversation is almost entirely about himself.

Do I enjoy the theatre?

I attend too seldom to be in a position to comment.

Ah, he had the privilege of seeing the wonderful Mrs Siddons as Lady Macbeth. They were performing in the Opera House, which gave the figures less effect. But the moment when she comes forth and Macbeth is in Duncan's chamber, and she says, "That which hath made them drunk, hath made me bold . . ." Ah, she was in a blaze! Why, it had the same effect upon me as my readings of *Macbeth* at home, at the dead of night, when everything was so silent that my hair stood upon end. I have begun another version of *Macbeth*, I fancy an improvement upon the great painting purchased by Sir George Beaumont. It would give me great pleasure to show you my studio and my latest works."

I foresee the inevitability of a visit to Mr Haydon's studio.

"I would be obliged if you would tell me, sir, what exactly is your connection with my uncle?"

"I do not know a man for whom I feel a greater reverence. Believe me, Dr Barry, he is much misunderstood. He alone is the champion of the heroic in art. He has travelled in Italy, seen the works of Titian and Michael Angelo with his own eyes. He knows that Art must draw its audience upwards, always upwards, towards the perception of greatness, to the beautiful, the true and the good."

"My uncle's unfortunate rejection of portrait painting and domestic scenes has principally been responsible for his declining fortunes, sir."

"But what Man of Genius considers these difficulties? Or remarks aberrant tricks of fashion or of fickle taste? Many men are jealous of your uncle's achievements. He has powerful enemies, Dr Barry."

"I am glad to hear that his paranoid fantasies have some foundation."

I rap upon the roof of the cab. "If you will excuse me, I will walk from here. Good day, sir."

As the iron wheels roll away I hear Mr Haydon's voice, gently receding, like a redundant god delivering his last oracle, importuning me to honour him with a visit to his studio at my earliest convenience. He is a man some ten years my senior. He is also very clearly after something.

James Barry is sleeping peacefully. But he has had a difficult night, with much coughing. I pull the curtains close, which we have arranged around his bed, so that he is shaded from the sharp, spring light. The wind is up, and London seems washed clean for the new season. I cannot understand how a painter survives in the smoky air and murky gloom which usually drapes this city like a cowl. James Barry often painted by candlelight. Patches of wax are ingrained in his coat, on the floor. I pull back the ripped drapes from the completed *Pandora*. And find myself peculiarly disturbed by the naked presence of Alice Jones; not so much her breasts and belly, as might be expected, but the curve of her calf, the slope of her ankle, and the oddness of seeing her feet so clean. She appears before me again, lifting her apron and her dark-blue cotton skirts, the mud squelched between her toes, as she steps out onto the rocks and the rushing cold of the stream.

"Rupert! We must find that girl. At all costs we must find her. And bring her home."

❖ ❖ ❖ ❖ ❖

Francisco comes with me to Mr Haydon's studio. The painter's rooms are at 342, The Strand. I am pleased to find his household modest, clean and so lacking in affectation that I begin to regard Mr Haydon in a new light. Francisco stands gravely to attention; his quiet mass of dignified solidity takes up a good deal of space in the little parlour, which is filled with sketches and books. Mr Haydon is a native of Devonshire and he once visited David Erskine's estate on his way into Wales, to which he repaired with the intention of sketching cataracts, torrents and mist-covered precipices in the new style. His detailed enthusiasm for the beauty of this country on the Welsh borders fills me with the pleasure of memory. He saw that house in the country, the barns, the gardens, the great curving fields, the donkeys cantering in the paddock, the dank picture gallery and the endless rising staircases. Ah yes, and the vegetable garden with the experimental greenhouses, and the machine for measuring the potential growth of cucumbers. And so, for the first time, I begin to look even more favourably upon Mr Haydon, with his tiny, round glasses, his impeccable linen, and sinister, clean hands. I imagine that all painters are like Barry, covered in paint and wax, his wig occupied by beetles. I have begun to associate genius with dirt. We rise up to the extended attics where Mr Haydon plies his trade. The window is open and we have a promising view out over the roofs and chimneys.

I look around.

The most awesome gigantic canvas takes up all of one wall. At first, as with the paintings of James Barry, it is impossible to make out the subject. We are standing too close. I step back as far as possible, leaning against the opposite wall, and my gaze encompasses the noble face of the king in judgement, with the temple's lofty pillars looming ponderous behind him. A man's naked torso glows in the dark. Haydon reads my desire correctly and brings more lights, which he places on either side of the picture. I am impressed by the massive formal structure and the drama of his faces. He has caught them all at the moment of decision. One woman offering up the naked child, and the other, palms raised, her throat exposed, begging the executioner to stay his hand. This is *The Judgement of Solomon*.

I stare at the painting.

Suddenly, I see her. She is running. Two children caught in her arms, her dark hair enveloped in a flying cape, but it is her face, her dark eyes, dimpled chin and fresh cheeks, more clearly her face than could ever be guessed from the erotic, coy goddess Barry drew. Am I so lost a man that I see her everywhere? No, I am not wrong. She is unmistakable. I stand transfixed in an attitude, like one of Mr Haydon's sketches of Lord Elgin's marbles, which have lately caused such a stir. Representations of them litter Mr Haydon's walls.

Francisco comes to peer at the object of my fascinated stare. Haydon intervenes.

"I took great trouble with that figure. You do not feel that she disturbs the balance of the painting?"

"She disturbs my balance, sir. For, as a matter of fact, I am in search of the original."

"Good Heavens," exclaims Francisco, adjusting his spectacles, "it's Alice Jones."

"Mrs Jones? Alice? Barry's model?" cries Haydon, surprised. He is irritated that we are concerned no longer with the grandeur of his painting, but with the verisimilitude of his portrait. I can hear it in his voice.

"You appear to know who she is."

"All the painters know Mrs Jones. She is quite a famous model. Artists will pay a good deal for her services."

My lips tighten.

"Will they, indeed?"

"She has given up her career as a model for a new career as an actress. She is a woman of great talent. I am confident of her success."

"I was under the impression that she was already well embarked on a career as a kitchenmaid," laughs Francisco, very amused. Mr Haydon is about to take offence. He will not have his model belittled. He steps back from his mighty canvas, a little flushed, and addresses me directly.

"Mrs Jones was peculiarly loyal to your uncle, Dr Barry. No matter how badly he treated her. They argued with considerable violence. But she would never hear a word against him. I always thought well of her for that."

"You don't happen to know where she is to be found?"

I try to keep the urgency out of my voice. But my caution is unnecessary. Mr Haydon notices nothing. He is a very assiduous salesman. He is trying to interest Francisco in some noble sketches of the famous marbles.

"Mrs Jones? She was here three days ago. She has joined a touring company at Greenwich."

The next half-hour nearly brings on an apoplexy of impatience. We are wasting time looking at this vain man's spatterings of genius. But I begin to examine his sketches and figures with close attention. And now I do see her everywhere. As Persephone, as Hermia, as Eve. Here are her strong arms, here is her merry face, and here it is, that wicked, calculating smirk when she has got her own way. I hear her voice, find myself watching the slope of her shoulder, the swing of her hip.

Francisco purchases a fine Greek torso, based on the marbles, worked in silverpoint, after the Italian style, and is negotiating an oil portrait of Mary Ann, depicted as Demeter. I peer at Mr Haydon's implements, chewing my whip in obsessive irritation. When did she begin to call herself Mrs Jones? Is Alice seeking some kind of specious respectability? She won't gain much more respect as an actress than she would as a model. No one becomes an actress, who is not born into the trade. What can she have learned from working as an artist's model? How to strike attitudes and take pleasure in immodest stares? I make the descent from the attic studio with indecent haste. But Mr Haydon wants one thing more.

"It would be an honour beyond measure, Dr Barry, if I were able to view your uncle's last best work, the famous *Pandora*, which has not yet been exhibited but about which we have heard so much."

I will not be so easily pacified.

"My uncle is not dead yet, sir. And I find it somewhat disconcerting that you should refer to the *Pandora* as his *last* great work. He is resting beside that very painting. I am his doctor. And he cannot be visited."

❖ ❖ ❖ ❖ ❖

Easter. The festival approaches with an uncharacteristic explosion of fair weather, early flowers and a fresh warm wind. The mud cakes and cracks in the streets. The streaked buildings begin to dry out. I hear the perpetual banging and hammering as the work on new houses accelerates with astonishing vigour. To the west and north of the park and into the fields of Marylebone, London comes creeping, putting forth smart new streets. The bulge of worked earth, spreading into the green, appears like a tumour on the town's best cheek. I spend the night with Barry and once I am certain that no change can reasonably be expected in the coming hours, I set out for Greenwich, on horseback and alone, filled with my terrible determination to recover Alice Jones.

I cross the river at the new Blackfriars Bridge. There is a chill wind coming off the water. The tide is out. The smaller boats and wherries lie enfolded in nests of ropes, their keels sunk into the mud. The crossing is like a medieval battle. I find myself engaged in hand-to-hand fighting with a struggling mass of pedlars, beggars and loaded carts on their way to the Easter fairs. We proceed, very slowly, locked together, like a millipede acquiring a fresh complement of legs. Once clear of the city I proceed at a brisk trot towards the hills of Greenwich, scarcely noticing, all around me, the greening of the world. But, as the stench of London recedes, I become aware of the fine, subtle odour of ploughed earth, the dew drying on the unshadowed side of the hedgerows. I observe two house-martins fluttering under the eves of a cottage a little to the left of the roadway. It gives me great pleasure to see people working their gardens, digging rows for potatoes. And here is an old man tending young seedlings. Can they be marrows, which he has grown under glass? The small coppice on the hill is alive with birds. My heart lifts.

When I reach Greenwich I find the fair already in full swing. Booths have been set up all along the streets, right down to the river, selling everything: farm produce, live animals, pottery, cakes, spices at fantastic prices, last year's honey and jam, fresh bread, fish, still alive and wriggling, piles of sweetmeats, sugar hearts, dried flowers and herbs in jars, furniture, textiles and candlesticks. There is a phrenologist, almost certainly a quack of the most vicious kind, reading people's characters off their heads. I listen to his patter for a moment. He is assuring two newly wedded couples that their domestic lives will be full of good-natured humour and their nights overflowing with pleasure in bed. This is so unlikely that I let fly an incredulous snort, only to find that everyone is enraged by my scepticism.

A troupe of performing dwarves from France is attracting a good deal of attention as they tumble through the streets. One riding a ball whirls under my horse's nose and makes him start. Most disturbing of all, a so-called doctor in a long black coat is doing magnificent business, with his pile of pink and blue medicines in little bottles, no doubt claiming to cure everything, from consumption to piles. He is telling the story of a huge cancer which shrivelled and withered before the pink potion's mighty powers. I listen to his discourse in considerable alarm. His assistant is conducting a very profitable trade, down below among the bottles. Out of anxiety for the good people of Greenwich, I persuade a young woman to buy me a sample, which I secrete in my coat pocket. I will analyse it in the hospital laboratory. If it be no more than sugary water, as these things usually are, the potion may prove efficacious. Most of my patients suffer from hallucinatory diseases. I have found that bracing speeches and accusations of hysterical malingering, although often more accurate as clinical diagnoses, do far less good than a dose of tonic salts, an energetic purge and a prescribed fortnight at the seaside. There is no gulf between the body and the mind. They form one another, just as a particular climate shapes the mind and character of a people, down to their most intimate habits and practices. Anxiety and depression of the spirits are therefore often alleviated by a change of air.

The theatrical booths occupy one side of the main square and already a large crowd is flocking around Richardson's jugglers and performing dogs, who are leaping over little pyramids and through coloured hoops, to the cheerful belching of a mechanical organ. Two grotesque dancing figures circulate on top of this machine as the clown turns the handle. His face is horribly whitened and his teeth have rotted away so that his red lips frame an open hole for a mouth. He looks like an animated mummy.

I stable my horse at one of the inns and return to the square, to watch and to wait. I am casually acknowledged by other soldiers in uniform. I am, once again, the visiting spy. The bright stripes of flapping canvas and the endless activity of selling prove irresistible. It is many years since I have last been to the fair. An artist is doing very fine portraits, a shilling a time, and has a long line of clients, already impatiently waiting. He has that rare talent for catching an undeniable likeness, but has not lost the essential ability to flatter. The boils and double chins are all there, but so is a fine shading which makes the nose more noble, softens the frown, and heightens the fire in the eyes. Arrogance is transformed into dignity, cringing sycophancy into humble virtue, meanness becomes commercial acumen, and preening vanity a refined *joie de vivre*. The public are delighted and convinced by these remarkable forgeries. Mr Haydon exaggerates. He is intent on inflating us all to his level of bombastic heroism, when all we need to be pleased with ourselves is a very little adjustment in the lines of our chins.

I wander among the booths. Here is a muscular man, covered in tattoos, encouraging a tiny monkey to fling peanut shells into the crowd. There are flower stalls overflowing with spring blooms, dark tulips, very fashionable, freshly imported. One booth sells nothing but buttons and has a new line in large, shiny metal ones, each commemorating a famous battle in the late wars. The one which attracts my attention commemorates the battle of Aboukir, where Bonaparte defeated the Turks. It has an intricate symbol showing the descent of the star and the sickle moon. I buy it for Francisco.

The first official performance of the play is announced at midday. A boy with a decorated drum, hung with spoons, does the round of the square, shouting to make himself heard after each drum roll. *The Siege of Troy* is to be performed today, ending in a *tableau vivant* depicting the massacre of Hecuba and her children. That we must see; half-clothed bodies tumbled across the stage, and the Greeks with real blood on their swords. It will be real blood. They bought it this morning. I saw a bucket being carried backstage, behind the frayed curtain. To follow: songs from Shakespeare, to be performed by Mr Richardson's tantalising new discovery, the beautiful and appealing Mrs Jones.

My first reaction is astonishment. Alice has many talents, but as far as I know singing is not one of them. She can whistle, certainly. I have heard her doing that, but I have never heard her sing. I join the crowd pressing inside the hastily erected canvas canopy which encloses the paying spectators. The walls of Troy are fetchingly painted around the front of the stage and above the action flaps a large white horse, painted on canvas. The same small boy who wielded the drum blurts out a loud fart upon the trumpet. Silence for the players! Let the performance begin!

I realise at once that it is the kind of audience where it is prudent to watch your pocket, and the smell of unwashed humanity, closely packed, is almost overpowering. But the people gaze entranced at the players, barely two feet above them, with so willing a suspension of disbelief that we need not fear for the future of faery land, goblins, elves, leprechauns with pointed ears, and general make-believe. Achilles is magnificent in plumes. He swears vengeance while standing over the colourfully bloody body of Patroclus, with thundering panache. And yes, indeed, it is real blood. Circulating in a pig until fairly recently, if I am not mistaken. It is drying nicely, and the smell is disgusting. Hector's wife has bad dreams after the manner of Lady Macbeth. Go not forth to battle this day. The omens were evil. A chicken with a baby's foetus, fully formed, cowering in its entrails, and a goose with three livers, sprawled upon the altar. I saw it with my own eyes. Ah! Ah! Here comes the wench. She has not slept one hour this night. For here she is, sweeping onto the stage, rejected, ignored, raving mad and prophesying doom. Here is Cassandra, her dark eye rolling, her curls loose, her cloak and veils in suggestive disarray. I can quite see why Agamemnon lost his head and chose her for his concubine. It is Alice Jones.

She gives a terrifying performance. She quivers and sways as if possessed. Her bosom heaves delightfully. But her eyes are demonic, staring, as brilliant as Mr Kean in full tirade. A baby starts howling in the front row. Cassandra lands a handsome fountain of spittle on the infant's head. The crowd cheers. The brilliant Mrs Jones steps out of character to curtsey, but then, with the rapid ferocity of an opera star who has heard her cue from the orchestra, she flings herself at Hector's feet, shrieking. To no avail. The story must unfold as it has always done. Cassandra is never believed. Hector takes on Achilles, is briskly butchered in a splendid sword fight and dragged off by the hair to tour the walls of Troy in the bloody dust, behind the chariot of Achilles. The audience is desperate to see this. It has been so thrillingly described.

Then, in bellowed asides, close to the audience, so that we become their fellow-conspirators, straining to hear, the Greeks plan their perfidious ruse to enter Troy. We are all agreed upon the plan. Tonight! Tonight! Make ready the ships. Douse the camp fires. Our enemies must believe in our retreat. The play proceeds at a cracking pace. Even I, against my better judgement, am captivated by the action. I notice too that we all change sides and support whoever is on stage, whether they be Greeks or Trojans. There are often up to five players, creaking in chorus on the frail boards above us. Their costumes are heavy and authentic, their faces whitened or reddened according to their parts. They are giving us the essence of Homer, at the double. What they communicate to the bewitched and delighted audience is a perilous sense of urgency. Something truly terrible is about to happen. Right there. Before us. Soon. We cannot leave. We cannot look away. We are the witnesses.

A master stroke has been prepared for the entry of the Greeks. There is an invisible slit in the canvas belly of the white horse above us. One by one, the Greeks ascend the ladder behind the stage, then tumble down the drop, emerging, monstrous infants, fully armed, from the Trojan horse itself. They fall expertly, clanking weapons, one after another, down onto the stage, enjoining our complicity with their rolling eyes and pursed lips. Shhhhh. We stifle our children, hush one another's gasps. No one in Troy must hear us come.

The massacre begins.

I notice that the young woman next to me, crushed in the press of spectators, is standing with her mouth open and tears in her eyes, as the infants, podgy, bumptious and pleased with themselves, are slaughtered at their mothers' feet. Hecuba literally does rend her garments, exposing a magnificent shelf of bosom to our expectant, awestruck eyes. The Greeks are bloodthirsty and pitiless. Which is how we want them to be. The women fling themselves upon the appropriate swords with terrible shrieks and yells, and above them all, seated on the altar dedicated to the forsaking gods, sits Cassandra, now revealingly *deshabillée*, with a tragic grimace fixed upon her lovely face. And here is Agamemnon, already lascivious, contemplating rape. In the *tableau vivant*, which they hold for several minutes, to thunderous applause, he grasps her gown, a lustful sneer distorting his lips. One of the dead children sneezes, but nothing else spoils the effect.

We make the canvas flap more vigorously in the spring sunshine with our shouts and gesticulations, as the players thaw, disentangle themselves from their violent ends, join hands and bow. Some of the audience leave the tent and others push forwards to take their places for the songs. We are promised the lovely Mrs Jones as Viola, in a plumed hat and breeches. Just as soon as she can get the blood off her face and transform herself into a rural swain gone a-wooing. In the meantime the children do a frolicking, tumbling act, dressed as tiny clowns. They bounce across the boards.

Ah, here is a rural cottage with a spring setting being unrolled as the backdrop. It is rather well painted, with a convincing perspective. A real bucket full of milk is placed near the painted cow. And here is Feste, with his cap and bells, carrying a lute. Would you like a love-song, or a song of good life? We all roar back. A love-song! A love-song! Ay, ay. I care not for good life. And here she is. A gasp goes up. Her tunic clings tight to her bosom and her fine legs are displayed for all the world to see. Natural and at ease in her buckskin boots, Alice saunters to the centre of the stage, a little melancholy, twirling a rose still in bud. She looks at us all reflectively. I turn my face aside. Has she seen me? No. She is wrapped in her own thoughts. She begins to sing.

> *O mistress mine! where are you roaming?*
> *O! stay and hear; your true love's coming,*
>   *That can sing both high and low.*
>   *Trip no further, pretty sweeting;*
>   *Journeys end in lovers meeting,*
>   *Every wise man's son doth know.*
>
>   *What is love? 'tis not hereafter;*
>   *Present mirth hath present laughter;*
>   *What's to come is still unsure:*
>   *In delay there lies no plenty;*
>   *Then come kiss me, sweet and twenty,*
>   *Youth's a stuff will not endure.*

And like Sir Andrew and Sir Toby before me I am forced to admit that she has a mellifluous voice, as I am a true knight. The public get three songs for their money and insist on a fourth.

>   *A great while ago the world begun,*
>   *With hey, ho, the wind and the rain;*
>   *But that's all one, our play is done,*
>   *And we'll strive to please you every day.*

A generous, sweeping bow, her plumes dusting the floor, and exit, to a monstrous chorus, roaring for more.

Alice can sing after all. Both high and low. But someone has taken pains with her. Her timing is perfect. She has been well taught. The confidence and daring are all her own. And always have been.

I take advantage of my uniform to insist upon my entry to Mrs Jones's dressing room. The green room is in fact a canvas flap, nailed to the back of a cart behind the booth. Hecuba is chewing a carrot and Mrs Jones is transforming herself back into Cassandra for the first afternoon performance. Troy falls at least five times a day if the weather is fine.

She doesn't notice me. Hecuba does.

"Alice, here come a courting soldier," says the woman dryly, as if this were a regular occurrence, and chomps her carrot. Alice stares.

"I didn't know you could sing, Alice."

Her face is suddenly transformed. And her joy is unfeigned.

"James!" she shouts and flings herself into my arms, covering my face with kisses. Hecuba gets up.

"She stoops to conquer," smiles the doomed queen, revealing a blackened tooth in the upper range. Alice is a good deal taller than I am and I vanish, engulfed in her embrace. Alice's manager, the portly Mr Richardson, appears, curious to see who is interfering with his leading lady. No gentlemen visitors in the green room.

"This is Dr Barry," says Alice hastily. "We grew up together."

It's true. We did.

Tell me everything.

Out it all comes in a giant rush.

"I'd been stitching costumes, backstage at the Lyceum. Well, that didn't get me anywhere except to watch women with legs like bent palm trees getting cheered for bugger all in the way of talent or charm. Then I met Lucy, that's Hecuba to you, and she introduced me to Richardson. And he saw me sing in Viola's costume. One of the songs I've just done. And off we go to the fair. Then I did Cassandra and I've also done Galatea in another classical thing where you have to sing. It's a beginning. The boss likes me. I'm paid per performance at the moment. He wants to see if I can stick it out. But if all goes well I'll get a proper contract in September. James, I love it. We're going on tour. Aylesbury, Oxford and as far afield as Worcester and Bath. I'm nearly home then. If I can get a message through to Ludlow. I've told my brothers where I am. But we daren't tell Mother yet. I will if I'm a success. Then she can't be very angry. Obviously you have to hope you'll get noticed. And go down well with the public . . ."

"Don't you worry, Alice. You'll get noticed."

She has the grace to blush.

"I can't believe it. All my dreams are coming true. I'm an actress. I earn my own money. And here you are . . ."

"Alice. James Barry is very ill. In fact, he's dying. And he is asking for you."

The darkness floods across her face.

"Is it about the box?"

I say nothing. I just stare back, gravely.

"You've never stolen anything of value before, Alice."

She puts her chin in the air. She is giving nothing away.

"The box is with a pawnbroker in Whitechapel. I pawned it."

"And I suppose you've sold the stones."

She says nothing for a moment. Then bursts out furiously, "He owed me wages."

The box alone was worth a year's wages. I say nothing. Then I ask her to solve the mystery of James Barry's urgent distress.

"Alice, listen to me. Was there anything else in that box?"

She looks up, puzzled.

"I don't think so. But if there was I've sold it."

She is unrepentant.

"Look," she says, anger just below the tension in her voice, "whatever I took, he owed me."

I take her hand in mine. I want to believe her.

"I gather that you were on quite intimate terms with my uncle, Alice."

"Who told you that?"

"Mr Haydon."

"Oh, him."

Pause.

"He said that you used to fight with Barry. Quite violently."

"What of it? How do you expect me to get on with someone whose ideal of womanhood is the Virgin Mary?"

There is a grim, antagonistic silence between us. But she does not withdraw her hand. Then she bends towards me, pleading.

"James, please don't be cross with me. I'm on stage again in less than an hour."

"When can I see you?"

"On a Sunday? We don't perform on Sundays. Mrs Richardson's a Baptist. But I can't come this Sunday."

"Where are you lodging?"

"With the Widow Dewey. By the river. It's filthy. But cheap. You can leave messages there if you want. Come next Sunday. And if the day's fine we can walk out to Batsford Warren. I know a way through the woods."

"Alice."

"Yes?"

"Do you promise to be there when I come? You won't disappear?"

"Will you tell your mother that you've found me?"

"No."

"Promise?"

"Promise."

"All right. Then I promise too."

And we look straight at each other.

"I don't forget things," says Alice. "You taught me to read."

❖ ❖ ❖ ❖ ❖

She pauses on top of the stile and sits there for a moment, with her skirts drawn up about her. All around us the earth unleashes fresh scents of early morning. I notice the tulips, hanging their heads in the cottage gardens, as if they have been pricked by the last sharp nights, and then, sure enough, at the corner of the barn, still in shadow, we feel the ground beneath our feet, the dew crisp with a faint, white frost. Yet all the world is green. Here are the fresh leaves, tender and unsteady, columbine and monkswood stirring in the wilder gardens. Out in the fields, dandelions are yellowing the short grass. We stand in the landscape of our shared childhood. Even the apple trees are in full bloom, unfurling their delicate pink and white flowers. Alice walks on fallen petals in the pitted dust.

"Shall we go on through the coppice?" she asks. "There's a stream just beyond."

"It's like Shipton, isn't it?"

"Not really," she says, with the pedantry of a country girl. "Up there the spring is longer in coming. Ludlow is always freezing at Easter. We'd have stormier weather later in the year. You wouldn't hear the crickets till the end of June. If then."

She pulls back her scarf and her dark curls are shining in the sun. My boots have heels and are a little unstable on the turf. I am hard pressed to keep pace with her. There goes the redoubtable Mrs Jones, her day's provisions flung over her shoulder, followed by her devoted toy soldier.

"Alice, slow down."

She stops a little way ahead, and looks round, jeering.

"You've got soft, Dr Barry. Too much riding about in carriages in the company of fine ladies. You're too good now for tramping across the fields with the scullery girl."

I take her hand and we walk on briskly.

"I see no kitchen slut. I see the famous Mrs Jones." .

Alice contemplates her imminent rise with just enough apprehension to suggest that she is not utterly immodest. But she smiles complacently all the same.

"Do you think I'll be really famous one day, James?"

"I have no doubt whatsoever."

"I pray for success every night."

And then it is my turn to smile. I feel for the unfortunate deity, besieged by pleas for money and fame in the kingdom of this world. Alice never queries her religion. It is part of the backdrop, in front of which she is in continuous performance. She accepts the Lord with the same easygoing good nature with which she accepts her lecherous admirers, these obsessive artists, anxious to paint her every crevice, and her temperamental, greedy employers.

Alice met Lucy, the matronly Hecuba, when the older actress was playing a bawdy dame in one of Farquhar's farcical romps. Lucy's animation with a beau and a broomstick had resulted in a huge shout of applause from the house and a major dislocation of her bodice, all of which, including the naughty revelations, were thought to be part of the stage plot. Alice did some emergency repair work in the near-absolute darkness which reigned backstage and sewed the actress safely into her costume, without pricking her nipples. These were dark brown and enormous, for she was nursing her sixth child at the time. Alice was rewarded with a kiss and Lucy's friendship. Lucy's family had always earned their livings in the theatre, as players, set painters, prompters and stage hands. Not one of them was famous. They were solid and essential, used to poverty, hard work, continuous travelling, mostly on foot, the rapacious public and a professional existence of perpetual Gethsemanes. Lucy, once a ravishing Juliet, was having an autumnal success in the related parts of Hamlet's mother, one or all three of the witches and various seventeenth-century bawds, for her girth had now expanded with much child-bearing. She took Alice under her wing.

And to some extent Lucy's protection kept the vultures, always on the watch for fresh pickings, at bay, circling. The old painter believed that Alice had gone home to Shipton to care for her ailing mother – that had been Alice's story – during the two months when she was in fact playing Katharina in *The Shrew* at Winchester and Faringdon. As I listen to this part of the tale I deduce the significance of that scene with Rupert in the kitchen. It was her role as Kate, played opposite a sadistic Petruchio with evil breath, who would clearly have liked to carry things further offstage, and even began the hopeful process in front of the public, which won her the arrangement with Richardson. Alice had been prudent. She did not abandon her regular employment until she was assured of at least a summer's income. Richardson had plans for her. But she was still learning her trade.

One night in Winchester, a well-heeled and, as it turned out, well-lubricated suitor followed them back to their lodgings and gained entry by describing himself as Petruchio. Alice found herself undressed and alone with a gentleman who would not be denied, while Lucy was down the street at the wet-nurse's cottage, handing out her ample nipples to one of the various infants. The gentleman, awash with good wine, was very anxious to arrive at the same state of undress as Mrs Jones, and made haste to remove all his clothes, crying out, "Katharina! It's our wedding night!"

"Well, he wouldn't be the first lord I'd seen without his underclothes after all the goings-on after dark in the upstairs corridors at Shipton. Men always think that you're going to be impressed by the scale of their desire. And that delicate persuasion is just a matter of force. But no one likes to be slobbered over, do they? He made all kinds of protestations and announced that he would fall at once into a fatal decline if I refused to yield. Utter nonsense. No man dies of a woman saying no. And he was too drunk to make me say anything otherwise."

Alice said no, decisively, with the aid of a warm poker. I wonder if she always says no. For there is only one point upon which Mrs Jones demonstrates that behind this pliant cheerfulness there is a wall of steel. Money. When she negotiates her price she is cunning, adamantine, and ruthless. Already Mr Richardson has found himself paying out substantial sums for potential performances. Alice never stints the work. I am heartened to watch how carefully she is studying her first parts. She stands beneath the willow trees and becomes one woman after another, before my enchanted eyes. Her watchword is nature. Her gestures and movements are fluid and unaffected. She inhabits her speeches with an ease that makes the words ring like a wine-glass, as if they were being spoken for the first time.

But Alice will never be a great tragic actress. She could never present terror, madness, infinite passion, repentance, anguish, loss. All these things are foreign to her very bones. Alice's world is one of comic disappointments, miraculous discoveries, naughty songs, hidden birthmarks which betray all, farcical revelations and dancing, dancing, dancing. Thalia is her Muse. She is fantastical-comical-pastoral, from her slender ankles to her practised smiles. I look at her carefully as she slithers down the river bank before me to a little cove of warm grey stones. Thalia, the comic Muse, from the Greek verb, *thallein* – to bloom. Alice ripens. Alice blooms.

The sausage she has brought with her is far too salty for my taste and I suspect that her coarse loaf of bread is inhabited by weevils, although I cannot track them down with any certainty. Even the cheese looks elderly and doubtful. I realise what my moderate wealth has done for me. I am accustomed to good food. We pull off our boots and paddle in the stream. She begins a water fight, which ends with both of us lying half undressed as our coats sway, drying on the willow branches, the sleeves hanging empty amidst the soft, fine green. We lie dozing in the grass.

"I've nothing against the profession, Alice. But don't you loathe being ogled and pawed? It's clearly one of the common hazards."

"James! What on earth do you think went on in the scullery and summer houses at Shipton? You don't have to be an actress to find men lying in wait behind sofas, mangles and hahas. I've never been a fine lady. I've always been fair game. But now that I earn my own money I can afford to say no. And I'm not a tiny creature like you. I'd take some overpowering."

She notices my irritation at her reference to my size. She reflects for a moment.

"Good thing that you can shoot straight, James. Do you have your own pistols now? Do you still go out shooting?"

"Mmmmm. Sometimes. When things are quiet at the hospital Jobson and I walk up to the hangers."

"Don't you have to go back and hack sailors' legs off?"

"Not every day. Not at the moment. David Erskine arranged extended leave for me. So that I could see Barry out of the world."

There is a sudden silence. Alice has laid her head in my lap, but I can feel the tension in the back of her neck.

"Alice, he's asking for you."

"I won't go back."

She says nothing for several minutes, then changes the subject.

"Lucy says that I could be as good as Peg Woffington if I worked hard, although no one could equal Mrs Jordan."

Alice now launches into the narrative of her ambitions, the great tale of what is to come, laying an unembarrassed emphasis on the fact that she has managed to save a little nest of florins. She still does not mention the old painter, nor does she utter the name of Mr Benjamin Robert Haydon. I see the pale shapes of cows in the fields across the river, unmoving, staring. And above them, the first sign of summer, a Babel's tower of tiny flies. Alice is fast asleep, her face resting on her shawl, but her cheek is taking on the shape of the pebbles beneath. I see the single earring, still there, pure gold, stolen too, no doubt. She has worn that earring since she was a child. It gives her the raffish look of a gypsy girl, a changeling. She wrinkles her nose against a fly's assault, without waking. I brush the fly away and reflect upon this strange and lasting love. I want her to stay with me always. I want nothing to change.

We walk the chalk ridges. A couple more miles to the east and the landscape opens out into orchards and oast houses. We keep to the shade of the woods. The foliage is not yet too thick, and the sun enters, streaming through onto a sweeping mass of bluebells, and paints the forest floor in broad stripes of pale blue and a deeper blue coated with gold. The forest floor is dressed with an untouched blue flood, a rustling river of blue, through which we saunter in single file leaving one trail of crushed stalks behind us, the sign of our quiet passing across the slopes.

Alice tells me about her daily world, the ogling and avaricious Mr Richardson, and Mrs Richardson, his Baptist wife, who assembles the entire company for prayers and sways with her eyes closed as she invokes the power of God over the theatre-going public with her holy rhapsodies. She acts out her struggles with the grasping landladies who overcharged them at Winchester, the generosity of the fertile Hecuba and her infant prodigies who upstage us all – "that was two of them you saw in the *tableau vivant*; the one who sneezed is called Jamie" – but she never mentions the old painter James Barry or Mr Benjamin Robert Haydon. *Alice? Barry's model? You appear to know who she is. All the painters know Mrs Jones. She is quite a famous model. Artists will pay a good deal for her services.* I am being given the selected poems, not the complete works.

Mary Ann taught me never to ask too many direct questions, on the grounds that you may not like what you hear.

So I don't ask.

I have also learned that sexual arrangements between other people are exceedingly mysterious. They have nothing whatever to do with official custom and practice. They cannot be regulated after any single law. We must be content to police appearances. I am a doctor. I do not believe that venereal infections or ending up with child are just punishments for sin. Or indeed that such a fate is evidence that my tearful patient is lost to the grip of the Evil One. It is simply all very unfortunate. But in this I am of an unusual and independent mind. I see the tell-tale purple blotches, the blood in the urine, the unhideable swellings. But I do not make judgements. I run a hospital, not a courtroom. And in any case, it is not my business.

I would never judge Alice Jones.

"We ought to go back."

Alice's eyes are cloudy with regret. And I should take that as my reward for this day. But I want more. We all, always, want more. I cannot bite the day to the core and throw the rind away. I want this moment, this day, to lie on the palm of my hand forever. I want time to stop.

I look up at Alice, who is chewing the bitter and probably poisonous stalk of a bluebell. I snatch at perpetuity.

"Alice, will you marry me?"

"Have you gone mad?" She wrenches her hand from mine. She is shouting. "Marry you? James! You're off your head!"

I turn scarlet. I know that all my freckles are suddenly visible.

"Don't insult my sanity, Alice."

She bursts out laughing. I am ready to box her ears.

"Please, James, don't be pompous as well as dotty. How can I possibly marry you?"

I assume that the challenge she presents to my masculinity is the reason for her refusal, and I therefore become intimidatingly dignified. But – *mirabile dictu* – this hasn't even occurred to Alice.

"You can't marry an actress, James. You're in the army. I'll get contracts that take me all over the place. I may even visit the Americas. You'll be posted overseas. You can't marry a woman who has no intention of following you wherever you go."

I burst into tears, all dignity flung to the winds. She takes me in her arms and produces a grimy handkerchief.

"Oh James, please don't cry."

We collapse in the bluebells and find that the ground is soaking wet. Alice hugs me close. Then gives me a violent shake.

"You don't love me," I wail. "You promised that you would always love me and now you don't."

Alice replies to this infantile moan with a ringing slap across my cheek, nose and left ear.

"Shut up. Listen to me."

My face stings from the intimacy of her assault. I stop sniffing and listen.

"Will you never understand me, James? Of course I love you. I love you more than my own soul. If I were to marry anyone it would be you. But I want my life. I want what every woman wants, if she's honest with herself. Money and independence. I don't want to be ordered about anymore and I won't be treated like dirt. I've got talent. I deserve to succeed and I'm going to do so. Don't you see? I want to please myself. I don't fall in love with any of my patrons, if that's what you'd like to call them. That's not the point. I need them. They like me. The contract is perfectly clear. And if they stop liking me, or I stop needing them, the deal's off. I please myself now, James. I've spent quite enough of my time pleasing other people. I want my life. For me. And I don't want to share it with anybody else. I will never marry. Neither you nor any other man."

She watches my face. I say nothing.

"Oh James, don't look like that. You must have known what I'd say. I want to make something of myself. It's very important to me. I want to do it. You had help from a gang of rich men. And I had help from you. I told you I'd never forget that you taught me to read."

I feel her hot breath on my bruised cheek.

"Go on writing to me. I adore your letters."

I begin crying again. She rattles my teeth.

"Oh James, don't pander to the plots of old stories. You want to live in the one where the son of the household takes up with the kitchen maid and turns her into a respectable woman. She gives a passable performance in the parlour but is initially not received; then wins them all round with her pious observances, eventually turning the rake in question into a religious man."

"I am not a rake," I explode indignantly.

"And you're not religious either. James, listen to me. I don't want your money or your life. I want my life. To spend as I choose."

The wind lifts above us and the first evening shadows are rushing across her face. I cannot say that I have not been fully answered.

❖ ❖ ❖ ❖ ❖

It is past ten and quite dark when I trudge into the hallway. The May night is cold and I have mislaid my gloves. I catch sight of myself in the great mirror, and I am fearfully humiliated: a pale smudged image, my red coat stained with grass.

Rupert flings himself up the cellar steps.

"Good news, sir. I've located Alice Jones. She's been taken on by Richardson's Touring Theatricals at Greenwich. She was playing in *The Siege of Troy* at the Easter fair."

I stand staring at him, eaten up by wretchedness. This was not the reaction Rupert had expected. And I see by the quickening of his eye that he would relish the task of laying his finger on the elusive Mrs Jones.

"Well, sir? Shall I set out for Greenwich tomorrow?"

"No, Rupert. It's not necessary. Bring me some hot water instead."

Slowly I climb the stairs, leaving Rupert standing in the hallway, open-mouthed, unthanked and, no doubt, furious.

❖ ❖ ❖ ❖ ❖

In the last week of May the old painter's condition deteriorates. He refuses to eat and it is with some difficulty that Mrs Harris and I persuade him to swallow a little chicken soup. He is now pitifully thin, his hands almost transparent, bony and frail as winter twigs. I order him to be carried to a cooler, quieter room behind the parlour downstairs, which has easier access to the kitchen. I sleep on a cot beside him. He does not miss his paintings because he is no longer aware of his surroundings. Mary Ann gazes at the shut and silenced face. He no longer rails at her, for he no longer knows who she is.

"Should I call the priest again? He's already had the last rites. Over six weeks ago."

Mary Ann is undeterred.

"Oh yes. Francisco says that you can't have them too often."

I look sadly at Barry. He believed in these scented charades. He thought they were mysteries.

Then Mary Ann whispers, "You can have last rites, very last rites, ultimate rites . . ."

I put my arm around my mother and I can feel the macabre laughter inside her slender body. She turned Papist all over again for the love of her soldier. She goes to church with Francisco three times a week, a fine black mantilla of lace covering her reddish curls. She believes in nothing. I admire her courage.

"Go and call the priest then, Mary Ann. We should do this for Barry and Francisco, if not for us."

But later, long after the priest has gone, and as the unseasonably hot afternoon ripens into cooler shadows across the street, James Barry's breathing becomes more laboured, more uneven. I doze in the cot beside him. Mrs Harris has gone home and the house is quiet. I have sealed the doors, so that the city's cries come from an ever-increasing distance. I have lowered all the blinds. Death waits on the doorstep, sensing my preparations. We are ready to receive him now. There has been no crisis, no marked transformations in this steadily yellowing, sinking face. The nose now protrudes, hawk-like; his habitual chubbiness has long since dropped away. But I awake at once when I hear the sudden shift in his lungs. His breath seems to come from somewhere far within his diminished frame, the last place where his angers still rumble, with ever-lengthening intervals between their manifestations. He drags up each breath with an effort, a great, rattling heave. I do not need my wooden stethoscope. I know at once that the end has begun.

I take his hand quietly. I watch. I wait.

Suddenly I hear muffled laughter and the unmistakable sound of footsteps upstairs. Mary Ann has gone, long ago. I sit still, wondering if I have imagined a presence in the upper floors. Who else is here to witness Barry's stately, measured dying?

Then again, a little cry, a voice saying hush, quiet murmurs far above me in the house. My first thought is simple. It is broad daylight. But that would not stop the assembly of criminals who live down the street and are given to persecuting Barry so assiduously. The old bugger is dying, or already dead. They have come to see what they can recuperate from the wreckage. I unsheathe my pistol and creep up the stairs.

There is more than one person in the studio. The door is ajar. They are making no attempt to conceal themselves, or to hide. I see Barry's empty bed, the old, stained, horsehair mattress folded up, as if he had already been called home. There is the chamberpot upended beneath the slats, next to a dusty pile of rags. At the other end of the studio, standing before the unveiled *Pandora* and inspecting every line and detail with enthusiastic gravity, is Mr Benjamin Robert Haydon, and on his arm, arrayed in lace, gloves, bonnet and veil, beautifully dressed as a lady of fashion, in what must be borrowed robes, is the elegant, the duplicitous, the gorgeous Mrs Alice Jones.

Neither intruder is immediately aware of my presence. The temptation to do away with both of them at once flickers through me. Alice turns around just in time to see me pocketing my pistol. She lets fly a little screech. I address myself entirely to Mr Haydon.

"Sir, I must ask you to leave this house immediately."

"Good Heavens! Dr Barry. We had no idea that anyone was here. The house looked closed. All the blinds are drawn at the front."

"Sir, were no one to be here you would still have no right to enter. I demand that you leave at once or I shall be forced to expel you myself."

Alice is tugging at his sleeve in alarm. She has not yet met my eye. Haydon has the gall to cast one last regretful glance at the *Pandora*, before Alice pulls him away. She stands open-mouthed, her naked double gleaming insouciant in fresh oils behind her.

"Mrs Jones stays here," I snap.

Haydon actually tries to argue. "Oh, I don't think that's possible," he begins.

I take one single step towards him. He hastily pushes past me and rushes down the stairs. It is quite clear, from all the clatter he now makes, that he thinks the dying painter is no longer in the house.

"I still had the keys," says Alice simply.

Her bonnet and coat are new, well-cut and expensive. She is wearing satin dancing slippers, not her usual thick-soled boots. She did not walk the streets to get here. I run my eyes over every inch of her plumage. Haydon is not a wealthy man. He never paid for any of this. She has the grace to blush, but then stares back, meeting my eye at last, obstinate and defiant.

"You said he asked for me. So I came. Is he already dead?"

"So you will never marry me, nor any other man. Is that because you can do better by taking as many husbands as you like? Why settle for one? Did you think I didn't recognise you in Barry's paintings? Or in any number of daubs by Mr Haydon?"

Alice becomes taller still. Her dignity is superb. All the colour is gone from her face. Nonetheless, I cannot fault the lines, nor her delivery.

"Excuse me, sir. I will not stay to be insulted."

Exit. And, this is a wonderful touch, which puts me exactly in my place, she does not hurry down the stairs. I am left confronting Alice's ravishing nakedness, while the lady herself closes and locks the front door behind her. I hear the keys fall onto the tiles as she posts them back through the box.

The whole affair is over in half a minute. I stand gazing at the *Pandora* for far longer than it has taken to send Alice and her artistic lover packing. Finally, shaken to the core, I stumble back down the stairs to Barry, who, preoccupied with the process of dying, is undisturbed, his chin sunk upon his chest.

Around midnight he opens his eyes and sees me watching, patient and exhausted. His voice is very faint, but uncannily normal, almost conversational.

"Bring Alice to me, my dear. She made an old man so very happy." These are his last words. Just after one in the morning his breathing ceased and he was dead.

❖ ❖ ❖ ❖ ❖

David Steuart Erskine, eleventh Earl of Buchan, is now seventy-six years of age. But there he stands, magnificent in knee breeches and powdered wig. His ruffled collars well starched, his medals level upon his chest, the whole exuding a faint concoction of rosewater and damp, the haunting musty damp of the tiles in back passages and the linen in long unopened closets.

We are considering a pile of documents embellished with official seals. We stand around a small, circular table upon which lie a silver tray and four glasses of cold champagne, untouched, the bubbles gathered on the surface. I have read the documents in question and hand them to Francisco. Mary Ann stands on tiptoe and reads over his elbow.

I have won a significant promotion. I am to be Assistant Surgeon to the Forces at the Cape of Good Hope on the most southern tip of Africa. The Governor-General of the Cape has personally intervened in the matter of my appointment. My work in Portsmouth and at Chatham has been brought to his attention. He is anxious to make my acquaintance. He hopes that I will do his family the honour of becoming their personal physician. He expects great things of me. He sends his compliments to his dear friends, David Steuart Erskine and General Francisco de Miranda. He remains their most devoted and affectionate etc., etc.

"It's a great opportunity for you, soldier."

"But it's so far, so far . . ." There are tears in Mary Ann's voice.

"I'm damnably proud of you, my boy," murmurs David Erskine. I notice a tiny growing cataract in his left eye.

My mind congeals with the clichés Alice so mislikes. If I cannot have her, I will wander the world.

— PART FOUR —

The Colony

THE ISLAND ROSE UP out of the sea in the early dawn. Just as the steady, distant line which divided the smoky air from the darker blue began to appear, the symmetry of sea and sky broke open and an uneven humped shape reared up, far distant but perceptible. Barry leaned against the rail. Distances were difficult to judge in the lurching unsteadiness of dark blue air. The storm had blown itself to bits hours ago and his stomach, emptied early on, was responding well to a basin of strong green tea. None of his fellow passengers had dared the decks. In fact, the boat seemed curiously empty, unmanned. The slap and wash of a low swell made the timbers stretch and creak beneath him. Barry passed his hand over his eyes. At one point in the night he was convinced he had actually felt his body leave the bunk, hover in the air for a second, only to be slapped down again into the foetid sheets, insensible. He looked out at the pale horizon. The island was still there.

One of the ragged boys, who appeared to be entrusted with their very lives, trotted past. His feet were streaked with tar. Barry caught his sleeve.

"Is that our destination?"

"Yes, sir," said the boy, indifferent.

"And shall we arrive before evening?"

The boy looked up at the lightening sky.

"Yes, sir, if wind. No, sir, if no wind."

Barry gave up. There had been sufficient wind the previous night. He concentrated on steadying the green tea, which was slopping from side to side in rhythm with the ship. When he looked out again the island was fainter, but still there. It had receded even further down the horizon. No one else appeared on deck. Barry undid his tighter buttons and leaned unsteadily against the rail. The quality of the light began to thicken, despite the earliness of the season.

It was February. You could have counted upon the sunshine in the Cape. In England, at this time of day, if the murky air cleared at all, you could see every crystal of dew upon the leaves. But here, at sea, far south, in the Eastern Mediterranean, the transparent wind of dawn drew breath and immediately thickened into the opaque white light of the south. As he watched, the island vanished. Barry gave up hope. They might never reach land again.

The swell deepened. He staggered back down the polished steps to his cabin, clutching the ropes. One of his fellow passengers appeared briefly on the gangway. It was the elder Miss Haughton, a maiden lady accompanying her niece. Her blouse was in disarray and her shawl stained with unmentionable liquids. She held her handkerchief to her mouth.

"Ohhhhh, Dr Barry," she murmured piteously.

"Lie down at once, madam. And take a very little sweet tea." This was his first and last attempt to treat the common malady. He dived hastily into his berth. Psyche was a sad mass of limp and wretched fur under the wooden desk, which was attached to the floor with brass rivets. She whimpered as Barry locked the door.

"Don't worry, my love," said Barry to the dog, crawling back into the unsavoury sheets. "No one cuts a fine figure when they are seasick."

The sun sent one terrible volley of light through the porthole. Barry pulled the sheet over his face and groaned.

❖ ❖ ❖ ❖ ❖

The boat docked that evening. As the light was darkening again the sheds of the wharf became clearly visible. The Health Officers rowed out to greet them and came on board to inspect the ship's papers and the log. They had last docked briefly in Italy so the quarantine period was probably unnecessary. All the officials wanted to meet Dr Barry. He spent some time shaking hands and dealing with openly inquisitive stares. All the lights on board the ship gleamed towards the answering lights on shore in the twilight. Port Health, a jolly red-faced man, bursting out of his uniform, waived the regulations for Psyche, who had permission to land with her master. Everyone was on deck now, gabbling with excitement. Barry had the younger Miss Haughton, still pale and interesting from the night's exertions, firmly attached to one arm and his white poodle carefully stowed away under the other.

"We shall see each other again, won't we, Dr Barry?" gushed the Misses Haughton. The ladies were fascinated by the courteous little doctor with his old-fashioned manners, his reputation for savagery and his irreligious opinions.

"I shall call upon you as soon as I am at leisure to do so. Now, can you pick out anyone in uniform down there?"

But nothing suggesting a military presence was to be seen in the early dark. The wind was still balmy and warm. Everyone declared their pleasure and surprise, and England was declared to be the damp, unhealthy isle, with a winter climate that was really quite unacceptable. They all agreed on a round of clichés: sea voyages were vile and to be avoided at all costs, all that had saved them from hurling themselves overboard was the pleasant society into which they had so fortunately been thrown and the herbal potions administered by our esteemed Dr Barry, who had clearly, singlehandedly, saved all our lives.

A loud cheer went up from all the passengers as the first rope hit the great iron rings fixed into the wooden jetty. A fainter answering cry arose from the little crowd gathered round the sheds. They had arrived in the colony. The group on board fragmented, rushing to amass hat boxes, suitcases, coats, shawls and bags. Barry stayed at the rail for a moment, stroking Psyche to prevent her from barking. There was no one in uniform waiting in the crowd.

But as Barry descended the gangway with careful steps, for it was damp and unstable and his heels caught in the ropes, a tiny swarthy man with a thick mass of dark curls clutched at his coatsleeve.

"Dr Barry, sir. I am Isaac. I am your servant, sir."

Isaac's statement of identity was accompanied by a deep bow. His assertion of servitude was probably meant literally, but was delivered with all the hauteur and austerity of a gentleman. And Barry took it that way.

"I am honoured, Isaac."

They shook hands in the flickering dark; two tiny men, both vibrant with self-conscious dignity.

Isaac described the vehicle which was to transport them up the hill to the hospital buildings as a curricle. He pronounced it "kurrikal". The thing turned out to be a cart, whose construction was of uncertain date. There was one lantern, insecurely attached. But the horse was small, powerful, and sure-footed, the only element in the entire equipage which inspired any confidence. The lights of the port dropped away behind them as they jolted and swayed upwards into the unknown whistling dark.

Barry was too disorientated to do more than comfort Psyche with a portion of his own vegetable soup and bread before retiring. He hardly glanced at his surroundings, but he left Isaac with detailed instructions as to where his trunks were to be placed. They were to remain locked. Barry would not give his servant the keys and clearly intended to unpack his trunks himself. No other master had ever done this. The houseboys were too timid to greet the new master, but they peered around doors and from behind screens, anxious to steal a glance at the tiny toy soldier with his red hair and fine manners. Psyche growled whenever Isaac approached and was gently reproved by the exhausted doctor.

He called for hot water, retired to his bedroom and took the jug from Isaac at the door. Then he locked himself in. The key turned decisively against Isaac and the houseboys, who retreated through the chilly shadows to the warm, private glimmering of their kitchen lamps, and settled around their table to share their first impressions of the new master.

❖ ❖ ❖ ❖ ❖

Reputations are like benign parasites. The carrier or the host is often unaware of their existence. Barry was cautiously open-minded when he encountered other people for the first time.

He made no distinction between titled lords and naked Hotten-
tots. His tone and manner never differed. Nor did he give any
hint of his assumption that the naked Hottentot probably enjoyed
better health than the titled lord and almost certainly had rather
less to hide. But Isaac entertained no suspicion that the doctor
was a democrat in the letter and the spirit. He greeted his new
master with well-masked anxiety. Barry's reputation had preceded
him by many months and the colony was seething with gossip. It
was a tiny tittle-tattle place, overflowing with the most turbulent
conduits for rumour and speculation, that is, stuffy drawing rooms
filled with bored English ladies.

Colonel Bird, on his way back to England, had wintered on
the island. Colonel Bird had known Barry well. They had served
together in the Cape. Colonel Bird let out a delighted roar.

"So! You're getting Barry, are you? Well, good luck to you.
He's a tartar and a tyrant. No quarter to anyone. He carried
through a veritable revolution in the hospital service down there.
And in his first year he established a leper colony for those poor
disease-ridden fellows that you must be damned careful not to
touch. Did well for himself, though. He was private physician
to the Governor's household. When he arrived he was nothing
more than an assistant staff surgeon and by the time he left he
was the Colonial Medical Inspector. Ordering people about like
nobody's business. And loved doing it!"

Colonel Bird qualified his views on Barry's high-handedness
with respect for his professional capabilities.

"Mind you, he's a damned fine doctor. He saved the Governor's life back in 1818 when Sir Charles went down with typhus.
We'd all given up the old boy for lost. He was yellow with fever.
Harrowing affair. The wife ordered all the children out of the
house. Nothing scares Barry, though. He's got hands of ice, that
man, and no nerves whatsoever. Or none that I've noticed. He's
a bit of a maverick. Follows his nose and is very sure of his own
opinions. But you'll never regret taking his advice. In fact, if you
don't, it's probably the last thing you'll do. And I've never seen
a gentler chap when someone's really ill. But you can't work
with him. You have to obey him. Or else. Give him his way and
he'd have all the malingerers shot!"

Colonel Bird threw back his head and roared some more. Then he began a fantastic tale of the great trek to the interior of the country. The ladies trembled delightedly at the descriptions of savage elephants, trunks raised and roaring, the rhinoceros, shimmering, white, which had almost charged, a lion snaffling one of the black boys from the camp in the dead of night, but which was persuaded to part with its prey when Colonel Bird himself burst forth from his tent, brandishing pistols, so that the lad escaped with an insignificant mauling. Yes, yes, a little blood, but there's no need to faint. The set piece of this predictably heroic tale of adventure was the moment when the Governor, attended by Colonel Bird, Captain Sheridan and the tiny Dr Barry, confronted Gaika, the Kaffir chieftain, with his guard of three hundred warriors, all stark naked apart from their feathers and tattoos, waving their assegais.

" . . . everyone kept their nerve, but they were grim fellows, I don't mind telling you, who could have run us through a dozen times if they'd had half a mind to do it. The Governor was very dignified. Polite, but unintimidated. Barry was his translator. I'd no idea that the chap could talk as fast and hard as the natives, even in their own lingo. He did all the negotiating. And he wouldn't give way on any of the original terms. He seemed to feel that it was his duty not to yield. And he knew how to hit just the right tone of haughty inflexibility, even when he talked Kaffir. Our retinue looked magnificent. Well, we were all laden with metal and feathers: full dress uniform, never mind the heat. That was Barry's doing. He wouldn't have it otherwise. He maintained that it was a question of respect. He may be a black savage, that chap Gaika, but he's every inch a king. That was Barry's opinion."

The fact that Bird did not like Barry, but was impressed by his performances, was not lost on the colonists. Two stories did the rounds: one about a quarrel in which Barry had sliced off his opponent's finger at the dinner table with a fruit knife. The ladies listened, thrilled. Everyone looked forward to inviting the irascible little doctor to dine at their houses. The other story was ripe for embellishments. In December 1820, the Emperor of St Helena himself had fallen ill and Earl Bathurst suggested that help should be sent from the Cape, where the finest doctor in the colonies served under Sir Charles Somerset. Napoleon died before the reply could reach St Helena. But, as the tale spread towards the furthermost outposts of the colony, it became widely believed that, during the Emperor's last illness, the famous Dr Barry had attended upon Napoleon.

Barry attracted attention wherever he went and this appeared to be deliberate. Mrs Lois Chance, who had known Barry in the Cape, on request, wrote a much-cited letter describing the good doctor, which also did the rounds of the stuffy drawing rooms, and was carefully scrutinised behind the fluttering of Japanese fans.

> He is a perfect dancer, and I have had the pleasure many times. He won his way to many a heart with his impeccable bedroom manners. In fact, he is a flirt. He has such a winning way with women and he has the most beautiful small white hands.

This was the kind of detail that Colonel Bird did not provide, but was manna to the ladies.

No household keeps secrets from servants. Isaac received a version of the drawing-room excitements. He did not believe that Barry would have sliced off a fellow officer's finger, even in a rage, simply because, in his official capacity as medical staff doctor, Barry would have been giving himself the trouble of stitching it on again. In any case, Isaac often polished the fruit knives at the residence, and they were barely effective for slicing through the flesh of a ripe apricot. But he firmly believed the story about Napoleon. Barry had closed the Emperor's eyes, with his cold, pale hands. And what he did gather from the rumours was the fact that Barry was autocratic and opinionated. These are not good qualities in a master.

✤ ✤ ✤ ✤ ✤

The first thing Barry heard in the cool dawn was the sound of bells passing outside. The jingling flood had surged over the white rocks and up the fragrant hills, covered with flowering rosemary and wild thyme. Barry flung open the shutters and looked out. The goats had long ears like floppy tongues and pert tails with white tufts. They tinkled effortlessly across the rim of a ravine and ascended the meadows, followed by a boy and two dogs. Barry watched them out of sight. He decided to order fresh goat's milk, to be delivered every morning.

When Isaac reappeared, carrying a bowl of hot water, the doctor was already dressed and inspecting the premises, his poodle tucked under his arm. He gave orders concerning his meals and linen quietly and without emphasis. Isaac listened carefully. The doctor preferred fresh milk, from the passing goats, fresh fruit and fresh vegetables. Then he asked a question.

"Do you ever have frosts?"

"Oh yes, sir. We have a frost every five years. And there is always snow on the high mountains."

Isaac delivered this information in tones of reassurance, imagining that the English doctor was already missing the chill of his native land. He was so anxious to say the right thing that he did not notice the ironic curl of Barry's lip. Barry turned away and looked out with satisfaction at the rough shapes of white rock protruding from the hillside above the colony. The house was surrounded by a small garden, which, from the smell of the red earth, had just been watered. Barry noticed that purple and deep-red bougainvillea was in bloom. He smiled at the sharp lines of colour: the cream walls and green roofs of the barracks, the thick blue of the sky in the early day. He was not thinking of England.

The army buildings were set apart on a little ridge above the town, occupying the view above the bay and far out to sea. The lights of the barracks were the only things clearly visible to passing ships, for the town was protected by a gentle curling finger of land which ended in a fat little Turkish fort, constructed in the fourteenth century. The bay was full of fishing boats, floating in shallow waters. Barry deduced that the wharf for the big ships must be on the other side of the hill, and invisible from his house. He liked the somewhat withdrawn situation of the Deputy Inspector's quarters, which enabled him to look down upon the esplanade lined with palm trees, the smart houses and their fragrant, well-watered gardens. He could even pick out the eighteenth-century columns and noble pediment of the theatre, which was decorated with one or two celestial Muses, organised around the chariot of Apollo. When he looked at it more carefully, some days later, he discovered that the seagulls had stained the statues in suggestive places with yellowing excrement and taken to nesting peacefully beneath Apollo's wheels.

The sun was already powerful. Barry sat on his verandah, very upright in the green cane furniture and cream cushions. He took his tea with sweet breads and fruit. Isaac watched over his silent master with cautious curiosity. The doctor's manners were gentle and considerate. He never raised his voice. But every gesture, indeed his very posture among the cushions, indicated that he was acutely aware of Isaac's presence and observation. The servant realised that he was no longer invisible, that he too was noticed and observed. This unusual fact alarmed him. He could no longer gather information with impunity. Master and servant negotiated their shared territory, circling one another, without a word spoken.

The white poodle, which had just wolfed down half a chicken without the bones, was not to be caressed. This creature, as delicate and fastidious as its master, was clearly vicious, and growled whenever he approached.

Then came the sound of several horses, taking the hill at a bracing trot. Isaac and Barry guarded the verandah, staring at the mounting cloud of dust. A few moments later, amidst a flurry of snorts and thuds, a very large man, formally but hastily dressed, loomed round the corner of the house, leaving a trail of slurred footsteps across the dew on the lawn.

"Dr Barry," he bellowed, long before he could possibly have shaken the doctor's hand, "I say, pardon me, won't you? Grovelling apologies and all that. I was meant to meet you on the quay, with due pomp and circumstance. But you were a day early. And I had a little band, all rehearsed. What's a fellow to do? I've been beaten by the wind, you might say. Never mind. I'll get them to perform the whole thing on another occasion. We're always getting up little ceremonies. How do you do, sir."

He arrived at last within hand-shaking range.

"To whom do I have the pleasure of speaking?" Barry stepped

forward, forever insubstantial despite his padded shoulders and high heels.

"Oh dammit, sorry. Walter Harris. I'm the Deputy Governor." Harris was never intentionally rude. He already knew so much about Barry that he treated the doctor like someone he had met many times.

Barry felt the sweating clamp taking possession of his cold hand. Harris looked like an unemployed privateer who had mislaid his brig. His hair needed cutting and his excessive jewellery suggested that he was not quite a gentleman. Barry liked him at once. Harris commented on the terrifying chill of Barry's hands.

"Bad trip, eh?" he thundered sympathetically.

"May I offer you some refreshment?" Isaac was hovering in the doorway.

"Don't mind if I do. Good morning to you, Isaac." Harris landed in one of the cane chairs with an emphatic thump. He had decided that Barry could not possibly be the medical Ghengis Khan of the colonial service that everybody said he was. He looked a bit odd, but was clearly a good fellow, and an independent, unfussy sort of chap. Colonel Bird had compared him to Robespierre, incorruptibly decked out in a satin coat of the latest pea-green Hayne. To Harris, this now seemed rather scandalous, and certainly uncalled-for. Harris was perfectly capable of carrying on a conversation without any outside assistance and did so now.

"But nothing cooked, if you don't mind. Just tea, Isaac. I've breakfasted. I came up to present the Governor's greetings. My own, of course, too. And everybody's apologies. First wind we got of the boat's arrival were the quarantine papers, delivered along with the Haughton girls. I say, you must have been out in that storm. Dreadful business. We lost a palm tree out by the fort. And a couple of roofs ripped off. No real damage. The fishermen were all home. And it didn't touch the north side of the island. How on earth did Isaac know that you were coming? Must spend his time watching for ships. Mind you, we've all been ready for days. Dinner at the Governor's on Friday? That's your formal welcome do. He wants to see you before then. Soon as you can manage, in fact. He lost his wife last year. But I expect you heard. I'm at your service. Whaddayou want to do? See the sights? Pop past the club? All the ladies are agog with excitement at the prospect of meeting you."

Here, Harris twinkled knowingly for a moment, creating a pause in his own bellowing flow. But it did cross his mind that, since Barry was clearly a delicate sort of a chap, he mightn't like innuendoes, and so the Deputy Governor rattled on again.

"The colony's a small place. But we all rub along pretty well together. The roads are dreadful, of course, so the social life is pretty much concentrated in town. I've brought you a horse. Compliments of the Governor. He keeps his own stable. Given you one of his best. He's a generous chap. Thanks, Isaac. Wonderful. There. I'll have another cup."

The horse was a gigantic bay mare with a fiery white streak down her face and four white socks. A terrific ride for a man with a strong seat and firm hands. She was clearly far too large for Barry, who would have looked odd on anything bigger than a child's pony. For a moment Harris was baffled.

"She's a big filly, though," he said doubtfully, as if reconsidering an unfortunate marriage proposal.

"That's fine," said Barry, with a slight, ironic smile. He had followed Harris's thoughts.

"Oh well – you'll manage. Gather you had a carriage and four greys in Cape Town."

Barry raised one eyebrow. He suddenly realised that a hurricane of gossip, probably consisting of adventures more preposterous than those put to amorous use by Othello must have preceded his arrival.

"Ah yes. All stallions," he remarked. "I put them out to stud for part of the winter season, and made a little income that way. Which helped pay for their upkeep."

This was in fact true. But a man who has handled four stallions is a man to be reckoned with, in anybody's book. The Deputy Governor was indeed winded for a moment, but he drew breath and then forged ahead. He let fly another inconsequential gust of gossip.

"Colonel Bird was here last winter, you know. Told us all about you. So we're forearmed!"

Barry decided that the conversation had gone far enough. He rose and indicated that he wished to visit the hospital immediately.

"By all means. I'll take you over there at once." The polished boards of the verandah shook as Harris achieved the vertical in two hefty jerks.

"Word gets about a bit, you know," said Harris, not altogether tactfully. "The hospital staff are somewhat apprehensive. They've heard that you're a little chap with a big punch."

He was suddenly very embarrassed. Barry had an open, encouraging manner, but Harris feared that he had overstepped the mark in directly referring to the doctor's proportions. He had no way to claw back his comments, and stood there biting his tongue. But Barry took no offence. He smiled up at the Deputy Governor, rightly detecting nothing but affable good will.

"We found that in Cape Town the smallest snakes are the most deadly." This remark, not altogether comforting, was delivered with candour and sweetness. "Well, Harris, let's have a look at this Trojan horse you've brought me."

Barry was good at reading other people, men and women alike. This was what made him an excellent physician and gave him confidence in his own diagnoses. He sensed malice, hypocrisy and malingering immediately. He had a very short temper and was often alarmingly violent in his responses. But he never imagined insults where none were intended. He liked this gigantic buffoon of a man whose hearty simplicity was warm, attractive and genuine. Harris was clearly unobservant and uncomplicated. He patted Psyche without thinking and almost lost a finger.

"I say, Barry, that creature's not to be trusted, is she?"

"My apologies, sir. She is still a little discomposed after our long voyage."

A sea breeze caught them as they rounded the corner of the house. The horses stood in the yard, flicking the first flies of the year away with their tails as they nibbled the sparse bush. Barry was undaunted by the precipice of the bay's long shoulder and simply led her over to the house steps, tightened her girth and used the steps as a mounting block. Once astride, he had to adjust the stirrups up to their highest notch, so that he looked like a jockey, perched on top of a prize racer. He noticed the glittering eyes of the house boys peering through the muslin screens. And so he leaned down into the rich-smelling, dim enclosure and called out with sinister authority, "I shall inspect the kitchens on my return. Be ready."

A small explosion of panic erupted in the wake of his departure.

✤ ✤ ✤ ✤ ✤

The hospital staff were advisedly anxious at the advent of Dr James Miranda Barry. The doctor interfered with everything. Habitual systems were overthrown overnight. New régimes were instantly enforced. Sensibilities were understandably ruffled and, in private, tempers were well and truly lost. Long before the transmission of infectious and contagious diseases was fully understood, James Miranda Barry had grasped an essential necessity for every hospital: absolute cleanliness. This was his obsession, his religion. On the question of hygiene he was neither liberal nor tolerant. He was a fanatic.

Barry insisted on a daily change of linen for every patient, frequent dressing of wounds and the boiling of all surgical instruments. He ordered his staff to achieve a level of disinfective scrubbing that prepared the way for godliness. His assistants were forced to hold out their hands like little children, for the doctor's inspection, before they trailed off behind him on the ward rounds. When he was called in for consultations he ordered all the previous doctor's prescriptions to be removed without even looking at them. Such tactics did not endear him to his colleagues. He opened windows, even in the coldest weather, and insisted upon what one rival described as excessive ventilation. Barry swept into overheated sick rooms on a gust of cold, fresh air.

The colony's hospital was fortunately placed, in view of Barry's fresh-air methods. It was situated less than a mile away from his quarters and built on a little hill. There were two main wards, both designated for men only, and a small female ward in a house with a verandah, a hundred yards away. This tiny building also served as a lying-in hospital for difficult cases. But most of the colonial wives who did not trek home to England preferred to give birth at home, aided by the midwife. Soon everyone wished the delicate Dr Barry to be there too, in constant attendance. The women's hospital was quiet and empty. A mountain spring that rose out of the earth a little higher up had been tapped to supply constant, fresh, ice-cold water from the belly of the earth. Barry had the water analysed in the first week of his command and found it to be rich in minerals that would do no one any harm. But he still insisted that all linen should be boiled, as should the water used for operations. Under Barry's rule, bed bugs became a thing of the past.

But on that first day, early on a February morning, when Barry trotted up the uneven narrow road, much pitted by erosion and potholes, the hospital staff, patiently engaged upon their usual business, did not suspect that they were about to enter the vanguard of nineteenth-century medical reform. Barry had spent most of his life banning medical practices that were centuries old, and that day was to be no exception. No word of the doctor's early arrival had reached the hospital and Barry caught them unawares.

The Deputy Governor abandoned him in the courtyard. "Well, here you are, old chap. I'll pop back in a couple of hours to take you down to the Governor. You'll have an office in Government House too, of course. And I must be there to make all the formal introductions."

Harris bounded back onto his horse and made off as fast as possible. Despite the fact that the hospital never knowingly took in contagious or infectious cases if they could not be isolated, Harris was quite sure that he was in danger of catching something that was either disfiguring or fatal. He stuck to the old methods and purged himself regularly. He had never suffered a day's illness in his life.

Barry was greeted on the step by the hospital's Superintendent, who was a big, serious-minded and unsmiling Greek. The doctor introduced himself and shook hands, ignoring the look of horror fixed to his colleague's face.

"Your name, sir."

"George Washington Karageorghis. Sir!" The Superintendent saluted. Barry peered at his armpits to see if his coat was clean.

"And from that I may gather that your parents are friends to the Republic?"

Barry's rare, warm smile appeared and the terrified Superintendent relaxed.

"Yes, sir. My brother is Thomas Paine Karageorghis."

Barry laughed. "I shall look forward to knowing him too. Let us proceed with our inspection. I want to see all the wards, kitchens, storerooms and offices. I want to meet all the staff and become acquainted with all your regular routines and procedures."

Despite this promising beginning the initial round of the wards did not go off well. Barry discovered that most of his assistants were still gripped by medical philosophies which were, at best, a quarter of a century out of date. A fully fledged doctrine of bodily humours was current among the native population, and blood-letting, as a preventive measure, was commonly practised. In the early spring, dozens of patients, a crowd of whom Barry encountered at the dispensary door, presented themselves to be bled, in order to evacuate the bad blood that had accumulated over the winter. This tradition generated a modest income, which was pocketed by the establishment.

Barry lost his temper and scattered the crowd, who decamped, bitterly disappointed and muttering discontent.

"Your namesake, George Washington, was bled to death by his doctors in 1799," snapped Barry. "This practice is to cease at once. On my authority, I will have neither venesection nor cupping practised in this hospital. I doubt that even the wealthiest inhabitant could procure leeches in this climate, but in any case, leeches are banned too. Listen to me, Mr Karageorghis, and remember this. Bloodletting has more to do with magic and quackery than medical science. And I will not have it."

The spirit of the real George Washington had unfortunately prevailed, and the wretched Superintendent had revealed the full truth concerning the spring bleeding. Barry never succeeded in stamping out the practice entirely. But he did drive it back into the remoter corners of the colony. And no one, ever again, dared to demand the service from the hospital.

The doctor sat down in his office, with his senior staff before him, and began asking awkward questions.

All his initial enquiries concerned the general maladies endured by the military and colonial populations and shared by the island's local inhabitants. Few diseases were common property. In the former case, they proved to be dyspepsia, boredom and sunstroke as a result of imprudent midday military parades. In the latter, the situation varied from general malnutrition, rotten teeth, numerous fevers, pleurisy, colic, diarrhoea, spots on the chest, a fluttering sensation in the lower body, consumption and plague. Barry at once arranged for a regular Friday afternoon clinic and dispensary, to be publicised among the townspeople and throughout the surrounding villages. No fees were to be charged.

Hospitals always attract the destitute and the mad. Barry's establishment was no exception. But the numbers of retired prostitutes, beggars, orphans, vagrants and thieves who descended upon the clinic, intent on free food and charitable generosity, were slightly smaller than was common, indicating the relative wealth of the colony. The doctor set about dispensing medicines and advice with the brisk and uncompromising humanity for which he was famous. In Cape Town he had indeed been responsible for establishing the leper colony, thus removing the mass of begging wretches from the streets to a clean place where they were well cared for and regularly fed by a noble batch of nuns. Barry made friends with the nuns wherever he went. He counted upon God's brides, rather than the Lord himself. Here, he found that the disease had not taken root and that, apart from one unfortunate creature whose face was half eaten away, there was no reason to set up another leper colony. But Barry was on the look-out for fresh needs to be met. The Friday clinic was always besieged.

It was Barry's custom to examine every person who came, even if it was already dusk, before he would depart for his evening's engagements. He knew that his patients had often walked miles to reach him, and would camp on the hospital steps if he did not see them on that day. Some of the villagers could speak rudimentary English, and within a few weeks Barry was barking advice in fledgling Greek. He had an uncanny aptitude for languages. George Washington Karageorghis sat firmly next to Barry as his assistant and translator. Thus, the Hospital Superintendent learned a great respect for his commanding officer. It was a measure of Barry's quality that, despite his ruthless and high-handed manner, despite his impeccable standards and sudden tempers, he inspired a passionate loyalty in his servants and inferiors. He was disciplined, but never officious. He was exacting, but never unjust. He had high expectations of his staff and flew into screaming rages if any one of his orders was not fulfilled in every particular. George Washington Karageorghis declared that the Deputy Inspector-General was the first doctor he had ever seen who threw an almost daily tantrum. He was exceptionally savage with all "Pedlars, Quacks, and Pretenders to Medicine". A good many self-styled Volpones found themselves out of a job, for it was Barry's firm belief that it was better to be without any advice at all than to receive bad advice, "whether in Lay or Physic". His manic cleanliness became an article of faith. The entire staff of the hospital cringed in helpless fright if Dr Barry detected "a stench".

❖ ❖ ❖ ❖ ❖

The English colonists were well satisfied with their fiery red-headed dwarf. He gave them lots to talk about. During that first week in the colony he scandalised – and delighted – the assembled company at the banquet given in his honour by partaking of a very frugal amount and yet downing several bottles of claret single-handed, without any trembling of the hands, reddening of the complexion or glazing of the eye. His reply to the Governor's polite enquiry as to what, in his opinion, was the most usual source of disease, became legendary, largely because it was delivered across a magnificent decorated edifice of shellfish and lobsters.

"The most common cause of disease in gentlemen of your

class, sir, is lack of exercise and bad diet. Most of what you eat, I may assert with some certainty, is at best rubbish, and at worst poison."

The sayings of Dr Barry, or at least the varnished truth, were repeated and embellished around tea tables and fireplaces, at picnics and on dance floors. Despite his abrasiveness, and his implied animadversions on the colony's collective diet, he became a popular dinner guest and was much in demand. Some of the ladies even adopted his régime of fresh vegetables.

One episode on the esplanade was worth several dinner parties. Captain William Boaden of the Royal Worcesters was drilling his men in full dress uniform and in the morning heat. Dr James Miranda Barry, wearing a staw hat with a muslin curtain hanging round the brim, so that his mouth was visible but not his eyes, and wielding a vast parasol like an under-arm cannon, trotted straight up to him. There was a moment's dreadful pause. Then Barry flourished his whip and screeched forth a volley of threats and attendant inevitable consequences if the parade were to continue in a temperature past ninety degrees. Boaden was about to fling Barry into the moat when some sixth sense intervened. He called off the parade and left the doctor yelling shrilly at the backs of his departing troops, who marched off with expressionless faces. Whenever he was asked to re-tell this episode, Boaden turned brick-red and tight-lipped. He would not be drawn. He avoided the doctor.

But the ladies sought him out. And the Governor's daughter simply could not get enough of him. In those years the colony was overseen by Sir Edmund Walden, an amiable epicurean who had been recently widowed. His young wife had been carried off by the same bout of typhus that had almost removed Sir Edmund himself to a better place, some eighteen months before Barry's arrival on the island. The Governor was unsuccessfully bringing up his seventeen-year-old daughter, Charlotte, and his fifteen-year-old son, Joseph, on his own, aided by much well-meaning and ineffective advice from the colonists' wives. He was intending to return to England the following year, where he had dozens of useful female relatives, to find a husband for Charlotte and another wife for himself. "You must waltz for your supper, my dear," he told his daughter cheerfully, making no bones about his purpose in renting a town house for the season.

Charlotte could vaguely remember England and retained unpleasant recollections of muddy gardens, drizzle and draughts. She loved the island's white rocks, the flaking red earth and the daily promise of cobalt-blue skies. She had no desire to leave the residence with its jasmine walks and Moorish arcades. But she also liked the idea of a husband who would give her status at the dinner table, the family jewels, and all his attention. He must be tall, very tall, but exactly like Dr Barry in every other particular.

Barry was often invited to dinner at the Governor's residence for the simple reason that he was very good company. He was sharp, but never pompous, and he could read Shakespeare aloud in a manner that was always delightful and sometimes extraordinary. Charlotte's favourite play was *Othello*, which, being filled with adult passions, made her feel breathtakingly complicated. Barry leaned against the mantelpiece, *pluming up his will*, warning against *the green-eyed monster, jealousy*, and grabbing the *uncircumcizèd dog* by the throat, night after night, in a variety of thrilling voices. When he became the outraged and abandoned father, he was especially stirring:

> Look to her, Moor, if thou hast eyes to see:
> She hath deceiv'd her father, and may thee.

Charlotte's one interesting flash of insight was to question Desdemona's traditional innocence. In the elegant drawing room of the Governor's residence, which sported some suitably Moorish archways, and fireplaces edged with tiles of pure Mediterranean blue, there was a genuine Venetian grandeur. Sensual possibility appeared to be lodged in the chandeliers. The decor was correct. The stage was set. Betrayal and adultery seemed all too likely, indeed temptingly possible.

"I wonder if Cassio was exceedingly good-looking?" Charlotte remarked dreamily. "She says he is *a very proper man*."

Charlotte's unspoken thought was that a black man would be daringly exotic as a lover, but not an undertaking for life. Barry regarded her with cynical interest. It would never have occurred to him to give his word and then go back upon a promise. Therefore, adultery was unthinkable. For heroines, at any rate. But Charlotte Walden clearly did not condemn women who organised their marriages according to a different set of rules.

❖ ❖ ❖ ❖ ❖

It was mid-June. Barry had passed almost half a year upon the island. The heat began early that year and there was much talk of a premature departure to the hills. The little company which dined regularly at the Governor's residence was still recovering from *Troilus and Cressida*, which had unfortunately been chosen for its Greek connections. One of the colony's residents was a mad antiquarian, who claimed to have discovered the original site of Troy. Every so often, during the readings, he was seized with the urge to deliver an impassioned discourse on the authenticity of Shakespeare the historian. Charlotte was considered too young and too unchaperoned to read the part of Cressida, but read it she did, with Walter Harris as Troilus, whom he portrayed with such excessive gusto that the rôle ceased to be credible. Barry was slippery and convincing as the perfidious Diomed. When Charlotte proclaimed her lines

> *Therefore this maxim out of love I teach:*
> *Achievement is command; ungain'd, beseech.*

she had looked straight at Barry, and the glance he gave her in return was generally considered to be rather shocking.

But the nights grew warmer and the ladies fanned themselves energetically in the late afternoons, inhaling the seductive scent of jasmine, leaning out over their balconies and watching for the first breath of evening and the sea wind. Shakespeare is well known for inflaming the passions, but this would not do for the sultry nights. And so they broached *Macbeth*, with their iced fruits and dessert wine, in hope of a change from the torrid aroma of adultery. *Macbeth* was a great success with the company of ladies, who all took turns at being witches. The events of the play had a military dimension and good battle scenes. This went down very well with the Governor, who had never been in a battle but liked to imagine that he had been.

Harris and Barry were reading the scenes where Macbeth and his lady work themselves into a frenzy, as a prelude to Duncan's assassination. At last, the sun dissolved peacefully into a mass of molten rose and gold behind them, and the breeze pulled at their sleeves. The ladies sighed with relief. The light turned blue, then purple. Barry's voice pierced the half-dark, decisive and uncanny, reading the lines quietly, as if they were a prayer.

> *Come, you spirits*
> *That tend on mortal thoughts, unsex me here;*
> *And fill me, from the crown to the toe, top-full*
> *Of direst cruelty.*

He paused, then called upon the elements of darkness, in a voice that thrilled the company. Charlotte, who had never taken her eyes off Barry, realised at once, that he was no longer looking at his book. He knew the words by heart.

> *. . . make thick my blood,*
> *Stop up th'access and passage to remorse,*
> *That no compunctious visitings of nature*
> *Shake my fell purpose, nor keep peace between*
> *Th'effect and it! Come to my woman's breasts,*
> *And take my milk for gall, you murd'ring ministers,*
> *Wherever in your sightless substances*
> *You wait on nature's mischief! Come, thick night,*
> *And pall thee in the dunnest smoke of hell,*
> *That my keen knife see not the wound it makes,*
> *Nor heaven peep through the blanket of the dark,*
> *To cry "Hold, hold!"*

Everyone gasped. Walter Harris gripped the cornice of the fireplace masterfully, to indicate his presence. He thundered his lines with bravado and panache, but Barry's lowered, serpent tones were the more telling,

> *Only look up clear;*
> *To alter favour ever is to fear.*
> *Leave all the rest to me.*

While they were waiting for iced sherbet and apricots in cooled liqueurs, the company dispersed into several rooms and scattered along the verandah. Charlotte cornered Barry and suggested a turn in the gardens. The Governor's gardens were famous for their Arab fountains, constructed in the twelfth century and decorated with the original tiles. The strange blue and cream patterns shimmered beneath the broken surface of the falling water. Oranges gleamed like lanterns in the dark. They strolled down one of the shaded paths by the fish ponds and Charlotte insisted on taking Barry's arm.

"Miss Haughton admires you tremendously, you know" was her opening salvo.

"We shared a very uncomfortable voyage from Portsmouth," Barry replied, noncommittal. He was already questioning the wisdom of allowing himself to be carried off through darkened gardens by a silly girl with a pretty figure.

"And you must know that I do too."

Barry bowed in acknowledgement of the compliment, but said nothing.

"When you were reading Lady Macbeth, I said to myself – it was very thrilling – but what understanding you bring to our Shakespeare! It is not only the excitement of the poetry. You know, just as he does, what it is like to be driven by ambition. To endure the frustration of your desires . . ."

Barry felt the ground cracking beneath him. Charlotte was rapidly departing from the high road of cliché. Her remarks, which should have been directed towards the coolness of the fountains and the beauty of the night, were about to become personal. He took evasive action.

"I have no idea, however, what it is like to murder someone in cold blood. Or even to desire another man's death, Miss Walden. I am a doctor."

For a moment she was checked.

"But you understood Lady Macbeth. You know what it is to be a woman."

For one terrible second Barry feared that Cape Town gossip concerning his identity and origins had followed him east with the steady accuracy of a carrier pigeon returning home. But Charlotte Walden flung herself unhesitatingly into a speech not about his sex, but her feelings.

"You must know how I feel – what I yearn for above all else. I cannot bear being a girl and having to wait, when I must speak."

Shakespeare's heroines were much given to speaking. Barry's relief caused his mind to wander for a moment. He did not notice that Charlotte had tightened her grip on his arm and was clearly working up to something. He re-assumed his professional tone.

"The reason why I can so well comprehend Shakespeare's women, Miss Walden, is that those parts were written for boys to speak. Women's lives were as limited then as they are now. Except, I imagine, among the higher classes, who have always enjoyed greater freedom of movement and had more opportunities to manage their property."

"I can bear it no longer. Forgive my frankness, Dr Barry. I beg you to kiss me."

Barry stopped dead beneath a fig tree. Charlotte could not see his face, as the lights from the house were behind him. She bounced in front of him and seized both of his cold hands. With great presence of mind Dr James Miranda Barry raised her importunate fingers to his lips and gently kissed them all.

Then he said very firmly, "We shall return to the house at once, Miss Walden, and rejoin the company."

Charlotte had no idea whether she had conquered or entirely missed the mark. But she knew that Barry was not to be crossed with whims or petulance. She took his arm again and they marched back past the pattering fountains.

"You won't tell Father that I asked you, will you?" she whispered like a schoolgirl, not at all embarrassed, but anxious not to be caught out.

"I am not in the habit of repeating private conversations" was the frosty reply, with which Charlotte had to be content.

James Miranda Barry had a very conventional, masculine notion of honour. Charlotte Walden was engagingly pretty, plump and pink, with dimples in all the right places. Barry was charming to her in company, but took good care never again to be left alone with her upon the verandah or to accept her invitations to wander down the jasmine walks, to admire the Chinese carp, drifting in green water, and to listen to the fountains.

❖ ❖ ❖ ❖ ❖

But Miss Charlotte Walden did get Dr James Miranda Barry into trouble, and this is how it happened.

The Governor's daughter caught the eye of Captain James Loughlin while she was singing a duet by Rossini with one of his closest friends and fellow officers, Captain William Boaden of the Royal Worcesters.

Loughlin had been absent on leave in England for nearly a year, following his father's death. He was a young man with a substantial inheritance. The estate was duly divided and settled, his sisters provided for and his mother comforted. Rather than buy himself out of the army, or resign his commission, as his mother had urged him to do, Captain Loughlin decided to continue his life of pleasure, adventure and fine clothes, on a significantly larger budget. And so he prepared to re-launch himself upon the social scene with all the *éclat* befitting a young man of twenty-two, who, all other things being equal, could hold his liquor with the best of them, and amply filled his trousers. He caught sight of Charlotte, singing away in a manner that was damnably attractive. It was not the singing itself that proved so irresistible, for her voice was middling indifferent and her style affected. No, it was the fact that she put her all into the high notes, which she just about managed to reach, and when she did reach them her bosom shook and trembled in a fashion that caught the eye and engaged the heart.

Miss Charlotte Walden's bosom was always the first thing that any new acquaintance remarked about her. Inevitably so, for it was the nearest thing on view and placed firmly in their line of vision. It was pale pink and had always been carefully protected from the sun. It was interestingly proportioned: twin volcanoes with a deep cleft between. Pale slopes rose towards the hidden cones, simmering, dormant, awaiting the fortunate lover who could kindle their tips into eruption.

Captain William Boaden was not above peering down into this delightful landscape as he bowed and kissed his partner's hand, complimenting her upon her singing as politely as he could without actually telling lies.

He caught James's eye at once and, with another courteous bow, abandoned Miss Walden to the queue of officers forming behind him and picked his way through the gossips hugging the sofas and the flat green baize spaces of the whist players.

"You lucky fellow," muttered James, as soon as they could hear one another above the chatter. "What a handsome girl."

"Tickle that fine tenor of yours into action with a few lessons and you too can get a close view of the treasures," said Boaden affably.

William Boaden did not much like Sir Edmund's daughter. He suspected, on the basis of her singing, that she was ill-tempered and spoilt. He liked women who were honest and humorous and had no pretensions. He had carried on a very successful affair with a married woman, who had since left the colony, much to his regret. This had been an ideal arrangement, which had resulted in many pleasant afternoon picnics and musical evenings. The husband was a liberal chap, much older than his wife. They had both lived in Naples and regarded the arrangement as positively Italian. The spinsters of the colony had been less enamoured of the mores of the south, and, once the affair became a matter of public knowledge, they cut Boaden's mistress dead in church. She pretended not to care. But she did. Boaden was irritated. He liked women who genuinely did not care.

"Do you want to be introduced to her?" he asked James, whose gaze was still fixed upon the Vesuvian landscape.

"Yes. At once."

They sauntered back across the crowded drawing room

towards the piano, carefully avoiding the trailing shawls and delicate hair arrangements, which presented themselves as obstacles
at every turn. James flung out his chest and filled his red coat to
good effect. He was sweating with anticipation.

No man likes to feel that he is being used to pass the time,
before the real object of interest enters the room. But that was
what James did feel and his irritation increased. Miss Walden
laughed and smiled at all his jokes. But she was watching the
door. The dancing had already begun and he was trying both to
interest her in a mazurka, which would animate the bosom
to delicious advantage, and to field the constant interruptions
from other men trying to catch her eye, when he felt her body
tense like a hound spotting the prey and her attention fix on the
doorway.

"Will you excuse me for a moment, Captain? I have my
duties to fulfil as the hostess."

She slid out of his grasp and vanished into the morass of
fashionable silks and lace. When she resurfaced beside her father
in the frame of the main doors to the drawing room, like a
swimmer reaching land, her generous figure prevented him from
discerning who it was that she was greeting so effusively. Boaden
appeared at his elbow, out of breath from dancing.

"Well, man? Where is she? Not lost to the opposition already?
I was expecting you to persuade her to dance."

James stretched up and peered through the crowd. He saw
Charlotte Walden's ample magnificence leaning towards a tiny,
dwarf-like, red-haired creature with pursed lips, who was half
her size. The mannikin was carefully groomed, impeccably
dressed, and dainty in his manner, if somewhat tightly buttoned.
He looked like a shrunken dandy, and a little ridiculous. He
nodded at Charlotte's animated queries and shook hands warmly
with the giant Deputy Governor as if they were on cordial terms.
One or two other ladies, perceiving his arrival, abandoned their
sofas to greet him. There was a little stir around the room. His
entrance had caused a mild, but enviable, sensation.

"Who in God's name is that?" snapped James, already jealous.

"Ah. The famous doctor," Boaden smiled. "He's a great
favourite with the ladies. That's James Miranda Barry."

And Boaden proceeded to inform his friend, in a surreptitious undertone, of the incident upon the esplanade. Something in Barry's manner had made the redoubtable Boaden back down. He sketched this out for James.

"Cross that fellow on something he cares about and you're a dead man."

And then, following his usual cautious procedures, Boaden adandoned the drawing room to the doctor and took refuge on the dance floor, leaving James Loughlin with matter for thought.

Nevertheless, in the weeks that followed, the young captain paid court to the Governor's daughter. He was far from penniless and he knew that he looked terrific in his uniform. He was very tall. And this ensured that Charlotte's tender glance would rest upon him. Indeed, she did find Captain James Loughlin to be a very proper man, and quite charming. Unfortunately, his hesitant tongue was nothing like as entertaining as that of the waspish and observant Dr Barry. Captain Loughlin made general comments. He saw the world as everybody else did. Dr Barry had an asperity and originality which made him teasing, piquant and desirable.

❖ ❖ ❖ ❖ ❖

James Loughlin did everything in the correct order. First of all he flirted with Charlotte in so public a manner that the connection began to be generally remarked. They were placed side by side at dinner tables, so that their whispered giggles could be observed by her father and the spinsters with knowing indulgence. No one, certainly not Charlotte, told him to desist. Then he made a formal call upon the Governor during his office hours. Sir Edmund was excessively affable. He had a large desk, a mass of documents and a very imposing polished crystal paperweight, which he employed to keep his bureaucratic importance stable and in order. The sea breezes were encouraged to enter the room, but not to depart with confidential reports. The steps leading down from his French windows into his gardens were still fresh from their morning dousing with cold water. The world was exceedingly pleasant, the wars were a long way off, and if this young officer, who had inherited quite enough money to keep his daughter comfortable, was willing to take her off his hands, so that the projected trip to England could become a wedding journey and a triumph of visits, rather than a husband-hunting foray, then, well, so much the better all round.

"Come in, my boy," boomed the Governor. And smiled.

Captain Loughlin was hesitant and embarrassed, which was as it should be. He presented a portfolio of credentials and assurances of high regard and filial duty. He exactly matched the Governor's expectations of what his son-in-law should be. This young chap looked the part and here he was, saying all the right things. The Governor tried to look grave and thoughtful, but a cheerful smirk greeted the finale of Loughlin's speech.

"Well, my boy," the Governor's approval illuminated the room, "if you have her consent, you have mine."

He had seen Charlotte strolling down the esplanade, twirling her parasol, with Captain Loughlin in assiduous attendance and he therefore harboured no suspicions that his daughter might be of a mind different from his own.

But she was.

Captain Loughlin was not obtuse. He knew that Charlotte was fascinated by James Miranda Barry, but, he believed, no more so than half the ladies on the island. And he had observed Barry's ironic, guarded distance whenever Charlotte flung herself into her flirtation with the doctor. The two men had hardly exchanged a word, but Loughlin had not missed Barry's twinkle of amusement when, white-gloved, pale-cheeked, not a curl disturbed, the doctor handed the flushed and gleaming Charlotte into his arms for the next dance. It was obvious. Barry was leaving the way clear for him. A Mediterranean dance floor is a stifling and noisy place, upon which misunderstandings could easily be generated. But there was no misunderstanding in this case. The two men may not have discussed the matter, but they bowed to one another across Charlotte's scented ringlets and came to a perfect agreement.

No sooner had he spoken to the Governor than James Loughlin leaped onto his horse and trotted the half-mile down the esplanade from Government House to the residence, on fire with sexual expectation. It never entered his head that she would refuse him.

When he was shown into the drawing room he found his lady strewn across a chaise-longue and giggling. She was in the company of one of her friends, a pert young woman, recently married, much given to flaunting her rings and boasting about her husband. She spewed forth an endless torrent of rumour and gossip and had earned the nickname "News of the Nation". This lady, upon seeing a young man hell-bent on making love, scrambled to her feet and excused herself at once.

James remained standing. Charlotte turned pale and sat up straight, her little slippers firmly together and her knees tense, as if she were about to execute a sequence of pirouettes. James presented a hesitant string of clichés. He was alarmed at how much harder it was to ask her than to ask her father.

" . . . in short, Miss Walden — Charlotte — I am asking you to make me the happiest of men, that is, I should be, if you would agree to become my wife."

Charlotte bit her lip, raised her chin, and said, "I am very sensible of the honour you do me, Captain Loughlin, and I am very sorry. But I can never marry you."

There was an awful silence. James went cold all over. He was unable to say anything. He knew that he should say something regretful and distressed, but he was unable to do so. Instead, he stood utterly still for a full two minutes, during which time Charlotte began to bite her nails in fright. Had he stood there any longer she would have begun sucking her thumb. James suddenly found that he was enraged.

"There is someone else." He spoke in a very low voice, chilly with rejection.

She nodded, terrified.

"Yes. There is."

"Dr James Barry."

She was unable to say anything, or even to raise her eyes to his.

"I beg your pardon for having intruded my feelings upon you," James snapped.

His anger was out now, the genie had escaped from the lamp.

He turned on his heel and stalked out of the room, forgetting himself so far as to bang the door behind him. He almost knocked Charlotte's friend down the short flight of steps in his hurry to leave the residence. She had been loitering in the hallway, behind one of the potted palms, as close to the doorway as she dared.

James snatched his horse from the servant in the stableyard and rode straight up to the hospital at a speed which was remarked from every window and shop doorway. Something was going on. Wasn't that Captain Loughlin, leaving the residence and taking the hill at a pace that was certainly precipitate, if not actually dangerous? Where is he going? Up to the hospital? But he isn't on especially friendly terms with Dr Barry, is he? Really rather the opposite. Has there been an accident? I must ask the Deputy Governor.

By the time James reached the crest of the windy white hills, he was sweating and trembling. This was the first time he had ever ventured to propose and he had been confident of his ground. He had no coherent plan. He simply wanted to hit someone. He wanted to vent his frustration by wrecking Dr James Barry's immaculate toilette.

George Washington Karageorghis saw him coming and met him in the tiled hallway, which smelt of ammonia and alcohol.

"Where's Dr Barry?" James found himself shouting.

George Washington Karageorghis was very taken aback.

"He's not here, sir."

"Then where the devil is he?" roared the injured Captain Loughlin.

Fortunately, the doctor was, at that moment, many miles away, at the bottom of a ravine, setting a broken leg and dealing with a bloody gash across the forehead of a man who had suffered a serious fall and was already badly dehydrated, having lain for two hours in the morning sun before he was discovered by hysterical relatives. The wound was nasty and covered with flies. The man's wife was screeching in the doctor's ear and the neighbours were taking far too long to construct a makeshift stretcher from green boughs. The doctor's careful red curls were damp with sweat, and upon his pale cheeks the freckles had become magnified by the heat. By the time he regained his quarters, exhausted, not having returned to the hospital, it was quite dark, and Captain James Loughlin was lying insensible with drink and rage on the floor of the officers' mess.

❖ ❖ ❖ ❖ ❖

"You refused him? Have I heard you correctly, young lady? Are you telling me that you refused him?"

Silence.

"Are you out of your mind? His elder brother is dead. He's just inherited a fine estate in Berkshire and enough money to buy you every damned trinket that takes your fancy."

Silence.

"You may never get another offer like that. What can have been going on in your head, Charlotte?"

Silence.

"And you gave him no hope whatsoever, you idiotic creature?"

Silence.

"What can have possessed you? I gave my full accord. You've danced yourself out of slippers in that man's arms. I had no idea that you wouldn't welcome an appeal to your affections."

Silence.

"You're seventeen, girl. You'll be eighteen in October. I married your mother when she was years younger than you."

Silence.

"What the devil . . ."

Silence.

"Oh no! Oh no, I don't believe it. You haven't set your cap at Barry, have you?"

Silence.

"My God, Charlotte, if your mother was still alive I'd have her permission to put you over my knee and spank you till you bellowed. Heaven help us all. You really are a greater fool than I ever thought you were. Do you have any idea who Barry is? You've no idea, have you? Nobody has. He's either the bastard son of old Lord Buchan or that crack-pot revolutionary general from Venezuela or Argentina or wherever. He has his salary to live on and damn all else, so far as I know. Barry has no family, land or relations. He's as good as the Wandering Jew. You couldn't possibly contemplate a life travelling the world with that man. You'd be dead in three years. Barry lives in climates where white men drop like flies. He only survives because he's as cold as a lizard. Don't get me wrong, my girl. I admire the man, of course I do. But he's not the kind of man you marry. Anybody can see that. Or at least anybody who isn't as silly as you are. He's a loner. He's . . . well, God knows what he is. But he will never marry anybody. Neither you nor any other woman. Men like that don't marry. And I don't believe that he's given you the slightest encouragement. He never says anything that isn't ironic. Charlotte, if you think that Barry will ever marry you, you're a greater fool than I took you for. You've sent a handsome young man about his business, who had no greater ambition in life than to cut a fine figure and to make you damnably happy."

Silence.

"I simply cannot understand your stupidity."

Charlotte burst into tears.

❖ ❖ ❖ ❖ ❖

She was still a little red-rimmed when she greeted Barry on Friday night, and he kept an eye on her across the card tables. The gossip had already hurtled round the colony. Yes, made her a wonderful offer. And she refused him. Ah, but there's another player in the game . . . I can't believe he's encouraged her. But she's not the only person wild about him. She may well have missed her main chance, for I really can't believe . . . The Governor and his colony were of one mind. Charlotte gazed pathetically at Barry from time to time, but she was also watching the door with slightly more anxiety than is generally considered suitable for a hostess to manifest if the evening is going well.

But in fact she missed Captain James Loughlin when he slunk through the door, too familar a figure to be announced. James had drunk more than was good for him and had puffed up his emotions so that they were all thoroughly out of proportion. The residence was full of laughing people, the dancing had begun and almost everyone had already served themselves at the supper tables. James was fortunate enough to find Barry on his own confronting the cold meats and savoury jellies.

The young officer appeared to be calm, but there were small beads of perspiration on his upper lip. Nevertheless, his hand was steady as he drew Barry aside from the supper table. The doctor was so small that once they were standing side by side James found himself gazing down onto Barry's pale-red curls. He stepped closer so that their exchange would be inaudible to anyone else. He had heard the rumours, of course, but was inclined to think that the surgeon's fine, elegant and carefully manicured hands were largely responsible, because the eyes which met his own were the eyes of a man who was unafraid and in control of himself and his world, a man who would never insult another idly or without deliberate intent. James felt his anger rising as he contemplated the insolent interrogatory stare of this mutant dwarf, a little pool of aggression, far below him. The waltz encircled the two men. But naturally, they were observed. Several people noticed their conversation. The doctor and the officer were the subject of immediate speculation.

"I must speak with you, sir."

"Do you desire a private consultation?" Barry realised at once that the man was drunk, and his tone of condescending irony became a shade more infuriating. James lost his temper.

"Declare yourself to her, man – or leave the field clear for somebody else."

The gossip had not reached the hospital, but Barry understood the situation in an instant. Loughlin must have proposed to Charlotte and the silly girl had refused him.

"Carry on, Captain Loughlin. I can assure you that the field, as you put it, is quite empty of my presence."

"That's not what Charlotte says."

"Then you may assume that Miss Walden is mistaken."

"How dare you trifle with a young lady's feelings!"

James wanted to quarrel and set about it with energetic determination. His moustache quivered. Barry's voice was calm and firm.

"Captain Loughlin, Miss Walden is seventeen and if I am not in error you cannot be much more. Seventeen is an age when we are all quite capable of mistaking politeness for proposals. Now, sir, I wish you a good evening."

And Barry turned aside to help himself to a bevy of cold meats, decorated with olives and tomatoes cut into serrated bowls, as if they had developed teeth. But Captain James Loughlin had passed well beyond the reach of reason and sensible argument. He had been insulted. Calmly and deliberately insulted. And so he presented his challenge as if he were an actor, dressed for his part in a comedy that was about to turn nasty in the fourth act.

"Sir! I demand satisfaction. My colleagues will call upon you tomorrow morning."

Barry acknowledged his words with the slightest of nods and a faint curl of the lip, closer to a sneer than a smile. Loughlin suddenly saw himself as the toy soldier, wound up and pro-grammed to do silly things. He discovered that his fists were clenched and that he was sweating with anger and alarm. He almost hit the doctor in the face, but withdrew at once as the tiny man turned away to give his full attention to the ladle in the fruit punch bowl.

There was an odd scent left lingering in the officer's nostrils, a strange, fragrant aroma that he could not identify, but which he had noticed in the hospital. This hallucinatory odour must have been present in the doctor's hair. He shook his head, trying to rid himself of the peculiar scent and the doctor's cold glance. Then he stepped off the verandah onto the pebbled walkways. He was followed by dozens of curious eyes, from behind fans, curtains, ornamental palms, and over the elbows of their dancing partners. And Charlotte, with her head tucked against her friend's shoulder, watched Captain Loughlin's exit, her mouth stricken with regret and distress. *You've sent a handsome young man about his business, who had no greater ambition in life than to cut a fine figure and to make you damnably happy.*

The night was alive with the sounds of toads, squealing in the undergrowth. Lanterns hung in the trees. He could see the thick white shapes of women's dresses, columns moving slowly up the gardens in the darkness. The darker shapes of the men were invisible. There was a warm night breeze from the sea. He could hear the waves breathing against the rocks. He looked back into the house. Every window was lit up; there was the music and the uneven beat of the dancing, excited cannonades of laughter and the chink of forks on empty plates. James was convinced that the momentous event had passed unnoticed. He had put his life on the line for the sake of a seventeen-year-old girl and nobody had noticed. The doctor had a formidable reputation for being both bad-tempered and a crack shot. Loughlin sobered up. He was no longer confident of the outcome. He began to wonder if he had put too high a price on his dignity and self-love. Then he began to feel very sorry for himself. He escaped from the luminous gardens and fled away down the beach.

❖ ❖ ❖ ❖ ❖

Well after midnight Loughlin sat in Boaden's rooms next to the barracks, explaining himself. William Boaden was very far from impressed.

"Are you out of your mind, man? Barry's a crack marksman. He's known for it. Why in God's name do you think he's here? The Governor of Cape Town had to move him on. He's already fought half a dozen duels and killed his man every time. Well, I know of two for certain. He's a quarrelsome devil, but he doesn't do it just for fun. You must have been excessively offensive."

"I was drunk," said James miserably.

Boaden leaped off his bed and circled the room like a bat.

"You're a fool, James. And you'll soon be a dead fool. Barry can drink an entire regiment into a vat of malmsey without a curl out of place or his hand shaking. I'll wake the others up. We'll have to try for a reconciliation. My God, the things you do to me."

Two giant moths battering the screen door came billowing in on the wave of his departure; one of them, hurtling down the glass funnel of the lamp, was immediately extinguished in the flames. James contemplated this sudden cremation. He was possessed by gruesome premonitions.

He slept fitfully, still wearing his boots, on a camp bed in Boaden's dressing room. Despite the fear that crept around his body with eerie persistence, affecting first his feet, with a glacial chill, then his chest, with sharp, shooting pains, and finally his brain, with an explosive headache, James fell asleep and remained unconscious until the moment came, just after six, when the sun streamed into the barracks and Boaden's servant stood over him, like a messenger from purgatory, with hot water and fresh towels.

Boaden himself, disturbingly awake and bubbling with irritation, slammed the screen door behind him as he came in, flinging his cap upon the unmade bed.

"No good. I called on Barry at the hospital. He's there every day from five a.m. onwards. He won't hear of an apology. Pistols at dawn tomorrow, before the Governor gets to hear about it all. He hardly lifted his eyes to speak to me and he didn't even offer to shake my hand. The man's a midget with a mission to exterminate damn fools like you. And he gets all his formal conversation out of books. *Please inform Captain Loughlin that I shall discharge my obligations to the letter.* Who on earth talks like that nowadays? It's as if he's repeating lines that have already been written."

Boaden flung himself flat on the bed, ignoring the servant, who was standing there, saucer-eyed, and who had of course taken everything in. James gazed at the ceiling, desperate.

"I felt that. Last night. I was talking as if I was in a play."

"That's because you're stupid. And you don't think. James, how could you be such an arse? You've got to go through with it now. The heat will be terrible today. For God's sake, man. Get washed, shaved. The boy's standing there, waiting."

Boaden got up and paced the room, attacking flies with a thick swatter made of patterned palm leaves. Then he flung himself down again. James sat staring at the steaming vat of hot water and the scrubbed black child in immaculate whites with gold buttons, standing to attention before him. He put his head in his hands. He had the most appalling hangover.

The heat shimmered on the gravel and unleashed the rich, wet scents of the gardens outside: the acacias, frangipani and purple torrents of bougainvillea, pouring over the wall. James shaved carefully, noting every curve and dip on his cheek and jaw. The mirror returned a handsome face, hollow-eyed, perhaps, and a little drawn, but a face worth kissing and preserving. The fear of death surged through him with all the force of a burst dam. What mattered? James was not a philosopher and what mattered to him was well-cooked red meat and good wines, the smell of a woman's warm skin close to his face, and winning at cards. All these things appeared before him, the temptations of Tantalus, shortly to be whisked away by a harpy with pale red curls, chilly hands, a peculiar aroma and the steady eye of a professional killer. James pitied his own fate from the bottom of his heart. He had not deserved this. He turned from the mirror and addressed Boaden's gleaming boots with their gentle coat of white dust, which was all he could see through the dressing-room doorway.

"I say, Will, is there really no chance of a reconciliation?"

"None whatever," snapped Boaden, gazing upwards, unseeing, into empty space. The boy leaned forward, pouring more water into the basin. The pattern of vine leaves swirled among the bubbles, delirious in china. James wondered if he was shaving his jaw and washing the magnificent brush of black hair on his chest for the last time. Suddenly Boaden was standing in the doorway.

"God dammit, James," shouted Boaden, terrifying them all, "I love you better than anyone else I know and tomorrow I shall have to bury you."

❖ ❖ ❖ ❖ ❖

Barry's second was one of his assistants at the hospital, whose clothes didn't fit. He looked nervous and embarrassed as he approached Boaden across the uneven clumps of grass, spangled with goat shit. The ungainly figure appeared to change shape in the mist slithering down the diminishing river. Sometimes he seemed to be small, shambling, at other times he was magnified, monstrous. It was an odd trick of the light. In a few weeks the water would have vanished and the mist would be gone in the dawn and the grass would grow among the rocks, flourishing at first, then browning into dead threads, until the winter rains came, and the river rose again.

Barry was almost invisible. Boaden thought he saw someone moving up and down, up and down, far away under the trees; but the bush was too dense for him to be certain. He was very upset. The entire affair was a mistake. Barry's choice of a half-caste hospital orderly was an insult to his fellow officers. The doctor was so convinced of his success that he had not bothered to comply with the minimum standards of courtesy demanded by the situation. As the man approached, Boaden set about adjusting his expression into a haughty sneer. Then he thought of James and tried to look more conciliatory. His thick jaw and heavy jowls accordingly assumed a look of lopsided cantankerousness. At least this man was also a doctor. But if Barry's reputation was deserved then an undertaker would have been more appropriate.

"George Washington Karageorghis. Your servant, sir," muttered the unfortunate subordinate.

Boaden let fly an indignant snort.

James stood to attention, virgin-pale but wonderfully dignified. He had spent hours dressing. For one indulgent second Boaden felt proud of him. Then he remembered his duty and stepped forward to propose a bloodless resolution to a futile dispute. This young lady's honour was not worth a good man's life. He bit his lip. Charlotte Walden was a bumptious little flirt who had probably allowed more than one officer to squeeze her pert little nipples and perhaps take even greater liberties. Her name was often accompanied by sly smiles and knowing chuckles. James was going to die for the sake of a cracked piece of pottery, not even a decent Coalbrookdale dinner service. What a waste. Boaden thought about the row of cheerful young prostitutes who looked forward to his arrival, entertained him heartily and had no honour to lose. But here was Barry's disgraceful half-caste colleague, executing a formal salute. Captain William Boaden's whiskers trembled with rage at his friend's foolishness.

No, it was just as he had feared, Barry would not negotiate. His second snapped open a polished walnut case, with a trim blue velvet lining and a brace of engraved silver duelling pistols, custom-built by one of London's finest gunsmiths, Cannon's of Leicester Square. As he checked the weapons Boaden noticed the initials in elegant italics: F de M. The guns did not belong to Barry, but F de M presented no immediate clue as to the identity of their owner. He nodded curtly to the orderly, and was somewhat mollified to notice that the man was terrified and embarrassed.

Twenty paces. Turn and fire.

Point-blank range.

James was already a phantom of his usual self and as he cocked his pistol he was unable to speak. They marched towards Barry in complete silence through the croaking bush and the eerie half-light. Boaden was already imagining the court martial. He was determined to hound Barry out of the colony as a pitiless murderer. This doctor saved lives with one hand and slaughtered them with the other. He should have embraced his friend for the last time. Then suddenly they were standing in front of him.

It was beyond Boaden's comprehension. They had all gone mad. His wonderful, handsome James with the gay laugh and the dark, bouncing curls, his friend, his beloved friend, was to be turned into worm's food by a tiny beardless boy in a formal white collar and a coat that was too big for him. It was not natural. But something in Barry's eye, for the second time, steadied Boaden's hands. However bizarre this tiny man's appearance and attire, he was not playing games.

The duel was played out like a formal piece of music. Every action was premeditated, deliberate. James, noble to the last, stepped away from Barry to Boaden's clear count, like the soldier he was, as courageous as he should have been. A single shot sent hundreds of birds no one had noticed, squawking into the air, and started a thunderous, sudden rustling in the bush. A dozen invisible creatures vacated the spot in flight, wrenching the vegetation aside. Boaden blinked. Barry's orderly had dropped the pistol case in fright. Far away the horses whinnied in alarm. The next moments stretched out into an eternity and a slight wind suddenly raised the dust into whirlpools at their feet. James stood, unmoving, his pistol raised and smoking in the cool air. Barry's gun was still vertical. No one moved as the doctor's arm levelled steadily towards his opponent. James leaned forward, all his weight on the balls of his feet, ready to take the bullet full in the chest, his face awash with tears.

There was a second shot.

James staggered back, his throat and left ear on fire. Barry had neatly sliced off one epaulette and a dark curl of hair. The shot had been careful and deliberate. Had he wished, Barry could have forged a channel directly into James's heart or laid his brains waste in the wilderness, as he had supposedly done to other men on other occasions. But he had not done so now.

Without a word, and with no explanations, Barry nodded to Boaden and his colleague and turned away. He stuck the pistol in his pocket and strode off towards his horse in the strengthening day, leaving the others staring at one another, shocked and baffled by his abrupt departure.

❖ ❖ ❖ ❖ ❖

Captain James Loughlin called upon Miss Charlotte Walden. He asked to see her alone. She was exceedingly pale and very excited. All pretence of formality was abandoned.

"You can tell me the truth now, Charlotte. And I think you owe me the truth. No one is listening. What is said here will go no further. Did you ever permit Barry to make love to you?"

Brazen as a bitch on heat, she never even lowered her eyes. Modesty was clearly a thing of the past.

"Yes" was all she said.

James gazed at her, amazed. Barry was half her size. He couldn't possibly have touched her. He would have disappeared between her breasts. Even Boaden, who was no friend to the Governor's daughter, admitted that it would be like entering a tropical rainforest. James decided that he still wanted to cover her breasts with kisses. Barry obviously had. The unfortunate young officer was transfixed with jealousy and regret. Then he shook his head, disbelieving. This affair was too unlikely, incredible.

He knew that he should ask no more questions, but he could not help himself.

"Where did you meet? Not here. It's impossible."

"I visit regularly at the hospital. I think he's an extraordinary man. I persuaded Father to invite him to dinner at least twice a week. He came. He talked brilliantly. Then, when Father was away in the north of the island, I invited him myself. I didn't tell him that Father wasn't here. Otherwise he wouldn't have come. He's desperately correct. But my brother was with us. Nobody else. It was all perfectly respectable. Dr Barry drank Joe under the table, and then put him – and me – to bed."

She smiled cheekily up at James, like a naughty schoolgirl. But his face was blank, like an atheist faced with a miracle. He stood up and bowed, speechless. She sprang from her seat and clutched his arm, angry at his open incredulity.

"I was in love with him, James. But he won't have me. Don't think I haven't tried. I've even asked him outright. He has vowed never to marry."

She was like a woman possessed. Her throat heaved and all her bracelets rattled. She was near to tears.

"There is no one like him. Now you know. Go on, get out. I don't care if you never speak to me again. Leave me, then. Go on."

She turned away to the window, biting her lip. Yet here was something odd, unexplained. These were not the words of a woman who had been seduced and abandoned, but of a woman obsessed, unashamed, who had tasted something unheard of, unknown, a magic nectar, whose life was laid waste without it. She spoke with her back turned.

"Oh, go away, James. Don't start getting concerned for me. I'll live. I'll marry someone else eventually. But I won't ever want anyone else. Other than him."

He was dismissed. Very quietly, James backed away and closed the double doors behind him. He stood on the steps of the Governor's residence, staring at his boots and at the gleaming hands of the man who was holding his horse. Now he faced a disciplinary action for fighting a duel with a fellow officer for the sake of a woman whose honour had never existed. She had admitted the whole thing. She had thrown herself at Barry, to whom he now owed not only his life, but the profoundest apology. He swung into the saddle and, despite the midday heat, rode straight up the hill to the hospital. Barry was not there. He had completed his morning rounds and departed homeward for his afternoon siesta. He was to be found at the green house, that one over there, with the mosquito mesh encircling the verandah. James was unable to look Dr George Washington Karageoghis in the eye.

Disconsolate, he waited until five o'clock and then presented himself at the door of Barry's residence. It was a house without eyes. The gardens were extraordinary: carefully tended green edges enclosing foaming colours. He recognised hibiscus and jasmine, wisteria and arum lilies, their white trumpets dusted with pollen, the carefully tended roses, cut well back since Christmas. There were flowering vines he could not identify, with trunks growing as thick as your thigh. An eerie precision characterised the doctor's garden. James stood upon the steps, staring at a lizard frozen in mid-flight down the wall and an army of red ants marching in step away to their lair under the house. Like all the military buildings in the colony, the house was raised up on little brick fortifications above the corrupting earth. James stood irresolute, certain in the knowledge of what he should do, but incapable of passing from intention to act.

Barry solved the problem by opening the frame door and appearing on the steps like the performing dwarf in the panto-mime. He made a comic entrance, tiny, courteous and impeccably dressed, his collar stiffly white with golden pins.

"Good evening to you, sir" was all he said. And there he stood, calm, unwavering, rocking on his heels, with his hands clasped behind his back. James stared. The unbidden spectacle of this man mounting Charlotte rose into his head. He felt like Iago, a sexual psychopath whose mind revolved on nothing but obscenity. Barry waited patiently.

"I . . . That is . . . Good evening, Doctor . . . I came . . ." James tried to get it all out in one breath and ended up coughing into his gloves.

"You came here to apologise." Barry glittered, looking up at him. "That would be the correct thing to do. But in this case there is no need."

"Well, I did . . . that is . . . I must reveal to you Doctor, that Miss Walden . . . I saw her this morning and she . . . well, she confessed everything to me. I owe you the deepest apologies for my behaviour, my insults, my . . ."

What precisely has she confessed to you?" snapped Barry. He was like a terrier scenting a rabbit, every sense alert. This did not help James, who had turned scarlet and was inarticulate with embarrassment.

"She . . . well, sir, I must admit that her frankness has quite startled me. She was very honest about her feelings for you."

Barry stood, chilly and impassive, on the highest step above him. Even then his eyes were only just level with James's collar.

"Miss Walden," Barry barked, "is a lady deserving of every man's courtesy and respect."

The terrier had the rabbit of reputation by the throat. Barry was clearly quite prepared to fight the duel again. James was reduced to mumbling.

"Indeed, sir . . . I had no idea . . . I am most deeply sorry . . ."

"Speak up, man," Barry retorted.

James pulled himself together.

"I beg your pardon. I was quite in the wrong and I make the most unreserved of apologies. I will of course take responsibility for the entire affair."

Suddenly, the lizard, which had hung perpendicular on the wall throughout their exchange, flickered, shifted, and vanished into the shadow beneath the building. Barry leaned forward. His thin, pale face became warmer and more generous.

"Come inside for a moment, Captain Loughlin," he said quietly. His welcome was still reserved, but the change in temperature was unmistakable.

James stepped cautiously into Barry's still, dim rooms. He had the impression of a ruthless, spartan orderliness. A stack of reports lay on the desk. Only the blotter, spattered with ink, demonstrated that Barry did anything other than polish his furniture day and night. The same strange smell, musk, alcohol and the sharper, heavy, burning odour, which he had detected in the doctor's curls, clung to the objects in the room and to the curtains that were made of French lace. James heard an unpleasant growl at his heels and almost stepped into a tiny mass of bristling white fur. Barry summoned the little dog directly and it pattered back across the boards towards him. No eyes or feet were clearly visible. The creature made one or two appalling noises and then sank at Barry's feet. Both the dog and its master looked peculiar and ridiculous.

"Please sit down."

Barrry's rooms were white and green. The floorboards glimmered in the half-light and the officer was forced to take small steps to avoid falling. By the fireplace a heavy green rug softened the effect. The evening sun was blocked by thick white lace across the blinds, so that the air within was murky and cool. James felt that he had been pulled underwater by the nymphs and was now lying, drugged and submerged, face upwards, in a stagnant pond. The doctor waited for him to sit down. The chair, with its upright, green-striped back, brought him to his senses. He stared at Barry, who was staring fixedly back at him. Barry rang a little bell on his desk. The sound hollowed out the green cavern. The heap of white fur stirred and growled again. The doctor now resembled an intelligent midget with a toy dog, about to perform in a circus. There he stood, holding a small silver bell. James realised that his stare had now continued well past the point of politeness.

"I will order green tea," said the Doctor, as if administering a tincture. "You should drink something hot in this heat. The water is always boiled correctly. My boy sees to that. And Captain . . ." here Barry smiled slightly "you should drink a great deal of tea to dilute the alcohol you are given to consuming in such abundance."

"Thank you, sir." James remembered his manners and that Barry was reputed to be cranky on diet. But he felt like a schoolboy, receiving a mild dressing-down from the headmaster.

Barry's servant was tall, swarthy and ironic. He appeared in the doorway, glanced at James, then grinned broadly at Barry. He had a wonderful array of teeth, all extraordinarily straight, like a military cemetery.

"Tea, sir?" He grinned some more.

"Indeed. And do you have any of those lemon cakes we made on Sunday? Or have we eaten them all?"

"I'll look, sir."

With an easy bow, the man strolled off, followed at full gallop by the little dog, its nails clicking on the polished boards.

"Psyche and Isaac are fond of those cakes," said Barry, sitting down at last. He vanished inside his chair. James had no idea whether the servants were called Psyche and Isaac, or if one of them was the dog. But he had noticed that Barry's domestic arrangements were casual and good-natured. The man had no fear of his master and clearly knew all about the abortive duel.

There was a long silence. Far away, James heard the rattle of crockery and low voices, interrupted by laughter. He felt exceedingly uncomfortable.

"You realise that I have already been sent for by the Governor himself?" said Barry suddenly.

"I didn't know. I . . ."

"I have an appointment to see him at eight o'clock tomorrow morning. I believe that the Deputy Governor called upon you last night, but that you were – how shall we put it? – indisposed . . ."

"I was disgustingly drunk."

Barry smiled. James realised that it was the first time he had ever seen this smile, a wonderful, transforming smile, which lit up the pale grey eyes, and covered the doctor's face with the cheerful glitter of a merry child. How old was Barry? He had no idea. How had he gained so much authority? No one knew. James smiled back, a little bewitched. He had entered the green domain of the Erl King.

"Shall I tell the Governor that we are reconciled and both heartily apologise for the disruption occasioned by our quarrel?"

Barry's actual words were still perfectly formal, but there was now an intimate complicity in his manner, which had never been there before. The doctor still had the whip hand, but the distance between them had narrowed abruptly. James could not fathom the register within which Barry conducted his conversations. The mixture of intimacy and menace was too much for him.

"I shall call on the Governor tomorrow," James declared. "I am entirely to blame. I shall make that clear. And I will explain everything."

"Not everything, perhaps," said Barry mildly. James blushed scarlet once again. Even his ears went red.

"No, sir. Of course not. But I shall say all that needs to be said."

Barry bowed slightly. There was another long pause. Then he said, "This is a very small colony, Captain Loughlin. There has already been a good deal of unfounded gossip, and I would be grateful for a few judicious words from you in the right quarters

on the question of Miss Walden. And it would be best, whatever
your sentiments, if, in public at least, we were seen to be on
excellent terms. May I count on your discretion?"

"Of course, sir." James floundered at Barry's candour. Then
he spoke from the heart. "I trust that we shall indeed be on good
terms. Whatever the circumstances."

"Thank you," Barry replied simply, but he smiled again. James
gazed at him and then sank, hopelessly and without trace, into
the spell of Barry's green kingdom. He was excessively relieved
when the servant reappeared with the tea.

The entire apparition on the tea tray was a miracle of elegance.
Here were delicate bone-china cups, thin as rice paper, huge
circles of lemon laid out like half moons on tiny saucers, one
each, a gleaming pair of sugar tongs wrapped in a miniature lace
napkin, with a hand-stitched design of two swallows flying in
formation, wing tips outstretched, silver spoons with little claws
and the familiar initials, F de M. James stared at this fastidious
demonstration of good taste. The service would have graced the
table of any well-bred lady in the empire.

"Thank you, Isaac. I will pour it myself. Where are the cakes?"

Isaac leaned forward and lifted another fine linen cloth with
a little flourish, like a matador, to reveal a charming array of
biscuits.

"Cakes all gone, sir."

"Wolfed down by you, Psyche and the boys, I suppose," said
Barry cheerfully. Isaac stood there, ogling James and grinning,
unabashed.

"Run along then," said Barry to the dog, which trotted out
of the room, with Isaac in her wake.

"I assume that you live in the officer's quarters?" Barry handed
James his cup and James found himself staring down at the tiny,
steady hands, pale, scrubbed, unshaking, with a gold signet ring
on the third finger of the right hand.

"Umm . . . Yes. I do."

"I prefer my independence and my privacy."

Barry's voice was quiet and even, but the timbre was that of
a boy, rather than a man. At that moment James wondered if the
rumours were correct. Could Barry be some kind of hermaphro-

dite, with a spectacular intelligence? He was neither man nor woman, but partook of both. He had a woman's delicacy and grace, but the courage and skill of a man. Barry's courage was legendary. James tried to order his thoughts and was unable to do so. There were very few men in the army whose aim was as infallible and murderous as that of James Miranda Barry. He had both saved and taken lives. He was the lord and owner of every one of his gestures and expressions. He knew neither hesitation nor uncertainty. He gave rather than took orders. The Governor himself deferred to Barry's judgement. But even so, he was not a man like other men.

James felt himself sinking down into the green tea, the green air and the green rooms, drugged by the pale oval of Barry's face and the odd, heavy scent that lingered about the doctor. Barry talked easily and pleasantly. James let down his guard. He heard the multitude of insects battering against the mesh. At dusk, Barry rang the bell again to summon Isaac with the lamps. The dog pattered softly back into the room and leaped onto Barry's lap.

" . . . and so operating conditions have greatly improved." Barry stroked the dog. "I am not yet able to offer these facilities to the native populations. But we have begun basic training for some of the more able apprentices."

James gazed spellbound as the doctor talked about his work and his plans for the hospital. The spell was cast not so much by his conversation, which was practical, even of a somewhat special- ised nature, and well beyond James's range of comprehension in all but the most general terms. There was something uncanny in the doctor's manner, but James was unable to make sense of the source. What was so hypnotic, strange and intense about this man, which began to appear like a deliberate tactic to beguile and seduce? He urged James to imbibe more and more green tea, until the young officer feared for an explosion in his bladder. He was increasingly anxious to relieve himself, but did not dare beg permission to step further into Barry's green kingdom or to take his leave.

Finally, when it was quite dark, Barry allowed him to go. As he rose to escape he ventured one personal question. He had no certain idea who Barry was, only rumours and gossip.

"We share a Christian name, sir." James hesitated. "Am I right in thinking that the painter James Barry was one of your relations?"

"He was. James Barry was my uncle."

"And forgive my impertinence, but I noticed that your silver was marked with the initials F de M. Is it indeed the case that you are connected to the famous Argentinian General, Francisco de Miranda?"

James did not dare to mention the pistols.

"Venezuelan. General Miranda was born in Venezuela. And yes, he was my patron. He was like a father to me. He lives yet. He is an old man now. But his intelligence is undiminished. He is at present engaged in important research into the conditions of the unfortunate Negroes upon his West Indian estates. It is my greatest privilege to merit his continuing good opinion."

This was delivered with uncharacteristic passion. For the first time, Barry flushed slightly. James bowed. He sincerely believed that his next observation was merely polite.

"I did not, of course, give credence to the rumour, but I was told that General Miranda fought with the French."

"Then, in this case, Captain Loughlin, you should have believed what you were told. General Miranda was, and is, a true son of the Revolution. He supported Bonaparte with his sword and with his life on precisely those grounds. He believed, as I do, that Napoleon was a great general. Napoleon towered above the Revolution, suppressed its abuses, preserving all that was good in it – equality of citizenship, freedom of speech and of the press – and that was the only reason he possessed himself of power."

Barry's voice was low and his manner was intense. James turned pale.

"The Revolution, sir, is the one grand event of our times. You and I are too young to remember that early blaze of enthusiasm, but we are fortunate enough to witness the first ripples of its aftermath in a changed world."

James sat open-mouthed at this torrent of treason and subver-

sion. Barry had a reputation for expressing himself with
unnerving frankness, but here he had exceeded all expectations.
James looked around in desperation for his cap. If he did not
rapidly escape from this green lair of odd smells, bone china,
fluffy dogs and revolutionary opinions, he was in grave danger
of urinating on the rug. The dog sniffed the air and growled.
Once outside, James staggered out of view and pissed at length,
up against a menacing hibiscus. It took him nearly an hour to
walk back to the town in the luminous, shimmering dark, with
the great sky and Barry's pale, oval face, vast and mysterious as
eternity, hovering before him.

James pondered his namesake all the way home. The man was
like quicksilver, fluid, indeterminate, yet utterly beautiful. He still
could not understand the perversity of Charlotte's passion. A
woman should, after all, fall in love with a proper sort of fellow,
not a creature outside the boundaries of this world. But he too
had succumbed to Barry's magic, and was, knowingly, a little in
love with this man who had been tempted to kill him. And had
resisted that temptation.

❖ ❖ ❖ ❖ ❖

But what on earth had happened? What on earth could have
happened on the night of that fateful dinner, during the Gover-
ner's absence? How had it ended? Barry was a man of honour.
He never lied. He had stated, without ambiguity or hesitation,
that Miss Walden was a lady who deserved every man's courtesy
and respect, whose reputation was beyond reproach. He was so
sure of himself and of her innocence that he had been prepared
to barter words for bullets. No honourable man fought duels for
whores. Either Charlotte Walden was lying, or Barry was. James
abandoned the struggle to imagine a scene of passion that was,
indeed, quite beyond the reach of his imagination. And gradually
he forgot all about it. This is what actually happened.

❖ ❖ ❖ ❖ ❖

There was something too knowing, too well informed, about
the boy's glance. Barry was an acute observer of every gesture,
every glance, even of the tension in another man's back or the

muscles in his neck. He was very quick to sense change. And here, from the flicker of a lash, the rapidity of the boy's gesture as he opened the door, his smothered grin, Barry knew at once that this was no ordinary dinner engagement and that something was wrong. He stepped inside the cool, tiled hallway with the tiny fountain exploding in intermittent bursts and the stairs curling away into the darkened storeys above. Nothing was out of place: the sound of a piano and Charlotte's laughter, uncoiling in the distance, were nothing out of the ordinary, but as Barry stepped into the bright, fashionable drawing room, already dominated by slightly too many china ornaments, hunting portraits and Chinese vases for his taste, he saw at once what was wrong. There was nobody there.

Lotte sat gorgeous at the piano, her famous bosom unaccountably revealed to great advantage. Her brother, handsome and gauche, barely sixteen, with still fewer hairs upon his chin, was mixing up her music for her and making a mess of things. He was dressed in a formal black coat, but giggling like a schoolboy. Neither of them had heard the cloche. When they saw Barry standing warily at the other end of the carpet, they both jumped up, excited and embarrassed, like two children meeting one of their parent's friends for the first time. Charlotte gambolled down the room, calling out long before she got within range of polite greetings, "Dr Barry! I'm so sorry that we didn't hear you come in. We were only fooling. How kind of you to come. It is wonderful to see you this evening."

She gabbled all this far too quickly. Then she cantered round him like a lively pony, as if she was trying to absorb him from all angles at once. Barry raised one eyebrow. Charlotte was being too silly and too gushing to be affected. On the other hand, she had never looked so pretty nor so young.

"Father's not here. It's just us. He had to go off to the other side of the island at short notice. He suggested that I should put you off until Friday. I told him I would. But then I didn't want to. We're so dull with nobody here."

The unfortunate brother, a head taller than the doctor but just as fresh-faced and pale, stood stifling giggles and scuffing his shoe.

"Lotte's an awful hostess, Dr Barry. Would you like a drink? We've made some terrific fruit cup. Enough for forty people."

Lotte pinched him, her face all puckered up and cross.

"Oh, Joe, don't say I'm no good at entertaining. I've only just got started. He's always teasing me and making me embarrassed. Please sit down, Dr Barry. Don't mind us."

She dragged Barry into the full glare of the candles and revealed the fruit cup in its vast silver bowl. There were apricots and cucumbers floating on its surface, and the entire thing had been excessively chilled.

Lotte was overdressed. She was wearing too many trinkets and looked like a saint's shrine in the aftermath of a miracle. She had the sense to allow the opals in gold that hung from her ears to set off a plain miniature on a red velvet ribbon tied tight in the French style, like a knife-cut round her throat. But she had gone quite mad with the bracelets and rings. Barry gazed at this child, this thoughtless, silly girl, and remarked the bizarre figure that she cut, aping her elders, and, no longer supervised by older hands, getting it all wrong.

"Did your father send a message to the hospital to inform me of his absence?" asked Barry curtly. He refused to sit down. These were the first words he had spoken. Lotte was beyond shame.

"Of course he did. I intercepted the messenger. You had been invited and I wanted you to come. I didn't see why you shouldn't. I wanted to see you."

Her brother exploded into giggles.

"Fruit cup, doctor?"

Barry nodded and peeled off his gloves. The fruit cup was laced with brandy and very strong. It was also very refreshing in the hot night. Barry drained two glasses and sat back. He could either disappoint her mightily by gathering up his dignity with his coattails and gloves, and taking his leave at once. Or he could give them both a run for their money.

"Dinner is served."

The servants in the Governor's household were Portuguese. They were clearly all vibrating with laughter in the kitchen. They couldn't wait for the second act, which, as they were serving at table, they would observe at close quarters.

Barry was taciturn over supper. The fish was well cooked with capers in a pepper sauce. Lotte chattered on, repeating all the gossip she had heard. She ordered up expensive imported wines from her father's cellar, about which she knew nothing. It was considered correct in good colonial society for a young woman to put her handkerchief in her glass to indicate that she did not take wine. All the young ladies in the colony followed the practice. Not Lotte. She sat at her brother's left hand and served herself with gusto. Had her father been present she would never have dared. And Barry did not try to stop her. By the time they arrived at the dessert, a lavish glass dish filled with dates, apricots and sweet peaches, she was wielding her fruit knife like a rapier. Her cheeks were deep pink and covered with tiny drops of perspiration. Her brother was slurring his words and asking impertinent questions about officers who were suspected of private visits to Barry's clinic after sorties to that part of town known as The Middens, a network of streets notorious for gaiety and disease.

"You must see very many members of our little world, Dr Barry," he guffawed, "in fact quite a cross-section!" He then sank into a jolly heap, quite overcome by his own vulgarity.

Barry insisted that Charlotte withdraw into the drawing room while he set the Governor's son straight on one or two points of unpardonable bad manners. Joe Walden was as contrite as a young man can be when impossibly, uncontrollably drunk. Barry finished the port, which was excellent and almost certainly taboo for general consumption. Joe joined him in a glass or two, then passed out, and collapsed over the table. Barry could hear Charlotte's polkas becoming ever more frenzied and inaccurate. Then, suddenly, the music stopped altogether and she appeared in the dining-room doorway, pink and white at the extremities, like a vampire's victim.

"Call one of the servants to help me carry your brother upstairs," said Barry quietly. He stood up. He was slightly paler than usual, but neither his voice nor his hands betrayed the slightest tremor. His collar was still stiff, white and straight, his cufflinks firmly fastened. Lotte's jaw dropped a little. She was unsteady on her feet as she crossed to the kitchen door.

"Antonio," she bellowed, far too loudly as it happened, for Antonio was bent double on the other side of the door, his eye fixed to the keyhole.

The debauched scene of the completed feast with the young master slumped beside his plate was not unknown in the Governor's house, but it was rare enough for Antonio and the other servants to be scandalised and delighted. Charlotte staggered on ahead with a lamp raised above her head, like the Bleeding Nun. She wobbled dangerously as she circumnavigated the landing. Barry caught the young man under the armpits while Antonio steered his feet up the curling staircase. They laid him out magnificently on his small cot bed, clearly left over from childhood. He was already snoring. Barry ordered a bucket, just in case he should be sick, and left him carefully propped upon his side, all his buttons undone, with a mass of pillows behind him. He ordered Antonio to check on the young master at hourly intervals.

The doctor then prepared to say his farewells to his hostess, who was teetering about in her brother's bedroom. As he raised his face to hers, she pounced. Seized with an excess of tact, Antonio scampered off down the dark stairs. Lotte abandoned her lamp in her haste to embrace the diminutive Dr Barry.

"Which room is yours?" snapped Barry, disentangling himself from Lotte's fragrant and abandoned grasp. Lotte was by now well beyond any form of rational discouragement and thrilled to the tips of her nipples by the doctor's authoritative approach to seduction. She indicated the room at the end of the corridor and then threw her full weight rhapsodically into the doctor's arms. She was far heavier than her brother. He half carried the drunken girl down the passage, bumping into invisible chairs and ornamental tables with a sequence of theatrical crashes. The door fell open and Barry threw Lotte down into a gleaming pool of white linen, simply because he was unable to carry her one step further. Lotte, dizzy with expectation, lost her satin slippers in the process. She closed her eyes in rapture. It was all exactly as she had dreamed it would be.

Barry looked round the room, vaguely expecting to see a rocking horse and a pile of china dolls. But no, Charlotte had begun to accumulate the symbols of young womanhood. Here was a dressing table, overflowing with pots of powder, brushes and ribbons, and numerous phials of perfume. Here was a pelisse draped over a chair and a smelly little pile of dancing shoes, with the left heels all worn out.

Barry shrugged in exasperation. Yet he had never seen Lotte looking so presentable. For once she was not trying to entice the doctor into ogling her bosom. She was natural, at last. And completely drunk. He imagined her headache in the morning. The fruit cup alone, which she had clearly been sampling well before his arrival, would ensure a darkened room for the entire day. He chuckled to himself and bent down to kiss her forehead before departing into the night. But Lotte was not as comatose as she appeared. Nothing stops a virgin hell bent on pleasure. Her bare arms flew up and encircled his neck. Then, demonstrating considerable strength and presence of mind, she capsized James Barry into her feather pillows. The buttons on his jacket were tangled up in silky ribbons and the soft white folds of her petticoats, which were strewn all across the bed. There was no escaping her now.

Barry's first thought was that he was still wearing his boots. Meanwhile, Charlotte was intent on stripping off all her clothes. She heaved in the dim bed like a porpoise. Barry pinned her down before she could lose every last shred of her remaining modesty. There was only one way to end this. He pulled her face round towards him and kissed her ferociously on the lips. Lotte sank back with a gasp.

Never before. No, not ever. Et cetera.

She was overwhelmed, intoxicated. She flung herself against him. He kissed her again, harder this time.

Lotte let out a ravished sigh, which turned into a somewhat less romantic whistle. She had all her desires at last. She had captured the alluring, the enticing, the mysterious Dr Barry.

Not quite.

With his left hand Barry pulled her skirts right up to her thighs and beyond, then reached down into her most secret places. She cried out, startled and amazed. The doctor's expert knowledge of anatomy came into play. She was soaking wet with involuntary excitement. He found out the source of her pleasure and rubbed her gently into ecstasy, his mouth hard against hers, stifling the little screams which poured forth, one after another. He waited until the soft electric shocks subsided, then began to liberate himself, with some difficulty, from her octopus petticoats. Lotte's breathing steadied. The alcohol was now racing frenziedly through her system, and she was almost unconscious. Barry found a little water in her floral pitcher that was not too stale. He soaked one of her handkerchiefs and wiped her face gently. Then he covered up her pretty, vulnerable form that was on display for all the night to see.

"Lotte, can you hear me?"

"Mmmmmmm . . ."

"Listen to me, Lotte. Don't ever get so drunk again with a man you don't know. Someone will take advantage of you. And you make it shockingly easy for them to do so."

Pause. Long drowsy breaths rose peacefully from the bed.

"Lotte, are you listening?"

"Mmmmmmm . . ."

"You may get away with it. But then again, you may not."

Pause.

"Goodnight, my dear."

She did and did not hear him. She failed to understand. She did feel the fatherly kiss, which he at last bestowed on her damp curls. But she no longer had any idea who he was. The entire affair had lasted somewhat less than seven minutes. Charlotte's magnificent bosom never did form part of the picture. Yet this young woman fell asleep feeling nothing but the warmth and dizziness of satisfied and completed love.

Barry let himself out through the front door, well aware that he was observed by dozens of admiring eyes, and strolled home beneath an aureole of stars.

❖ ❖ ❖ ❖ ❖

Speculation about Barry's sexual past was as dense as the mosquitoes outside the screens at every dinner party in the colony;

indeed, at every social gathering where he was not present and at many where he was. Inevitably, his connection with the famous Mrs Jones leaked forth into the stream. Barry had been seen at many of her London performances. He had even once accompanied her on a tour of Ireland and the northern provinces. He had been a frequent visitor at her London house. During a year he had spent in England between his foreign tours he had begged her to abandon the stage and follow him through all the world. Are you sure? The very idea! Everyone was titillated by the piquancy of the attachment, the famous doctor, nephew to Mr B, the painter, and a very close relation to Lord Buchan, in love with the actress of humble origins who had taken London by storm. It was shocking, delightful, perfectly delicious. And quite charming to talk about. But the incongruities were also unavoidable. They were a most peculiar couple: the statuesque Mrs Jones, on the one hand, with her magnificent figure and breathtaking legs, her comic charm and saucy jokes with her devoted audiences, and, on the other hand, the tiny, serious, ice-cold doctor with his sharp tongue and exaggerated dignity. No, the colonial wives, delighted as they were by the oddness of this picture, simply could not see it at all. Mrs Harris, who had wintered in London, attempted direct and provocative action in a bid to ascertain the truth. She took up her position behind the teapot and fired all her guns at once.

"Our visit to town was quite wonderful. We were invited everywhere. And I had the pleasure of hearing Mrs Jones as Rosalind. I assure you, she was every bit as astonishing as the reputation which precedes her, quite glowing, one would even say radiant, with a very pleasant singing voice. She seems to take charge of everyone on the stage. Even when she is silent, she is somehow at the centre of every scene. The slightest shifts in her emotions are so pretty and convincing. When she appeared in the forest dressed as a rustic gentleman she was quite transformed. And her second metamorphosis from a saucy page boy into a perfect lady was bewitching indeed. As for her performance in the pantomime, I have not laughed so much for many years."

She paused, expanding her bosom with predatory significance.

"I gather that you had known Mrs Jones, Dr Barry. When she first began her career . . ."

"I did."

"How interesting this is! Do tell us, Dr Barry – for you will certainly be able to do so – what sort of a person is she in private life?"

The company leaned forwards with a little crescendo of cups, agog to hear what Dr Barry would tell them about the famous actress, the woman who was reputed to have caught the eye of the King himself, if these wicked cartoonists were to be believed. And gossip is never without foundation. No, never.

"Mrs Jones is a clever, astute and unscrupulous woman," said Barry flatly.

The ladies clamoured for more.

"But she has real talent . . ."

"I am told that she is very witty and well read . . ."

"She is our greatest comic actress . . ."

"But she bests Mrs Siddons in many of the tragic roles . . ."

"She played Desdemona, with Kean as the Moor. All London was talking of it . . ."

"Mrs Jones is excellent at portraying injured innocence," said Barry bitterly, turning away.

The ladies redoubled their attack.

"But Dr Barry, she is a great artist . . ."

"She must have suffered when she was young . . ."

"Yet she is believed to be quite rich . . ."

"She was raised in Lord Buchan's household . . ."

"Am I correct in asserting that you, Dr Barry, are an intimate of that family?"

"She has a house on the river in a most fashionable district . . ."

"And her own carriage . . ."

"Her costumes alone are worth thousands . . ."

"Her breeches were quite daringly tight . . ."

But, not even upon the interesting subject of Mrs Jones's breeches could they draw Dr James Miranda Barry back into their conversation. He refused to play their game. They were not satisfied.

❖ ❖ ❖ ❖ ❖

Captain James Loughlin began to make formal calls upon Dr James Miranda Barry. This fact, like every other event in the colony, was much commented upon. James Loughlin was an impulsive, unreflective man. He had no idea how he should behave towards someone to whom he owed his life, but he had acquired a peculiar sense of intimacy with and admiration for the doctor, who had so generously spared him. They never referred to the incident again. But Barry's bullet continued to slice the air between them. James moved cautiously towards the pale, cold doctor. He befriended Isaac and sent any game he had shot, usually the best cut of the wild boar, round to Barry's kitchen. He tried to beguile the beast, Psyche, and was bitten for his pains. Barry apologised on the poodle's behalf. He explained that he had always had a small white poodle called Psyche, but that the last one had been very friendly and gentle, and had loved being kissed and caressed, settled on the ladies' laps. The present occupant of the post was altogether more cantankerous. James wondered about this. It was a little odd to harbour generations of identical dogs called Psyche. He finally decided that the doctor had so loved the first one that he could not bear to lose the creature, and had therefore settled upon a system of eternal replacement.

"Nonsense," said William Boaden. "Dogs all have utterly different characters. He just can't think of another name."

In fact, the reason was far more existential than either of the two men could ever have supposed. Barry had no constant markers in his life. He moved onwards from land to land. He had no close friends. He was a public figure in every place where he had lived. He was rarely alone. The first Psyche had been his only unquestioning, loyal confidante. He could not afford to lose her. And so there began the sequence of white poodles, trotting briskly behind him, waiting patiently at doors, on verandahs, under awnings, snapping at flies, gazing suspiciously at ladies who revealed their petticoats, growling on steps in the dark.

James Loughlin sent Barry's household regular gifts of a sensible, practical nature. But, at the beginning of the hot months, when the ladies had already departed for their summer residences high in the hills, James sent Barry a huge cluster of wild orchids, which he had gathered in the mountain gorges. Barry sent Isaac with a formal note of thanks. Loughlin understood this as permission to visit and called on the doctor at once, despite the oddness of the hour, following Isaac back up the hot rocky hill to the green verandah overlooking the sea. The light was painted into the air, like a breathable cream glaze. The path simmered under his feet and the shrivelled vegetation hung limp under the congealing heat. Isaac walked slowly. James realised that his impulsive visit was very ill-advised. He stood, sweating and wilted, at Barry's green door.

The doctor wore white shirt sleeves and was sitting smoking in a draught.

"You're a very imprudent young man," he said, offering James an ice-cold hand. "You shouldn't move at all between twelve and five. As your Chief Medical Officer, I may well order you onto the sofa for the rest of the afternoon."

The room was disturbed with the heavy purple of the orchids. James looked again into their deep streaks of yellowish white, which addressed the antique lace of Barry's gently stirring curtains. They had no scent, but they dominated the deep green rooms.

"Thank you. I love flowers," said Barry quietly, uneffusive.

James sank onto the sofa. Barry ordered a tumbler of cold water for them both and Isaac vanished. They spent the afternoon smoking and exchanging occasional comments. James dropped off for nearly an hour, and awoke to find Barry gazing at his face, concentrated, unsmiling, intent. James apologised for his bad manners, and sat up, dizzy and embarrassed.

"I am told that you spend the nights dancing, drinking and gambling, Captain, rather than sleeping. It is therefore perfectly suitable that you should spend the afternoons asleep."

"I say, Barry, don't you think . . . I mean . . . I wanted to ask whether you'd like to go up to the mountains . . . for a week or so, or even ten days. Just us, and Psyche, of course. My shout, although I can't think it would cost us very much. But, you know . . . We'd have a terrific ride. There's plenty to see and you haven't got much on at the hospital. You could be back in time for your Friday clinic. That's if you wanted to go . . ."

James trailed off. He had kept on talking because he was too frightened to give Barry the opportunity to say no. Barry was still staring at him, unabashed.

"Thank you, James, for a very kind invitation. I should be delighted."

It was the first time that Barry had used their common Christian name. James leaped off the sofa and shook Barry's hand. Psyche set up a frenzied barking.

"Terrific. That's all settled then. When shall we start? We must get out of this heat."

Barry went on staring, but he added a very small, ironic smile.

"At dawn tomorrow. If you don't burn the candles at both ends tonight."

❖ ❖ ❖ ❖ ❖

They spent most of the first day marvelling at the views. In the dull chill before dawn they crossed the irrigated plain beyond the town, trotting briskly down the soft sandy tracks between the green maize fields. Psyche wobbled unsteadily inside Barry's coat, her nose black and wet, raised to the cool air. By the time they began climbing slowly on the rougher paths through the white rocks, the sun was upon them, baking their backs and heads. But they were already a long way above the bay, turning inland along the ribbon cliffs. Far below they could pick out the aquamarine thread close to the shore, outlining the port and the promenade, which anchored the island into the darker wash of blue. The air shifted its weight, exhaling hot breath against their faces. They dismounted and picked their way carefully up the uneven track towards a huge head of rock, cracked, jagged and stained with giant stripes of yellow ochre, buried in the rifts. The rock cast a twisted shadow across the rough scrub beneath. As they crushed the vegetation beneath their boots and the horses' hooves, the green threw up the sudden smell of rosemary and wild thyme. Barry rubbed a twist of herb between his gloved fingers and sighed. In the rock's shadow the air changed and drew away, but there was no water.

Barry had a map.

"There's a spring about four miles further on and the path should get easier. Do you think we can climb up there by midday?"

"Easily."

Psyche flopped down beside James. She was too hot to negotiate anything other than a truce with the handsome soldier, of whom she was intensely jealous. James looked at her warily.

"Do you clip her nails?"

Barry nodded.

They sat silent, side by side, puffing with the horses, gazing at the empty vanishing line of blue.

"Beats England, doesn't it? "said James.

"Not for beauty," Barry replied. "Nothing could ever do that."

James laughed.

"Never had you down as a patriot. You're always so sharp about our fellow countrymen."

"That's because their idiocies are magnified abroad. I don't think that you will ever have heard me criticise the country itself."

"But what is the country other than the people and what they've made of it?"

James was a little puzzled. He was attached to people rather than to places. He never did understand why he should venerate the flag. His regimental world was one in which honour and tradition were things about which you ranted with vehemence when magnificently drunk. He entertained no abstract ideas of England as a psychic entity which could be the object of nostalgia. But as it happened, neither did Barry. He was remembering somewhere quite specific. The doctor sat prim and serious, perched on a rock, smoking a thin cigar.

He was silent for a moment, then he said, "I spent a significant part of my childhood in the country. My family and I were frequent visitors to Lord Buchan's estate in Shropshire. After I had begun my studies I returned there every summer. From May to September I lived on the farm, in the kitchens, in the fields. Look out at those dry white rocks, James, where nothing grows, and think of the fresh dew on cow parsley, lacing the hedgerows. Think of purple foxgloves on the woodland floor. Imagine the squirrels racing across your lawns. Breathe the smell of cut grass. Remember the candles of the horse chestnuts, pink and white, jaunty and elegant, swaying above the green, this year's green, the new spring leaves, folded like napkins, high above you. Think of that fine, soft rain, delicate as a woman's silk sleeve, touching your face. Remember the late white frosts? Just a faint crust of white among the daisies. Hear the birds chanting the dawn. Remember those long summer evenings, of blue shadows and thick gold, that long, evening sun you only see in the north. See the hills, those soft, swollen, rounded bellies of green. And smell the water, clear water, spring water, ice-cold, battering the stream stones, the irises yellow against the green and the cows browsing in the shallows."

James sat up astonished.

"Good Lord, Barry, you're a poet, not a doctor! But I could certainly do with a drink."

Barry laughed. He seemed surprised by his own oratory. He went to pull the water flask from his saddle-bag. The huge bay snorted hopefully and dipped her head down towards her master. He peeled off his gloves, poured a little water into his bare hand and wetted her nostrils. She blew a damp blast of heat into his ear and stamped twice. He rubbed her head gently. James stared at him. The doctor had to climb rocks to mount the creature, which he did a little self-consciously but with aggressive dignity. Yet the animal, which Harris had described as hell on four legs, trotted out for Barry like a seaside donkey. All Barry's animals appeared enchanted. They bit anyone else who approached. It was very peculiar.

"The mare goes well for you," said James, puzzled. There had been some merriment in the colony at Barry's expense when the Governor had first proposed the gift. The bay had been intended to take the doctor down a peg or two.

"Yes, she's a good horse," Barry answered absently. He looked out at the sea. "Don't you miss England, James?"

"Not at all. Or at least I've never thought about it. I grew up in Berkshire. But I can't say that I thought about the country like you do. I just remember flies and mud. And Father shouting. I couldn't wait to get to town. See the world. I hated school. Didn't you hate school?"

"Never went. I had tutors at home."

"Lucky you, like my sister."

Barry looked down sharply at the soldier sprawled beneath the shadow of a great white rock. But there was nothing more than idle chat behind the remark. Barry handed over the flask.

"I didn't know that you had a sister. Here, drink up. Let's move."

The water ran over James's fine moustache and gleamed on his red underlip. Barry watched a drop fall onto the front of his uniform. James flopped back against the rock, groaning. Barry was fitter than he was. The soldier looked like a marionette with the strings sheared.

"My God, Barry. Pull me up."

"Consider which one of us is likely to win a tug of war," laughed Barry, suddenly dapper, merry, game for anything. They grasped each other's wrists and pulled like children, James winning easily against Barry's slender weightlessness. He noticed once more the doctor's fine, cold hands, each nail cut short, each oval cuticle pale, perfect, unbroken. He understood why all his patients spoke of the doctor's light, tender touch and the gentleness of his authority. He gazed down at the other man's hand, resting in his own. Cautiously and slowly, Barry withdrew his hand.

"Shall we go on?" he asked quietly, looking up into the young soldier's confused and bewildered face.

❖ ❖ ❖ ❖ ❖

At sunset they stopped to watch the giant glowing ball, illuminated like a Chinese lantern, sink with all theatrical splendour into the black pit of the orchestra. The heat was sucked out of the air. They found the mountain hut easily enough. It stood directly in their path and they would have had to struggle round it to go on upwards in the closing dark. The distances between the hut and two of the local monasteries were written in Greek on the wooden wall, but with no indication of directions. James found the stones where the last visitors had lit their fire and began to grub about in the dark bush for sticks. There was nothing to hand, so he set off over the rocks. When he returned, bitten by mosquitoes, scratched and cursing, Barry had already lit the fire from the neat little pile of brushwood stacked inside the door of the hut. He was sitting on a rock, calmly slicing a sinister sausage.

"You try my patience, sir," said James, laughing at himself and flinging down the hard-won sticks.

"Regard it as one more piece of evidence that James I was more successful than James II," smiled Barry.

"And had more luck. Both the doctor and the king."

James flung himself down beside the fire, almost crushing Psyche, who was too exhausted either to growl or to move.

"And you've no doubt hobbled and fed the horses, discovered a pile of hay and refilled the bucket from the spring."

"Indeed. But the spring is merely a trickle. It's fifty yards away up a rather dangerous track and I would not advise it in the dark. I propose that we put up with each other's stench tonight and wash in the morning."

"*A vos ordres, mon général*," murmured James, stretching out. "And are you as competent at cooking?"

❖ ❖ ❖ ❖ ❖

The doctor slept close to the door, wrapped in his cape, with Psyche tucked against his shoulder, like a warm, curled cushion. James got up to relieve himself in the middle of the night. He had to step over the doctor's legs. As he did so he heard the sudden unmistakable click of a pistol being cocked, and the poodle's low growl.

"It's all right, Barry," he whispered, a little dazed, "it's me."

When he came back into the dark space, which reeked of goats, he was wide awake from the night cold and the apprehension of being shot. Barry's accuracy was no doubt still invincible, even in the luminous dark.

"I say, Barry, are you asleep?"

"Not now, my dear, I'm talking to you."

"Sorry."

James lay down again.

"I wasn't asleep."

There was a comfortable pause.

"Barry?"

"Yes?"

"So far as I know we aren't surrounded by brigands and we haven't been followed. Do you always sleep with a loaded pistol on your chest?"

Barry chuckled.

"I do indeed, sir. I have my honour to defend."

Then they both fell asleep.

❖ ❖ ❖ ❖ ❖

The monastery was attached like a leech to the upper edge of a perpendicular precipice. They could see the stone walls growing out of the rock: Οικος αγιος Πνευματικος, The House of the Holy Ghost. It was a fortress against all comers, pilgrims and pillagers alike. Everyone was equally unwelcome, both the terrestrial invaders and the heavenly hosts. The doctor and the soldier were descending from the north through the pine woods. They had seen no one for days. But now, as they looked out towards the hotter, dryer peaks of the southern range, they could pick out a steady trail of pilgrims, some on donkeys, others on foot, creeping up towards the Holy Mountain. This was not in itself an unusual sight; but the numbers were astonishing. A long caravan, seemingly without end, toiled onwards and was lost to sight around the rising curve of the crag. It was still early in the day.

"Looks like they've got visitors." James wondered aloud, "Do you think they've got space for us?"

Barry stared at the endless trail of veiled women and bare-headed children far below them. Some of the wanderers were old, poor, crippled. Some were being carried on makeshift stretchers. There were wealthy men on fine horses, surrounded by attendants. Bearded priests mingled with the flock. As they came closer they could make out camps and groups of pilgrims, clustered in tiny pockets of woodland or secreted in ravines. Some had lit fires. They saw the pale blue smoke rising in the early light. Others were simply resting before beginning again the long climb upwards in search of holiness. Barry picked out a bishop in full array, surmounted by a parasol, and entire families, calling to each other, accompanied by a Noah's ark of animals, scuttled over the rocks, up the slithering paths. It was like the last pilgrimage, the medieval dance of death, strung out across the mountains.

The first person they passed was a ragged herdsman, seated on a rock, surrounded by a dozen goats. Barry addressed him in Greek. The old man gurgled out his reply from a toothless mouth.

"What'd he say?" demanded James, who, despite three years' residence on the island, had never learned a word of the language.

"He says there's been a miracle."

"A what?"

"A miracle."

"What sort of miracle? One worked by God?"

"I wasn't aware that there were any other kinds of miracle."

"Dammit, Barry. Explain."

"An icon of the Virgin is shedding tears for the world on a regular basis."

"Oh, come off it, Barry. All these people can't be climbing three days' worth of mountain on the off-chance of seeing a damp piece of painted wood."

The herdsman peered into their faces, trying to decipher their words and ascertain whether they were quarrelling.

Barry smiled faintly and offered the man a few coins.

"Spoken like an Englishman, my dear James. I'm proud of you. But these people have the kind of faith that makes three days' journey up a precipice a mere step towards heaven."

James shrugged. He was not in fact an unbeliever, which would have required an intellectual effort of which he was quite incapable. His God was a decent sort of chap with inexplicable preferences, who did not operate abroad and who certainly never interfered with the world. He should be invoked on the occasion of births, sicknesses, marriages and deaths. Not otherwise. The icons at the House of the Holy Ghost were very famous indeed. The sanctity of the monastery had been preserved for centuries.

No woman had ever seen them. All these veiled creatures carrying their sons to be blessed would be left, derelict of benedictions, waiting at the gates. Books had been written about the icons by travellers James had heard of and he had expected to enjoy their beauty and antiquity without being surrounded by a mass of illiterate and smelly peasants, weeping with devotion. He said as much to Barry.

"I don't expect it will come to that," replied Barry ironically, "but we shall have to join the flow."

Their uniforms guaranteed that the crowd parted before them like the Red Sea, but, to James's amusement and surprise, Barry was frequently hailed by his regular patients. The doctor was well known, both to the people he had actually treated, and by reputation, among the native populations. His healing skills were, in any case, regarded as little short of miraculous. So it was considered entirely suitable that one miracle worker should pay homage to another and that the doctor had come to call upon the Virgin.

The monks had not yet opened the church for the evening's viewing of the miracle when the two dusty soldiers trotted through the gates. Obsequious and sinister, the black figures poured forth a smooth welcoming patter in Greek. Barry nodded, but said very little. James handed his horse to a small boy who was already clutching the bridle with one hand and holding out the other for payment. One of the monks slapped the outstretched hand.

"Let's take a look at the bloody Virgin," James snapped irritably, "and then see if they've got anything that we can eat, rather than worship."

The interior of the church smelt of incense and damp. It was like entering a decorated egg. There was a wooden screen, smothered in icons, which divided the space in half. James stumbled over the clawed feet of a huge lectern, surmounted by a mass of intricate gold turrets on the corners with a huge leather Bible laid out upon it. The scriptures were locked with ornate gold clasps, as if they were a box of jewels, and bound to the lectern by two solid golden chains. Everything was locked, shut or kept behind bars, as if the monastery was perpetually expecting an incursion of raiders from the valleys below. James tweaked the golden chains with his riding whip and they clattered against the wood. One of the monks twittered in Greek. Barry peered at the dusky icons littering every surface. There was one representing the Virgin that was supposedly painted by St Luke himself, and was so holy and efficacious that it had to be covered with a curtain. James bent down to read the text beneath the magic icon, then caught Barry's sleeve flirtatiously.

"It says here that St Luke, being a master physician, put all his healing powers into the icon and that it has cured many men of rattling in the body, fits of the evil thing and the bloody flux. I thought only women suffered from the bloody flux. You should prescribe icons, Barry."

"It says nothing of the sort! You can't read Greek. And I do prescribe icons. Frequently. They are exceedingly effective with the *malades imaginaires.*"

Barry wandered off round the dusty interior of the church with its oppressive blackened pictures leering through braided pearls and coloured stones. He loathed all the paraphernalia of religion, and could not understand why they were tourist attractions. So far as he was concerned, religion transmitted nothing but fear and ignorance, like a contagious disease. The miasma of superstition rising from the smoking icons was palpably visible, smouldering with medieval prejudice and the spectral presence of the Holy Ghost itself. Barry never underestimated the power of religion to heal bodies, arm nations, destroy lives. He simply longed to see it abolished in his lifetime.

A tiny priest with arthritic, freckled hands stood at the back of the church making fluttering gestures towards the wall of icons, one of which was supposedly weeping with contrition. This was the miracle! James strode over to look, curious to see how it was done. Barry hesitated, peering at the other icons, which rested propped against the walls. Outside he could hear the indignant murmur of the crowd, who had been excluded while the colonial rulers took their time. The locked doors, old wood shot through with nails like the body of St Sebastian, shook slightly with the presence of accumulating bodies.

Barry stood staring at the icons.

Some of them were in poor condition. The paint was cracked and flaking, the colours obscured by smoke from the devotional candles. Some were clearly being consumed by woodworm, others buckled with damp. Yet there they had stood for almost a thousand years, a rogues' gallery of saints and bishops, some of whom he recognised easily: St Catherine clutching a tiny wheel, St Agnes presenting a plate with two breasts, St George, ubiquitous on a geometrical horse, with the dragon indignant beneath his hooves, laid out flat, without any perspective. Some saints had bishops' mitres. The faces gleamed, contented with power, from behind their ornate, grey, curling beards. Barry's upper lip curled slightly with contempt.

He peered at the numerous representations of the Virgin. And, even in the eerie thickening half-light of the blackened basilica, he began to notice something peculiar about the icons. Each painting of the Madonna was subtly different from every other one. The Virgin's face was a disturbing, pale nuanced green, but her expression, by no means uniform, became subtly attractive to James Miranda Barry. The woman gazed outwards, unblinking, unafraid. Her identity was self-contained, remote. She received all comers with indifference. Barry had seen that peculiar, insouciant detachment on the faces of prostitutes dying of consumption. He stared at face after face after face. The Madonna stared back, her pure indifference now bordering on transcendent grace. James Barry stood transfixed before the incorruptible, eternal body of the woman whose mystery saturated the dark.

"I say, Barry, come on." James was at his elbow. "Let's view the miracle. This chap running the show wants to let in the mob."

Barry nodded, taking the other man's arm, and they stepped into a tiny chapel, a mere indentation in the wall, which contained the miraculous icon.

Here was yet another green-faced Madonna. But she was not like the other icons in the squat medieval church. She was unsmiling, but bolder in her glance than the more secretive Virgins. The child, a dwarf, painted out of scale, sat ignored in her lap. She had a round chin with a festive dimple and huge dark eyes. There was something about the set of her shoulders inside the jewelled robes that was determined and fierce. Barry peered up at her. The icon was unusual. This was not the hieratic, remote face of the saint, but a woman larger than life, larger than any man who looked at her. As he watched, the painted wood glistened strangely, and then, uncanny yet undeniable, two huge tears rolled down her inflexible face. A woman who cared so little for the daily griefs of this world would never weep, never pray for us sinners, neither now, nor at the hour of our death. She reminded him of another woman whose gaze was as deliberate and unashamed. She reminded him of Alice Jones.

Barry's eyes were barely level with the Virgin's calmly folded hands. On the shelf beneath the icon a communion plate overflowed with coins. Barry touched the money, which was surely the point of the exercise, and the hovering priest lunged forwards. James gazed up at the damp face, impressed. The priest began clucking gently. He indicated that the soldiers should kiss the icon. His long grey beard was yellowed round his lips and his black robes white with dust. Barry surveyed him from head to toe. His feet were bare and purple with ingrained dirt. His body smelt stale, unwashed. Barry wrinkled his nose in disgust.

"Give these creatures some money, James. I wish to leave."

Barry's imperious manner amused rather than offended the younger man. James grappled in his pockets for some loose coins while Barry strode out of the basilica. The side door was very low and narrow, but he did not stoop and he cast not another glance at the weeping icon.

When James caught up with him, Barry was standing smoking in the cloisters. He looked tired and two fluid spots of red illuminated his pale face. James knew the signs. Barry was very angry.

"Good show, eh?"

"That weeping piece of painted board is quite clearly a theatrical fabrication on the part of these foul-smelling monks to delude and rob the innocent and credulous," Barry snapped. "Come on James, we're not staying here."

Barry delivered his opinion as if he were giving an order, but what he did not say, even to himself, was that the icon had disturbed him because her face had reminded him of a woman he used to know.

✤ ✤ ✤ ✤ ✤

In April of the following year, when the acacias were already blooming with honey blossom, and James Barry was walking among his lemon trees in the sun, wondering at the precocious heat of the season, he noticed a figure in black toiling up the rocky track towards his house. There were two ways up to Barry's residence, either the longer winding dust road which circled easily up the hill, where each visitor paused to look up at the white mountains and then down to the sea far below, or the far steeper eroded rock path, which became an informal and impassable torrent during thunderstorms. This route was the more direct, but the more exhausting. The figure was an old woman, veiled, but as sure-footed as her own goats. Barry recognised her at once. The witch woman was coming to call upon the doctor. It was a very unusual hour to visit anyone.

Barry's high-handed arrogance in medical matters did not extend to shamans, faith-healers, herbalists, sorcerers or the keepers of cauldrons. Upon his arrival in the island he had immediately demanded the identity and address of the local witch. The Deputy Governor was taken aback. The witch had no official existence and could not therefore easily be traced. Barry called in his servants. They were too frightened to give him a direct answer. Barry went down to the village and sat on the low wall that surrounded the spring, by the recently installed and therefore suspect pump, and there he waited for her to come to him. And sure enough, before many minutes had passed the little square had emptied, and here she came, very graceful and steady, like a black ship in full sail, all flags hoisted, festive in the rigging and atop the mast.

The witch was an elderly widow, wealthy and respectable, cocooned in swathes of handsome black lace. She lived in a grand house with copious plantations masking the verandah. Her vines stretched up the hill behind her. She employed three workers, full-time. She boasted a weird collection of china dolls. She had a sense of the literary, could read English perfectly well, and possessed not one black cat but two. She was very honoured to meet the famous Dr Barry. The entire village watched through the cracks in their shutters as Madame Diaconou welcomed Dr Barry into her house.

Barry asked about the weather. What climatic changes and seasonal variations affected the patterns of illness among both populations on the island? He took careful notes concerning the location and efficacy of particular icons. He asked which local saints concerned themselves with childbirth, wounds, the shakes, infectious diseases, putrid fevers and general paralysis. He enquired after the herbs which were easily available and possessed powerful healing properties. He reported his suspicions concerning some of the unappetising local fish, which were nevertheless considered delicacies, and asked for her opinion. He was informed, affable and courteous. Madame Diaconou was disposed to reveal that she put a great deal of faith in the antiseptic qualities of wild thyme and had had great success with sore throats and bronchitis. She spoke an intriguing mixture of Greek and English. Her husband, God rest his soul, had been a converted Turk, who had seen Venice once and who, to her relief and the personal desperation of her mother-in-law, had died in the arms of Holy Church. He had been particularly susceptible, poor man, to violent inflammations of the lungs. Barry revealed that he too was a great believer in infusions. They were both very small people who sat eyeball to eyeball, and as the conversation continued, the red curls and the lofty coronet of black lace drew closer and closer together. The omens were favourable.

The witch was perfectly clear in her own mind that Barry had come to do a deal, preferably cash on the table and all above board. She was waiting for him to reveal his hand. And so, to gain the advantage, she moved into areas where Barry's expertise was bound to be unequal to her own. She was an expert on all forms of possession, either by evil spirits, the unquiet dead, passing malfaisances, or the devil himself. Her charms, which took a day or two to concoct, had caused many a ghoul to depart, consumed with a white-hot burning rage, gnashing his fangs in frustration. Upon the departure of his satanic majesty, the victim always reported an agreeable sense of freshness and restful cool. Her love potions were expensive, but much sought after. Barry confessed that he had never mixed one and the witch raised her eyebrows in feigned amazement. She also had the power to cause spontaneous abortions in sheep and goats, but she was too amiable to market this considerable facility. She preferred to avoid village disputes about land.

Matters became tricky when the subject of fees was broached. It was Barry's practice never to charge the indigenous populations. The Friday clinics were therefore subsidised by the hospital and at times out of Barry's own pocket. The witch was, in terms of the average fisherman's income, very expensive. Barry had hoped to draw a clear demarcation line between their separate areas of professional concern. He had no knowledge of love potions, which was the most lucrative side of Madame Diaconou's business, and, listening to her confident pronouncements, he was unworried about her expertise in childbirth. The fluids she dispensed to ensure the birth of sons were a little alarming, and would have dramatic consequences for the digestive tract, but they were not dangerous. Her advice on sexual technique – how, for example, can a young bride be cured of frigidity? – was flawless. But there remained the difficult issue of demonic possession. Barry had come across many demons in Africa, but in the worst case he had seen of agony sent by the evil spirit, the man had also suffered from stomach ulcers and gallstones. Demonic possession had occasionally been proved to coexist with a wandering pregnancy and an inoperable cancer where, when he peered into the interior, he saw the tumours wonderfully intertwined like a lush black vine throughout the dying body.

Barry looked speculatively at the mass of china dolls, hoping that one of them would wink to him with some knowledgeable advice on how to handle the witch. But they sat, rigid and unblinking, all along the dresser in the dim rooms, ranked according to size, taking up the usual place of household plates. The doctor was relieved to hear, upon further enquiry, that cases of demonic possession were increasingly rare and that the local priest, a close friend of Madame Diaconou, was a noted exorcist.

But they could not agree upon fees.

For the first year of Barry's tenure in the post of Deputy

Inspector General, there was an uneasy truce established between the doctor and the witch. Their first clash came over the spring blood-letting. When Barry forbade the general release of bad humours from the blood of the village population, the people gathered before the witch's house in droves and often came down with infections or anaemia, and were carried back up to the hospital. Within a year or two Barry had put a stop to the practice, but he could only do so by buying off the witch with an enormous sum, and giving his official blessing to her nettle tonic, which purified the blood by other means. Nettles were good for the blood, as Barry well knew, but the witch's clients could have brewed up the potions themselves, far more cheaply, with the same results. Barry could not grasp that this terrible spending of money on a prophylactic they could not afford was, in fact, part of the cure.

Then there was a breakthrough. Somewhat to the doctor's surprise, the widow appeared at the head of the queue during his Friday clinic. Everyone else stood aside, murmuring, as her prodigious bosom breasted the crowd.

Barry saw each patient separately with his interpreter, George Washington Karageorghis, resplendent in uniform, standing to attention behind him, and delivering the translation, if necessary, with a military bark. "He says he has pains everywhere, sir!" was a common description of the symptoms. And it took Barry a few weeks to realise that this was often simply an opening gambit to impress the gravity of the case upon the doctor. But it was not easy to see each patient separately. Illness was a family affair. And the entire family usually came too, each brandishing a medical opinion and years of experience of all known diseases. Barry systematically separated wives from their husbands and mothers-in-law, thus generating a lot of scandalous gossip and bruised feelings. He insisted on subjecting the unfortunate sufferers to an interrogation in tongue-tied privacy and sometimes ended up shouting at the patients. Very few were malingerers. But the psychological labyrinths from which these narratives of illness emerged often defeated the doctor. Some diseases were hereditary and some were obligatory. Particularly intractable were sodomy and incest, both of which produced alarming, incurable symptoms. Some illnesses proved to be the guilt caused by not being ill, like my mother, my father, my aunt. He confronted women stricken with marital breakdown. He could not prescribe divorce. He never knew how to help them.

Barry became grateful for running sores, venereal seepages, varicella, dengue fever, measles, trachoma and hookworm. He knew what he was looking at and what to do.

But here was the witch, Madame Diaconou, in his clinic for the first time, beaming.

"Good day, Doctor," she said, in English, majestically.

Barry rose, bowed, kissed her hand. Everyone in the waiting room peered round the door. The witch had not shut it and Barry did not either, realising that their conversation was intended to be public.

The widow sat down.

She bent forward, black drapes crackling, and unbuckled her shoes with some difficulty. Then she presented him with a magnificent smelly yellow corn, upon which her charms had proved fruitless. The doctor's first look of surprise blossomed into a merry smile as he reached for his scalpel and his antiseptic swabs, reeking of alcohol.

After that, the witch and the doctor became not only colleagues but friends.

And now here she came once more, picking her way up the hill by the shortest route, the witch woman coming to call upon the doctor, at a most unusual hour.

Barry met her in the shadow of a gigantic grapefruit tree, hung with gleaming yellow balls. She was a fat woman, and a little out of breath. The doctor took her arm, smelling the sinister kindling of the sun impregnating her fronds of old black lace. At first she did not speak. She gazed out to sea.

"I have come to report a death, Doctor," she said in Greek. "But this is not an ordinary death. The man was brought to my house early this morning from another house in the village, where he had lain, without my knowledge, for two days. He was terribly emaciated. He vomited even the clear water we gave him and his faeces were black and putrefying. He had a high fever. An hour ago he expired. I could count his ribs. He was not yet thirty years old. He had been a fine strong fisherman, from the outer isles."

"Not dysentery?"

"No. He sicked up the black bile."

The doctor's hands were cold. He said nothing. The witch read his silence.

"The visitation is upon us, then," she murmured quietly.

Barry nodded.

Cholera.

✤ ✤ ✤ ✤ ✤

The year was 1817.

The disease rose up in the hot swamps of Bengal and set forth upon its journey down the rivers, devastating the villages through which it passed, leaving in its wake the bonfires of damp wood, the incense-ridden pyres, and the sound of weeping behind locked doors. Gathering up its dark cloak of heat, the stench of vomit and bile, the hectic cheek of fever, and the sweat of superstition and fear, the pestilence moved steadily east towards China, dividing its force, turning back to Persia and Egypt in the west. The slum quarters of Cairo were the first to be attacked, but the disease did not rest among the poor. Remembering the first plagues, it crossed the well-swept tiled thresholds and fountained gardens of the rich, crept through the ornamental patterns on their alabaster screens, swept past the doors of mosques and cathedrals, climbed up from the servants' quarters, every step up, up, up to the well-fed tables of each reigning class to become a member of the feast.

All climates, all lands, fell victim to its passage. The pestilence moved northwards, adapting swiftly to the dead wastes of ice and snow. After 1824 it circled towards the great steppes, hurried across the mountains and the wheatfields of Russia, traversed the vast expanses of deserts and the rich black earth, softly awaiting the plough's touch, rushed onwards beneath the great skies. By 1831 the pestilence had reached England.

Its spread was attributed to miasmatics, or bad air. Bonfires were supposed to have powerful disinfective properties. Their purifying, guttering breath was like a beacon, marking the passage of evil. But in fact no one knew how the disease was transmitted or spread from the outlying villages into the cities, how it clambered up from the poor man's hovel to the beds of the rich, crossed empty tracts of barren land, leaped oceans with one giant stride. Nothing was safe from its touch. No one knew why one person was taken and another spared. The disease was a judgement, a warning, the herald of a prophecy, a message from those heavenly powers, now clearly displeased, who destroyed the peasant, the burgher, the bishop and the king alike, without hesitation, without pity, without compassion. Whole families were wiped out, both the decrepit and the newborn.

The pestilence could not be held at bay, neither by penitence nor by supplication. Clusters of candles weathered the icons, to no effect. The strictest quarantine enforced by the army proved useless. Whole sectors of cities were cordoned off, streets disinfected like firebreaks in a forest. But the scourge stepped effortlessly over the barriers, evaded the guards, rode with the death carts out to the perimeters of every zone. Then swept on. The disease stole past the watch at the gates, at the doors, by the ports, its paw marks silent on the roadways, invisible in the dust. This eyeless enemy moved in a thousand forms, ignoring the Passover marks on every door.

Cholera.

Barry stood for a few minutes, alone among his lemon trees, watching the witch renegotiate the uneven descent. Then he called Isaac and ordered him to saddle the bay. He was going to call upon the Governor at once. No, he would eat nothing.

❖ ❖ ❖ ❖ ❖

The Governor was taking a siesta. He lay peacefully asleep in his oriental suite, overlooking the sea. He was still red-eyed and confused when Barry was shown into his private rooms. But it was not his midday somnolence which accounted for his difficulty in understanding Barry's alarms and demands. It was the seductive colours of his gardens and the pure, tideless blue of the Mediterranean in the spring. It is impossible to believe in impending catastrophe when you have taken up residence in an earthly paradise. Barry's talk of blockading the port, severe quarantine restrictions on all shipping, suspension of the fishing industry between the islands, and the possible destruction of The Middens, fell not so much upon deaf as upon uncomprehending ears. He also demanded a vastly increased budget for the hospital, permission to transform the maternity ward into an isolation unit, and money for more staff.

The Governor sat shaking his head. He had enormous respect for Dr James Barry. But surely the doctor was exaggerating. After all, there had been only one isolated death. The disease was not confirmed. The fisherman was not even a native of the island.

"I say, Barry, aren't you being a bit premature?" The Governor splashed his face with cold water from a pale white bowl.

Barry lost his temper.

"Sir. I am your Chief Medical Officer, responsible for the health and well-being of every inhabitant in this colony. I am giving you early warning not of the possible advent of a serious epidemic, but of its presence among us. There may well be thousands of deaths. We have no idea how this disease is spread, and so far there is no treatment and no cure. Our only hope lies in prevention. And the measures to be taken will be unpopular and expensive. I am not offering you my candid advice, sir. I am telling you what has to be done."

There was a terrible pause. The Governor was dumbfounded.

"I wish you a good day, sir," snapped Barry contemptuously. He turned on his heel and stalked out of the Governor's private chambers, his boots ringing on the tiles as he strode away.

❖ ❖ ❖ ❖ ❖

As expected, the first deaths came among the native populations. At the edge of the town there was an unsightly agglomeration of makeshift huts inhabited by the dissolute and the depraved. The Middens was a sort of growth protruding from the smooth white walls, neatly painted porches and brilliant gardens belonging to the richer residents. There could have been no greater contrast with the fragrant enclosures filled with jasmine, oleanders and arum lilies. The Middens was constructed from discarded bricks, driftwood washed up on the beach and old sailcloth abandoned by the fishermen. It looked like the last camp of a defeated army. A foul gutter ran down the central street into which the inhabitants poured waste water mixed with raw excrement and old food. In hot weather the stench was appalling.

Barry had ordered a pump to be installed at a little distance from this heap of disreputable dwellings to provide the inhabitants with clean water. This was a popular move, but did little to alleviate conditions inside the slum itself. A grog shop in the middle of the mass was a popular haunt of visiting sailors, fishermen and prostitutes. It formed the rotten heart of The Middens and there was much coming and going at all hours of the night.

The Governor had not been inclined to leniency when he first took office and was quite of the opinion that The Middens should be razed to the ground, the rat-infested dwellings burned and the populations dispersed. Barry had argued against this policy on the grounds that the pustule would simply reform elsewhere. He proposed improvements in the housing provision and a proper sewage system. But the Finance Committee was unwilling to subsidise the evidently criminal inhabitants and regarded Barry's ideas as a dangerous method of rewarding vice, which smacked of Jacobinism. Barry now wondered whether he should have supported the proposed burning as he entered The Middens some weeks later to inspect the first cadavers consumed by the pestilence.

Here lay a mother and child, browned and fleshless creatures, already frail from immoderate alcohol, venereal infections and persistent hunger. The woman's breasts were shrivelled and lined like old limes, hanging down from her body, the nipples puckered and enlarged. No one had helped her to die. The child lay in a bundle at her side. Barry had the impression that putrefaction must have set in well before death had occurred. An old man hovered in the doorway. He was too fearful to enter.

"Mother of God, have mercy upon us," he droned.

"How long have they been dead?" demanded Barry.

"A day and a night," squeaked the elderly prophet. "May God spare us, spare us. Our sins are counted. The day of His Coming is upon us. The night of our souls has begun."

"Bring me two men. Tell them to wear masks over their faces

and that they will be well paid. Go! Do it!" shouted the doctor, enraged. The old man hovered for a second, then disappeared. Barry sat down beside the dead.

Her mouth hung open, revealing many lost teeth; a result of malnutrition since childhood, Barry guessed. Her eyes were already covered in flies. Barry brushed them aside with a gloved hand. As he did so he noticed a marching line of ants entering the bundle and knew that they were already excavating the corpse before him. She was young, younger than he, pitiful, vulnerable, exposed in death, her fingers crisped, emaciated, clutching at nothing. She lay alone. No candle burned in the wretched semi-dark of the shack. The hovel was empty of possessions. Either she had nothing, or, more likely, the vultures had already passed as she lay dying. Outside, the heat shimmered in the stagnant gutters. The stench of rotting flesh was overwhelming. Barry waited in the silence. Far away he could hear the sound of dogs barking and barking.

At last two desperate-looking men appeared in the doorway, carrying an old blanket. One of them wore a large earring and had a black hat pulled low over his eyes. Barry gave the other his own handkerchief as a mask.

"Wrap the baby together with the mother. Don't touch them. Then follow me."

All the doors of The Middens remained closed as the bizarre cortège passed by. There was no cry of grief or formal orchestrated weeping, no followers, no family to mourn the young lives lost to the first kiss of the pestilence. Barry learned later that she had been the dead fisherman's mistress, and that she had worked as a prostitute in the grog shop. They carried her out beyond The Middens through the rim of bush surrounding the town and into a deserted vineyard. The old roots were still flushed with fresh green, but unpruned, struggling, smothered in bright weeds. And it was here that they dug the first pits consecrated to the disease. Barry ordered lime to be thrown upon the bodies. There was no priest, no prayers. Barry stood above the grave, gazing past the burning hills to the dark sea beyond.

Late that night he called upon the Governor again. The Middens were burnt to the ground.

Despite this terrible step, the disease would not be checked. Like a dog who has had the pleasure of the first kill, the pestilence set off through the dark streets, hungry for the slow slaughter by black vomit and liquid excrement. Barry's usual hygiene precautions had improved the level of public health in the poorer quarters of the town. The regular burning of the rubbish piles, once picked over by stray hounds and cats, had reduced the usual levels of dysentery. The morning passage of the closed wagons, emptying the privvies, became a popular sanitary improvement, and the education sessions at the maternity clinic had made a little difference to the rates of infant mortality. But the pestilence, certain of its ground, tenacious, enterprising, stepped casually past all his barricades, evading the bonfires, which became a regular and dangerous sight on the streets. During the first few weeks of May the early summer heat increased and the number of deaths rose alarmingly. Barry ordered the immediate cremation of the bodies and a total blockade of the port. The English inhabitants retreated to their summer mountain homes in panic. The economy was paralysed; the Governor's nerves were in shreds.

No one knew how the disease was transmitted, but Barry suspected that the water supply was contaminated. He became even more fanatical on the subject of cleanliness and gave emphatic commands concerning the spring source above the hospital. All water was to be boiled. No matter what its provenance. Official notices concerning the new sanitary regulations were posted on walls all over the town. The hospital incinerator worked overtime. The danger of fire increased. Their stock of sheets and dressings was almost exhausted. Some of the colonial ladies donated their silk petticoats and fine curtains, which were duly shredded and restitched. Mrs Harris set up a committee, The Ladies Health Defence League, which met to discuss fundraising for widows and orphans and pronounced freely on all subjects. The loose morals of the islanders were responsible for bringing the pestilence down upon them all. Significant changes would have to be made. The Ladies set about the process of moral rearmament with zeal and gusto.

Stray animals were killed on sight. The schools were closed.

A curfew was put into effect, which curtailed the activities of the taverns and the grog shops. The usual pilgimages up to the monasteries on particular saints' days were cancelled by order of the Governor. Against this order there was much murmuring and dissent. If ever the island needed the intercession of the saints it was now, in the time of judgement and despair. Some of the people made the journey anyway, only to find the monastery doors locked against them by the terrified monks.

Barry hardly slept. From his office at the hospital he kept track of the disease on a great blackboard to which he pinned a detailed map of the island. He calculated the number of deaths, the locations of fresh outbreaks. He feared that it looked like the cricket scores. He could chart the progress of the pestilence, but he was powerless to stop it. The disease, indifferent, arrogant, mocked him with its success. The blockade of the port was complete. The island was solitary, adrift.

❋ ❋ ❋ ❋ ❋

When the first deaths came in the barracks Barry evacuated the camp. Isaac was the bringer of bad news. He came to the hospital in the first cool of the evening. Barry was completing his ward rounds, exhausted. Two more of the villagers in St Helen's had been found dead in their beds that morning. His staff, who had, miraculously, been spared until then, were no longer reliable. One of the nurses had fled back to his relatives on the other side of the island, leaving them short-handed. Isaac rattled the screen door, but did not wait for Barry's voice. He entered at once.

"Corporal Jarret, the trumpeter, is dead," said Isaac flatly in Greek, knowing that Barry would understand him all too well. "He complained of pains, a burning mouth and the fever. He vomited at four yesterday afternoon and died at six this morning."

Barry looked at him steadily. Isaac returned to English.

"Master, what is to be done?"

Barry passed a hand over his eyes.

"Well, there is no one left to blow the last post," he said gloomily. Then he turned to Isaac.

"The plans are laid. We are ready for this. Tell the Deputy Governor that we must evacuate the barracks now. Today. Start this minute. Leave only a minimum force to protect property and prevent looting. Call for volunteers. I want the rest of the regiment to take up their summer quarters in the mountains."

Barry gazed at the blackboard with its map and lengthening list of the dead, the stack of hospital reports, his great leather account books, untouched for weeks. His usually tidy office was now dusty and cluttered.

Isaac stood close to his master, waiting. Barry patted his arm affectionately.

"Go now. Tell Walter Harris to act quickly."

"Sir. Come home. Sleep," said Isaac firmly in English. Barry looked up, surprised. Then he said, "Thank you, Isaac. I believe I will."

Barry had been interred in a terrible dreamless slumber when Psyche's growling pulled him back into the unyielding heat and the brutal consciousness of the epidemic pushing westwards, into the tiled courtyards and papered salons of the colony's heart. He sat upright abruptly, alarmed by the implications of the young corporal's death. You are here to heal the world, to bind up wounds, to cure fevers and putrefactions, to greet the newborn and alleviate the moment of departing, you are here to cut out the diseased flesh, so that the body may possess itself again. You are here to wipe the tears from their eyes. Barry was ruled by the desire to control all the world he touched. He was not a man who found it easy to delegate. He hated the uncontrollable and the unknown. Yet this pestilence was always ahead of him. He had been outwitted.

Someone was knocking at his locked door.

Barry pulled on his jacket. His red curls stuck to his forehead. The room smelt of sweat and eau de cologne. He opened the door. Captain James Loughlin stood over him, red-faced, impatient and anxious.

"I say, Barry. Sorry to barge in. Isaac didn't want me to wake you. But we're leaving. Now. I know it's on your orders. But I couldn't go without saying goodbye."

Loughlin took his leave with the suppressed emotion and iron control expected of a soldier. But he was unable to leave unsaid the very things that were still simmering in the air between them.

They stood facing one another in the half dark. James lost the thread at once.

"Listen, Barry, I know that you're in the front line, as it were. And you know how much your friendship means to me. Well, it's just that, you know, we're both called James. And I've always felt, you being older and all that, well, you've got such authority and know so much, I never studied like you did . . . By God, James, you're the man I could have been."

"I hardly think so, my dear," said Barry and Loughlin could hear both his affection and his smile. "Now off with you. I want the regiment gone before midnight."

James made one more effort to tell Barry how much he loved him and how terrified he was that he would return to find that the tiny, heroic doctor was dead.

"I don't know how to say this," he mumbled.

"Then don't."

"It's just that – I mean – I might never see you again to say it . . ."

A look of exquisite pain passed over the doctor's face. Suddenly he reached up to James and embraced him tightly.

"I know. But don't say it. You'll bring bad luck upon us. I'll miss you too. Take care. Boil all your water. Don't forget that. Don't do silly things. Keep William company."

Having delivered this motherly advice in so intimate a way, Dr Barry executed a brisk salute and sent Captain Loughlin off down the steps, away down the dark roads, on the first stage of his journey to the cool safety of the mountains. James looked back and saw the small, tense figure of the doctor, holding up the lantern, back straight, head up, peering out into the night.

✤ ✤ ✤ ✤ ✤

By September the hottest part of the season was over and the daily tally of victims began to drop. Barry's scoreboard registered the retreat of the disease. Gorged, satiated, the pestilence gathered itself up and withdrew from their gates. The cremation fires no longer blackened the eastern aspect of the vineyard. The lime pits were marked and sealed. By October the churches, freshly painted, were reopened and the thanksgiving mass shook the brilliant, coloured domes. The icons were carried gleaming through the streets and then replaced in their ranks before the screens on beds of fresh, scented pine. Like a summer storm, the visitation had passed over the island, then blown itself out beyond the seamed white cliffs in the great expanse of blue.

Out of a population of roughly fifteen thousand, nearly three thousand were dead. The English colony had escaped largely unharmed, as had the rural poor, the solitary shepherds and their families, lost in the mountains. Some never even heard of the epidemic until the danger was long past. But the town itself and the fishermen's habitations had been mercilessly liquidated. The people regarded the pestilence as a judgement, paid over their fortunes to the churches and wept for their sins. Barry attributed the rapid spread of the contagion to poor hygiene, bad housing and inadequate sanitation. The Governor shook his head sadly. His daughter had prayed for the doctor's safety, with increasing fervour, every night in the mountains. It was high time that she was removed to England.

The blockade of the port was maintained three weeks into November. When no fresh case had been reported for over twelve weeks, Barry lifted the quarantine regulations and the boats which had been stranded, bobbing all summer in the blue water, could finally enter the harbour or depart. Sometimes the owners were dead and lengthy histories of insurance and inheritance were told in the refurbished grog houses and taverns on the wharf. Some of the sloops lay rotting, subsiding gently at their moorings until they were dragged ashore and dismembered to rebuild The Middens. For the pustular swelling on the cheek of the town was regrouping its forces and preparing to rise, like an already putrefying Phoenix, from its own ashes. Barry watched over its corpulent swelling, helpless and depressed. He could not simply order the people not to be homeless, drunk and poor. But when the first winter rains came, tender, grey and misty in the mountains, the streets smelt fresh and clean, as if the earth wept for the lost and promised a gentle restoration. The redcoats marched back into town with a spring in their steps, returning victorious to retake the territory once the enemy had long since departed.

The first boat from England sailed into the harbour, carrying a six-month mountain of outdated newspapers and longed-for rolls of cloth, with new patterns and fashions from the best haberdashers and outfitters in London and in Paris, to be greeted by a makeshift band and a cheering crowd. The port health authorities and the customs officers were jostled by the excited colonists as they climbed aboard. Barry watched the arrival through his telescope from the eyrie on the hospital verandah. George Washington Karageorghis was somewhere among the mass, searching the cargo hold for the hospital stores. The doctor left instructions at the hospital for their unloading and then returned to his house and his studies.

He was reading Pierre Louis's *Essay on Clinical Instruction*, a volume which exactly corresponded to his own views on scientific hospital medicine. Barry believed not only in diagnosis based on the patient's symptoms, but also in the importance of each patient's individual and family history. Observation, watchfulness, intuition were the hallmarks of Barry's methods. He kept abreast of all the latest developments. He now owned a wooden box containing three mono-aural stethoscopes, each handsomely polished, and, being Chief Medical Officer with a licence to terrify the sick, he now used them openly, spreading consternation and relief in equal measure among his patients, who were convinced that he possessed infallible methods of detection. He listened to their bodies, bubbling and rasping at the other end of his long tube. He did not believe that Nature was implacably opposed to him. Indeed, he sought to understand the elements in her struggle with disease and to fight alongside her. He was impressed by the Paris school. He wished he had studied in Paris.

James Barry was completely absorbed by Louis's quantitative categorisations of symptoms. The first chill of evening had descended when he heard footsteps, which disturbed him strangely, advancing up the dusty roadway. He stood up and looked out at the two figures approaching in the faint light of a lantern attached to the pack on the side of a donkey. He knew Isaac at once, here he came, bringing the doctor's new books, equipment and tailored clothes, ordered direct from Bond Street, carefully cut according to his diminutive specifications. And he knew the figure who strode alongside Isaac's stooping lurch. At first just an outline in darkness, the hangman's wide shoulders, the mane of white hair falling onto the collar, the mass of white whiskers, which would have looked pretentious and ridiculous on a younger or a smaller man. But above all, Barry recognised the proud turn of the head, the sure stride, still there in a man of sixty, the curve of his shoulder as he turned to look back at the town, lit like a chain of glittering trinkets, a necklace around a faceless black void.

Barry flung himself down the steps and into the old man's arms.

"Hello, soldier!"

Francisco took Barry's small form into his embrace with a father's tenderness. Barry leaned into that gigantic warm strength, still there after all the years travelling the world. The tears he had not let fall for over a decade washed down the doctor's cheeks. But he spoke quite clearly, and without hesitation or fear.

"You must tell me every detail, Francisco. I want to hear everything. But there is no need to speak the main news. If it were not so, you would not be here. My mother is dead."

❖ ❖ ❖ ❖ ❖

This is the story told by General Francisco de Miranda.

"The guava has an intense musky, sweetish smell. Here. This confiture has been made from the fruit. No sugar has been added. Taste it. There. Exceptional, isn't it? I remembered that you used to like sweet things. Even when you were a baby, you used to dip your finger into the apricot preserves. The flesh of the fruit contains dozens of tiny seeds. I remove them when making the jam. The taste is especially distinctive in my planter's punch. Here is the rule of proportions: one of sour and two of sweet, three of strong and four of weak. For sour I use squeezed limes, for sweet I take the cane molasses which darkens the mixture, for strong the island's rum. And for the fourth measure I use the juice of oranges, grapefruit, mangoes, and guavas. Some of the colonists drink this for breakfast! We served it later in the morning, and then slept well during our siestas.

"Mary Ann loved the tropics. She was like you. She thrived in the heat and never suffered from the insects. She wasn't like the other white women, who wilted into the mountains. We intended to sail on to Venezuela next spring. I wanted her to see my country. I had no fears for her health. She was full of good spirits, ideas, adventures. She armed herself with loose white shawls and parasols. She hired a guide with a mule. She learned Spanish. She had the soul of an explorer. You should be proud of her. The colonial wives received her well enough. The place is rather like it is here, I imagine – too small to support old scandals. Or at least nothing bad enough to ostracise someone blown in upon the fresh wind of curiosity. We installed ourselves in a very handsome residence, where the biggest slave market on the island used to be held. You could have watched the sales from our front verandah. The slaves have some rights now, some channels of justice to which they can appeal. They cannot, without their consent, be sold on to other masters. But it still happens. As for the freed slaves, after seven years as indentured labourers they are free to work where they can. But I feel dreadful pity for the offspring of the two races, whose numbers are increasing. Often they belong nowhere, and to no one.

"I cannot imagine being owned. All my life I have fought for the freedom of men to lift up their heads and look the next man in the eye, proudly and without fear. God created all men in His own image. But I suppose this is a man's view. For when I said as much to Mary Ann she declared that women's bodies are always for sale, to the highest bidder. But that only harlots manage to keep the cash. Condorcet was of the same opinion. He was a great advocate of the rights of women. I knew him when I was in Paris. Poor fellow. He died an unjust death.

"Well, we lived within sight of the docks where the slave traders were unloaded. Our own servant, Immaculata, witnessed these things, for she has been on the island for over twenty years. The slaves were made to stand upon blocks to be sold. They were sold a day or two after their arrival, so that the planters could be given due notice of the sale. On the day of the sales the captains of the slave ships used to raise their ensigns and fire off a gun to give notice of the event. The indentured servants were sold on the wharf, but some of the plantation slaves were sold on board ship and then deposited directly into the waiting wherries. Many of them died of infections, or the bloody flux. Some were found dead in the hold. The planters were prepared to pay substantial amounts for a healthy slave. Many of the townsfolk, especially the women, took pity on these poor people and rushed to give them food and clean water. Immaculata used to prepare fresh fried fish for them as soon as she heard that the slavers were in dock. The general outrage at seeing these half-starved, maddened creatures emerging into daylight sometimes caused trouble in the port. One of the captains, known to be a cruel man, was mobbed and beaten. Immaculata told us proudly of her part in this riot. Like Simon Peter, she was personally responsible for slicing off the tyrant's ear. I think this is why so many of the sales were conducted on board ship. For my part I am glad to hear a tale of such simple humanity.

"For the freed slaves they now hold hiring fairs, as they did in the stableyard at David's house when you were a child. Sometimes I think it is much the same. But at least the Negroes negotiate their own terms.

"Here is your mother's first drawing of our house. She has signed and dated this one. We had tiled floors and a handsome verandah circling the house on the first floor. There was always a sea breeze at Port Royal, so that the heat was never oppressive. We enjoyed the daily excitement when the ships came in. The dockyards are on the sheltered harbour side. You can see them clearly here, these wooden buildings, capped like pagodas. Most of the buildings are in the Spanish style, raised on stakes, with walls of wood. These resist earthquakes far better than the British-built brick buildings do. Earthquakes are terrifying, but what are they but old mother earth yawning and stretching out her bones. Did you read of the earthquake, soldier? No, the famous one that happened long before the Lisbon catastrophe. Port Royal used to be a wealthy place. Some of the ruined buildings are still there. Look, this is the graveyard. While I was a resident in Port Royal, I witnessed the pious burial of many of those unfortunate, unwilling travellers from the slave ships. Not only the slaves but convicts and dissenters from their own nations, are laid to rest here, outside Palisadoes Gate. This is the same graveyard which split apart in the earthquake of 1692, yielding up its dead some-

what before the appointed Resurrection Day. People still tell
stories of that day. Here are your mother's sketches of the graveyard. All the shattered and cracked stones date from that time.
Look at this one. DIEU SUR TOUT. With the skull and crossbones
beneath. It is the tombstone of Lewis Galdy, who survived the
earthquake. And here on the other side she has copied the
inscription."

HERE LYES THE BODY OF

LEWIS GALDY

WHO DEPARTED THIS LIFE AT
PORT ROYAL
THE 22d DECEMBER 1739 AGED 80

HE WAS BORN AT MONTPELIER IN FRANCE BUT
LEFT THAT COUNTRY FOR HIS RELIGION AND
CAME TO SETTLE IN THIS ISLAND WHERE HE WAS
SWALLOWED UP IN THE GREAT EARTH-QUAKE IN
THE YEAR 1692 AND BY THE PROVIDENCE OF GOD
WAS BY ANOTHER SHAKE THROWN INTO THE SEA
AND MIRACULOUSLY SAVED BY SWIMMING UNTIL
A BOAT TOOK HIM UP. HE LIVED MANY YEARS
AFTER IN GREAT REPUTATION BELOVED BY ALL
THAT KNEW HIM AND MUCH LAMENTED AT HIS
DEATH

"A curiosity, isn't it? I smiled too when I saw her sketches. A
strange history. Lewis Galdy's life was remarkable not for his own
efforts but for the miracle which preserved him. What will they
write upon our graves, soldier? What will they say of our lives?

"Mary Ann enjoyed the markets. We inherited two domestic
servants. The passionate Immaculata, who assaulted the captain,
and an indentured black called True Repose. She was on excellent
terms with both of them because she was strict, but fair-minded.
They marched off three times a week in a convoy of rippling
baskets to the central market on High Street, which was the
source of all our fruit, herbs and poultry. Mary Ann purchased a

grotesque brace of live turtles and turned them into delicacies. The fish market was on the wharf near the wherry bridge. She always bought her fish from one man, whom she befriended, a giant freed slave. He never worked for whites again, but earned his living as a fisherman. No one knows how he purchased the boat. His two front teeth were missing and he whistled when he spoke. A peculiar mixture of Spanish and Creole. I couldn't understand him, but she could. They stared at one another as if in recognition, and I thought that this was a silent form of haggling. And then she would choose fine crabs, great flat fish with a marline spike for a nose and lobsters moving slowly in a damp straw-lined crate. But only from this man, no matter how importunate the other piscadores became, pressing their wares upon her. True Repose was very frightened of the black fisherman and said that he was a *maraboutier*. If for some reason Mary Ann did not buy the fish, our boy went elsewhere.

"Your mother knew what everything cost, soldier. She never overspent. Your mother was a canny, thrifty woman. It was a quality I always admired.

"Our residence fronted the western end of Queen Street, and we had a handsome row of palms lining the walkway. Our salon faced away from the dockyards towards the public gardens and the fortress. There was a brick yard at the back, with the cookhouse, storerooms and access to a fine vaulted cellar, built after the earthquake with bricks from the old house. The wood warps and fades with the sea storms. We painted the façade every year in the calm, cooler weather before the spring rains.

"There's a well here to the left, with a pump behind it. We never used that water. In fact we had our water imported from the mineral springs at the Rock. But even then I took your advice and had it all boiled. Even for domestic purposes. But we drank fine wines from Madeira, which I bought from the importers at a good price. And Mary Ann enjoyed the punch I made. She could hold her liquor as well as any man. As well as you do. But of course she never touched a drop in public.

"These are the red clay pipes which the local craftsmen made. Only two appear to have snapped during my voyage. Look at this geometric design, here, on the top of the stem, where it meets the bowl. This is typical of the West Indian pipes. All the Negroes use them. The whites still use the kaolin clay imports from Bristol. It's a form of snobbery. The red ones are just as good. Here, I'll make one up for you. And we can enjoy a tropical smoke together. Mary Ann used to joke with the rough women down by the fishing port. They sit, bare-footed and half-dressed, smoking pipes like these on their front steps, and shouting advice at anyone who passes by.

"All the cooking was done outside. We imported wood and charcoal from the mainland. Mary Ann meddled with the cooks, but they grew to respect her. She rationed out all the meat and fish for the household and was never parted from her keys. But she learned to master the oven and the chimney. Her hands were sunburnt and hard by the end of the first year. She used to complain about that, but never gave up her policy of domestic interference. Salvatore soon spoke Creole as fluently as Spanish, and they both operated like unpaid spies on the yard workers.

"Ah, Rupert! Did Mary Ann never tell you? No, Rupert was dead by then. We lost him on the voyage out. We were on board HMS *Hercules*. There was a good deal of sickness during the trip. He died from a screaming fever, which he had caught during our time in the Azores, and which returned some weeks later as we entered the tropics. I nursed him myself during the last days. I wouldn't have Mary Ann in the cabin for fear of her health. How he clutched the crucifix in which he had no faith. I miss him still. He was not an old man. I could have expected to die before him. We buried him at sea. And despite the weights the body did not at once vanish. The thing floated, beautiful in the green Atlantic, and set sail, cresting the waves, carried on a fair wind, choosing its way back, back to the cold north. We watched him bobbing away, his shroud white against the grey waves. Then the feet pitched downwards and he sank down into the dark. We turned once more in the direction of the islands. Rupert turned back, taking the way we had already come.

"Mary Ann wept many days for him. I am very surprised that she said nothing about it. I find that most odd.

"Ah, that is not one of the drawings I can let you have, soldier. That one I must keep with me always. It is the outline of her stockinged left foot. Almost as small as yours. The cobbler at Port Royal was a young Portuguese man, originally a fine-tooled leather worker, fallen on hard times. She ordered some tough riding boots for her forays into the interior. There are snakes, not, on the whole, dangerous, but many insects and jiggers in the wet earth. She needed a strong pair of boots. In the hills we saw dozens of peenie-wallies, which is what they call the fireflies, shining numinous green in the dark. The Negroes in the kitchen yards collect them in glass jars and use them as lanterns. I remember the fireflies in the evenings, caught in the folds of her white shawls as she walked in the warm nights. We stayed here, in this house, The Heights, at Silver Hill. She has used watercolours for the ferns, but the house was sketched first, in ink. It was very plain inside. Polished hardwood floors, with scuttling cockroaches. The smell is repulsive if you have the misfortune to tread upon them. The beds were giant fourposters with moth-eaten drapes. The day of the great houses is already past. We saw mansions ruined, overgrown with vines and guinea grass, their slatted shutters grey and buckled, like driftwood parched and bleached by the damp heat and the great rains.

"I was there to investigate the conditions of the slaves. Not only on my estates. It was very difficult to find blacks who were willing to talk to me. This was why we made numerous journeys into the interior. I found that the prospect of emancipation made little difference to the wretched conditions of these disinherited people. I found whole families living in insanitary huts on the brink of famine. Those whose old masters had been declared bankrupt were the most unfortunate. I was shown empty, derelict houses where the people had perished of starvation and disease. Sometimes they fled, looting the great houses for anything they could find, and lived, half savage, in the wastelands and smoking bushes. Sometimes their hovels were adorned with porcelain plates and candlesticks stolen from the plantation residences, but they had no candles and no food. Mary Ann was unable to draw the people who lived here, in this shack. They were too afraid to sit for her. And too ashamed.

"Here is their church. See, the porch is neatly repaired, and the stone steps swept clean. I have rarely seen such courage and such faith among any people. A group of rebels formed on one of the Trelawney estates. I tried to make contact with them. They lived together like the early Christians, and held all things in common. They had decided to draw up a proclamation setting out their grievances, but none of them knew how to write. A people that cannot read and write can never be free. Eventually the rebels were tracked down, rounded up and shot. They had no weapons, only their sickles and hoes. The master's tools are the only ones we can ever use to pull his house down. Sometimes I think that I should have been a schoolmaster, not a soldier, my dearest child. The most precious thing that I gave you was your education. All those hours that we spent together in the library. They are dear memories for me now. We were very happy then, were we not? The three of us, with Rupert and Salvatore robbing me blind downstairs. Sometimes you have a look of her. Just a hint of her beauty. You have the same pale skin, and ah, it hurts a little, even now, you have the same smile.

"She gave up the parasols and hats when she took to going out fishing in the little boats, and her arms and nose were spangled with small brown freckles. Just like the ones you are sporting now, soldier. I thought that she had never looked more beautiful.

"She could swim, my dear. Your mother could swim. She wasn't afraid of that eerie blue-green water, where you could see clear to the bottom. I don't know what happened. No one will ever know. She went out early in the evening. I heard her voice below, in the yard. She left by the back door. I always looked out when I heard her voice. From the balcony I saw her hair and ribbons, jaunty as a ship in full trim, under way, taking the corner of Queen Street, avoiding the docks and going straight on past the fortress walls. She often went out alone. There was no danger. It was still bright at five-thirty, but the night hour was approaching. When she did not return at the usual time, I went out calling for her. Salvatore and True Repose came with me. I wasn't alarmed. Even when we saw that the skiff was still missing. There was a fair breeze and a rocking sea, but the air was gentle and tender. It was a peaceful evening. I expected to see her, far out, her lines set, waving from the cradle of the sea.

We went out among the cacti and the scrub grass along the inner arm of the Palisadoes spit, looking out at the steady waves, the brisk white tips, appearing, vanishing, again and again. We called and called along the shore, Mary Ann, Mary Ann. And there was nothing there, only the windswept sand against our boots and the last light, naked and red on the sloping stone walls and the bobbing masts.

"I sounded the alarm. We gathered men, boats, horses. Every inch of the shoreline was searched that night. The sand was a mass of shouts and torches. As the hours drew on I became desperate. But I could not believe that she would not be found, sunburnt and chiding, barefoot on the roadways. I heard her voice, soldier, in the night birds, in the lapping waves, in the gull's cry over the spit in the early dawn.

"They came to me at first light. The priest's eyes were terrible with the news.

"We hurried to the little port at the far end of the docks where the fishermen's boats come in. It was the giant black fisherman she had always chosen, the man she had singled out, his huge frame bent over her in the bottom of his boat. As I looked down from the dock, he made space for her body among his lobster pots and the stirring claws of his creatures on the damp planks. His huge black arm was around her shoulders. He pushed the wet hair back from her face and gazed into her cloudy, drowned eyes.

" 'Yoh woman, Massa?'

"He looked up at me, the words whistling through his lost teeth, the gums skinned and pale in the fresh light.

" 'Pretty-pretty woman.'

"Her face was still hers, for it had been masked and covered by her full skirts, but her hands and arms were almost gone, eaten away to the bone. How long does it take to drown, soldier? How quickly would she have perished in that clear mass of translucent green? The boat was never found. The verdict was accidental death, based on the fisherman's testimony. He said that he had pulled her up in his nets just as dawn was breaking. I believed him. He loved Mary Ann. He was telling the truth.

I saw how gently he touched her dead body, his giant hands tender on her cold, white skin.

"What was left to me then?

"I knew that I would go back to Venezuela to end my life there. But first, I had to find you.

"Turn over the drawing she made of Lewis Galdy's tomb. Look at the back. That is the inscription I chose to be carved on her gravestone. She is buried in the cemetery at Port Royal, within hearing of the shouts from the port, the quiet rocking of the boats and the fresh sea wind.

"On the last night we were together she talked about you. We sat there on the verandah in the coming dark and she talked about you. I know that she wrote to you, soldier, almost every day. But she hardly ever spoke about you, except to share her letters. And she never spoke about the past. That's why I noticed the occasion. It was out of the ordinary. There is hardly any twilight in the tropics. Maybe ten minutes of dusk. Then the rush of darkness, with Tarquin's ravishing strides. It is very sudden. When we were inland we drew the blinds at once, for the mosquitoes are drawn to the light. But there are fewer insects down by the sea. There is a fresh wind. There, we used to watch the night come. From our perch we could hear the creeping rise and slap of the sea. At first light we would sometimes go down to watch the fishermen unloading the night's catch. We lived by the rhythm of the sea. It is eternal there. There are no great tides. There are no markers, no seasons, just the May rains and the October hurricanes to map out the year. I was afraid that she would miss the northern spring. But she never did. That was our last night together. And she talked to me about you.

" 'I have had so little satisfaction in my life, Francisco. I think that, until now, I have never been completely happy. I have always wanted something other than what I had. I was never accepted, never acknowledged. What was I? A rich man's wife, a drunkard's poor widow, another rich man's mistress. Always a man's possession. No, don't say anything. It's true. I was always a man's possession. Even yours. That's why I asked you to do it. You were the three men I had every right to command. I asked you to give my child the life I never had. My child has a position in the world. She will be respected, remembered. My child will have the freedom I never enjoyed. My child will be a gentleman, well-educated, well-travelled. My child will see the countries of which I dreamed, but never saw, will eat foods I have heard of, but never tasted. What else can a woman desire for her child, but a larger, wider life than the one she has inherited? Oh yes, I wanted to give her happiness and joy, but more than that, I wanted her to have the power to choose. There was no other way to manage the affair.

" 'You said it was a masquerade, a lie. How could anyone think that, Francisco? I have acted a part every moment of my existence. Even now. Even with you. No, don't speak. For once, let me have my say. What is my role here? I am the famous general's pretty mistress. Even you – with all your radical opinions – you couldn't change what people think of a young widow woman who lives with an older man. Of course they are polite to me. They wouldn't dare to behave otherwise. But out of respect for you, fear of you, not out of regard for me. It was always so. My life has been made safe by your money, and your fame. My child has protected herself, fought for herself, made her own life, earned her own name. And that was my doing. I set her free.' "

"I think that she was more honest with me then than she had ever been. There was love in her eyes, and passion in her face, in her gestures. She was thinking of you. Her whole heart was with you. She sent you to us on that damp midsummer night. She was the source of the plot, soldier. It was her idea. We all loved her so much. What was she asking of us? To give you the chance to live something other than a woman's life. She gave you up to us, my dearest child, because she loved you more than anyone else in the world. More than she loved me, more than she loved any one of us. She was the woman who held all the cards and the dice. She set the rules of the game. It was a game worth playing, don't you think so, soldier?"

"I don't know," said Barry.

PART FIVE

Tropics

THIS IS UNHAPPINESS. Sitting alone in the night, listening to the cicadas, the frogs and the great white owls, watching the moonlight move on the mosquito net, knowing that I have grown old. I hold a letter in my hands. I have read this letter again and again. There is now but one person in the world who remembers me when I was a child. The others are all gone, all gone. The first woman I loved, so cunning, duplicitous and brave, slipped away into this transparent sea. Hers was a kind of vanishing, an uneasy, ambiguous death. And my revolutionary General, for whom I imagined an heroic finale in battle, a grand public funeral, his horse following the gun carriage, the boots reversed in the stirrups, flags at half-mast and endless eulogies of praise? No cannon sounded at the last for him. He died of old age, under house arrest in his own country, decrepit and incontinent, in a sea of piss and dribble.

Here, even at the most angry height of summer, I feel the sea wind on my cheek. I watch the lizards freeze on the mill wall, blending quietly into the lichen and the stone. I cannot hide. And no disguise is necessary now. I have no fears of discovery. What should I fear? The mask has become the face.

Nothing is sadder than these men with their twisted hands, these women with their lined and silent faces, waiting for me, waiting for me. One of the women holds a child wrapped in a filthy cotton shawl. The thing is dying. Its skin is already grey and flies are gathering around the mouth. There will be nothing I can do. I will administer a pink tonic from Volpone's bag and tell her that the Lord giveth and the Lord will very probably take away. She has ten children already, by several different men. She sits gazing at me, silent, waiting. She loves this child. This one. Bone of her bone, flesh of her flesh. As my mother loved me. The baby's eyes are vacant, glassy, yellowing at the rim. Better dead, better dead, better dead.

I stroke the child's tiny ruff of hair. The woman breathes her blessing over me and I retreat to my surgery, hot, angry and ashamed.

But don't forget, these people whom you serve sell their children too, sell them – boys and girls of eight or ten – as workers, prostitutes, servants. There is not enough food in this place to feed them all. Sometimes I find the children brutalised, bleeding, cowering like animals in my surgery. A small boy was left before the door last week. He had no guardian, no clothes and no name. His collar-bone was fractured, his face cut and bruised. He was bleeding from the anus, which I found to be rotting with venereal disease. He can have been no more than six or seven years old. The child shrinks from my touch. No white man has ever touched him gently. He has been beaten, raped, abused. His eyes are huge as he listens to me, talking to him softly. He understands nothing. I leave him sitting quietly, stroking Psyche, his arm in a sling, and cross the road in the boiling dust to call on the Augustinian sisters in their cool white corridors with their blue shutters, closed against the heat, and I beg them to take one more, just one more. When I come back into the surgery the child has his arms around Psyche and he has fallen asleep. She licks his face. I stand over them, my fists clenched.

My hair is heavy with grey streaks and grey dust. My hands are covered with liver spots. What difference have I made? What difference have I ever made? I gather up the sleeping child in my arms. His elbows and knees project bonily out of his black skin. He snuggles his head against my neck.

Why can I achieve so little here?

If they live, they live. If they must die, then nothing I can do will save them. This place has defeated me, this sweating humid bush, jiggers in the dust, white nights drenched in stars and the clinging yellow fever. The colonists lie sweating beneath their silk mosquito shrouds.

Only in the mountains does the air thin and chill. Here, in these beautiful steep, wooded hills I catch my breath in the night air. I stopped my guide so that I could identify a tree orchid, shedding its humid torrent of scent upon the overgrown dirt of the pot-holed road, one single track, wolfed down by green. The flower was nothing much, white spindly petals and coiling tendrils anchoring the plant to the damp bark. It was not there to be seen, but to be smelt, a gift handed down to a tired and lonely man.

For this is unhappiness. But I will not shrink from my melancholy, nor from my loneliness. The letter falls from my hand. I will spend this night remembering. Sitting here alone in the shrieking white night and knowing that I will always be alone, no matter how long I watch at the open door, no matter how many nights there are to come.

❖ ❖ ❖ ❖ ❖

The first days when I came to this place become more luminous and vivid with the ebbing years. I can remember the boat coming ashore in a rocky cove to the west of Montego Bay. The shouts of the blacks on the beach, and the men in straw hats rowing together, and the lap and splash of clear water against the coral reefs, rocking like planted gardens beneath the sea. I smelt cooking in the clear air. We drove into town aboard a rickety cart drawn by two mules, covered in fly-blown sores where the harness pinched. I gazed out at the hills sheathed in the slender bright green tapers of the bamboo forest. The colours were too bright and too close. There was no perspective, no distance. I made many studies of the vegetation during those first weeks. Behind my garden there was a morass of log-wood, prickly yellow broad-leaf and trumpet trees with the wild fig pushing a curtain of green against the grey branches of a dead cotton tree. In this place I bear witness daily to the resurrection. For nothing stays dead for long. The entire world appears to be in the grip of a perpetual metamorphosis.

The vultures who assist this process of destruction and rebirth are protected by law. They gaze confidently back when you approach, their evil red eyes surrounded by hideous, wrinkled flesh, as they pick at the stinking carcasses of dead animals, thrown out on the rubbish mounds alongside the usual household waste. I have been unable to suppress the practice of abandoning dead animals in the open air and it is true that the John Crows pick them clean within a day. But the town waste pits are now situated at a healthy distance from the habitations, and the rubbish is regularly burnt under the supervision of my sanitation inspector. He once found a dead child wrapped in a sack, carefully stowed away in a wooden crate. The vultures, perched expectantly on the crate, alerted him to the dead flesh within, and upon kicking the crate aside, he discovered the child, which rolled out, its legs bent and shrivelled, unravelling its shroud. The poor thing was less than a year old, so I did not call for an official investigation.

Life is of too little value here. The days are too hot, too bright, the rain too rapid and powerful, the vegetation renews itself too rapidly. The tropics may resemble paradise, at a glance, from a great distance, but living here I can never rid my nostrils of the smell of putrefaction. During the annual epidemics, too many die for me to investigate them all. In 1840 we buried the new regiments in mass graves. If Gomm had not seconded me, and thrown all his influence behind the plan, we would never have established this station in the mountains. Often it appears that I have passed my life here fighting a paper battle with the bureaucrats. Ah, but I shall never forget the thunderous tones of the Field Marshal, bursting into my hospital office with the wild cry of victory: "We have carried the hill, Barry, we have carried the hill!"

And so I was able to build my airy fortress in the Blue Mountains.

I have sat here upon my verandah in the early day, watching the mist thinning into damp drops on the cannons, and then seen the far, low lines of Kingston and the coastline, laid out beneath me, a painted map, delicate at my feet.

We had the illusion of victory, of command. We are a nation of rulers. But no one holds this country. The land itself crouches, flexed and tense, opposing all I am and all I do. No one holds this country. Except perhaps that classic figure with the scythe and the hourglass, who, in the end, will cradle us all in his bony arms.

When I first came here the planters in residence still lived in the grand style. Their huge balconied houses were covered in bougainvillea and deep purple wisteria blossoms. Their irrigated gardens flamed with hibiscus and poinsettia. When they sat down to dine their tables overflowed with meat and fish, land and sea turtles, quails, snipe, plovers, pigeons and doves, mangoes and guineps, pineapples, fresh oranges, plucked from their own groves. But the most excellent fruit is the grenadillo, reduced in its ripeness to a mulch of juice and seeds, well sugared and then scooped out with a spoon. I sigh to remember the exquisite deliciousness of all the meals I have ever eaten in this insect-infested paradise world, from which, for me, there has been no escape. It seems that the tree of life and death is no longer forbidden.

Each white member of the planters' households had a black servant: their personal, domestic slave, to attend upon them, to prepare their wardrobe, enhance their toilette, anticipate all their desires and clear out the shit from their chamberpots. There were no horses in all the King's Stables that were better fed, watered, nourished and groomed than these spoiled and indolent people.

I myself inherited an elderly Negro. His name is Abraham. He is only slightly taller than I. If we let out the seams to their limits and lengthen the sleeves, he can wear my cast-off clothes. He cannot read or write, but I am teaching his sons to do so. He is patient, discreet, white-haired. We stand side by side.

The Creoles were deeply inbred. Inherited diseases were rife within their families. The women were addicted to pleasure and demonstrated a loose sensuality that was shockingly overt. I was once forced to retire from a late supper party by a beautiful lady from Haïti, resplendent in white lace, who deliberately persisted in brushing her fan against the front of my trousers in a vain attempt to arouse me. I was amused by her gesture, in itself flattering, but alarmed that she did not care who saw her.

And yes, the balls and fêtes continue here, and there is a great splicing of patterns and studying of journals, including the latest designs in *The Ladies' Magazine*. What are they wearing in Bond

Street and Paris? We do not ape the fashions of the mother country here, we reproduce them with exaggerated excellence. The boats bringing cloth, already several months out of date, are eagerly awaited. I gaze at a pale mass of bare arms and shoulders, ferociously defended against the sun, drenched in powder, sweat and citronelle, to baffle the mosquitoes. I lead the ladies from the floor, their gloveless hands moist with dancing, and present them with softly opulent shawls and fans.

The estate I came to know best was Montpelier in St James, which then belonged to the Ellis family. Charles Ellis was an absentee landlord, for he was much occupied with his parliamentary duties. But he was not an irresponsible man and his second brother, Edward, a man some twenty years younger than myself, was sent to take care of the estate, after an undistinguished career in an unfashionable regiment.

Edward was a weak and languid man, given to an excess of lace shirts and Portuguese sweet wine. He was exceedingly effeminate and sought the company of ladies at every opportunity. In the hottest season he was unable to stir from a pale draught of warm air which traversed his bedroom and his study, where he lay on the sofa like a discarded damp handkerchief.

I rode over to Montego Bay every six weeks at least, to inspect the hospital and see to the needs of the regiments garrisoned in the north of the island. If the interior was considered unsafe, I made the voyage around the coast, for spontaneous rebellions were, and are, frequent and violent. On each visit I did not fail to spend time with Edward and to observe the life on his estate. To my knowledge Edward never once entered the infirmary, constructed under my personal direction, in all the years he lived in such close proximity with the noble, yet often wretched, creatures upon whom his life, and theirs, depended. He assured me that his aversion to the stench of illness was insuperable and he had promised himself that he would faint at the merest drop of blood. Yet he was a kind, if idle, master, and would not tolerate the grosser punishments, which were freely administered on other plantations.

I supervised the births of many Negro children born at Montpelier. I eased their passage into this world, and, all too often, their rapid departure into the next. One of Edward's slave women, whose name was Jessica, a handsome girl with fine, high cheekbones, velvet black, with a face full of valleys and shadows, gave birth to eight children, only one of whom survived. Who the fathers were, I never knew. Lockjaw is the most common killer, and, as the midwife assured me, "Oh Massa, till de nine days over, we no hope of dem." My most rigorous régime of hygiene and cleanliness was followed at Montpelier. Yet still the infants died. Jessica told me that the souls of her children, liberated from slavery, fled back to Africa. She herself has never seen Africa. This land is her land, for she was born here. This is the only place she has ever known.

The Negroes bury their dead in their own gardens. I was puzzled by this practice at first, as they are an extremely superstitious people and live in terror of ghosts, or duppies as they are called here. But Jessica explained to me that she and her sisters had no fear of the beloved dead, but trembled before the menacing spectres of their enemies.

These people are deeply religious, and each corpse is accompanied to its grave by a whole community's passionate singing and lamenting. I attended the ceremony for the last of Jessica's babes, a child that was stillborn. The slaves were given permission to bury their dead at dusk, when the day's work was over. Despite my advice that she should rest, the woman accompanied the coffin as the principal mourner. At the head of the cortège she sang the most heart-rending melody to the quiet grave in her own language. Her people are called the Eboes and their language is forbidden to them upon punishment by flogging or even death. They eat no meat and have been known to fall ill after eating the flesh of turtles. As she sang, the company stared at me, the only white man present, transfixed with alarm. I took her hand when she had finished, wiped her incessant tears away and cast the first handful of dust into the tiny grave. My shadow leaped across the earth's opening. The company gathered round, crushing inwards. I realised that something was expected of me and so I spoke the *Nunc dimittis* as loudly and as clearly as possible.

"*Lord, now lettest thou thy servant depart in peace, according to thy word: For mine eyes have seen thy salvation, Which thou hast prepared before the face of all people; A light to lighten the Gentiles, and the glory of thy people Israel."*

A huge wail went up as I finished speaking and the rhythmic chanting began. I extracted myself gently from the crowd, gathered in the purple twilight, and left Jessica alone with her people and her dead.

But Death is my companion here, my fellow rider, perched beside me, silent and rattling on his pale horse. The numbers of the deceased in the army alone make my pen falter as I copy them out for my despatches. According to official records, one in nine of all the British soldiers stationed here between 1816 and 1836 was surely doomed to die.

The station at Montego Bay was notorious. The barracks were sited in the town, an evil position in a stone building, cut off from the sea wind. The sweltering temperatures never ebbed. At night the men sweated naked on their foul mattresses. Even the civilians who lived in that malodorous place scarcely passed a year without falling victim to some appalling disease. Ants and termites undermined the buildings. Everything rotted and festered, no matter how carefully it was wrapped or cleaned. Yet still the town grew, alongside its expanding graveyard. Sometimes the seamen entering the harbour emerged spotless and hopeful from their quarantine, only to succumb to the malignant vapours emitted by this unhealthy cauldron. On several occasions I closed the barracks down myself. How could the troops defend the planters when I had scarcely a man who could stand upright? Even the hospital, which was scrubbed daily and maintained with Prussian rigour and fortitude, on my orders, proved to be a lazar house. In 1832 I buried a third of the garrison, with minimal ceremony, in shallow graves.

Part of the solution, as in Spanish Town, was to rebuild the barracks; not on low, swampy ground ridden with mosquitoes and general pestilence, but up on the purple slopes of the volcanic hills, in the cooler air. I demanded buildings with large windows and airy balconies, a muslin mesh firmly fixed to the frames against the nightly armada of insects. We eventually won the station at Newcastle, when Field Marshal Sir William Gomm so memorably "carried the hill" after ten years of persistent bullying.

The north coast was the most unhealthy place in all the world. At Buff's Bay seven out of twenty-five men were dead within the year. In Manchioneal they were all dead, sick or dying when I arrived. There was not a man left in the guardhouse. I rode straight in, unchallenged, followed by a little mob of shrieking children in love with my uniform. The visiting killer is usually yellow fever: our notorious Yellow Jack, who hastens them away to a painful end. In the case of the barracks at Manchioneal, which could have been overrun in a matter of minutes, I took the precaution of sending Abraham out to the rum shop, to spread stories of the good Dr Barry battling with the recalcitrant duppies of the dead soldiers, who, having died so far from home, refused to rest and wandered the fort at all hours. I had the satisfaction of seeing members of the local population scuttling past at high speed, casting fearful glances up at the red brick fort. I'm afraid that Abraham half believed my stories.

In the hot months I could not leave the camp at Kingston. I was needed to fight yet another useless battle against these rapid, clammy fevers and to reconcile myself to inevitable defeat. It was in the cooler months when the stormy season of violent winds and rain, what Abraham calls "de big blow", was safely past that I was able to travel the island without anxiety. I always visited Montpelier towards Christmastime. Sometimes, when the roads had seen little passage for many weeks, they were so overgrown with vines and creepers that Abraham rode ahead on his mule, slashing to left and right with a machete, forging a passage through the smouldering green like Moses faced with a thick green sea.

On one of these December expeditions, shortly before Christmas, on our way to Montpelier, while Abraham was attacking the vegetation some way ahead, I paused to stare at a palm tree, which was afflicted with a strange variety of blight. The large fruit, or rather vegetable, which had formed at the top of the tree, was crawling with a species of strange black roach, and the usually brilliant seeds, often scarlet and purple, were faded and dull. The feathery palm leaves were curling and brown at the tips, yet from its size the tree could not be more than twenty years old. My horse nuzzled the grass as I peered at the dying tree. Then I felt Psyche's muscles tense and she let fly a low growl. Directly before me, uncannily close, inside the steaming, damp cave of bush,were several pairs of eyes, cautious and dark, surrounded by reddened white balls. I could make out a fine nose, then a pair of straight red lips, a jigsaw of black faces, watching from behind the green. I was certain that they were runaway slaves, but I could not pretend not to have seen them. I was armed, both with a sabre and with a musket, but I did not reach for either.

"Step forth." I spoke calmly to the undergrowth, meeting the glare of three pairs of eyes without flinching. Three desperate, ragged-looking men obeyed, and stood, blocking my path, leaning on their ferociously sharpened sticks, cradling their machetes in their arms.

The tallest of the three was instantly recognisable. This was Plato, a runaway black, who had abandoned the Lewises' estate in Cornwall and had then set about terrorising the neighbourhood with many thefts and beatings, and the occasional murder. He was exceptionally good-looking and was rumoured to have a harem of women living with him in the bush. He had robbed many carriages on the Blue Mountain roads and stolen jewels and rings to decorate his numerous brides. A fine fob-watch adorned his frayed waistcoat, underneath which he wore no shirt, so that his magnificent naked chest and shoulders were fiercely visible. We all stood looking at one another. Nobody moved.

"Good morning, Plato."

It was as if we were meeting one another, not for the first time, in perfectly congenial circumstances. Nobody flinched. Then I heard Abraham crashing back towards us through the bush. I could make out the unsteady gleam of his top hat, which he always wore on journeys, and which still bore the name of its maker in Bond Street on the rotted silk inside the brim. The runaways glanced quickly at each other.

"Gud mawnin', Dr Barry," replied Plato suddenly, and smiled. The upper teeth at the front of his mouth were disconcertingly missing and many others were black and loose, from sucking raw cane I supposed. Sucking cane was rumoured to preserve the teeth, but I never noticed that it did. Nevertheless, Plato presented me with a superb and generous smile, his upper lip curled in insolent defiance. We bowed to one another like visiting diplomats and they vanished rapidly away into the wall of green. Psyche set up a frenzied barking and would not be hushed. Abraham, grey with terror, arrived just in time to see them vanish.

"Massa! Dat's Plato!" he hissed in dramatic tones, as if we had both already been murdered and were breathing our last in the dust.

"It was indeed," I replied, "and he seems to know my name."

"Erribuddy know Doctor," snapped Abraham indignantly, as if he would have been personally insulted had Plato and I not recognised one another.

I never mentioned the incident to the military authorities. The poor fellow was caught soon enough. His weakness for rum drew him into the town at Montego Bay and he was betrayed by his regular supplier, the night watchman at the port cargo store, who was tempted into treachery by a handsome reward. Yet Plato went to his death as he had lived, cursing all those who had mistreated and betrayed him, promising them that his vengeful duppy would walk the earth until his blood was appeased. I did not witness the hanging, but I was told that, as he died, one arm shot up in a final salute, like a finger of doom, pointing out the guilty, who were now at his mercy forever.

And sure enough, the night watchman fell victim to a slow wasting disease before the year was out and spat blood as he died. Within a month of Plato's unnatural death the October storms had laid waste a great part of the estate where he had been so brutally whipped and punished. The cane crop was reduced to pulp. There was a great nodding and shaking of heads as Plato's curse took hold. Everyone knew who was responsible. And so Plato's power increased tenfold in death.

The slaves were, on the whole, very cruelly treated. On many of the estates they were kicked and beaten for the slightest offence. In their master's absence, the whites, that is, the attorneys and overseers, were transformed into petty tyrants with the first grasp of power. They were brutal, violent and crude. They took whatever women they wished to possess, often by force. One group of slaves from the Beckford estate was forced to fling themselves on the mercy of the magistrates after some monstrous incident when a young boy was so violently assaulted and flogged with a cartwhip for stealing food, that he died from a punctured lung, in a bubble of blood. The magistrates duly reprimanded the violent deputy, but he was so far departed down the rum bottle that I doubt he paid much attention to the authority of the law. In any case, Savannah la Mar was a long way away from the estate. The abuse continued and the overseer was found with his throat cut, a neat slick slice from ear to ear. There was a certain amount of scandalised murmuring and anxiety among the resident planters, who all expected to wake up one fine morning to find themselves murdered in their beds. There was even a move to arrange some exemplary lynchings on the Beckford estate. I pointed out that slaughtering every Negro the Beckfords owned was an unlikely route to justice, for the incident had taken place in the hills, where, at that time, Plato and his band were still on the loose. The overseer's solitary returning horse had raised the alarm among his people and they had found him shortly thereafter. The body was not yet stiff, although already draped in a red shroud of ants, and the blood was scarcely blackened and congealed upon his collar. A band of runaway slaves, I maintained with some force, was almost certainly responsible. Other travellers had been robbed near the spot, although no white man had ever been murdered there.

But it was my private opinion at the time, and remains so to this day, that an intelligent conspiracy of slaves, for they were many more than one, had followed the tyrant up the bush trails, moving silently through the bamboo forest, and slaughtered him in the very manner he deserved. Justice cannot always be achieved by due recourse to the law. I cannot say that the emancipation has dramatically improved the living conditions of these people. But they are now able to negotiate their terms with the plantation owners and work longer hours upon their own land if they wish. Above all they hold their lives and deaths in their own hands.

Their deaths, ah, their own deaths. Some years ago a dead

child was handed into my arms, wrapped in an old silk petticoat, the very garment in which it had been christened. There were no outward signs of illness or violence. And a woman stood before me, accusing her sister's husband of murdering the infant. She claimed it was her sister's child. I looked down at the small brown face, peaceful in death.

What motive could he have had for obliterating this defence-less fragile thing? It is an offence, punishable by death, to murder a healthy slave child. Their strong working bodies are the only things for which they are valued.

"Him say chile no his, Massa," she shouted in grief and rage.

That is still no justification for murder, if murder is what we are here to witness.

"Justiss, Massa, me wan justiss!" she cries.

I look to Abraham for clarification. He recites the litany of prejudice as if it were written on the wall before him. The offspring of a white man and a black woman is a *mulatto*; the *mulatto* and the black produce a *sambo*, from the *mulatto* and the white comes the *quadroon*, from the *quadroon* and the white the *mustee*, the child of a *mustee* by a white man is called a *musteefino* and the children of a *musteefino* will be free by law and will count as whites.

"Dat chile mulatto, Doctor," Abraham explains patiently. "If de mudder black, den she go wid white man."

Well, even if she did she probably had little choice in the matter. I have already assisted at some of these dangerous and embarrassing birthings in the Cape. I have known the white wife of a Dutch farmer give birth to a dark child. A woman's virtue can always be challenged and she can never be proven innocent beyond all doubt. But I have seen this often enough to suspect that the dark blood can lie dormant for as long as a generation, and then reappear with no warning, to the terrible conster-nation and surprise of everyone concerned. I kept these matters quiet as a matter of course and I have never accepted the money I was frequently offered to sign a false death certificate and to remove the child. I look sadly down at the perfect ears, the small round cheeks, of a healthy baby, who has almost certainly been smothered.

Bring the man to me.

But here he is, being dragged towards me by two constables, who empty a small sack on my front steps, a sack which has been found in his possession. Here indeed is a strange variety of objects: thunderstones, cat's ears, the feet of various animals, human hair, fish bones, the teeth of alligators, finely polished.

"Dis Obeah man's magic, sah." Abraham retreats at once to the kitchen.

"Ah so him kill baby," yells the weeping woman. I look up at the tall, fierce African, too dignified and ferocious to defend himself. He makes it clear, with a gesture of contempt, that he is seeing all these Obeah objects for the first time.

I organise a decent Christian burial for the baby and a hearing before the magistrate. Cause of death: suffocation. The pillow or a mass of rags, lightly pressed upon the sleeping face. And so our sleep becomes dreamless and we step lightly into the life to come. This is a woman's way of killing, not a man's way. Not this man's, at any rate. But they are waiting for me to give the crucial testimony in a case that is too darkened to admit of any resolution. I cannot leave these incidents uninvestigated. Now that the importation of slaves has been stopped, each child born on the estates becomes precious. Another child, another slave. I make arrangements to visit the child's mother, and find that her sister has walked, weeping, across fourteen miles of bush through the wild mountains, hoping to find me, because she has been told that I am a just man.

I used to consider myself a shrewd judge of character. I thought that my capacity to unmask the liars, tricksters and malingering soldiers was all but infallible. My own disguise made that of others so simple to detect. I was a master not only of masquerade but of revelation. Now, truth eludes me. There are no truths, there are only layers of lies, what should be and what is. I, who have lived so long inside a chrysalis of ambiguity, find that I no longer see clearly. Yet I see that not I but the world is murky with deceit. I took the part of this poor people, spoke for those who had no words with which to defend themselves, and found that freedom and justice, whose meanings were so clear to me when I began, in the days when Francisco taught me to recite the Rights of Man, have become cloudy with power and divided interests, muddied with the lies of an Empire's rule over an island that still teases us with its promise of paradise.

I have no idea why I was so fond of Edward Ellis. He was an indolent creature, hypochondriacal, terrified of fresh air and spicy food. He was at the mercy of Newton, a ruthless black servant who ran the household, and without whom the entire régime at Montpelier would have collapsed. Newton wore a gold signet ring which the old master had given him and held the keys to the storerooms and the armoury chained to his belt.

Edward lay upon moth-eaten satin cushions from which insects and dust occasionally spiralled upwards, ringing a bell and yelling as loudly as his enfeebled lungs would permit, "Newton! God help us all! Newton! Confound the man. Where the devil is Newton?" He subsided, moaning. Then said, "Listen to this, Barry. Isn't it beautiful?

Now more than ever seems it rich to die,
To cease upon the midnight with no pain . . .

Why, I feel myself sinking into eternity. And were it not for this damnable climate my descent would be quite blissful."

I gazed down at the inert form of a handsome young man, whom all the ladies cherish.

"A little sherry, Edward? To oil your forthcoming slither to oblivion?" He held out his glass to receive the decanter.

"Bless you, Barry. You're the only man on the island who has heard of Keats. Who sends you the books?"

"My stepfather, General Francisco de Miranda. He sends a regular parcel every three months."

"Your stepfather! Oh Lord, you know, Barry, my mother used to send me all the latest reviews. The last contact we ever had really, before she was called to her reward. Some years ago now. At least she never saw this place. The climate would have been the death of her."

I sat silent for a moment, remembering. Francisco had given me precise instructions. I was to visit my mother's grave on her anniversary. I was to lay the golden lilies she had loved on her stone blanket and to remember that our deaths are but a passage, not an ending, and that the love we bear within us for each other lives forever. I love Francisco, but I do not believe what he believes. I am too close to death on a daily basis not to know that his dark mystery cannot be fathomed and should never be underestimated. In the faces of those I have known, who have died calmly, I have never seen anything but an absolute indifference to all things. Death comes, whether we wish to live or not, at his appointed hour. But to those who are blessed, life and death are no longer in opposition. This is our final night, which makes the odds all even.

I had been working on the island for over a year before I made the decision to visit my mother's grave. I rode out along the dusty, windy peninsula to Port Royal, alone in a small buggy, and was bounced rudely back and forth among the potholes. I saw few people, for it was late in the day. The road is rudimentary, for most of the supplies and, indeed, the visitors to Port Royal are transported across the bay by the regular ferry. But I wanted to drive that road, see the beaches where she had walked, put my hand on the warm pebbles where she had stood, her silk shawls tugged and jostled by the wind.

This was my sentimental journey, a punitive voyage, undertaken in solitude. For I had so loved this woman once. I had loved her lightness, her elegance, her wit, her bright hope. And when I stepped away from her, across the margins of my sex, I saw her anew and ceased to love what I saw. For she became smaller in my eyes. She became just another woman grubbing for money, flirting like a paid whore with a man who was already hopelessly in love with her. She could have robbed him blind. Perhaps she did. How she fought to keep her looks, her figure. She was still slim and light as a girl when she died. And suddenly my memories betray her. Here she is, hovering in damp English conservatories, whispering with Louisa, calculating every gesture. Everything that I once believed to be natural and charming became manipulative and callous. She never laughed with her whole heart. She listened to herself laughing. Why was James Barry so ruthless to his sister? Why did Alice Jones never relate any kitchen gossip about her? The servants talked about her, I know they did. But Alice would never be drawn, beyond the comment that she's your mother and you should show some proper respect.

This woman had a double existence. She lived entirely in her own reflection. She waltzed before the mirror of her own life. Oh yes, she was beautiful. But she treasured her own beauty. It was a commodity, the only one she had to sell. It was her passage on the survivor's ship, her voyage out of Ireland. I wonder if she ever really loved Francisco? Or did she simply set out to enthrall a rich man? Was she just a young widow, whose feckless husband had done nothing but fornicate and drink, trying to remake her wretched life? Was that man, the drunkard whom she married, really the man who was my father? She says so. But I do not believe her. Did she love my General? She played the child to him, all smiles, damp eyes and dancing. But did she love Francisco de Miranda with all her heart, as I did?

It matters to me that I should be certain of this. But I shall never know.

I have her to thank for who I am. "*She sent you to us on that damp midsummer night. She was the source of the plot, soldier. It was her idea. What was she asking of us? To give you the chance to live something other than a woman's life. She gave you up to us, my dearest child, because she loved you more than anyone else in the world. More than she loved me, more than she loved any one of us.*" Well, every child owes his being to the mother who bore him.

She taught me to believe in fair play, generosity, openness. Yet she gave me an identity within which I could never be anything other than an imposter. Who is James Miranda Barry? No one but her mother knows. And she has gone to her grave without telling. I am alone on the grey beach, watching the great roll of the windy sea, remembering a woman without whom my life can never be disentangled. She remains unforgiven.

I ride on to Port Royal.

The graveyard is outside the town, to the left of the road. A woman tries to sell me melons and fresh fish as I pull the horse to a standstill. I look around for a water trough and my horse and I both stand restless, shaking our heads clear of the flies. The woman plucks my sleeve and lays out a brace of fine snappers on an oil cloth.

"Janga, Massa," she cries, menacing me with a basket of crayfish. I give her money to guard the buggy and take refuge in the graveyard.

The gate clangs shut behind me and I fumble in my inner pocket for Francisco's folded letter. There is no shade in this graveyard, only gravel and stone, and iron crosses rusting on the graves. Flowers lie dead and dried in the little vats near the headstones. I calculate the distances. There is a wall all round the graveyard with many memorial plaques, now mostly illegible, affixed to the crumbling brick. The gravestones fractured by the earthquake of 1692 are heaped together like a crazy puzzle all along the wall. I remember Francisco telling me one of the myths of Port Royal, that the graves were opened on that day when the earth heaved its heart into its mouth, and the dead walked. I pass by the broken stones. Fragments of writing in several languages are still legible. HIC IACET, PRAY FOR THE SOUL OF . . . and most menacing of all, the sinister promise WE SHALL MEET AGAIN IN HEAVEN. There are no names written on this tombstone, but I can make out two hands clasped in a Masonic gesture of union. There is another gate on the far side leading out into nowhere, for beyond the wall there is nothing, nothing but the dunes and the sea. The wind smells strongly of the sea. My hat rises in the gust. I set off firmly towards the more modern part of the graveyard and almost stumble over her grave.

I stand staring for a moment, empty-handed. I have no flowers. I have brought nothing. The stone sarcophagus is cracked across. There is a huge fissure in the lid of her grave, as if the last day has already been announced and her spirit has escaped. I peer superstitiously into the crack, but see only lichen, earth and broken stone. The headstone, a plain white shield with a small black cross inlaid in jet, is untouched, as is the inscription.

MARY ANN BULKELEY
Née BARRY
1785–1823

DEARLY BELOVED NOW AND ALWAYS
HER BEAUTY AND VIRTUE SHALL NEVER FADE

But doth suffer a sea-change
Into something rich and strange

DEEPLY MOURNED BY HER ONLY SON
JAMES MIRANDA BARRY
&
F de M
WHO LAID THIS STONE

I take out my pocket book and note down the date, the time of my visit and the inscription. I include a few comments on the condition of the grave, simply to give myself something to do. For I know that I am being watched. I feel nothing whatever. Only puzzled curiosity that the grave should be so violently broken open. When I turn around two long-legged black children are sitting astride the graveyard wall, grinning wildly and banging their heels against its grainy surface.

"Evenin', Massa," they shout out in chorus, and a little shower of sand and red grit descends onto the gravel beneath them. Their feet drum the wall in rhythm. Their voices ring like the avenging Erinyes.

"De erth she done move, Massa."

"De lady she drown."

"Duppy walk. Duppy walk."

"Dat grave never close. Dey close her. She open."

"Buckra man pretty woman drown. But duppy walk."

"She ol' higue, suck yo blood, man."

"She duppy woman, but she pretty pretty duppy woman."

"She devil woman, Massa. She higue woman, duppy woman. Irri night she walk."

"Irribody see her when her duppy walk."

And there they sat, pounding the wall and grinning, like mad masks on All Hallow's Eve.

I stayed in Port Royal that night with the Governor's relatives, who informed me that one of the milder earthquakes, which regularly afflict the town, had indeed caused some damage in the graveyard. He promised to repair my mother's grave. He told me that she had been very popular in Port Royal and that many people remembered her; for her generosity of spirit, her graceful slenderness and her remarkable red curls. Some people, and not only the Negroes, claimed to have seen her ghost walking the streets and the wharves, or, with her skirts pulled up to her knees, pushing her little boat out to sea. But he gave no credence to such stories.

I looked down at Edward, realising that I had been silent too long, remembering. His face was filled with anxious concern.

"I say, old chap. Have I said the wrong thing?"

I told him that I had recently visited my mother's grave.

"I had hoped to lay my unquiet memories to rest, Edward. But I found that I was unable to do so. My feelings about my mother, who was a very secretive woman, are not resolved. I fear that now they never can be. I shall just have to live with them."

"Must have been damned upsetting. I never go on these pilgrimages. I just can't face things. Fearful thing to admit, but there you are." Edward shook his head regretfully.

"Pour me some more of that sherry, there's a good chap. I say, you will stay on for Christmas, won't you?"

The six months leading up to that Christmas had been extremely difficult. The early rains did not come and the island suffered an appalling drought. We were not so badly affected in the Blue Mountain district, but Edward wrote me miserable letters about the streams drying up, leaving a few stagnant pools in the hollows and the gullies, which were clogged with green weed and vibrated with mosquitoes. His Negroes had drained their wells dry to water their provision grounds with an endless chain of buckets. This land, from which the blacks feed themselves, apart from their usual rations of meat, flour, salt fish and sugar from the estate, is crucial to their well-being. They grow plantains, bananas, yams, coconuts and ockra. Ockra is the one native vegetable to which I am very partial. It tastes like asparagus. Ackee fried in butter is also delicious, if it is quite ripe and perfectly cooked. On Montpelier the crops failed in the provision grounds and the people went hungry. The planters suffered too, but, as always in these cases, the white masters tightened their belts and the blacks faced starvation.

Edward Ellis was prepared to break the locks on his stone

stores to feed his people. Other owners, or their overseers, were not so generous, and there was unrest in St Thomas in the east, and in the area around Montego Bay. The troops were sent in to two estates and quelled the riots easily. How could they fail to do so? The people were armed only with pointed sticks and cutlasses and were easily dissuaded from their intentions. Eight men and one woman were flogged at Beaulieu, some twenty miles from Montpelier. I was concerned by this development and asked to be kept informed. A sequence of smallpox outbreaks among the troops stationed at Up Park Camp kept me busy and I feared that, were a rebellion on any larger scale to develop, there would not be enough men healthy and upright to defend the Crown.

The Maroons had indeed several militias, supposedly ready to answer the Governor's behest, but, given their history of subversion and dissent, their loyalty could not be counted upon. One condition of their autonomy was that they should return runaway blacks to their estates forthwith. But I am not convinced that they always did so. Plato and his band survived many years in the bush and could not have done without shelter or sustenance.

Then in October the rains came with a vengeance. We were not forced to endure the excessive tempests which struck some of the other islands, but for six weeks together torrential rain washed away the roads, brought down huge trees in landslides of mud and rock, made the mountains impassable and destroyed the untethered land. Where there was no terracing in place, such as you often see in the Mediterranean, the earth was swept away. Entire crops were ruined, water supplies polluted and the cattle drowned. Many people faced ruin. Totty Kilman, our local storekeeper, suffered a disaster when the roof of his store gave way and all the contents, flour, seed, sugar, cloth, were wrecked. We set up a disaster fund to help those whose lives had been savaged by the extremities of this intolerable climate. An outbreak of dysentery detained me in Kingston for several weeks. Every population on the island was affected and my colleagues sent me gloomy tales of many deaths. Dr Cullinan, stationed in Port Antonio, warned me not to come. He had written so many death certificates that he was considering what he was pleased to describe as my medieval measures of lime pits and mass graves. Cullinan had a mordant sense of humour. My own report for the Governor made depressing reading. But fair weather came before Christmas and my projected visit to Montpelier, despite the state of the roads, was a pleasure I could permit myself.

Edward and his brother owned several hundred slaves, who worked the land on the Montpelier estate. They worked shifts so that the sugar mill was constantly fed with raw bundles of fresh cane. I went down to the mill to find Jessica, early on the morning of the day after my arrival, but her shift was finished and she was lying asleep and exhausted. I would not allow her sisters to wake her. Instead, I walked on in the heat, looking for the headman, who could give me a general report on the condition of the slaves.

The rulers in the slave hierarchy were often the offspring of the whites. The Montpelier headman was no exception. He was a handsome, aggressive mulatto with orange hair, tightly curled, and he sometimes claimed kin with "Brudder Edward" when he had had enough rum. He was almost certainly the bastard son of Edward's father, who had, reputedly, been magnanimous in all things. He had not only given freely of his supplies – flour, sugar, salted meat, herring and rum – on special holidays but had scattered his personal seed among the house slaves and upon any young woman in the cane gangs who happened to catch his eye.

This practice, although not common on the estates, was quite beyond me. The plantation owners regarded their slaves as animals, valuable livestock to be sure, and indispensable, but an inferior species nevertheless. Now that the slave ships were forbidden, the planters encouraged the slave women to breed with other slaves. Edward's father, however, often entered into the most intimate relations with the African and Creole women. The headman's mother used to wear her mistress's clothes, once the lady of the household was safely underground. She lorded it over the other house slaves and sat fanning herself among the accumulated crystal and porcelain in the dining room. Her unlikely name was Waterloo. Her rise to power spawned some sharply satirical songs, which did the rounds among the plantation slaves. One told the story of a black woman who dressed up "like Frenshie" and gave herself airs. The chorus of this song ran:

Ay! hey-day! Waterloo!
Waterloo! ho! ho! ho!

I myself heard the returning cane cutters singing this as they marched home through the dusk. Clearly, they were not praising the Duke of Wellington's past victories.

The field workers led an appalling existence. Edward's benevolent neglect of Montpelier meant that the management and control of the estate was left in the hands of the most unscrupulous sadists I have ever had the misfortune to observe at close quarters. What is it that turns a man of fair intelligence and some education into an unprincipled tyrant like Godwin's Mr Falkland? The slave drivers in charge of the plantation gangs should, according to the law, administer punishment of more than ten lashes only in the presence of an overseer. But in fact they were as generous with the lash as old Mr Ellis had been with his sexual favours. And for the afflicted blacks there was neither retribution nor redress.

Montpelier was a tiny nation, sufficient unto itself. But it was not well governed. I loved Edward and he was not an evil man, but he was a careless one. The consequences were alarmingly similar. I suspected that, in my absence, he was not above continuing his father's tradition and taking his black women into his bed. I received several resentful glances from Hecuba, one of the serving girls, while we were sitting at table. Newton was so indiscreet as to reveal that she liked to sit upon the master's knee and to cut his meat for him, but that she did not dare to claim her rights "wid de Doctor dere". I imagined Edward's affection for her. He probably regarded her as an amusing child, a pretty toy to play with in the evenings.

Edward was not sufficiently responsible to govern his tiny nation. Yet it was a very beautiful place, lodged on the first slopes of the purple hills.

The mill was one of the few stone buildings at Montpelier,

that and the infirmary. I stood on the steps and watched one of the gangs coming down the tracks. Their shoulders were bent with the weight of the cane. They carry the raw shoots directly into the cavern where it is to be ground, and feed it into the grinder. Once the juice has been extracted, the pulped trash is used for fuel. Sometimes the slaves carry it away to thatch their houses. Nothing is wasted. The white juice is propelled down the ducts in a foaming, thin liquid into the boiling house, where it is collected in the hotcock copper and slaked with lime. The pure liquid then flows through into the second copper. The boilermen work hard, but it is a skilled job, and they are usually privileged in the plantation hierarchy. Even the coarser parts of the fluid are re-used in the distillery, where they are mixed with molasses to make strong dark rum. The remaining liquid is finely skimmed, then skinned off, that is, transferred to the coolers, where it is left to crystallise into granules. This is raw sugar, which is then carried into the curing house, put into hogsheads and left to settle. The remains, which will not form sugar, are used in the distillery to form "low wine" and, after the second distillation, real rum.

I like the fact that nothing is wasted.

I stood, watching the pure fluid sugar rushing through the wooden gutters. One of the boilermen, whose arm I had mended the previous season, came up to me, bowed, hesitantly took my outstretched hand, and asked if Doctor was staying for the New Year's John Canoe masquerade. I assured him that I was.

"Dat gud ting, dat gud ting," he said several times, most mysteriously. We shook hands again and I wished him a good day. Only months later did I attach any significance to his words.

The blacks celebrate Christmas with an extraordinary festival pageant in masquerade. Indeed, I had found the estate already in something of a holiday mood. Looking back, I can see that the high spirits among the slaves were partly attributable to their raised hopes of freedom. The anti-slavery measures advocated by the Home Government were widely discussed and many blacks were of the opinion that the Emancipation, rather like the Second Coming, was close at hand. There was wild talk of free land for all slaves as a present from the Crown. I attended a chapel service in Montego Bay, where the Baptist preacher, a passionate young black man in a stiff white collar and brushed suit, was carried away by the radical significance of his text, which he declaimed in thrilling tones before applying himself to the knotted business of exegesis.

For ye are all the children of God by faith in Christ Jesus. For as many of you have been baptised into Christ have put on Christ. There is neither Jew nor Greek, there is neither bond nor free, there is neither male nor female: for ye are all one in Christ Jesus. (Galatians, 3: 26–28)

No one is a slave in God's eyes. When Jesus proclaimed, "I am the way, the truth and the life," he offered himself as the gateway to freedom. Ye shall know the truth and the truth shall set you free. In Christ there is no place for the distinction between a free man and a slave. For ye are all one in Christ Jeeeeesus, he boomed.

The argument was obvious and irrefutable. Newton, who was by my side, found all this very persuasive, and ventured to demand my opinion. I did not have the heart to tell him that I was not a believer. Nor, indeed, to explain that the consequences of my atheism demanded still more radical solutions than a paradise of love in the beyond. For it is here, in the Kingdom of This World, that we shall find our salvation. Or not at all. I think of Francisco and all his contradictions. He was a devout Catholic. Yet the very fluid in his veins was that of a republican. Slavery was an invention of the tyrant Satan, who was himself enslaved by pride, envy and desire. When God made the earth He gave it freely to all men, regardless of their race and origin. For Francisco, and in this we were never divided, the abolition of slavery was a simple and inevitable thing, the justice of which did not admit of argument or discussion. All men are born free and equal to one another. And from this great truth flow all the Rights of Man. He lived at least to see the emancipation throughout the Caribbean, if not in the Americas.

How to answer Newton, whose huge, round, urgent face was now pressed close to mine?

We had sung the last hymn and were leaving the little chapel

in the dust. I gestured to the people around us, who were all
races, all colours, although the majority were black.

"Well, Newton. Here are God's people, who have knelt down
before Him. If all manner of men are prepared to pray with one
another, to the same God, then indeed, we are, and should be,
all one in Christ Jesus."

That remark of mine, overheard and accurately reported,
almost led to a formal charge of sedition. Given what was to
come.

This was a few days before Christmas. The situation at the
hospital in Montego Bay was not good, but was far from disas-
trous. I spent the morning making notes of what was most
needed in the storeroom, in terms of both linen and medicine.
I checked the account books and accompanied my doctors on
their ward rounds. Then I went out to buy Christmas presents
for Edward's household and for Abraham. He had requested a fine
knife with a horn handle. Edward had, somewhat shamefacedly,
repeated Hecuba's desire for a petticoat with pink ribbons, so
that I found myself riding back to Montpelier in the evening with
a medley of weaponry, leather belts and frilly female underwear.
Newton was very amused by the petticoats, lacy aprons and
decorated bloomers destined for the ladies of his household. We
trotted into Montpelier, still grinning at one another.

There had been a good deal of excitement in town, but no
more than was usual for Christmastime.

The slaves always had a holiday at Christmas. That year the
day fell upon a Sunday, but Edward, well aware of the long
months of hardship, which now seemed to be past, granted
Monday as well. Although this was characteristic of his generosity,
it was not a universal practice among the plantation owners in
the district and caused some irritation and dissent. Edward
avoided adverse comment by declaring that he was severely indisposed and unable to attend the December assizes. He was a
local magistrate, who usually took his responsibilities seriously. I
upbraided him gently at his defection, but he defended himself.

"Dash it, Barry. What I don't hear them saying won't warrant
a reply. And I can get out of traipsing over to Kingston for the
New Year dances. All of which I loathe. I am mobbed by

dozens of matrons trying to marry me off to their affected shady daughters. You'll vouch for my indisposition, won't you? There's a good fellow. And in this climate you can always be suddenly seized by the unquenchable shits."

He settled himself more comfortably into the crumbling chaise longue.

"And if I don't go to the Governor's ball I won't have to listen to the end-of-the-worldism from all the planters resisting the abolition. It must come, you know, Barry. And soon. We will just have to negotiate a different arrangement for planting cane."

He told me that a week before my arrival there had been trouble at the Salt Spring estate, where the slaves had turned on the attorney. Edward was sure that the man had been enjoying his little moment as the tyrant king, but the mob of slaves actually disarmed the constables who were sent to suppress the troublemakers. Edward should have been sitting on the bench to hear the full story and pass judgment.

"The people's heads are full of freedom, James. And we must reap the consequences. How was that Baptist preacher you went to hear yesterday? I'm told that he's sedition incarnate and that it's only a matter of time before they haul him out of his pulpit, along with the Jacobin missionaries who put him up to it!"

Newton must have overheard this. He was in the room, searching for the best linen and silver candlesticks with which to lay the table.

I remember the dining room with terrible clarity. The portraits of Edward's parents over the oak sideboard and all the chairs, when not in use, standing in tiny dishes of water to save them from the white ants. The windows on that side of the house were masked with Venetian blinds, made of bamboo, which left huge bars of sun on the opposite wall. One of Edward's English visitors, who had stayed here eight months, nursing a consumption, had painted a huge oil portrait of the estate, fastidious in its detail. Here were the barracks where the book-keepers lived, and there the overseer's house and offices, with the hospital well placed on the breezy rise, the cattle sheds, water mill and the boiling house, shaded by coconut trees, and beyond them, the purple hills. We sat staring at the picture.

"There isn't a coconut tree to the right of the main gates," I said pedantically.

"Yes, there was," said Edward. "It blew down after the painting was complete. Poor old Halliwell. Don't you remember? You dealt with his hookworm. Well, he died of his consumption as soon as he got home. You need a hot dry climate for consumption, not a hot wet one."

Edward glared gloomily at the painting for a moment, then cheered up.

"We'll die here, won't we, Barry? We won't bother sailing back to England."

"Very probably," I agreed wearily.

There was a strange quiet on the estate throughout Christmas Day, apart from the usual hymns, sung on the house steps by Edward's little band of devotees. This was a group of his slaves, not only the houseworkers, to whom he had been especially kind, but also others from among the fieldworkers, and they often prevailed upon him to watch them dance or to hear them sing. I observed their approach, dressed in their Sunday best, carrying their Eboe drums and two curious instruments, shaky-shekies, which were calabashes filled with pebbles, and kitty-katties, which were nothing more than a flat piece of board and two sticks with which they energetically pummel the board. The musical instruments may have been primitive, but the singing was wonderful. A young girl led them, her high, clear soprano echoing across the yard. Her companions followed in a chorus. I saw Jessica among the singers.

When the song had ended, Edward ordered drinks and cakes for his Christmas singers and we retreated inside from the heat. As I wished them all a merry Christmas and turned to go, Jessica caught my hand.

"You stay here, Doctor?" she asked urgently.

"Yes. Until New Year," I replied. She withdrew at once, apparently relieved.

The following day was even quieter than Christmas Day had been. Even Edward remarked on the lack of drunken good cheer among his people. We heard nothing but the chickens, geese and guinea fowl engaging in the occasional raucous scuffle across the yard.

In the early dawn of 27th December the slaves rose up, formed their gangs as usual and departed into the cane fields. Most of them never came back. But we did not know this, for the overseers never returned to report their vanishing. The first sign we heard, as the light failed, was the sound of the conch shells.

Yes, the first signal was the sound of the shells, calling to one another in the first misty cool of the mountains, the shells calling across the purple slopes, the waiting, then the echo coming, damp from the ferns at the mouth of the waterfall, the shells calling and calling across the mountains. The sound is unspeakably sad, and I will never hear it again without remembering the taste of those bitter years, the tingle in my nostrils from the smell of coffee beans roasting on jute sacks in the sun, and the stench of sweet, thick, fermenting rum and the trickle of sweat streaming inside my shirt which hangs sodden against my belly.

We went down the steps in the advancing dark and saw the luminous red glow of Kensington on the Hill. This was the beacon, the signal to all the surrounding estates that the uprising had begun. From the intensity of the blaze, we realised that many of the neighbouring estates were already in flames. The light transformed the skyline. What so many of the planters had always feared had at last come to pass. Newton stood beside us in the shadows. He had clearly been converted by the Baptists on that very morning in Montego Bay, for he rose to the moment with apocalyptic fervour.

"Di Day o' Judgement is a' han', Massa," he cried, "whe' di blessed will be clasp to Him Bosom, an' di wikked will be cas' into de everlastin' fire!"

"Don't talk nonsense, Newton," snapped Edward.

We could by now see the Everlasting Fires of the distant estates, blazing clearly across the hills. And coming closer. The sky was like de Loutherbourg's famous paintings of Coalbrooke-dale, an inferno of smoke and flame. The house servants had vanished, and all the estate – usually so busy and so thriving, with the sound of singing and the slaves calling to their children, running footsteps, the thud of buckets at the pump and the nickering of the horses being led back to the paddocks – was silent and deserted. The buildings loomed, suspended in the red night, as if testifying, like a malignant prophecy, to their coming destruction.

Edward set up a little cache of arms on the back porch. He prepared a row of four muskets, firing off one or two into the blackness, to see if they were functioning.

I sent Newton over to the stables and told him to release all the horses, apart from my bay and Edward's piebald mare. The animals were to be set free into the bush: cows, chickens, geese, guinea fowl and all the dogs. This was easier said than done, for I went to the chicken house myself and opened the pens. But the fowls, fluttering, gibbering and terrified, simply clustered together as far away from me as possible. I left the door open and the dim-witted creatures to their fate. The buildings were all silent and locked, the silence uncanny. I could smell the coming pall of smoke on the warming air.

One lamp burned in the infirmary. There were two men, sick with fever, abandoned in their beds, and the nurse sitting quietly in a chair, hands folded on her lap before her.

"Good evening, Elizabeth," I said softly. But she was too terrified even to reply. I checked that both men were as comfortable as possible and that she had plenty of fresh water. It was unlikely that the rebels would be able to set fire to the roof. I stroked the woman's head and then blew out the lamp.

"Stay here," I whispered, "but don't burn any candles or light the lamp again. You will be quite safe." She said nothing.

And I was by no means as confident as I pretended to be.

Edward had abandoned his musket practice and was out searching in the undergrowth by the abandoned village for Hecuba and her companions. She had been delighted with the petticoat and had even gone so far as to kiss him quickly in my presence. Now, she too had vanished.

"Well, Barry," said Edward calmly, all his illnesses forgotten, "what are we to do? Flee the coop or wait to be butchered and roasted? Newton, bless him, is washing up the supper dishes on his own."

I had never seen Edward so calm, relaxed and indifferent to his fate. I told him that we would do best to watch for the rest of the night, armed with muskets to face whatever came. If the estate survived the night I would set out for Montego Bay at first light. We sat down on the back porch and watched the distant infernos, as the Trelawny plantations were reduced to ashes. But we heard nothing close to us, and we saw no one.

As dawn lightened behind the fires on the morning of December 28th, I saddled the bay in silence and nodded my goodbyes to Edward and to Newton. My place was with the army and the Governor, for as soon as news of the rebellion reached Kingston, troops would have been despatched from all the ports. The small militia at Shettlewood was almost certainly already in arms. I rode away into the burning shroud of smoke at a brisk trot, leaving Newton and Edward alone, in all that empty land.

It was clear that the rebellion had been planned in advance. The conch signal indicated an intelligent conspiracy. I was aware, as soon as I left the Montpelier track and turned onto the red dirt road towards Montego Bay, that I was being watched and followed by rebels hiding in the canefields. Suddenly a group of black shadows solidified out of the murky green before me, their cutlasses gleaming. My horse started and reared, but was calmed at once by Jessica's familiar voice. She caught the bridle and looked straight into my eyes. A young black man, whom I did not know, waved his machete in my face and sneered:

"We wont be slaves no more. We wont lift hoe no more. We wont take flog no more. We free now! We free now!"

I did not answer him. What could I say? They had justice on their side, if not the law. What desperate longing for dignity and liberty drives a man to take up arms against his fellow men? Their very humanity had been betrayed. And now they stood before me, armed and ready for vengeance, colour for colour, blood for blood. The consequences of our cruelty now stood before us.

Jessica must have read my thoughts. She held the bay's bridle firmly and peered up into my face.

"Den come wid us, Doctor."

"I will tend the wounded of both sides, Jessica. Both sides. And I urge you to spare as many lives as possible. A man's life lost is the only thing he can never regain."

There was a pause as her companions looked around and away into the lightening sky. I could see the great house at Roehampton, still standing, but I could now hear howls and shouting in the distance. Jessica raised her hand quickly and the small gang of rebels parted before me.

And then I was alone on the road in the midst of the uprising, my horse snorting uneasily in the red dust.

It is in the nature of events such as these that one man has only a confused and muddled understanding of all that has passed. That night I saw the countryside in flames, but although many people passed by me on the road, some armed, some running, some carrying torches, I continued on my way, unchallenged and unharmed.

The town was in uproar. The population had panicked. Some fled to the boats and put out to sea in terror. One man had overloaded a small fishing craft with all the worldly goods he could carry. The skiff overturned in the bay and he was drowned. His body was identified many weeks later by the cutlery hidden in his pockets, but his skull had been picked clean by the sea.

I regarded the rebellion as an inevitable consequence of slavery. The people wanted what is desired most passionately by every man or woman who is humiliated and oppressed: their freedom, and the right to live in peace on their own land. In all the pages of history there is no tale of tyranny that is not followed by the story of resistance and rebellion. The one will follow hot upon the other, as the dust rises before the wind. It seems that my political sentiments and sympathies were known in Montego Bay, as, on two occasions, I was spat at by townsfolk who ought to have known better and accused of being a white nigger.

In fact, the rebels advanced on Montpelier as soon as I had gone. I have reason to believe that this was no coincidence. The militia, which had taken a more devious route through the canefields, confronted them in the forecourt of Montpelier. They lost the day, although they managed to inflict some losses, and retreated back to Montego Bay, bringing Edward and Newton with them. The rebellion then spread into the hills, and thick smoke from the burning plantations laid a pall over the sun. All the estates along the Great River valley were set alight. The people rose up throughout the counties of Westmorland and St Elizabeth. The roads were impassable as far as Savannah la Mar, for they were in the hands of the rebels. Freedom was in the mouth of every man who held a cutlass in his hand.

Weeks later we learned that some slaves had remained loyal to their masters and defended both property and lives. In fact, there were very few direct attacks upon the whites. True, it was Christmastime and many of the owners and their families were absent from their properties. Many more slaves, not sufficiently courageous to join the rebellion but fearing reprisals against themselves, simply vanished into the bush, as Edward's people had done.

But those things were still to come.

The militia was powerless to stop the destruction and looting of the estates. We defended the town as best we could while awaiting the arrival of Sir Willoughby Cotton and his troops. The townspeople were terrified by rumours of atrocities and slaughter as the rebellion spread.

The most common wounds were burns and cuts from machetes. Those who had been shot were usually beyond my help. We worked shifts at the hospital, to deal with the people who scrambled into the town from all sides. Edward was despondent concerning the fate of his estate and the loss of his sweetheart Hecuba. He drank heavily over the next few days. He stuck two muskets in his belt and reeled down the main street, but I doubt that he would have been able to shoot straight had he been confronted with a desperate battalion of insurgents. Newton was in the grip of a religious conviction that all was lost and Satan stalked the land. He spent his days in prayer at the Baptist chapel where we had heard the fiery black preacher, now known to be one of the ringleaders of the rebellion.

The troops from Kingston arrived before the week was out

and as we watched the man-of-war entering the harbour with her cannon at the ready there was little doubt of the conclusion to this violent episode in the island's history.

The following proclamation was issued forthwith.

NEGROES!

**You have taken up arms against your masters.
Some wicked persons have told you the King has
made you free.
In the name of the King I come amongst you
to tell you that you are
MISLED.**

**All who are found with the rebels will be
PUT TO DEATH WITHOUT MERCY.**

**You cannot resist the King's troops.
All who yield themselves up, provided they are not
principals and chiefs in the burnings that have been
committed, will receive
HIS MAJESTY'S GRACIOUS PARDON**

**All who hold out will meet
CERTAIN DEATH.**

I thought then, and I still believe, that Sir Willoughby Cotton was a humane and enlightened man. But the land was under martial law and we had not reckoned with the fury of the militia. When the troops entered the ruined and smouldering fields they often shot dead the first blacks they saw, regardless of their history or intentions. All blacks were potential rebels and deserved to die, as an example to the others. Those estates identified with the origins of the rebellion bore witness to the most brutal floggings and summary executions, often without trial. And at Montpelier, where I returned during the second week of January, I found the maggot-filled cadavers of the two men I had left lying helpless in the infirmary. Each man, almost certainly too ill to move, had been shot in the brains at close range. Elizabeth's body was lying at a little distance in the bush. She had clearly been attempting to flee, for she had been shot twice in the back.

Edward strode away, stormy-faced but quite grey, to protest to the brigade commander at this act of mindless barbarism. But other whites were indifferent to his tale and to what they regarded as his mistaken sense of outrage. The blacks were all potential rebels. And they had it coming to them.

Newton and I were digging the graves of the unfortunates massacred in the infirmary when we were surprised by a mass of terrified black faces peering over the cemetery wall. These were Edward's slaves, many of whom had fled on the night of 27th December and who only now dared to return.

Montpelier had been ransacked and the stores had been looted. There was not a scrap of china remaining in the house and all the beds had been stripped. But the buildings were still standing and the fowls, which had been so cowardly on the night when the uprising had begun, now returned to the yard, cackling greedily and scratching among the trails of grain left by the plunderers. The cost of the damage was enormous. But even so, the house still stood, and the returning slaves resumed their work, largely in silence and watchful wariness. I do not know how many had gone with the rebels, and I did not ask. Neither did Edward. One of the house slaves came telling tales and offering names in the hope of favours or rewards. Edward, quite rightly, booted him straight down the steps. Neither would he listen to tittle-tattle or denunciations among the house girls. But some slaves never returned. Edward never saw Hecuba again. I assume that she was one of the slaves shot and buried under white lime in one or other of the mass graves across the countryside, for many of the bodies were not identified. And the circumstances of their deaths were never investigated. There was little singing on the estate at Montpelier for many weeks to come.

I did, however, see Jessica once more. The court martial was a desperate affair, hastily constituted; and so anxious were the magistrates to liquidate the troublemakers that innocence or guilt was largely irrelevant. It sufficed sometimes that a particular slave belonging to the rebel estates had once expressed a desire to be free, or to till his own land, for him to be condemned to death.

An offence that would have called for ten lashes in peaceful times now merited the gibbet. And the gibbet stood for many days before the courthouse in Montego Bay.

Three or four men were hanged, and left hanging, their bodies turning slowly in the sea winds. They were only cut down by the hangman when he had fresh victims ready to replace them. The pile of corpses was left in the square to be sniffed at by passing dogs until the workhouse blacks appeared at dusk to take them away in carts to their communal pit, into which, without prayers or tears, they were unceremoniously flung. I supervised the digging of these unholy trenches and prescribed the level to which they should be dug so that no risk of infection should menace the population of Montego Bay.

Over three hundred men were hanged.

But sometimes the rebels were taken back to the estates from which they came, and there, under the vindictive eyes of the overseers and constables in the militias, they were executed among the ruins of their former masters' wealth and power. I witnessed many of these executions and I was impressed by the cold courage with which the rebels went to their fate. Many were religious men, who died convinced of the justice of their cause and their role as martyred servants of the true God. They wore their white caps as condemned men with the pride of martyrs' crowns. No criminal ever goes to the gallows fearlessly. But these men did. They believed that they had earned the right to die nobly in the struggle for freedom.

It was at one of these plantation executions that I saw Jessica for the last time. The blacks on the estate were gathered in the yard to witness the doom awaiting all those who plotted insurrection. The method of execution was primitive indeed. Each condemned man was fixed onto a board placed over two barrels with his hands and feet tied and the noose about his neck. Then the plank was kicked away, and as the bodies jerked and struggled one of the soldiers would pass among them, drawing the noose tight and breaking the man's neck. If this was not effective and the prisoners still shivered and wriggled at the end of the rope, another man laid hold of the legs and pulled hard.

Thus, they died. It was a slow process and I often wished for the spectacular rapidity of the guillotine.

At this particular execution, held at one of the neighbouring estates, I saw Jessica among the crowd of slaves who had been forced to watch. I did not recognise the young man who was about to die. He stood tall, head erect, as the sentence was read out. There was the Eboe woman, watching intently, her eldest and only surviving daughter at her side. They had not been seen at Montpelier since the beginning of the uprising and had been reported as missing blacks. I saw her cover her mouth with her hands as the plank beneath the young man's feet was kicked away. Apart from a slight sigh from the watching crowd there was no sound. The men waiting to die rarely spoke or cried out and audible weeping was a flogging offence.

I looked hard at Jessica. Her eyes bulged as she strained forward. Her daughter's grasp upon her arm tightened. I followed her gaze to the swaying corpse and remembered him at last.

"*We wont be slaves no more. We wont lift hoe no more. We wont take flog no more. We free now! We free now!*"

Jessica looked up. We recognised one another. Neither of us gave any sign of having done so. When I stared again into the dispersing crowd I could see her no more.

❖ ❖ ❖ ❖ ❖

What is freedom? Who is free? In the years since the Emancipation the fall in the market for sugar has bankrupted many of the plantation owners and brought destitution and poverty to their former slaves. Now they must pay rent for their provision grounds and the rent collectors are hated men. The blacks believe that the land their fathers tilled is theirs by right. On some of the estates many have refused to pay and had their livestock confiscated by the bailiffs. Wages are often pitifully low. The people go hungry during the bad times. It is not often that the future is clear to me, but of this I am certain: a major rebellion will come again in this colony, gripped by an irreversible decline. We will see the return of the killing time and the hanging tree. When I read the words of so eminent a philosopher as Thomas Carlyle, maintaining that the blacks are an inferior race who are not worthy of their freedom, I wonder if I can ever return to England. All these years and nights in the islands of the great winds and the red dust have convinced me of the justice of Francisco's simple faith in the inalienable, unchanging Rights of Man.

Edward died of drink a year or two ago. He sank down the bottle gradually, and his company became intolerable. He still read poetry aloud, but it was interspersed with drunken meanderings. He is buried at Montpelier, in the very cemetery where Newton and I laid the murdered victims of the militias to rest. Hecuba's successor ousted Newton and ran the household, very successfully and to her own advantage. If the master died poor, she was not going to do so. Nor did she. When I last saw the house, the sash windows at the end of the long corridor were broken and smashed and the rain had stained the wallpaper and the paintings.

Newcastle Station, where I live now, is thriving, and I find myself less able, as I grow older, to endure the wet heat of the lowlands. I have bought some good land in the Blue Mountains for Abraham and his family, so that he will be able to retire in comfort and in peace. We signed the papers together and I vouched for Abraham's teetering signature with my initials. He has never learned to read or write, but we spent a week practising his mark so that he should not be ashamed in the attorney's office.

Since then Abraham has grown a successful crop of Indian hemp, which has become very popular among the plantation workers. I have tried it myself, but found its soporific effects undesirable. Ordinary tobacco keeps me awake and has done so all through this long night.

I can no longer see the peenie-wallies glowing against the bush. The outlines of the verandah railings are glowing more clearly in the damp cool. My coat hangs down behind me on the tiles, and my bones feel old and chilled. I hear the faint rustle of the dogs in their outside sheds. Psyche lies peacefully sleeping in her old basket at my feet. As the light outside suddenly, rapidly, shifts from black to deep blue, I relight the candle. One lone bird cries out in the half-dark. I take up the letter, which has precipitated this endless night of remembering.

PART SIX

Alice Jones

Lincolnshire, 22nd June 1859

My Dearest James,

I haven't rewarded you very well for your refusal to forget me, have I now? But I have kept every single letter you ever wrote. They are all dated, ordered and wrapped in fine tissue. Layers of it! Some of those loving angry ones you wrote at the beginning are falling apart, with age and re-reading. I have ordered two of them to be repaired by the museum restorers. They were stitched onto a jute backing with a fine mesh, and now they can only be folded over once. Of course they are all locked in my desk, and I count them among my most precious possessions: love letters from the famous Dr Barry! But I will never part with them. Not unless I fall upon exceptionally hard times.

Why did it irk you so much to hear of my success? I never ceased to hear of yours and bore the news with great equanimity, good humour and not a little pride. After all, l knew you when you were just a bright tiny child who didn't look as if he'd live to be twenty. And be honest, without a bracing from me from time to time you might not have done. I still remember those summers we spent together when you taught me to read. But they were only my beginning. I was no one then. Nobody had heard of me. Well, they have now.

You've been gone for thirty years, James. You're like the Wandering Jew. But nobody forced you to go. I certainly didn't. And you aren't under a curse. You could come home now. Why don't you come home?

I have officially retired from the stage. You can't go on prancing about dressed up as a boy forever. And although I wouldn't admit it to anybody but yourself, my voice is not what it used to be. I gave a sequence of acclaimed farewell performances, one of which the young Queen herself attended. I received exceedingly flattering notices in all the papers, one especially charming account from Mr Dickens himself. He said that I was as fresh and charming as my reputation and that he had no need to imagine what I had been, for there I was! Or something to that effect. Did you know that he is exceedingly interested in the theatre and once wished to audition? He fell ill on the day. Is it not sad? I imagine playing alongside him. He is a most thrilling reader. Well, his kind words have pride of place in my Memoir Book, along with Adolphus's pressed roses. The first he ever gave to me.

My poor Adolphus is dead. But I expect you did know. It was in all the papers. He had a very handsome funeral, which I attended, sitting just behind the family. I was perfectly discreet. But his sister came right up to kiss me and to press my hand. The reporters had the insolence to wonder what would now become of the adorable Mrs Jones. As if I'd be put out in the streets! I would never have allowed Adolphus to be swept to his reward if he hadn't left me well set up and comfortable. I have the house, of course – that was a gift – and a handsome annuity. But I can't be idle. It's not in my nature.

I have a new profession. I'm telling you about it now so that you won't be shocked or try to stop me.

I have become a noted and fashionable medium. I won't do it for just anybody. But I have my regular clients, all very respectable, and some from the very best society. It came upon me after Adolphus died. I so wanted to be in touch with him. After all, we had shared so much in the past. Death needn't be the end. It's only the end if you want it to be. And if I was feeling lonely and bereft then other people must be too. I made some discreet enquiries among the wealthy widows. There was one poor woman who had lost her baby boy to the smallpox and was utterly distraught, two years on. All she wanted to know was that her child was safe and happy. What harm could there possibly be in giving that woman a little reassurance? After all, if a two-year-old can't get to paradise, there's not much hope for the rest of us. So I can't be doing any harm, can I? All I do is open the pearly gates, just a crack.

I was always excellent at children's voices. And sometimes I do feel that there is something speaking through me. If the mood is right. I don't charge fixed rates, of course, or anything so vulgar and commercial. I just welcome donations. It's a little embarrassing how much people are prepared to give. It's as if I am involved in one long benefit performance. I have always made my audiences happier people. No one can say that I haven't done that. They go away, down my wide staircases, comforted and reassured. I give them back their faith.

I have no idea what lies beyond the grave. No more do you, James, for all your fashionable atheism. Very shocking, really. But if my work helps other people to believe that all shall be well and quenches their sorrows and their fears, I see no harm in it at all.

I have all the machinery, of course. I do winds and lights and voices. Even in overheated curtained rooms the effects can be quite striking. And the table always bounces a treat when the loved ones acknowledge their summons from the other side. These details are very important. It puts the clients in a state of heightened anticipation. I want them to be on tenterhooks of expectation, ready to receive their message. It doesn't much matter what the message is, it's the fact that they have spoken from the beyond that counts. I never allow daylight to enter the room where I hold my séances, and my maid ensures a musty smell of rose petals. The small upstairs parlour is a very suitable stage for my performances. I always wear black lace out of respect.

Of course I ensure that the clients tell me a good deal about the dear departed in our first interviews. I'm always well informed about the details. Sometimes I think that this does them more good than anything else – to pour it all out to someone sympathetic and to tell me how guilty they feel. Why do people always feel guilty about being alive when other people die? There's no need to blame yourself, unless you're the murderer.

I will not handle suicides.

Did you know that my poor Haydon was one of that unfortunate company? You found him insupportable. Well, the abandoned creature came to be of your opinion and could no longer tolerate his own company either. He blew his brains out in front of his unfinished painting of Alfred. Oh, my dear James, it was a terrible business. I was playing at the theatre in Kew and was not in London. The weather was extremely hot and he had been unable to sleep. His exhibition was not a success and his affairs were very embarrassed. He had sent me a desperate note appealing for funds. What could I do? I sent him a draft for £50 by return. But £500 would not have solved Haydon's debts. There was no limit to his needs. He had a wife and children by then, who did nothing whatever, but sit there, rapacious as baby pelicans, while Haydon tore his breast and painted yet another unfashionable historical monstrosity which produced not a drop of blood at all. Nor any cash either. It was thirteen years ago this summer. He went out to Rivière's in

Oxford Street and purchased a pistol. He arranged his studio and wrote numerous farewell letters to his family.

Then he wrote down his last thoughts and shot himself. Poor, unfortunate man. He did not have enough money to buy a sufficiently fatal weapon and the bullet bounced off his skull, inflicting, nevertheless, a terrible wound. The *malheureux* then staggered to his painting table, snatched up a razor and slashed his own throat, covering the Alfred with his life's blood. Thus he died. He was found by his daughter, who came into his studio at midday.

Naturally I was one of the first subscribers to the benefit fund for the widow and the orphaned infants. His wife, Mary, was a foolish, simple woman. He took better care of her in death than he had ever done in life. She gave me the last volume of his diary, by which to remember him. She could not bring herself to read it, for he always tried to be cheerful with her. And, indeed, it makes sorry reading. He was just sixty years old. Only two months before he so untidily dispatched himself, he wrote, "My situation is now of more extreme peril than even when I began Solomon 33 years ago." I was a pretty young woman, James, when I posed for his Solomon.

Poor dear Haydon. His fate grieves me still. The last entry in this doleful volume ends thus:

"God forgive – me – Amen.
Finis
of
B. R. Haydon.
'Stretch me no longer on this tough World' – Lear
End."

He'd set it all out like a tombstone! I copied that from the original. And even the quotation is incorrect. When I am playing Cordelia I am always laid out, hanged, at this point, my wig pathetically arranged in long tresses about my face. But I'm right there on stage and the line is spoken by Kent. It should be delivered as follows:

Vex not his ghost: O! let him pass; he hates him
That would upon the rack of this tough world
Stretch him out longer.

Haydon could get nothing right. Not even his suicide message. He was pathetic, James, and his death affected me deeply. Mary lived until 1854. She died peacefully, in comfortable circumstances, on a civil list pension. But it is a terribly sad tale.

I would not have you die like that, my love, despairing, alone, among strangers. You have been gone for thirty years, James. Thirty years is a long time to sulk. For you have not forgiven me, have you, for refusing to marry you. But I kept my word, did I not? I never married anybody else, even if I did make my own arrangements with my generous protector. Well, I am an independent woman now, sir. And quite rich.

Come home, James. Thirty years is quite long enough to wander the world. Look how many pages I have taken up before I come to the point. This is my simple request. I have always loved you. I have never forgotton you. We are old people now. We have our lives behind us. Come home to me. My waist is not as neat as it used to be and my step is not as quick, but with a little assistance my hair is as black as ever it was and you will find that I am not so very much changed. Write directly, James. And tell me that you are coming home.

I remain, your loving friend,
Alice Jones

✤ ✤ ✤ ✤ ✤

I set about rebuilding the house. The roof was sound, but the tenants had done little to modernise the kitchen. It was still as vile a pit as it had been when my uncle died. The walls were white-washed, but huge patches were blackened and peeling as if there had been frequent fires in the domestic underworld. The pantry and the scullery were rat-infested and stank. I ordered them to be destroyed. An army of workers moved in with me. I stood over them, day after day, making decisions and impeding the steady trickle of petty theft, which is characteristic of building sites in London. My neighbours all came to greet me, delighted at the restoration of the master. Psyche growled at each one of them in turn. In so many years the street had improved beyond all recognition. The tenements and children's gangs were gone. There were lime trees planted at intervals down my side of the pavement, so that Barry's old drawing room, the room that had once harboured his notorious *Pandora*, looked out into a mass of fresh green.

I had the garden's brambles razed to the ground and the roots dug out and burned. The great elms, which now dominated the long walk leading down to the mews, were sawn briskly into shape. One of them was rotten and had to be felled at great expense. Nothing extraordinary could be achieved in the first year and without advice I was never an effective gardener. But once the internal alterations had reached the question of wall-paper, and the brick-layers' tools had vanished from the vegetable patch, I planted a quantity of bulbs and shrubs. This was my gesture of faith in the following spring.

The house had no furniture and no curtains, and so I bivou-acked in the topmost rooms below the attics on a low camp bed with the barest minimum of comforts, despite the disconcerting summer heat and the dust storms rising from the works below. I was very happy. I saw no one. My acquaintances were all in the country and many of the theatres were closed. London had poured its contents out into the countryside for the duration of the summer, and I took advantage of the fact to install myself in all tranquillity.

During the first week of September I had one or two rooms nearing completion, although the odd sofa and oak table that had caught my fancy looked like little vessels lost on a sea of polished boards.

I was out walking in the park when she called.

The maid was waiting for me, hysterical with excitement. When I entered the house she pounced upon me in the hallway. She wasn't sure, she couldn't be sure, but the lady had left a card. And she had peeped. And yes, it was. It was her. The famous, the beautiful, the legendary Mrs Jones.

"Oh, a lady, sir, a real lady. And so gracious. And so handsome."

You've done it, Alice. You've pulled it off. You have become respectable.

"And she didn't stand on ceremony, sir. She was very emphatic. She says that as soon as you've received her card you're to go to her instantly. She doesn't care what time of day it is, sir. And I hope I did right. I said you weren't in. Well, you weren't. But she insisted on looking all over the house. Not your rooms, sir, as you keep them locked. But she did try the door and she looked everywhere else. And she really admired the new kitchen. A real lady, she is, but she knows what's what. Did I do right, sir?"

I pat Jesse's hand.

"Yes, my dear. Of course you did right. Mrs Jones is not to be resisted when she sets her mind on anything. And she is very welcome to view the premises."

Ah, Alice. You were at the mercy of your own memories. This house has meanings for you too. I am glad to hear that it is so. Well, despite my weariness, I must call for a cab and go to you at once, like a young man in love. You are an old lady now. But I can see you, your step still vigorous, your ankles slender as ever, your stage face perfectly painted, conquering the streets through which you pass. Ah, Alice.

I peer at the card: her name in flourishing swirls and a very good address. But I already know the house. I drive past at least twice a day, watching for lights. But the blinds are firmly in place and the shutters up at nights. Even the servants, who are clearly used to being bribed for information, say that they do not know when she intends to return, but certainly not before the end of the month. She is three weeks early. At least three weeks.

I sway around the corners, leaning against the padded door of the cab, clutching at Psyche for comfort, hoping that it is no coincidence, that she has heard rumours of my return and set forth directly to town, by train, without maids or baggage.

But she must have sent news of her arrival. The dust sheets are off, the lamps are blazing, there are fresh flowers fragrant in the hallway, a frenzy of rushing on the staircases, a fire full of pine cones roaring in the grate against a windy, damp night. She is at home. She is alone. She has been waiting for me and I am to step upstairs at once. Psyche scuttles at my heels. I hover on the threshold, with all my life behind me.

I had not expected quite such vulgar luxury. She sits like an eastern queen in an orgy of glass and gold. Every surface is marbled, inlaid, polished, precious, opulent. And the lady herself glitters with an excess of silk and jewels. She is rich. Every heavy bracelet, necklace, earring proves her wealth. Her satin slippers hit the floor with an astounding thump. Psyche slithers on the parquet, reaches the safety of Aladdin's carpet and gazes desperately around at her reflections. I see myself, echoed to eternity in two opposing Empire mirrors. An arrangement of flowers and peacock's feathers brushes my cheeks. A row of sil-houettes, set in silver and pearl, descend the wall beside the pale marble column of the fireplace, and I see myself again, prominent amongst them, my black profile captured, like a shrunken head. There is too much dramatic vanity on every surface. I cannot concentrate. I cannot understand the distances. Alice has buried herself under a mountain of expensive *things*. This is exactly what she has always desired. And here she is. In the midst of her possessions.

She has both her hands in mine.

She is kissing me.

She is dragging me down onto the sofa beside her.

Psyche is barking at our feet.

We are looking into one another's eyes.

She is exactly the same.

"James, tell that wretched dog to shut up."

This is the first thing she says, rearranging her armada of green and gold silk skirts around her.

"Shhhh, Psyche. Come here." Psyche bounds onto the sofa and sits jealously between us.

"Not on my dress," growls Alice. We all change places.

"You faithless beast. I've a good mind to sack you as my lover. You've been here since mid-August and you never sent a word to me. You knew perfectly well where I was. You had the address in Lincolnshire. I heard quite by chance that you were back. Some stupid youth told me that you were in London, and asked, was all that old gossip true? That we had once had a romantic attachment? I nearly pushed him down the staircase. I don't know what made me crosser – his insolent insinuations or the fact that you hadn't written to me. Explain yourself."

"I'm here now, Alice."

"Well, that's something, at least."

She is suddenly smiling, a huge merry glow of satisfaction. Her face is rounder. She is altogether heavier. But her smile is exactly the same. We sit looking at one another. She squeezes my hand. Then she reads my horror at her décor off my eyeballs and looks round the room complacently.

"What on earth did you expect, James? To find me starving

on a straw pallet and repenting of my sins? Or did you expect me, at my age, to have become another rich man's mistress? Or to be still dressed up as a soldier and showing my legs on stage? You've been gone for thirty years, James. Things change in thirty years."

Indeed, they do. I look at her carpets, her porcelain vases with Chinese dragons coiled around them and her opulent Venetian chandeliers. I look at her raw silk sofas, her inlaid rosewood tables, the thick gold braid which borders the velvet of her drapes, her endless rows of china shepherds warbling along the sideboards, her life-size Moorish boys bearing fruit and flower baskets, her seventeenth-century Flemish tapestries. What do they represent? Dido and Aeneas embracing in the cave, Dido ascending the pyre, Aeneas on board ship in the distance, his back turned, gazing towards Rome. The Greek sequence on the other wall depicts various classical rapes with Zeus transformed into bulls, swans, thunderbolts and showers of gold. The thunderbolt is particularly interesting. Here lies Semele, heaving on top of a sarcophagus, at the very moment of ecstasy and conception. And here is Zeus, his pointing finger luminous in gold stitching, indicating the exact spot. The image is reminiscent of the more dubious Italian Annunciations I had the misfortune to view in Rome. It is decidedly obscene.

"Don't you find these tapestries disturbing?"

"No. Why? They belonged to Adolphus. I don't think I've ever looked at them properly."

"They all represent women being raped or abandoned. And in this one" – I try to decipher a myth I don't know – "being violently sodomised by a group of satyrs."

"Really? How shocking. I didn't know they were so unsuitable. Although Adolphus did keep them in his private rooms . . ."

Alice peers at the shadowy walls. I realise that she is now very near-sighted and too vain to carry spectacles on her breast. After a moment she settles back into her rustling skirts.

"Never mind. They may not be moral, but they're worth a fortune."

I shrug ruefully. Alice has not changed at all.

"Don't sneer," she snaps, "You always had all the worldly goods you ever wanted without even asking."

"That's true."

Like an old-fashioned moralist I want her to tell me that money doesn't matter, that what really count are loyalty and passion, but Alice is on Satan's side and loves The Kingdom of This World. She has satisfied all her desires and she has no regrets. She is a little relieved that her sins are all forgiven her. What were those sins? Charming lecherous old rogues whose skin hung flabby round their necks like turkey roosters?

"James! Don't exaggerate. Adolphus was really quite good-looking. Even in his fifties."

. . . Hoodwinking the gullible bereaved into believing that Paradise exists, with an astonishing mixture of pots, pumps and wind machines . . .

"Why is that any more immoral than what the Church does? You tell me. I give people comfort and hope. Are they better off for believing in me, or aren't they?"

. . . And being excessively grasping with her theatrical managers over the terms of her contracts . . .

"Now there I won't hear one word of criticism. No one should ever perform for free. If I hadn't hustled and higgled they'd have paid me off in old shoes. I was a big star, James. You've got to know your market value and then up the odds. Maybe you'll get it and maybe you won't. But you owe it to yourself to fight for the highest price. I owe it to myself. I always fought for myself. No one else would ever have fought for me."

I sit silent. I have spent my life fighting for those who were too frail even to raise their heads in protest. I suddenly realise that Alice knows what I am thinking. I do not have to speak.

"I know, James, and the wretched of the earth are somewhat less wretched for your passage. But neither of us is out of step with the times. You went in for humanitarian philanthropy and I bettered myself by my own efforts. If the rich and the poor met halfway up the ladder we'd all have more comfortable lives."

We sit holding hands in the firelight, meditating, with a proper theological objectivity, on the morality of our methods and desires. The maid brings in a handsome platter of wine and cakes.

As soon as the goggle-eyed girl has retreated Alice falls upon the cakes.

"When did you last eat? Did you have supper before you came? You can't have done. It must be after midnight. Quick, James. Grab a slice of this. I had it soaked in rum to remind you of that God-forsaken volcanic rock you have just escaped. Eat up. If you don't, I'll scoff the lot."

I had feared that we had spent too many years of our lives apart. Who am I remembering? A child's love is a potent and enduring thing. I am Ariel, returning from Caliban's isle, searching for my elderly Miranda, my first love. Does she see a sixty-year-old man, dwindled to the size of a gloved puppet, still perilously stiff in his elevated soles? Or does she see the child in the fields, his shirt wet with the summer damp from the grass in the early morning? I doubt, I hesitate, I take heart.

Alice is concentrating on a large slice of cake, soaked in rum and filled with cherries. Once, when I was serving in the eastern Mediterranean, a lady of the colony celebrated her fiftieth birthday, and her husband ordered a dress for her from England " . . . and oh dear, Dr Barry, I hardly like to tell you, but you understand these things. It was in the very latest style, charming, but three sizes too small, at least three sizes! And so I had my dressmaker insert a few judicious darts and panels, but covered in flounces and ribbons, that a woman my age simply cannot wear. And of course, I had to tell him I was utterly delighted. We toned it down a little and hoped he wouldn't notice. My daughter was very clever at removing some of the more ostentatious frills. He didn't notice. But, oh dear, oh dear. Well, I'm not eighteen any more, but it seems that he hasn't noticed that either."

"Madam, you are a beloved woman and therefore very fortunate, for your husband still sees the girl he married."

I remember my reply and I see Alice now, more honestly, with a woman's perspicaciousness. And I see a menacingly energetic old lady, with a calculating glint in her black eyes, a woman to be reckoned with, a woman who knows the cost of everything, a woman I still love with all my heart.

"What are you looking at, James? Have I got crumbs on my chin?"

Time to be gallant. Alice loves that.

"I was looking at you and thinking how beautiful you are."

Alice is disarmed. She rewards me with an enormous serious smile. She has a cherry stuck to one of her teeth, most of which, I note, she still has. She always said it was vital for a radiant smile on stage and took good care of them.

I listen to her bright talk, and note the frequent justifications for her new career in spiritualism.

She is admitting that she is not received quite everywhere.

"As an actress," she sighs, "you can't expect to be. We aren't respectable, no matter how well off we are. There are some people who shut their doors to me, whom I could buy out twice over. It's not so much what you do on stage, although that's bad enough, it's what they think you do when you're not working. Sometimes I imagine it's because we earn our own livings and are beholden to no man. And Mrs Jones I may be, but who was the late Mr Jones? That's a very complicated story."

"Indeed, who was he?"

"An Irishman," she glitters, "a very small, but clever man, with adorable red curls."

She leaps up, scattering crumbs and shouts with joy, "James! You're blushing!"

For the first time in thirty years, I surprise myself.

"Come and live with me, Alice."

I hadn't planned to say it, but it was what I wanted now, more than all the riches in the world. She doesn't take any time to consider my proposition. She merely reflects for a moment, staring intently into my face, reading whatever thirty years has written there. She must recognise what she sees, because her smile is the same smile that I had learned to love in David Erskine's haybarn, down by the river where the flies buzz wearily in the August sun, out in the woods where her arms and legs glimmer brown under her stained white apron as she hunts for mushrooms. It is the same smile that I catch for a moment, glancing up, as she sits counting her pleasures and her coins. It is the smile her audience howled to glimpse appearing under her wide hat and plumes. It is the smile I have remembered for over thirty years.

"All right," she says. "I will."

The trouble started a few days later when I informed her that she could not, under any circumstances, bring everything with her.

✤ ✤ ✤ ✤ ✤

I courted Alice Jones, formally, for the look of the thing. I called on her daily at the correct hour. I put up with the tribe of sycophants, arselickers and toads which trooped past her door and up her staircase. I found that one or two of the playwrights, if you were foolish enough to flatter their entertainments with the description "plays", were independent, witty people. They sometimes prevailed upon her to sing to us. Her voice is not as strong as it once was, but her delivery and freshness proved to be as moving as they had ever been.

We quarrelled violently over her table – rapping séances, as I was disposed to describe them. I remained adamant on this point. I stipulated that when she found the right moment and chose to remove herself to my house to enjoy a genteel and loving companionship in her retirement, she must let it be generally known that her services as a professional medium were no longer available. Alice sulked. I insisted. Her public begged. Stalemate.

I persuaded her to moderate her desires concerning the interior decoration of my drawing room, and was forced, in return, to purchase another piano. Her black dinosaur would never have passed through the first-floor windows without extensive demolition of the structural wall. She refused to auction off the rapist tapestries. I faced the prospect of them hanging in baronial folds all down the staircase. Her bed she must have, a four-poster mock-medieval edifice with thick velvet curtains edged in gold brocade and trimmed with fleurs-de-lys. This means that the entire third floor of the house must be hers, boudoir, dressing room, front room with three windows and the small bay alcove with the low seats, all of which she has had to have re-covered with a slimy satin finish and matching cushions.

The old painter once kept all his canvases in these huge spaces. Alice must have posed for him here, in this room, which now has a fresh green view of the trees' blooming. I had been anxious that she would find the house disturbing, but I need not have worried. Alice is quite free from sentimental angst about the past.

"Back at last!" she announced, stepping briskly over the threshold on her first official visit, "I must say, I'm glad that the neighbourhood has improved. Do you remember those children who threw stones at the windows and rubbish down the steps?"

There was talk, of course. I was invited to become a member of the Garrick, given my intimate connections with the theatrical world, as the case was tactfully put. Naturally, I refused. One or two of my old colonial acquaintances called upon me. The gentlemen were suitably impressed. Alice's name, especially among the older generation, still has a magical quality, which awakens an erotic nostalgia for the past. Some of the women were dying to meet her. Others firmly declined, even before they were invited to do so. We spent our time in the company of men.

There were many portraits of her at large in society, including a very provocative one in which she is dressed as the saucy soldier in *Will She? Won't She?*, which hangs in the Garrick. I have never seen the original, although I have inspected many engravings. It is barely decent. Alice had, and still has, the most marvellous legs, long, slender and shapely. It appears that they have been widely appreciated.

I helped with her packing, sorting out endless boxes of playbills and souvenirs. London must be filled with her lovers if the insinuating *billet-doux*, all of which she has kept, are anything to go by. I read many of them carefully and must confess to one or two jealous spasms. The men seemed to think that any actress was fair game. If she was available on stage, then she must be so immediately afterwards, in the green room. The wealthy and the well-connected often left printed cards with discreet initials and locations on the back. Some of these proposed assignations were half a century old.

"Why on earth do you keep all this compromising offensiveness, Alice?" I banged down the box, with its decades of dusty lust, carefully recorded.

"Useful if I want to blackmail someone. Anyway, how can I be compromised? Actresses don't have reputations to lose, James. They just have reputations. Deserved or otherwise. Here, come and help me sort out the hatboxes."

I was submerged, shortly thereafter, in a sea of hats, soft velvet, starched linen, straw and feathers. We spent the rest of the morning trying them on. She could not be persuaded to throw any of them out, even though it was abundantly clear that she would never wear any of them again. But the packing was a useful thing to do. I spent days rummaging in Alice's past lives. She never appeared to hold back any secrets from me. And I – I fell in love with her extraordinary courage all over again.

We were drinking sweet wine one night in her dressing room, having given up on her jewellery, half of which I had immediately despatched to a strongbox in my bank, when our shared past erupted into the present in an unexpected way. Alice's private rooms smelled overpoweringly of musk and attar of roses. All her furnishings were too heavy and overcrowded, even for the fashion of the times. I often felt that I was already interred in a pyramid, surrounded by treasures in decorated urns and mummified slaves. Then Alice began, somewhat nervous and offhand, which was very unlike her.

"I say, James, I know it's going back a bit, but do you remember the spring before your uncle died?"

"How could I forget? It was the first time I proposed to you. Why?"

"Well, in February, when he had his first attack and before you came up to town, we were alone in the house. I'd sent for your mother and the doctor, of course, but the old boy got desperate. There was something he had to tell you. He didn't make sense when he talked. It was all slurred. And so he wrote you a note. He couldn't dictate it to me and he was too weak to write more than a line or two. But he said it was very urgent. And he made me seal it up and promise before God to give it to you."

Alice coloured slightly. She held out a yellowed, crushed slice of paper with the red wax seal crumbling away.

"Well, here it is. It's from James Barry."

I stared at the dead man's message, which fluttered across almost fifty years.

"I should have given it to you. But you were behaving like a dictator. I certainly wasn't speaking to you. And then, to be honest, I forgot. I found it yesterday when I was packing up."

I took the letter from her fingers. It was still sealed. I looked at the yellow paper and the tiny unsteady hand. My name. Not one letter faded, smudged or illegible.

"Where did you find it?"

"In an old jewellery box."

"Was that the box you stole from my uncle's house when you ran away?"

"Stole?" Alice's hackles went up, all down her back. "That's a bit strong. And anyway I've told you this. I remember telling you. I took the box in lieu of one half-year's wages and modelling fees. I needed the money to buy costumes. Your uncle was a skinflint, James. If I'd asked for my wages and he'd got wind of the fact that I wanted to run off and be a heroine on stage, he'd have told me to go to the devil. I took what he owed me."

"Alice, that box was worth three years' wages. At least. Never mind what was in it."

"So? I was very well paid."

"You said you'd sold the box."

"Well, so? I lied, didn't I?"

We sat glaring at each other. I was the first to realise that none of this mattered. Not a damm. I fingered the folded note. The seal looked genuine. And unbroken. Alice watched me angrily.

"You've never read it?" I asked, incredulous. Alice was perfectly capable of forging Barry's seal. She was even capable of prising the signet ring from his dead hand.

"No, I didn't read it. Why should I? It was addressed to you." Alice exploded in a burst of righteousness. She was still sensitive, after all these years, about the theft of the box.

Suddenly, she relented.

"Oh, what does it matter, James? I sold all the stones. Some of them weren't polished, but they were worth quite enough. I never sold the box. James Barry must have known I'd put the letter in the box, but to be honest, I'd forgotton all about the note. The old bugger left you everything anyway. So he can't have had anything significant to say. Well, go on. Open it."

I sat still, silent.

She sat down with a resentful thump on the cushioned stool in front of her dressing table, and all the pots rattled. I broke open the seal. It dropped off the paper. The ink had faded a little and the writing was crooked and unstable. James Barry was dying. He could hardly hold the pen. I peered at his words.

"Well, what does he say? Go on. Any last minute revelations?" Alice was anxious.

I read the letter aloud, one word at a time.

My Dearest Boy I fear you may not come home to me in time I have so much to tell you I have not the strength go to your aunt Louisa Erskine tell her I wished you to know everything and that I loved you and your mother forgive me I am so proud of you

The letter was neither dated nor signed. I handed the note silently to Alice, whose near-sightedness made the re-deciphering of the note a painful process. She wanted to read it herself to check that I had not left anything out.

"So much for that," I said. "I lost touch with Louisa years ago. She must be dead by now."

"Oh no, she isn't" said Alice, lighting up like a gas lamp. "The old hag is fit and well. Quite blind and nearly ninety. She lives in a house on the park with a dozen servants. I know exactly where she lives, because I called on her last year."

"You spoke to her?" I demanded incredulously.

"No," Alice bristled, "she wouldn't see me. The woman's a snob." Alice mimicked Louisa's scalpel precision, " 'Miss Erskine begs to inform Mrs Jones that she is not and never will be at home to receive her.' What a bitch!"

I laughed.

"Well, Alice, Louisa clearly still thinks of you as the scullery maid. Bad luck."

I got up and put my arms around her.

"Don't worry. We'll go together. Let's see if Louisa Erskine will refuse to receive a combination of Dr James Miranda Barry and Mrs Alice Jones."

❖ ❖ ❖ ❖ ❖

Louisa's house must have been elegant once. It was not one I remembered. The style was old-fashioned and ponderous. The wrought-iron frames for torches, held aloft by a brace of muscular stone gods, now useless in gaslight, were still there nevertheless, one either side of the front steps, naked and blackened in the early spring light. There were yellow and purple crocuses carpeting the park, but the wind was cruel. We arrived at eleven o'clock and encountered her doctor, just going away. Miss Erskine was as comfortable as could be expected, if not in the best of tempers. She no longer receives visitors. I doubt that she will be able to see you. Psyche was intimidated by the huge front hall, chilly in the corners and filled with gloomy portraits. A hideous umbrella stand made out of an elephant's foot lurked behind the coal scuttle. We huddled together in front of the fire. Alice was immaculate, but overdressed. She had put on her most beautiful and expensive coat, with lavish fur trimmings and matching muffler. I was not concerned. If Louisa was completely blind it was unlikely that she would notice this exaggerated affluence. In order to appreciate Alice's grandeur she would have to finger the layers, one by one. Psyche growled at the dissected elephant. There was nowhere to sit.

The maid descended the staircase.

"Miss Erskine will see Dr James Barry" was all she said, clearly very embarrassed.

But Alice understood the message. She swung round on her heel and swept out, slamming the front door behind her, leaving me to confront the domestic astonishment. Alice was always good at exits. I hesitated. Her carriage was waiting. I was a little surprised. Usually, Alice was extraordinarily phlegmatic whenever she was snubbed and ignored. She once told me that being cut dead in society was a different form of being ignored from that which she had endured during her life as a scullery maid. Now she knew that she was visible, and threatening. As one of the servant class, she explained, you just don't exist. But if you were a public scandal, then behold, no matter how vehemently you were ignored, the more you increased in size. I wanted to speak to Louisa. I wanted her memories. Here, against all the odds, was someone else who remembered me, who remembered our shared past. And so I left Alice to deal with her anger and strode up the staircase.

Louisa's rooms were stifling. A huge fire burned in the grate and the world was shut out by screens, curtains, shutters and bolsters. There sat Louisa, tiny, crooked and antique, in the midst of this grim, overcrowded airlessness. I took off my jacket as well as my coat and gave them both to the maid. I bent to kiss the old woman in a state of undress I would never normally permit in company. But this woman had known me as a child. She knew more about me, perhaps, than I would ever know myself. Her cheek was the texture of a wrinkled apple, left to ripen for too long in the barn. She wielded a large hearing trumpet and wore a plain white bonnet, so that her skull, which I suspected of being nearly bald, was no longer visible. She gazed sightlessly in my direction. Her eyes were milky, but still fierce. She reached for my cold hands. Our conversation was conducted in a sequence of high-pitched shouts.

"James? Is that you?"

"Yes, it is."

"You haven't brought that grasping harpy with you, have you?"

"If you mean Alice, no, she's gone."

A noise somewhere between a snort and a cackle emerged from the old woman's throat. She then demanded her tea. This was served in a baby's dispenser with yellow flowers painted on the porcelain, so that Miss Erskine did not douse herself regularly in Darjeeling.

"I have the papers read aloud to me. Including the advertisements and the gossip columns. I know that you're carrying on with her. Sometimes, James Barry, I think that you're as bad as your mother."

Suddenly she laughed. An unearthly cracked howl from the last century broke out from her sagging throat.

"Welcome home, James," she croaked.

I said nothing.

"You thought I was dead, didn't you?"

"Well, yes, I'm afraid I did."

"Not unreasonable. Everybody else is."

There was a long pause. I studied the furniture. I didn't immediately recognise any of the pieces. Her desk, yes, that had been in the old house. And perhaps one or two of the paintings, animals in landscapes. But here was over a hundred years of unsorted clutter and all the books she could no longer read. Louisa had been something of a bluestocking when she was young. She had even known Fanny Burney. Why had she never married? She had been beautiful once. The kitchen gossip had been one long story of rebuffed suitors turning tail before her serpent tongue and retreating back to London. Psyche sniffed at the footstools. I could smell the age of the old woman's body, a musty, acrid smell.

"Don't let that creature shit in here," shrieked Louisa, jabbing at Psyche with her stick. My poodle retreated, timid and alert, into my arms. I sat staring at Louisa's black layers and the pearl brooch that was pinned on upside down.

"Why have you come?" she demanded.

"To see you. And to uncover the past."

"Well, that's honest."

I told her about James Barry's letter.

There was another long pause. I noticed the rubbed corners of the chairs, their ancient shabbiness. Moth and rust had begun their inevitable process of corruption. Louisa mumbled and spat into her yellowed handkerchief.

Then she snapped, "What do expect, James? That I should justify your mother's life to you?"

"Does it need justifying?" I asked neutrally. Louisa's tone was unnecessarily aggressive. But she relaxed back into her chair, casting the child's cup aside. She folded her hands on her lap and turned her sightless eyes upon me.

"Yes, my dear. I think it does need justifying. Mary Ann wasn't given to self-explanations. When did she die? Wasn't it in 1823? It doesn't seem so long ago, but it's nearly forty years since Francisco's letter came with the news. She must have killed herself, James. She had a constitution like mine. She could have lived to be a hundred. I always thought that we would both bury the rest of you."

Even at this great distance from my mother's death I find that hearing that obvious fact stated, that she took her own life, makes me catch my breath. Was it so? Was it true? Why did she choose the sea, rather than the arms of a man who loved her?

Louisa appears to guess my thoughts.

"We'll never know why for certain, James. But she wasn't a happy woman, not in herself. She was never married to Francisco, you know. He could have cast her off at any time."

"He never would have done."

"Well, so you say. And he may well have given you that impression. But I don't suppose he ever told you about his wife and children in Venezuela. That's why he never married her. He wasn't about to disinherit his sons. To whom do you think he went home on all those endless journeys to the other side of the globe? I'm told his wife was beautiful, cultivated, from a famous, wealthy family. Why do you think he didn't leave you his fortune?"

Madame Isabella de Miranda
regrets to inform Dr James Miranda Barry that
General Francisco de Miranda
passed peacefully away early this morning at home,
surrounded by his friends and family

MAY HIS SOUL REST IN PEACE

I sit frozen before the sightless eyes of this evil sibyl. Yes, of course I had known. But the gulf between knowing, somewhere in the cleft between your shoulder blades, where the knowledge can do you no harm, and being told, clearly, aloud, so that you cannot escape or deny knowing, so that you cannot pretend not to know – these are two different things. And no, he never told me.

But Louisa has lost interest in the dead. She is remembering her girlhood in Ireland.

"The Erskines always knew the Barrys. We had land in Ireland. Your grandfather used to go hunting with my father. We celebrated Christmas in each other's houses. My brother held your mother in his arms when she was christened. It's a very old connection. David and your uncle travelled on the continent together. I knew your mother before she could walk. Apart from those last two years when she went off travelling to all those pestilential islands with Francisco, I saw her almost every day. I knew your mother all her life. Not that I knew anything about her.

"She was very beautiful, James, very, very beautiful. Francisco always loved beautiful women. Would he have gone on being in love with her when she was no longer beautiful? She must have asked herself that question. Wives can develop thick waists and heavy steps, but a mistress must always be light and laughing, with shining eyes and a pretty smile. Why do you think I never bothered with the whole merry-go-round of sexual capers? I never married because I won't trouble myself with dishonesty and pretence. But if I had been a man like you I would have begged your mother to marry me.

"My brother was in love with her. I was in love with her. We all were.

"When she was sixteen she was extraordinary, that pale cream skin, grey-green eyes and a vast cloud of red hair. Red hair is often thin and fine, not hers. She had the most beautiful, heavy mass of red curls. She was clever too. She read widely. She wasn't shy and she had a sharp wit. Her temperament was egalitarian. She was equally at home with the gentlemen farmers as with the county aristocracy. She was invited everywhere. And she never sat out once at the pump-room dances."

Louisa stretched out a twisted claw to find the child's cup with the thin crack from which she sucked greedily.

"She always loved dancing," I remembered sadly. "Tell me about her husband."

Louisa screwed up her milky eyes, and spat into her handkerchief again. Her face darkened.

"Him? You want to know about him? Well, that's easily told. She married him when she thought Francisco had abandoned her to cook up revolutions on the Continent. Her husband had a lot of money. But there was nothing else to be said for him. He was drunken, abusive, off his head most of the time. But he was in love with her. That much was clear. He wanted her to be his private possession. He threw my brother out of the house once. And that caused a scandal. Bulkeley threatened legal action, divorce and what not. He even appealed for evidence by putting advertisements in the newspapers. Of course, no one came forward. But it took some living down afterwards. Drunken fool, he accused David of seducing his wife."

"And had he?"

"Look, James, I can't see your face, but I can read your tone. And you needn't take that line with me. In these times, appearances seem to count for everything. What you do is your own affair. The great thing is never to be found out. I'm not saying that the formalities and civilities counted for nothing then. But we were more honest about liaisons in my circles. Mary Ann was a beautiful, sensual woman. She had many lovers. And my brother was one of them."

She paused.

"You must have known. You spent all your time in the kitchen. Everybody knew."

"I suppose I half knew. I suspected. I guessed. He was so much older than she was."

"Age is no barrier to sex, my dear child. Men never retire from the bedroom. And neither would women if the opportunities were to go on presenting themselves. Well, when Bulkeley died she went to live with David and Elizabeth. I was there too most of the time. We were old family friends. Your grandparents were dead. James Barry was in Rome. It was all perfectly respectable. Apart from the echoes of Bulkeley's legal tub-thumping. Francisco was in jail somewhere in France. I can't for the life of me remember why. But they got along together perfectly well. These arrangements are more usual than you think. Elizabeth loved Mary Ann. I'm not saying that she never felt any jealousy. But we were all very discreet."

For the first time Louisa weighed her words.

"You were the problem, really."

"I was?"

"Yes, of course you were. David was desperate for children. And like all men, he wanted sons. Elizabeth was barren. It was her greatest grief. David loved his wife too. There was no question of putting her aside or anything like that. His younger brother had three sons. It wasn't likely that they would all be carried off by the scarlet fever. The estate would stay in the family. And so it has. But he wanted to adopt you officially, as his child. That was his overriding desire. Elizabeth was willing. All he had to do was persuade your mother. Mary Ann appeared to accept her position. She was his mistress and that was her role. The only person who could not accept any of this was your uncle, James Barry.

"He came thundering back from Rome, breathing moral fire and Catholic slaughter. He made trouble. He made scenes. He abused Mary Ann to her face, in front of us all. He was an impossible man, James. Impossible."

She tapped her stick on the floor. Psyche froze, fearing another reprimand. She stood poised on her paws, like little pig's trotters. I gestured to her to lie down. She collapsed on the rug with a profound sigh.

"Keep that dog out of my workbox," snapped Louisa. I realised that her hearing was still uncanny and accurate.

"Of course Elizabeth knew that David made love to her. And it's my belief that she hoped Mary Ann would bear another child. She had offered to bring you up. The second one would have been hers by right. Her position was secure. She wanted nothing more. Mary Ann was playing the role of Hagar to my brother's Abraham.

"Then General Francisco de Miranda broke out of the French jail where those ungrateful insurgents had locked him up for safe-keeping. In the Palais de Luxembourg, I believe. He escaped the guillotine by a whisker. And he arrived back in England, full of mad politics and atheistical opinions. He fell in love with Mary Ann all over again. And she with him."

Louisa is a romantic, after all. She has clasped her hands, remembering.

"James, you have no idea how good-looking Francisco was in those days. He was a giant of a man, with a weight-lifter's shoulders. He bulged out of drawing rooms. When he sat down on sofas, they collapsed. He had the most magnificent moustachios, long before they were fashionable. He was daring, outspoken, well-read. We were all in love with him. Every one of us. He had such magnetism, such authority. He swept into our quiet lives like an army, galloping through history. He was full of enterprise, ideas, plans. He entertained us with fabulous tales of his voyages in lands where the ice never thaws and the sun never sets. He had crossed deserts dressed up as an Arab in long white robes. He rode like a corsair. He was one of Byron's heroes. He had a beautiful bass-baritone voice. He sang with such passion, such feeling. He had no inhibitions."

Louisa smiled, remembering. I too, saw him again, as I first had, at a house in the country, long ago, when the century began. A huge puff of smoke floats out of his mouth. As if he were a dragon. There is a chain hanging from a pin only a few inches away from my nose.

"Dragon. Gold."

"Stand to attention when you're addressing me, my girl." He peers into my eyeballs. I see that his own eyes are grey, but flecked with gold. "You don't look like your mother yet, you know. But there's hope that you will."

Is he wearing a uniform? Gold, shiny buttons and a silk cravat? I put out my fingers and touch the gold. I unleash a strange smell: herbs, musk, forests. And the weariness of immense distances.

"Travelling dragon." I look up at him, already in love with his adventures. "Give me gold."

"When he was in the room," said Louisa, dreamily, "we looked at no one else."

And I believed her.

Then she continued, "Mary Ann? Well, she was a woman

who loved first and asked questions afterwards. You may think she always had an eye to the main chance. But it wasn't in her interest to fall in love with Francisco. Yet she did. We all did."

"So long as Francisco was there, nothing mattered. Everybody knew. Nobody cared. Not even David. He was a much older man, James. A girl of eighteen cannot be expected to stay faithful to a married man who is nearly fifty. And he loved Francisco too."

"The only person who wasn't caught up in the glamour of it all . . ."

I finished the sentence for her.

" . . . was James Barry."

Louisa was irritated by my interruption.

"Do you want to hear all this or don't you?" She pulled a face at me and her skin folded into a thousand wrinkles.

"Go on, go on." I said sadly. And the reason for my sadness was simple. She has conjured up the drawing room with the damp brown water marks by the bay window, the stuffed fox under the glass dome, the oval silhouettes in hierarchical order across the yellow patterned wallpaper, all the jewelled and jowled outlines of the Erskine family, renowned for their breeding and their inherited diseases. I see the straight-backed chairs, pushed against the walls of the dining room, the glass cases of fossils, each hand-written label pinned gently down upon the baize. Here are all the shells and stones, which David Erskine gave me to hold, closing his huge, dirty hand gently over mine. The smell of polish in the hallway, the clock's sudden whirr before the chimes, and damp rain on the great pots of geraniums outside the front door, the uncarpeted, treacherous staircases, the Welsh slate floor in the pantry and the kitchen, cold, cold under my bare feet. Why is childhood so sensuous, so bitter and so poignant? I cannot displace this past.

Out in the patterned sunshine, in the brick yard peppered with chickens, sits Alice Jones. She has been shelling beans. Here they lie, bright green ovals in the basket at her feet. I have watched her work, her fingers hard and rapid as the potter's hand, thumbing the slits open, and from the cradle of her apron there falls a shower of vivid, fresh, green beans. Now she plucks at the seams of her dress, retrieves a small loaf from her pocket and leans back, crumbling stale bread between her grimy fingers. The chickens gather, expectant, all around her. She gazes up, into the sun.

I hear the nicker and stamp of the horses, shouts from the gardens, far away on the other side of the house, and above us, the great rustling sway of the horse chestnuts, a green shining tent of leaves, the pink and white candles luminous in full bloom.

I smell the scythed grass, see it lying in uneven yellow rows as the whole earth breathes the warm damp of early summer. Violets and aubretia cover the rock garden, and on the other side of the ha-ha, screaming with pleasure because he has discovered a giant toad among the wild irises and cowslips, is an old man with a musty wig and a dented straw hat. I hear his excited yells.

"Elizabeth, Mary Ann, come and look, come and look."

I am the first one over the ha-ha and he catches me in his arms. He is like a Hogarth cartoon, all red cheeks and breeches.

"Here you are, my boy! Look!"

And I see the broken veins on his nose and his contented happiness when I stroke the unwilling toad, delighted, and look up to return his smile.

"She loved two men, James. My brother and Francisco de Miranda. But they all loved you. David's opinions on the education of women were very advanced for the times. It's true that he had always wanted a son. But he didn't want you to be wasted. So they decided to share you too, as they shared Mary Ann, and to invest in you together. But it was all Mary Ann's doing. They'd never have dreamed up this scheme on their own. They wouldn't have dared. She put them up to it."

"The meeting in the labyrinth," I whispered.

Louisa peered at me sightlessly and leaned forward. Her collar smelt of musty lavender.

"What? What did you say? Speak up, child."

For a moment I said nothing. Psyche jumped up, her claws catching in my trousers. I cannot believe that I am over sixty years old.

"What of James Barry?" I asked carefully. I wanted to avoid all the obvious questions.

"Ah," Louisa stiffened, "this is not easy to tell. You're a doctor. You must have seen these things many times."

But there was a terrible pause, nevertheless, as Louisa's sightless eyes bulged and glistened. She lashed out a little with her stick and Psyche growled softly.

"Keep that animal quiet. Or put it out."

She dropped her cup. I felt like a canary under a bell jar, running out of oxygen. The old woman went on talking softly, as if to herself.

"What does a man see in his sister? The lost female part of his own soul. James Barry loved Mary Ann too. He was already a grown boy when she was born and her mother died giving birth to her. Mary Ann was therefore his charge, his responsibility. He brought her up. She looked to him for everything. And he worshipped her every gesture. She was so graceful, so sinuous, like a young sapling. When she was a child they were inseparable. You have her eyes, James."

"They were Catholics, all mired up together in a big draughty house in Ireland living through the winters with next to no company. The old father was quite mad. He sat in the kitchen, spitting into the fire, when he wasn't openly engaged in doing unspeakable things with his housekeeper. I think our house was a sort of refuge for the children. Barry kept all his paints at our house. My father fitted him up with a studio.

"Your grandfather opposed his son's ambition to be a painter for as long as was decently possible. But David Erskine and old Burke, Edmund Burke, the philosopher, talked him into putting a little money into Barry's education as a painter. Then he won the Prix de Rome and that was it. His vocation was settled. But he already carried the enemy within, his father's nature, which erupted in rages and paranoias, like a sequence of wens and boils. Barry always believed that everyone was against him. He behaved as if they were. And then, mostly, his fears came true."

She paused. Psyche had closed her eyes, overcome with heat, and was beginning to snore slightly.

"And Mary Ann?" I asked.

"Well, he couldn't take her to Rome, could he? She was left behind in Ireland. Left to grow into that beautiful young woman who liked making trouble and breaking hearts."

Louisa paused again. Then she yawned.

"Remember James, I've only ever had her version of her brother."

The muted rattle and crash of the passing cabs shield the silence from becoming oppressive. But the stuffy thickness of the old woman's cluttered rooms tickles my throat. I have lost the thread. What does it matter if my mother and her brother were once lovers? The passionate intensity between them was their affair, their business. Mary Ann was never the kind of woman who could have been seduced or forced. Not even by a bully like James Barry. She was never powerless. If she posed naked for him in his studio, it was because she wanted to do it. If she lay down beneath him when they were young, to draw him back to her in the world of wet green, which they had shared as children, then it was because that was what she had desired.

Louisa is right. I am a doctor. I have seen terrible things. I have seen human lives casually shredded and thrown away. I have watched the endless wretched toll of poverty and disease. I have seen men turn upon their own children, gluttonous as Saturn for their shrivelled, wasted flesh. But my mother loved her brother in ambiguous, private ways. He made her angry. But she was never afraid of him. She never adandoned him. She was not his victim.

Louisa's mouth drops open and she gurgles slightly. She has fallen asleep in the midst of her own narrative.

I rise quietly, scoop Psyche off the floor and tiptoe out. The maid is waiting anxiously at the door. I leave a note on the back of my card, assuring Louisa that I will visit her again tomorrow, that I am neither offended nor distressed by her stories and that I will cherish all that she has told me as a sacred confidence. With any luck she will entirely forget whether she has revealed anything at all, either vital or incriminating, and the past will rest like an ageing grave, where the lovers slumber in peace beneath the lichen and dead leaves.

I walk out into the terrible damp chill of a February afternoon in London. The murky light lifts a little in the gusts which splatter drying flecks of mud against my trousers. Psyche whimpers and demands to be carried inside my coat. We stride away across Hyde Park Gate towards the mansions of Mayfair, while the damp collects in drops along the rim of my hat.

Alice is waiting for me, dressed up for battle like a Christmas tree. She is wearing an array of expensive trinkets which Adolphus no doubt hung upon her over the years. Her cheeks are slightly flushed and her black eyes polished and glittering. I am certain that she has been drinking.

"Well? And what did the old cow have to say?"

"Watch your language, Alice."

She glares.

I fling myself down in the nearest chair and Psyche flies up onto my lap. I gaze at Pomona's naked bottom as Vertumnus grabs her robe. I can see it through the open door. The tapestry is hanging on the landing. And then I see James Barry's painting of the same scene, the nymph's basket of apples strewn across the unlikely marble floor of a neo-classical building. I remember the woman's face, my mother's face, open-mouthed in fear, confronting the satyr's treacherous, leering grin. And now I see the grimace of elderly lust, the wicked caricature of his rich friend and patron, which James Barry has embedded in the painting. The old goat rampant before young flesh. Age is no barrier to sex, my dear child. Men never retire from the bedroom. And neither would women if the opportunities were to go on presenting themselves. But how can I know if that version was the truth? James Barry never painted the reality. He painted his jealous desire for revenge. And yet . . . I sink into my chair, uneasy at the images which return. The truth lies beyond my grasp. But I cannot bring myself to care, no matter how disturbing my memories become. They are dead, dead, dead decades ago. I am past sixty years old, and I have walked two miles in windy spring cold.

"Any money going? Was that it?" Alice demands, in character.

"Oh no, nothing like that. She wanted to talk about the past. She wanted to give me a list of my mother's lovers."

"Oh, the lovers!" Alice loses interest a little, but takes up battle stations on the hearth rug anyway.

"And could she tell you which one was your father? We always speculated about that in the kitchen. Cook practically had the odds worked out on a slate. But you had us confused. You contrived to look like all three of them."

"Did I? All *three* of them?"

"You still do. You're a red-headed dwarf like Barry. Yet you stand up straight with your chin in the air like the General, and you've inherited all his mannerisms of command. But then, you have David Erskine's gentle mouth and smile. Your best features! Both still quite charming."

I have no answer to the past.

She comes over and kisses me, long and hard. I smell cinnamon and alcohol on her breath.

"And am I forgiven for staying on with Louisa? Even when she wouldn't receive you?"

Alice nods.

"Have you been drinking?"

She nods again, shameless, smiling.

"How many glasses?"

Two fingers shoot up.

"Just two? Port wine? My best? And you had it mulled! Alice, you're a criminal. I keep second-rate port for mulling."

She laughs out loud and jingles the household keys on her belt, just as Mary Ann used to do.

"Listen, James, I know just what the old witch will have said. And whoever gives a damn who their father was. As long as you get the financial backing. Which you did, James. You had enough fathers to keep you happy for a lifetime. And a very pretty mother, who left you her French accent and her surgeon's hands."

❖ ❖ ❖ ❖ ❖

Louisa died peacefully a year later. I visited her regularly until her demise and I followed her coffin to the grave, along with the younger generation of Erskines, who regarded me as much a relic from the past century as their great-aunt. Louisa left me a handsome bequest, with a specific message that not a penny was to be passed to the "grasping harpy". Alice rejoiced in the money and I suppressed the message. Visiting Louisa had been more problematic than I had imagined, for Alice sulked whenever I made ready to depart. Her equanimity over the old aristocrat's refusal to receive the servant who had made good was never quite restored. Louisa had once combed the lice out of Alice's hair while they sat on the back steps, years ago, in the house where we had grown up together, and Alice felt that this memory should take precedence over everything else. She was family, after all. Louisa didn't see it in exactly that light. She refused to hear Alice's name mentioned in her presence and gave Alice as the principal reason why she had ceased going to the theatre. I resisted Alice's attempts to have herself reinstated, on the grounds that an old lady of nearly ninety-four must be left to die with her prejudices intact. Alice never accepted this and we quarrelled from time to time, always going over the same ground, and never achieving a resolution.

In fact, I was surprised how often we did quarrel. If I had expected a tranquil and harmonious life with Alice Jones, I would have been mightily disappointed. Alice would not accept the role of peaceful old lady. She loved scandal and intrigue. She kept up with all her theatrical cronies and gave frequent raucous dinners, after which I often found several of the guests, stained and snoring, asleep on the couches downstairs, and once, peacefully laid out on cushions, behind an armchair in the breakfast room. Jesse had laid the table carefully without waking him, stepping over his boots as she cleared away the debris of the previous night. The now comfortable dinner guest looked like a dead soldier in the battle for pleasure, laid to rest where he had fallen.

Alice was very apologetic. But it happened again and again.

I was used to spending a great deal of time on my own and could not accustom myself to much company. Yet I had no public duties to occupy my days and therefore, I imagine, my unease and restlessness increased. My public and professional life was over. I was left living inside the shell of the man I had once been. I read. I studied. I visited exhibitions. I went to public lectures. I kept up with the new developments in medicine. Yet it seemed that there was no reason to do so, and no purpose to give direction to my days. I had been a servant of the Crown. I was not a scholar, neither by nature nor by acquired inclination, and apart from my life-long love of Shakespeare and the English poets I was only an occasional evening reader of the new novels and magazines. I rarely attended the opera or the theatre. Tastes had changed radically in my absence. Often I found that I had passed an evening of utter boredom in uncongenial company. I disappointed Alice, who flung herself into the pursuit of pleasure, night after night, with undignified abandon.

Things came to a head in the spring two years after Louisa's death. I discovered that Alice had continued, all her life, to send money back to her family in the country, and now her youngest niece was to be married. She decided to go home for the wedding. And I decided to go with her.

The journey was quite different from what it had once been. We travelled all the way to Shrewsbury by train, in our own compartment. Alice adored watching the landscape bouncing past, interspersed with great puffs of steam. She loved watching the rain streaming diagonally across the glass. She liked the varnished elegance of the interior and the ubiquitous smell of soot. She wolfed her dinner in the dining car, drank wine in public, autographed the waiter's menus, and strolled along the platform whenever we stopped for any length of time, twirling her umbrella. She was on the lookout for what she described as "improvements". Some country people found the advent of the railways a disturbing phenomenon. Alice loved change for its own sake. She was born into the right century.

Two of her nephews and her youngest brother were waiting for us, armed with hired carriages, umbrellas and cushions. Every conceivable development in the weather had been envisaged and alternative plans carefully laid. The family had improved its state during my long years in the tropics. The girls were no longer in service, but in the dressmaking industry, and the boys worked in the Coalbrookdale porcelain factory and out at Jackfield, making decorated ceramic tiles. There was more money to be spent. Everyone now wore shoes and owned a dinner service. Alice's elder brother, a retired Nonconformist patriarch with foaming whiskers, had purchased an old ironmaster's house, with a proper conservatory and two parlours, one of which was reserved for Alice. And there she sat, enthroned.

As soon as I could disengage myself from the collective domestic excitement, I borrowed a horse and rode out to the old estate, despite the fact that it was late in the afternoon.

The chestnut trees in the park were just escaping from winter and I saw each bud, lurid and green, barely unfolding from the soft fledgling down of the paler underleaf. The grass still wore its winter brown and the air was sharp. I was glad that I had left Psyche by the fire with Alice. My horse snorted like the locomotive, giving out thick gentle puffs, as we trotted down the gravel ways, looking out to the hills on the Welsh borders. The timber was well tended, but the house itself looked empty and sad as I approached. All the shutters were put up on the second floor. The front garden was not as opulent as it had once been. But the huge sweep of daffodils, brilliant doubled trumpets, still flowed over the rough lawns, a great gust of colour in the pallid light. The window sills needed re-painting, but it was all much the same as it had always been. A stranger answered the door.

The family were absent, said the housekeeper, and the main rooms covered in dust sheets and darkness. But I was welcome to wander in the park and gardens for as long as the light held. I left her my card and tied up my horse in the stables. There was no one there. The kitchen yard was unchanged, but deserted. The laundry door was ajar. There were no animals nesting in the outhouses. The dovecot was empty and none of the dogs came to greet me. Here was the locked house, married to time. Upstairs, in one of the small windows, I saw a faint light. There was fresh straw laid in one of the stalls, and a pitchfork balanced across an empty wheelbarrow. Two wooden buckets stood stacked one inside the other. My footsteps chimed hollow on the brick path as I set off towards the fountains in the eastern gardens.

Here, nothing had changed. All the flower beds were neatly turned and the roses were properly mulched. But the fountain at the foot of the stone steps was thick with moss, and the brackish water slaked with dead leaves. Hermes sat disconsolate on top of the greening stone. The cupids drooped, waterless, astride the dolphins. The sundial was still there, but that too had acquired a sinister tint of fresh green. The alley way of rhododendrons had been cleared, giving that side of the gardens a naked, unprotected flank. The wooden Chinese pergolas had been replaced and a row of stone statues, the old stone gods, unappealing and aggressive, marked the entrance to the maze. They were men's gods: Mars, Zeus, Hercules, Vulcan and Apollo. The women's gods were hidden within. I entered the maze.

The yew hedges were lower than I remembered, but well trimmed, and the old stone seats which had punctuated the labyrinth were still there, cold slabs perched on stone balls. The maze no longer seemed to be an endless threatening prison. Now it was simply a dated garden curiosity, a harmless amusement of hexagonals which would baffle no one for very long. I reached the core. The fountain's goddess of love, modestly hiding her breasts, the huntress poised for flight, her dogs beneath her and Zeus's only begotten daughter, the owl perched on her shoulder, were all gone. No trace remained. Instead, there was an unmarked paved square in the last box, at the heart of the puzzle. I looked round at the unyielding banks of yew. The scene was blank. In the fading light of a spring day, two reflecting empty squares of hedge and stone had nothing to reveal to each other or to me. The sound of the fountain had always led us to the core of the maze. Now, for those who had achieved the centre, there were no clues and no rewards. There was nothing to see.

I stood alone at the heart of the labyrinth and listened to the rooks calling in the early dusk.

❖ ❖ ❖ ❖ ❖

When we returned to London I told Alice what I intended to do. She leaped to her feet and began shouting.

"James! Are you out of your senses? Do you think that your pension would be paid to some nameless Irish woman who'd hoodwinked the army all her life? They'd probably say you couldn't possibly have been a real doctor either – if you'd been a woman all along!"

Alice spat out the word "woman" with perilous contempt.

"Anyway, what on earth do you mean? Imposture? Mas-

querade? Your real identity? What is your real identity? You're
James Miranda Barry, near relative to David Steuart Erskine,
eleventh Earl of Buchan. You even attended your Aunt Louisa's
funeral. You've got aristocratic connections that you're proposing
to deny? I don't want to live with a public scandal. Think what
they'd say about me. They'd say that I knew all along and was
some sort of Sapphist. Adolphus would turn in his grave. Just
when we're received almost everywhere together. What were you
intending to do? Disappear? How can you even think of it?

"And what is genuine? This genuine inner soul you say you
want to discover? Nothing's absolutely genuine! You aren't the
same person with everyone you know. You act out different roles.
I've acted every minute of my life. I'm always on stage. We all
are. It's all a performance. Does your inner soul call for the hot
water every morning and then dismiss the maid so that you can
start washing? Or is that someone else you've always pretended
to be? What I know and what you seem to forget is that we've
only got one play in which to act. And you make up the lines
and the plot as you go on. Did you need Shakespeare to tell you
that? There's no rehearsal and no second night in which to do
better. We're on stage now. This is it. And you got the breeches
part, James. Oh, you're such an idiot. You've played that part
with verve and gusto. You've been marvellous. You've done it.
Now, do you want to speak the epilogue – where you turn up
in skirts to point the moral before being booed off the stage?
You're mad!"

She paced the room with a handkerchief pressed to her face.
Two fine red spots of rage gleamed on her cheeks. For once,
despite all her disclaimers, Alice wasn't acting. She was very angry
indeed.

"What do you want to do? Go around saying you're a woman?
Wear my clothes? What do you think will happen? Do you think
that they'll try to cure you or make drawings of your anatomy?
Or sell you to a circus? For Heaven's sake, James . . ."

She reached the hearthrug and picked at one of her appalling
china shepherds on the mantelpiece. Then she actually stamped
her foot.

"You'd be spitting on people who've moved heaven and earth

to make your life adventurous and interesting. You've got money. You've done well for yourself. Plenty of people look up to you. Are you going to turn on them too and say, look, I didn't mean any of it? It's all been a mistake? Because that's what you'd be saying.

"Damn you, James! How dare you? Why have doubts at this stage? Why have doubts at all about who you are?"

She stood biting her lip.

"Who is Alice Jones? I'm a great English actress. There are paintings and play bills and God knows how many ecstatic notices to prove it. No one bothers with where I came from. Well, very few people, anyway. It's not where you come from, it's where you get to that counts. And are you really telling me that you want to undo it all?"

She turned on me.

"James Barry, you listen to me." Now she was standing on the toes of my boots, glowering, and I could feel her anger in my fingertips.

"You are who the world says you are. And the world says you're a man.

"I'll hear no more about it. Not one word."

She flung herself down beside me.

"Alice," I said quietly, "I haven't said a word. You've done all the talking."

Alice burst into tears, the huge indignant howl of a child who has just been told that playtime is over, and now it's time for bed. I took her hand in mine and squeezed it gently. When the first storm of tears was past and she was sniffing crossly, I began again.

"Alice, I've spent my life in disguise. I don't know who else I could have been."

She cut me off.

"But you loved dressing up. Don't you remember your first uniform? And how you danced for me in a swirl of red? You looked wonderful. I was so jealous. You loved the power, James. You did, you did. You loved ordering people about and shooting at Zulus – "

"Alice! To my certain knowledge I never shot anybody who hadn't agreed to be shot at."

"Duelling! You fought duels, James. You took mad risks. You courted discovery."

I was silent. I remembered that heady rush of fear as I walked away from my opponent, knowing that, were I even to be wounded, my career would be over. Yes, that had been part of the glimmering, unspoken motive. Alice was right. I had courted discovery.

"You didn't exactly make yourself invisible either, did you? You quarrelled with everyone you had anything to do with. Your staff adored you and your masters all shuddered when they saw you coming. You provoked trouble. You did it on purpose. You were talked about, James. You had a public life."

"Exactly," I shouted, suddenly as angry as she was, "I had a public life. But what else did I have? I had no one there at the end of the day. I didn't have you."

For a second she is silenced. But I've never known Alice let someone else have the last word and she didn't now. She pulled me round to face her.

"You've got me now. I love you, James, and if I'd ever once felt that I could have lived my life with you I would have done. But you'd never have been upstaged by any other woman. There was only room at the top for you. You'd never have let me tour on my own. I had to. I wanted to get on. You'd have ended my career as surely as I would have supported yours. You knew too much about me. I needed besotted, darling idiots like Adolphus, God bless him, not a man who asked questions like you did. Of course I loved you, James, but I wanted my life too. I didn't want to be dragged off to the tropics to die."

"I would never have let you go there," I snapped, alarmed.

"You see. I'd never even have got to dance at the plantation balls. James, you're too used to giving orders and having them obeyed. I can't bear arguing and you love it."

"But you like having your own way, Alice."

"So do you."

We hissed at each other like scrapping cats. She tugged at one lock of my greying red curls, then leaned over and kissed my cheek. She tried a wheedling, begging tone.

"Oh James, we're so happy now, please don't spoil it."

Then something terrible occurred to her.

"Don't tell me that you aren't happy. That you want something different? Something else? Oh, please don't tell me that."

These were real tears.

She had conquered once more. What could I do but reassure her? For in the course of our quarrel something had become clear to me. I was no longer in any danger of being discovered. And it was the danger of the disguise that I had loved. I had been obsessively preoccupied, for so long, with the fact of my loneliness, with the secrets of my hidden being, locked away from the world, that I was unable to understand the change. I was no longer a solitary man. James Miranda Barry was at last reunited with the only person left in the world in whom he had a complete and absolute trust and whom he had always loved.

"The story has a happy ending, James," she smiled. Her face was a little swollen from crying. "We found one another at last. Shall I ring for tea?"

I am unable to resist her.

We walked along the river front at dusk, watching the lamplighter moving rapidly between the streetlights with his long rods, like a burglar scurrying from house to house. And what would other people have seen? The little doctor, moving stiffly but still ferociously straight, his military bearing undiminished, and the gorgeous figure of the famous Mrs Jones. Who is to say that the old actress is slightly overdressed? No matter. It is all the very latest style, down to the short cape and trimmings. She bows to her passing public, always gracious, never haughty, heroine of the boards and applauded to the echo. Bravo! Bravo! Bravo! But perhaps the most subtle performances are never detected, and cannot therefore be admired.

❖ ❖ ❖ ❖ ❖

I look out over the Atlantic. I hear seagulls crying, following the ship, weaving back and forth in patterns, swooping and diving into the wake. I notice the creak of the ropes, the wind singing in the rigging. The water level shifts in one of the buckets by the mainmast and the gust bulges the sails. I neither move nor stir. We are moving steadily westwards. I know this from the position of the sun. I can hear no other human voice, only the gulls circling, calling. Is the ship abandoned? This cannot be. I am here and the decks are well scrubbed, the brass polished and gleaming. The ropes are new, the hatches closed. I listen to the steady rush of the waves against the keel as the sloop thrusts ever westwards and I feel the sun on my left cheek. Far out to sea, I can see the dolphins, forked flashes, leaping, vanishing, then appearing again, two or three playing together in the bright water. All around, as far as the flat line of the horizon, stretches infinite, illuminated space and the ship moves onwards. I hear no voices. I am alone. I gaze out into this endless clear distance, this great dome of pale ether and this grey-green blue. I close my eyes. When I stare once again into the great spaces of ocean and sky, I feel that the wind has freshened. We are moving more swiftly and the jib is now full. The buntlines and bowlines are taut. Someone has hung stern sails on the mizzen-mast, and we are now taking all the wind there is. Here are the flying fish in vivid colours and the sea is an extraordinary, deep, transparent blue. The light has changed, from washed white to gold. We are entering the tropics. And is it to be so? Am I returning there to die? Is this my last voyage home? Was my home there with you? In the place you chose – for I can accept it now – that you chose to slip quietly over the rim, away from the great hot light of the sun, down, down, down, into this unending, deep transparent blue.

❖ ❖ ❖ ❖ ❖

"James, can you hear me?"

A slight shiver moves across his features. The barest of nods.

"James, shall I send for the priest?"

The mouth tightens.

"Well?"

The answer comes in a tender, slipping breath.

"No."

"James, you godless fool! You were baptised a Catholic. You

can't die without the last rites of Holy Church. What would your uncle, your mother and your stepfather have said?"

There is the faintest glimmer of a smile.

❖ ❖ ❖ ❖ ❖

25, Duke Street
Westminster
25th July 1865

Sir

**Inspector-General
Dr James Barry**

Disease: Diarrhoea

I have the honour
to report that
the officer named in
the margin died at
4 o'clock am this morning
I have the honour to be,
Sir,
Your most obedient
humble servant
D. R. McKinnon M.B.,
S. Surgeon Major

Somerset House
25th August 1865

Staff Surgeon Major D. R. McKinnon

Sir,

It has been stated to me that Inspector-General Dr James Barry, who died at 14, Castle Street East on the 25th July 1865, was, after his death, discovered to be a female.

As you furnished the certificate as to the cause of his death, I take the liberty of asking you whether what I have heard is true, and whether you yourself ascertained that he was a woman.

Perhaps you may decline answering these questions: but I ask them not for publication but for my own information.

I have the honour to be, Sir,
Your faithful servant,
George Graham
Registrar-General

25 Duke Street
Westminster
26th August 1865

To George Graham
Registrar-General.

Sir,

Further to your enquiry as to the sex of the late Inspector-General Dr James Barry. I had been intimately acquainted with that gentleman for a good many years both in the West Indies and in England and I never had any suspicion that Dr Barry was a female.

I attended him during his last illness and for months previously for bronchitis, and the affection causing his death was diarrhoea, produced apparently by errors in diet.

On one occasion after Dr Barry's death I was sent for to the office of Sir Charles McGregor (Army Agents) and there the woman who performed the last offices for Dr Barry was waiting to speak to me.

She wished to obtain some perquisites of her employment which the Lady who resided with Dr Barry as his intimate companion in the house in which Dr Barry had died had refused to give her.

Amongst other things she said that Dr Barry was a female and that I was a pretty doctor not to know this and that she would not like to be attended by me. I informed her that it was none of my business whether Dr Barry was a male or a female and that I thought he might be neither, viz. an imperfectly developed man.

She then said that she had examined the body and that it was a perfect female. The woman seemed to think that she had become acquainted with a great secret and wished to be paid for keeping it.

I informed her that all Dr Barry's relatives were dead, and that it was no secret of mine, and that my own impression was that Dr Barry was a hermaphrodite.

But whether Dr Barry was male, female, or hermaphrodite I do not know. I am prepared however to swear as to the identity of the body being that of a person I had known well for eight or nine years, and I myself see no purpose in making the discovery, given that Dr Barry's professional reputation is above criticism.

I have the honour to remain, Sir, your obedient servant,
Major D. R. McKinnon
Staff Surgeon

From Edward Bradford
Deputy Inspector of Hospitals
To The Editor, *Medical Times*

Sir,

The stories which have circulated since the death of Dr James Barry
are too absurd to require serious refutation. There could not have
been any doubt, among people who knew him, on the subject of
his physical constitution which was really that he was a male in
whom the development of the organs of sex had been arrested from
the sixth month of pregnancy. It is sad that no qualified persons
took the opportunity of his death to examine closely the physical
condition of the deceased.

I remain, Sir,
Yours, etc
Edward Bradford

The Old Manse
Winderton
Cumberland
20th September 1865

Sir,

I had the honour of serving with Dr James Barry for many years
and of knowing him first at university, where we studied under Dr
Fryer, and subsequently at Guy's Hospital, where we were both
apprentice surgeons of Sir Astley Cooper. We were then colleagues
at the Military Hospital in Portsmouth before his removal to the
Cape. I was his life-long correspondent and had the pleasure of
visiting him at his London home less than three years ago. Dr Barry
was a dedicated doctor whose primary concern was for the welfare
of his patients. He was a short-tempered man and would not tolerate
inefficiency, incompetence or uncleanliness. He made many enemies
in the profession and elsewhere on account of his championship of
the weak and helpless. His diminutive stature and the fine hands
which were so advantageous to his work as a surgeon, combined
with the above-mentioned professional jealousy of many years'
standing, have led to the insulting slanders published in the press
over the last weeks. Dr Barry was a perfect gentleman and a

courageous man. We were intimately acquainted and I am prepared, on my honour, Sir, to vouch for his reputation.

I remain Sir, your obedient servant,
Robert E. Jobson
Surgeon-General (rtd)

Poynton Hall
Berkshire
3rd October 1865

To The Editor
The Times

Sir,

I have read the rumours concerning Dr James Barry published in your organ with mounting amazement. I served in the IV ★★★★shire regiment along with Dr Barry on the island of C★★★★ over forty years ago. Our paths in life may have diverged, but I have never forgotten him & no one of his acquaintance ever would. An unfortunate misunderstanding led us to confront one another with loaded weapons before Dr Barry had been on the island above a year. It is well known that the doctor was an expert marksman, and had his magnanimous generosity not spared my life I had been a dead man. No woman would be capable of such a deed. No, Sir, Dr Barry was a small man in stature alone; in all other respects he was generous, compassionate and in every way admirable. I owe him a great deal and I will not tolerate these insults to his honour and his memory.
I remain, Sir, your obedient servant,
James Loughlin (Bart)

5th October 1865

My Very Dear James,

I saw your letter concerning Dr Barry in The Times and I could not *resist* writing to you again. I know that we agreed to maintain a decent silence for the time being, so please forgive me. But tell me at once, is it true that Dr Barry commenced a *liaison* with the actress Mrs Alice Jones, upon his return from the West Indies? We have heard rumours that they were actually *living together*! Although they went so very little into society. Can this *really be* the case? If you have any *positive* information, please do write to me directly.

As to the rumours concerning the good doctor's true identity, I am in a position to *quite positively affirm* his masculinity, although I could never admit to that in public, but I imagine that you are too. For you travelled alone together many times. Yes, I do believe you did. And I *simply cannot imagine* that the extraordinary Mrs Jones would ever take up with a man who was unable to give her *every satisfaction*. She has *that kind* of reputation.

I have sent this under separate cover as we used to do, so that your wife need not know that we are in correspondence, as I am sure you would prefer that. But pray *do write* to me by return.

I am, as always, your devoted
Charlotte

Charlotte, Lady Fraser (née Walden)

The journalist's name was Henrietta Stackpole. She had a neat, quick step and was freshly trimmed at all the edges. She swept into the front hall, smelling of energy and America. Alice watched her through a crack in the dining-room door, while she gave her name in ringing tones and began opening her smart leather attaché case and extracting notebook and pencils. Alice was used to the press, but not to lady journalists. The maid set off up the main staircase carrying the embossed card, and Alice ran for the back stairs. She crashed into Jesse on the upper landing, snatched the card and hurtled, breathless, into the drawing room.

"Shall I show the lady up, ma'm?" Jesse demanded anxiously. Jesse was only just weathering the scandal. She had adored her master.

"Let her wait a minute while I compose myself. Then show her up."

Alice paced the floor.

None of this would have happened if I'd laid James out myself. I never thought that Sophia would blab. The unscrupulous chit wanted money from all sides. Can't say I blame her. Shhhhh, Psyche, don't whine. We've got to get along together now, without him. He wouldn't want us all to fall to bits at the final hurdle. I can't get rid of the Army Agents. They want to control and suppress the whole thing. If that man

McGregor comes round here again I shall show him the door myself. What would James have done? Does it matter? He was the one who lost his nerve at the last. Not me. What on earth did he want to do? Retire as a woman to some secluded cottage like the last Poet Laureate? Ridiculous! You can't suddenly become a woman. It takes years of practice. He knows nothing about clothes, manners, gestures. He wouldn't even know how to walk up and down a staircase, let alone climb in and out of a carriage. Or how to manage the servants. I can't see James learning how to ask people to do things instead of telling them. And he didn't even have a name. I suppose it must have been Miranda. But so far as the army and I are concerned it's still James Barry, after his uncle. But what am I supposed to do in the face of all this gossip? Silences cease to be dignified if the scandal persists. They become positively sinister. And certainly suspicious. I'm the talk of the town already. Again.

Alice smiled to herself, with not a little satisfaction.

Everybody's waiting for me to speak. Well, if I never knew, then that proves one thing. That it was an entirely virtuous connection, with separate bedrooms. The lot. And ever so much more interesting than an ordinary liaison. Eyebrows will go up all over London. I'll be invited everywhere and able to get out of this reclusive confinement – into which James had us so securely locked. Freedom! I could go up to Lincolnshire for Christmas. I may be an old lady now, but there's life in the old bird yet. I was still dancing last season. I'll be able to receive a lot more visitors. Instead of Mrs Jones being endlessly indisposed at Dr Barry's command.

I'm not saying that it wasn't wonderful, being together with him at last. But I did feel all gobbled up. Like a theatre that the bailiffs have closed down before the last performance in the run was over. He'd been on his own so long he couldn't imagine what a social life was like. Locking his bedroom door at night, too, so that I was reduced to stratagems, like Iachimo, to get a peek at Imogen's breasts. And sometimes he didn't speak for hours, just sat there like the Sphinx. Mind, you, he always was like that. Even when we were children. He'd read, or sit silently, thinking. Too much thinking isn't good for you.

All right, then, yes, we'll talk to the Americans.

How do I look? Mmmmm? Past my best some years ago. No amount of paint is going to change that, but in a dimmer light not so bad.

"Jesse, draw the blinds and show the lady journalist up to the drawing room. Bring us some cold champagne.

"Yes, I did say champagne. Why not? Here's the key. Quick, girl. Run. She's been standing in the hall for long enough."

Alice arranged her black mourning into a becoming torrent of grief and bowed her head. She heard the brisk click of Miss Stackpole's boots on the stairs, then the soft thud of her arrival in the drawing room.

"Miss Stackpole, ma'am," whispered Jesse, terrified.

Alice raised her stricken head slowly to meet Miss Stackpole's curious green gaze. *Oh God. She's taken her hat off and the woman has red curls, just like James. What a shock!*

"Mrs Jones, it is very good of you to see me." An American twang. The voice was sympathetic, but direct.

Alice allowed a lengthy pause to become almost alarming, then murmured, "Miss Stackpole, you must be very tired after your long journey. Will you take a little champagne?"

"Thank you, no. I never drink while I'm working."

Out came the notebook and here was the fresh white page, folded back with a snap.

"Will it disturb you if I take notes?"

"No, not at all," whispered Alice, with the Egyptian dignity of a mummified queen. Miss Stackpole looked about the dim but laden room, blatantly inquisitive, taking in all the paintings and the bibelots.

"Thank you, Jesse. Put the bucket here, beside me." *Silly prig. I'll drink it all myself.* Alice imagined that she had complete control over the situation. But there was no holding Henrietta Stackpole. She had a public to inform.

"Am I right to assume, Mrs Jones, that you had known Dr Barry since childhood?"

"Indeed, I did," said Alice calmly. *All right, here goes. Take the plunge.*

Noli me tangere, said the doctor. I am not for human hands. But no one knew why, not until the final revelation. The leading lady, much deceived, became the heroine, nay, the lover, in this version of the tale, consumed with an enduring childhood passion for the bastard son of David Steuart Erskine, Earl of Buchan. *Be definite about that. This is being written down for history.* And all her life she had loved in vain. Until her affection, if not her ardour, was finally returned in a tender meeting of minds at the moment when the fires of the flesh were dampened down.

Dampened down, my eye, but the public expects that. It's not considered decent to enjoy a squeeze and tickle once you're past sixty. But I've known plenty of old goats, still standing about with their beards shaking. Louisa was quite right about that one.

Then the last illness. The lamp burning day and night. *Make it sound more like consumption. Diarrhoea is decidedly unpicturesque. America doesn't want to hear about soiled beds and boiled sheets.* The midnight hour passing. The priest withdraws. Those last vows exchanged in whispers, and the quiet end.

Alice wiped her eyes. Miss Stackpole had the decency to cease scratching with her pencil and to suspend her insolent interruptions when Alice got to the deathbed scene. There was a pause in which the actress sipped her champagne. On to the shocking revelations and the truth of the body as the winding sheet was peeled back.

"And not only was it the perfect body of a woman, Miss Stackpole, but a woman who had borne a child. Of this I am quite certain."

Alice had invented the stretch marks. She had them on her own belly and did not see why James should get away with being so handsomely preserved at nearly seventy. After all, they weren't going to dig him up now to find out. Henrietta Stackpole sat looking at the most scandalous scoop of her career. She pressed Alice for more details.

"But you have lived in the doctor's house for years, Mrs Jones, and known him since childhood – did you really never suspect anything?"

"Never," lied Alice, with emphasis, "never. Not once."

"There have been rumours that Dr Barry was an hermaphrodite. Were you never tempted? . . . I mean, there must have been opportunities . . . ? Given the perfect intimacy which existed between you . . . ?"

Alice indicated that she needed another glass of chilled champagne to steady her vocal chords. She calmly decided to up the price, and in so doing indicated that there might just be the possibility of photographs. She flung herself into the role of revelatory angel. And at this point, Alice tells all. Well, not quite all. But she presents America with a marvellous narrative, filled with secrecy, passion and adventure, the story of the actress and the doctor, the obsession that stretched across decades, continents, the love that never died. If it was a good enough story the *New York Post* would certainly pay. Alice Jones was a professional performer. And no one should ever give their best performance for anything less than the highest possible price.

— AFTERWORD —

THE PEOPLE AND EVENTS described in this book are not
entirely fictitious. James Miranda Barry really did serve as an
army doctor from 1813 to 1859. He was a well-known, contro-
versial medical reformer, who quarrelled with Florence
Nightingale in public. His ambiguous sexual identity caused considerable speculation and debate during his lifetime. Readers
wishing to know more about the facts of his life should consult
June Rose's biography *The Perfect Gentleman* (Hutchinson, 1977)
as I have done. Rachel Holmes is writing a new biography of
Barry, so we can look forward to further revelations. Other
histories of Barry include Isobel Rae *The Strange Story of Dr James
Barry* (Longmans, Green, 1958) and a novel by Jessica Grove and
Olga Racster, *Dr James Barry: Her Secret Story* (G.Howe, 1932).
On the significance of cross-dressing see Marjorie Garber *Vested
Interests: Cross Dressing and Cultural Anxiety* (Routledge, 1992),
which includes a section on Barry.

The following texts and reference books were extremely
helpful to me. On the life and art of Barry's "uncle", the painter
James Barry, I consulted William L. Pressly *The Life and Art
of James Barry* (Yale University Press, 1981) and his catalogue of
The Tate Gallery exhibition *James Barry: The Artist as Hero* (The
Tate Gallery, 1983). For nineteenth-century diseases and their
treatments, both what they looked like and what people thought
they meant, I studied *The Cambridge Illustrated History of Medicine*
edited by Roy Porter (Cambridge University Press, 1996).
William Cobbett's *Rural Rides*, ed. George Woodcock (Penguin,
1967), first published in 1830, gives a vivid impression of the
countryside in southern England in the 1820s. I also drew on
Gilbert White's Year: Passages from The Garden Kalendar and The

Naturalist's Journal selected by John Commander (Oxford University Press, 1982). Jennifer Stead's *Food and Cooking in Eighteenth Century Britain* and Maggie Black's *Food and Cooking in Nineteenth Century Britain*, both published by English Heritage in 1985 were very helpful on cooking and kitchens. I have used Benjamin Robert Haydon's own words; see *Neglected Genius: The Diaries of Benjamin Haydon*, ed. John Jolliffe (Hutchinson, 1990). For images and information about nineteenth-century theatre I drew on Simon Trussler's *British Theatre* (Cambridge, 1994), and Claire Tomalin's superb biography of Dora Jordan, *Mrs Jordan's Profession* (Penguin, 1995). Also useful and fascinating was *Women Reading Shakespeare: An Anthology of Criticism 1660–1900*, eds. Ann Thompson and Sasha Roberts (Manchester University Press, 1997). The following texts were especially suggestive for that part of the book set in the West Indies: M. G. Lewis's *Journal of a West India Proprietor 1815–1817* (George Routledge and Sons, 1929), Gad Heumann *"The Killing Time": The Morant Bay Rebellion in Jamaica* (Macmillan Caribbean, 1994), Michael Pawson and David Buisseret *Port Royal, Jamaica* (Clarendon Press: Oxford, 1975) and Mary Turner *Slaves and Missionaries: The Disintegration of Jamaica Slave Society 1787–1834* (University of Illinois Press, 1982), which gives a detailed historical account of the slave rebellion in 1831. I have drawn on her work in Part Five of the novel and am grateful both to her and to my mother, Sheila Duncker, for their bibliographical help and historical advice. The real James Barry, who was working in Jamaica at the time of the rebellion, wrote: "I served under Sir Willoughby Cotton during the Rebellion and the burning of the plantations by the Negroes."

This book is a work of fiction, an imaginative exploration of particular aspects of what must have been a very strange life. I have therefore taken the liberties which all novelists, who are not strictly historians, always do take with history. Alice Jones is entirely fictional. It did not suit the shape of my story that the painter James Barry should die in 1806, and so I insisted that he should live on until 1816. I hope he will forgive me. Francisco de Miranda lived from 1750 to 1816 and died a prisoner in Spain. I have changed his dates to 1770–1836, as I imagine that he would have liked to see more of the nineteenth century. And

I sent him home to die. Barry's last posting was in Canada. I have decided that he ended his career in Jamaica. It was, in any case, a climate he preferred. Where people have suffered and died in pain, as was the case of the slaves in the West Indies, I have remained as true to known historical fact as possible. As to the inner reality of James Miranda Barry's life, here we can only guess at the truth, for there is very little evidence. And it is here that the novelist will always have the edge over the historian.

I finished the first draft of *James Miranda Barry* while I was a visiting fellow at Künstlerhaus Schloss Wiepersdorf in Brandenburg, Germany, during the autumn of 1997. I am grateful to the Ministerium für Wissenschaft, Forschung und Kultur des Landes Brandenburg, who financed my stay in Wiepersdorf and I would like to thank the Director, Frau Doris Sossenheimer, her staff and all the other "Stipendiaten" who were working at Wiepersdorf at that time, especially the painter Sati Zech. My first reader, S.J.D., heard most of this book over the telephone, then carefully read the manuscript. This book and every other book I have written are dedicated to her. I can never thank her enough.

Patricia Duncker
France, 1998